Four Women
(Quattro Donne)

A North End Love Story

Bennett R. Molinari and
Richard C. Molinari

ISBN: 978-1-4834-9391-6 (sc)
ISBN: 978-1-4834-9392-3 (hc)
ISBN: 978-1-4834-9390-9 (e)

Library of Congress Control Number: 2018913733

Lulu Publishing Services rev. date: 06/12/2019

In Memory of
Our Parents, Mary and Louis, and
Our Brother, Louis (Junior) and
Deceased Members of our Family

CONTENTS

ACKNOWLEDGEMENTS

We would like to thank our Mom, Mary, whose extraordinary memory and love for the North End, enabled her to pass on to us many of the stories related in this book

We would like to thank our Dad, Louis, whose absolute integrity served as a guide through our formative years, and our brother Louis Jr, whose writing skills (a great sports writer) and wry sense of humor were a constant source of inspiration.

We would like to thank and remember our cousin Ethel and her husband Larry for being a constant encouragement through the nine years it took to write this book. They were our biggest fans and constant supporters.

We would like to thank our cousins Rita and Marie for critiquing the early manuscript, helping to shape the course of this book, and our cousins Audrey and Tommy for constantly urging us to complete our book.

We would like to thank our cousin Vilma, (author of Pasta, Popes and Passion), whose intrepid nature and writing skill served as both inspiration and encouragement, and our cousin Dina for never giving up on us.

We would like to thank our cousin Laura and our friend Jim for the hours they spent editing this book.

We would like to thank our cousins Carolyn and Barbara for their constant support and encouragement.

We would like to thank our friend Elvira for the hours she spent translating the many passages into Italian found throughout this book.

We would like to thank our friend Susan, the most erudite person we know, who provided us with the title of this book.

Finally, we would like to thank the Scalabrini Priests of Sacred Heart Italian Church, the Sisters of Saint Joseph, the Saint Mark Society and the many Religious who were invaluable in helping to shape our character, providing lifelong values to the descendants of the many immigrants in our North End Community, whose lives are echoed within the pages of this book.

INTRODUCTION

Permit me to introduce myself. My name is Antonio, I will be commenting on the story you are about to read, popping up from time to time, helping to shed light on the lives and times of the people depicted in this novel. It is my pleasure to be your guide. I was on what I believed to be a permanent retirement, having made it into heaven, but a Higher Authority thought it would be a good idea for me to do this, and I plan to enjoy the experience.

This is a story of another time, one we will never see the likes of again. The North End of Boston in the late 1940s was a time of immigrants and Church on Sunday with the family, a simpler time of neighbors helping neighbors in Boston's "Little Italy." You will be reading about my daughter Lucia and grandchildren, many of whom I had not met when the events in this story took place. This is also the story of my grandson Pietro, who is very close to my heart.

Pietro is the son of my youngest child, Gerardo, who became a successful lawyer, and married into a noble Roman family. Pietro is meant to carry on the Contes' age-old tradition of having a priest in the family, and perhaps, like his great uncle, possibly become a bishop. He is sent to America to visit his relatives before entering the seminary, and unexpectedly falls in love with Carla, the beautiful daughter of an overly protective father, Egidio Ricci, who with his five sons are successful hardened fishermen. Like a modern-day Romeo and Juliet, their forbidden love could lead to a tragic ending, promising to tear my family apart.

Before I leave you (for now), perhaps, I should tell you something of myself. I was born in 1850 in Prato la Serra, a tiny village outside of Naples, Italy. My family was poor. We had a small plot of land which

Papa farmed, doing his best to feed us. Mama divided her time, working beside him in the field while taking care of me and my brothers and sisters. I loved reading the lives of the saints and attending Holy Mass daily. By the time I was nineteen, I entered a monastery in Calabria, where I thought I would spend the rest of my life. One never knows what God has in mind for us. Just before I was to be solemnly professed, my plans changed when my monastery burned to the ground. I returned to my village, where eventually I married and raised eight children. I never lost the desire to enter religious life and became a church sexton, a job I held to the end of my days. I was known as *il topolino della chiesa* (the church mouse).

It was through the Port of Boston that immigrants flowed, drawn by the promise of a better life, leaving their homelands in successive waves. Millions of Italians left Italy toward the end of the 19th and the beginning of the 20th centuries, many settling temporarily in places like the North End of Boston, neighborhoods often known as "Little Italy," before moving on to become assimilated into their adopted country. My daughter Lucia was among those immigrants. How proud I was of Lucia when she announced she wanted to become a nun, but like her father, entering religious life was not meant to be. In Lucia's case, it was a handsome Neapolitan named Bernardo, who was madly in love with her and swept her off her feet. She probably would never have left Italy, but Bernardo was restless and ambitious, so he took his bride and they set off for America, passing out of my life and breaking her mother's heart. We were left behind to worry and pray for them. It was a hard time for all of us.

Basta (enough)! Now that I have set the scene, I will remain quiet, inserting myself every so often into the story, only when I want to make a point. For the most part, I will let my great-grandsons speak to you through the pages of this book.

CHAPTER 1

Il Villaggio (The Village)

Cities were darker when we were growing up, street lights dimmer, shadows between them forming threatening voids. Doorways were seldom lit. Looking back, it is hard to believe, lighting your doorway was once considered a luxury, but it was in the tenements of the North End where we grew up. Narrow, grey, cobblestone streets led to grey unpainted doorways of two and three-family "walk-ups", mostly cold-water flats, many with shared bathrooms in dingy corridors. Dimly lit interiors were brightened by the intense family life within their worn brick walls.

Boston in the 1940s was not the bustling city it has evolved into. It was a city of ethnic neighborhoods, and the North End was its "Little Italy," a forgotten place. It was a place its residents sought to leave, exiting to the suburbs, as they assimilated into America. Of course, some families were different. Our family adjusted to life in America without leaving the North End and our Italian traditions; we were the die-hards who comfortably lived in our Italian cocoon.

A visit to the North End by an outsider in the 1940s was considered an adventure. Thinking back, we must have seemed quite exotic to anyone from beyond the limits of our tiny villaggio, who ventured into our Italian enclave. We were a walled city without walls, an Italian village in the heart of Puritan Boston, supposedly, an "unsavory" place to visit that never lived up to its reputation. Our villaggio was a beehive of activity where many families scratched out a living through their tiny stores and pushcarts, generously sprinkled throughout the streets. There were fruit and vegetable stores, grocery stores, bakeries, countless butcher shops and because the Atlantic was at our doorstep, fish markets with the freshest fish found in the City, thanks to the fleet of trawlers docked at the end of our street. The whole place smelled of food. It was a supermarket one square mile in size, where streets were aisles and store windows were showcases.

Back then, the North End had many street vendors, each staking out a corner where we would find them every weekend. Others wandered through the neighborhood in a set pattern. There was the Shoelace Man, with the big, black, mole on his face. Then there was the Rag Man, who constantly shouted, "Rags! Rags!" as he wended his way through the narrow streets and alleys. There was the lady with the leatherette shopping bags, whose constant chant was, "Shopping bags, a leather bag, shopping bags, a leather bag." There was the Eel Lady, who sold the slimy creatures from a huge, chipped, enameled white basin. She had leathery, dark skin and a thin, wrinkled, boney face accentuated by her grey-streaked hair pulled back in a bun. Kids would dare each other to grab one of her eels and throw it down a sewer. If one of us succeeded, she would let loose with a torrent of curses in Italian. Her shrill voice was even more frightening when coupled with an obscene gesture, causing us to run for our lives.

The Crab Man was the most popular vendor. He was an old Sicilian fisherman, short and fat, whose weathered face revealed his many years at sea. He wore a brown, leather apron that covered him from his neck to his knees, and sat on a little, wooden stool while shouting out, "Crabs! Five cents a crab! Crabs for sale! Five cents a crab!" He piled his crabs up into a huge, red, steaming mound of tangled legs and claws that smelled of the sea. Kids would gather near the cart, while screaming, "Give me a crab! Give me a crab!" He would then gesture to the cardboard sign on top of the crab pile, scribbled on it: 5 cents a crab. This was a challenge. First, one of the kids would shout, "You cheap bastard!" The Crab Man, knowing trouble was coming, would shout back, "Get the hell out of here, you little shits!" while trying to hang on to his crabs, anticipating what was to come next. Someone would purposely bump the cart, causing crabs to fall onto the street, while the rest of the kids would swoop down like birds of prey, grab a carcass, and be off down the street. The Crab Man would invariably give chase, abandoning his cart, exposing it to the kids and more mischief.

The other thing about these street vendors was the eerie visage about them, prompting the kids to call them names, such as - "The Boogie Man"- for the scary faces of the men or - "la Strega"- for the witch-like faces of the women. We travelled in small gangs. Pushing a gang member or friend into the grasping arms of one of the vendors, was just about the most frightening thing you could do. Making a victim piss his pants from fright was the best; if you succeeded, you hit pay dirt, for you could taunt the kid for weeks to come. The taunt went something like this: "The Eel Lady made 'Little Baby' Jimmy piss his pants!" 'The Little Baby', really drove the taunt home. You could then count on the kid's father or mother searching you out with shouts and curses. With a little luck, you could keep this going for weeks.

Whenever you misbehaved in public, you could always count on the parents or someone in the neighborhood reporting the incident to the Principal of your school. At least that's how it was in the North End. Sister Francine was the principal of our parish Grammar School. If one of us who attended the school was reported to her, she would call us incorrigible and a lot of other names we didn't understand. Sister Francine, who had been a nun for almost fifty years, was a tiny woman with a saintly face. She was very kind but also very strict. Being strict was a necessary attribute for any nun who had to teach a bunch of kids caught between the Italian and American cultures. Many kids were angry and confused by the two conflicting worlds, never staying long enough in one to fully identify with and call home.

It was a time when nuns still traveled in pairs and wore full black habits that reached down to their ankles. Our nuns were identified by the white headdress that covered the sides of the face, and a black flowing veil affixed to the top of the headdress that flowed down the back. The nuns were mostly of Irish descent. They seemed to be as intrigued by us as we were of them. Our names like Vito and Vincenzo were a long way from James and John. We had dark skin while they were light. We smelled of garlic while they smelled of soap. We were from different cultures, trying to understand each other, finding common ground in our religion.

On top of it all, we kids were always acting up. Frequent incidents like that of the Crab Man and other street vendors, were only some of many reasons to discipline us. Stickball provided another reason. We played with complete disregard for traffic and pedestrians. In the classroom, putting tacks on Fat Joey's seat, throwing a frightening banana bug, caught in the back of a fruit truck, down the shirt of whoever was sitting in front of its captor, was reason enough to send the "wise guy" off to Sister Francine's office. There, any number of punishments could be selected from her rich and seasoned treasure chest.

There was one disciplinary action Sister knew the boys dreaded, giving her power even over the most mischievous offender. When you walked into her office and found her holding a bucket and scrub brush, you knew she had pulled from her repertoire, her most dreaded weapon. She was sending you to the Saint Theresa Society to join the girls on Friday, the day they cleaned our parish church. She always said the same words as she handed you the bucket and brush: "You will be doing God's work and you will be a better boy for it."

Some of our parents worked or volunteered at the school. Our Mom, Carmela, managed the cafeteria. She ran it exactly as she ran her kitchen at home, which meant it was a blizzard of pots and pans with lunches served at the speed of a short order cook. She ran the original fast food restaurant. Mom was a good cook but an impatient one. Her real joy was talking with the kids and stuffing them with food. Our role in this food fest was to set the tables for over 250 kids. Each kid was to have a tray of his or her own with forks, spoons and napkins arranged every which way. When we were really flying, we could lay all the settings out in fifteen minutes, coaxed on by Mom, shouting from the kitchen, "Bobby and Charlie, hurry up and set the tables, then get in here and help peel the potatoes!"

The potato peeler was an adventure. It stood by the sink at the far end of the cafeteria kitchen, an odd-looking contraption, we would fill with potatoes twice a week. Once turned on, it would send the potatoes into a frenzy, bouncing off the sides of a stainless-steel cylinder that looked something like a giant cheese grater. Mom once got beaned by a runaway potato, from then on, she wouldn't go near the thing, leaving it to the two of us to get the job done. This was a good idea, but also a bad idea, because when we weren't peeling potatoes, we would throw all sorts of things into the contraption. We threw in anything from tomatoes to Joanna Romano's brand-new falsies that were shredded in an instant. This really made Joanna crazy because they cost her a week's wages working at Jack's Candy Store. When Mom saw the falsies in the potato machine, she at first couldn't figure out what they were. When she finally recognized them, she reported us to Sister Francine who was waiting for us with a bucket and brush along with her usual sendoff: "You will be doing God's work and you will be better boys for it."

If there was one thing Mom hated to do, it was washing pots and pans and serving trays. This she left to her sidekick Connie whom Mom said had the strength of a man and worked like a wild woman. Connie was a friend of Mom's. She was a large middle-age woman with the ruddy complexion of a farm worker. Her apartment faced the rear of our building, across a narrow alleyway, spider webbed with clotheslines. Connie, wearing a rubber apron, stood over a double stainless-steel sink. She tore through the pots and pans in a slam bang manner, water and soap suds splashing everywhere. When the job was done, and the kids returned to their classes, Connie would slip off her soapy apron, light up a cigarette, and shoot the breeze with Mom.

CHAPTER 2

One Big Family

The North End in the 1940s was well populated with priests and nuns, the result of having four Catholic Churches and three parochial schools within one square mile. One of the churches was distinctively Irish, a holdover from the mid-19th century when the North End was an Irish immigrant community. The other three churches were essentially Italian. They were responding to the most recent wave of immigrants settling in this port of entry during the latter part of the 19th century.

In addition to the four Catholic churches, there were private chapels associated with societies, dedicated to the patron saint of a town in Italy. Some of these societies were for men only, others for women, while a few were mixed. Back then, whenever the men of the society got together in a chapel's function room, they would cook spaghetti and meatballs, always in a battered pan that supposedly enhanced the taste. The designated chef would dole out meatballs as if they were diamonds, eating while standing over the pot, and would often eat nearly as much as he doled out. The function rooms were always lit with fluorescent lights, making everyone look sickly grey. A statue of the patron saint, standing in a niche, watched over the proceedings. The furnishings were always the same: red Formica tables banded in chrome with matching red, leatherette chairs, standing on shiny, chrome legs. The walls were covered with dark-brown, Formica wood-like paneling usually trimmed with a string of Christmas lights that remained hung the year round, and always the worn black and white linoleum floor. Faint smells of tomato sauce and beer permeated the air, while Frank Sinatra crooned through a crackly speaker in the background.

Another distinct feature of the North End was the Prado. The Prado was the only green space in the North End at that time. It was a place where old men gathered to play cards, and grandmothers sat in the sun to exchange gossip and pass the time of day. There was an old guy named Giuseppe, who would show up at the Prado once or twice a week. He would find a seat in the sun, take from his pocket an old piece of string, set on the ground as a noose, controlled by a long string held in his weathered, bony hands. Patiently, he sat for hours, occasionally tossing a piece of bread into the middle of his noose. Pigeons apprehensively approached the noose with a built-in sense of danger prey animals always seem to possess. Every so often, after making several attempts at snatching a piece of bread, a frustrated pigeon would pluck up its courage, step into the noose, and Giuseppe would spring to life. With a quick pull of the string, twist of the neck, and into his sack, accompanied by a scream from an on looking old lady, it was pigeon cacciatore that evening.

Growing up in the North End in the 1940s was fun. We were a family of forty thousand people jammed into one square mile, privacy was not an option, for gregarious Italians, it was heaven on earth. Everyone was your uncle, aunt or cousin. We were all related, if not by blood, then by common circumstance and way of life. In the summer, because our flats were small and hot, we spent as much time on the street as possible. We took folding chairs and tables from our flats, set them up on the sidewalk, where we ate and drank as if we were at our kitchen table. Mothers and fathers, children and grandparents, and any friend who happened to walk by, were welcomed to the table. This scene was repeated in every alleyway and along the broken sidewalks of our villaggio, creating a feeling of family throughout the North End.

In every family, there are certain rituals that bind them together. One such ritual is a rite of passage into manhood. These rituals can be expressed in many ways. For some of us in the North End, it involved a visit to Scollay Square.

CHAPTER 3

Scollay Square

Hanover Street was and remains the heart of the North End. Restaurants and coffee shops line both sides of the street, their tables spilling out onto the sidewalks. Hanover Street was longer when we were growing up. It had a Jekyll and Hyde personality. The good Doctor Jekyll passed through our neighborhood where Hanover Street began, but Mr. Hyde was loose and having a great time at the other end of the Street, where it emptied into Scollay Square, its seedy colorful terminus. The overhead expressway had not yet severed the street separating Scollay Square, the storied red-light district, from the North End. It was a place where tattoo parlors, strip joints and barrooms beckoned sailors on shore leave and anyone else looking for a good time. It was also the place where some of the guys of the neighborhood went to receive their right-of-passage into manhood.

The ceremony began when we sneaked our way into the local Burlesque House, a smelly, grimy place, where fans and tassels were artfully manipulated to the cheers of a sweaty audience. Body odor, dim lights and a stale stench of cigars, built up over many decades, saturated everyone and everything. The old theater looked, smelled and sounded like Burlesque. We entered through a little-used side door, worked our way to the garishly lit stage up front, passed old guys looking for a thrill and drunks sleeping it off. The new inductee, who we referred to as a shithead, was surrounded by former shitheads. We kept the inductee between us, just in case he decided to bolt, getting as close to the stage as possible, where the ladies seemed to be performing just for us. The smell of their cheap perfume washed over us with every wave of their fans. Once we were in our seats, we would start our cat calls. Catching the attention of one of the strippers, we would call attention to our latest inductee and shout out: "Toss one at the shithead!" If it all went right, one of the ladies would oblige by coming to center stage, begin a series of bumps and grinds, with a final bang in the direction of the shithead. All of this had to be done quickly, because we knew we were going to be thrown out at any minute. The ladies came to recognize us, knew what we were up to, and always co-operated. A minute or two later, a couple of bouncers would make their way down the aisle to where we were seated. Before they could grab us, we clambered over the seats, making a beeline to the exit.

Next, we would search out Old Sadie, for part two of the ritual. Sadie was an over-the-hill hooker with flaming red hair and a white powdered face. She stuffed herself into an assortment of cheap, tight-fitting bras, breasts billowing half-out of her dress. She could always be found occupying her favorite stool at the Old Scollay Bar. "What will it be guys, 'a quickie' or 'the works'!" Sadie would shout out. Two dollars bought you 'a quickie', consisting of Old Sadie grabbing her unsuspecting victim and shoving his face into her billowing breasts. She would hold him there until he was ready to pass out, then release him, catching him before he hit the floor. For three bucks, you got 'the works'. Old Sadie would throw in a couple of 'feels', which would just about finish off her victim. We always opted for 'the quickie', never having enough money for the works. After completing her part of the ritual, Sadie would shout, "Go on home before I tell your mothers where you hang out!" With that warning from Sadie, the ritual came to an end. We would run into the North End screaming, the newest inductee into manhood leading the pack.

CHAPTER 4
Our Family

We lived in a three-story building on Richmond Street. There were three street-level shops in our building, always very busy. There was Nick the butcher whose store front was often festooned with carcasses of goats and skinned rabbits. Next to Nick was a tiny cigar shop, owned by a fat guy, who everyone knew as Smokes. Finally, there was Nicolino's espresso bar. It was a lively place with people coming and going all day and late into the evening. Nicolino had these wire chairs with round, brown, wooden seats that never stood straight, giving the feeling the chair would collapse from under you at any moment. He was always washing the pavement in front of his restaurant, spraying trash into the gutter from a black rubber hose. He finished the job with a yellow straw broom that seemed to be grafted to his hands. Nicolino was a stick-thin southern Italian, well into his 60s. He had dark, leathery skin and no teeth, causing his cheeks and mouth to collapse into his face. His grey streaked hair was always combed straight back and slicked down, his crackly voice was heard constantly throughout the day, as he took orders from his patrons and shouted them on to the kitchen help. Rumor had it, Nicolino was a relative of Joe DiMaggio. This gave him instant celebrity status with regular customers, hoping to see "The Yankee Clipper", despite Nicolino's bad coffee and hard biscotti.

Our flat was located on the second floor. You entered through a tiny reception hall that led directly into the kitchen. The kitchen was the focal point. Every day, we would gather around a small table wedged into a corner. The table was square with a pale blue, metal top, extensions on both sides slid out from under the top with a thud. The table stood on four sturdy, wooden legs, which Dad was constantly painting in the vain attempt to make the table look new. When family visited, a card table extended the kitchen table practically to our front door. There was a small refrigerator that stood on four bowed legs. The refrigerator stood about 5 feet tall with flat sides, a flat door, and a silver metal handle. A white, metal basin sat under the refrigerator to catch its constant drips. In the corner of the kitchen was a white and black, cast iron gas stove, also with bowed legs, that was Mom's pride and joy. A window in the kitchen looked out over a small parking lot and a large, brick building that totally obstructed our view. A door on the right side of the kitchen led to a long, narrow, bathroom with wainscoting running halfway up the walls. There was an old bathtub with ball and claw feet, and a toilet with a square water tank that sat directly over your head, operated by pulling a long chain connected to the water tank. Completing the bathroom was a square, white enameled sink, attached at its rear to the wall, supported at its front by two white metal legs.

The rest of the flat consisted of a living room with two wing chairs, and a large studio sofa that turned into a double bed for Bobby who was 9 years old, and Charlie 6 years old. Dad converted a storage room, just off the living room, into a bedroom for our oldest brother, Anthony, who was 15. On the opposite side of the living room was a small bedroom shared by Mom and Dad and an alcove that functioned as a play space. We had just enough closet space for our clothes; everything else was stored in the basement in a chicken wire enclosure that Dad called the woodshed.

Our Dad, Joseph, was a newspaper man, working the evening shift, for one of several Boston newspapers, which flourished at the time. His shift ran from about four in the afternoon to midnight. He was a typesetter, that is, the person who designed and laid out the page, arranging type, making it all intelligible to the reader. Dad was an excellent typesetter, but he was no Mr. Fix It. Whenever he tried to fix something, we all prepared for the worst. This was particularly true when he tampered with anything electrical, especially the fuse box. Mom would warn us in advance, "Get out the candles." You could always count on him getting a shock, lights going out, and his yelling out, "Jumpin' Mosses!", the closest he ever came to an obscenity.

Mom, like most married women in the 1940s, was a housewife whose job was to bring up the kids and keep house. When we were old enough, as we wrote earlier, she took a part-time job managing our Grammar School cafeteria. She was happy to be back at work after so many years and loved working with the children. Grandma Lucia, who lived just up the street, visited us almost every day and always brought something delicious, left over from her dinner the night before. Mom loved this, for it meant there would be that much less she had to cook. Mom was a good cook, but not an enthusiastic one, she much preferred spending her time visiting friends and family.

The late 40s had to be the best time to live in the North End. The exodus of second-generation Italians had not yet taken place, entire families still lived within shouting distance of each other. Most of our family lived within two blocks of us. Grandma Lucia was the matriarch of the family. She always dressed in black, out of respect for Grandpa Bernardo who passed away in 1940. Grandma was slightly under five feet tall, wore a little pug at the top of her head, and constantly fingered a rosary in her pocket. Many people described Grandma as looking like a china doll. She was in her sixties and still had a wonderful complexion. Grandma lived with her unmarried daughter Stella. Auntie Stella was the tallest of Grandma's children. As a child, she was rail thin and known as "Skinny Stella." She had light brown, wavy hair, parted in the middle, which delicately framed her Neapolitan features. Auntie had a caustic wit and sharp tongue. She was the family bomb thrower.

Auntie Angie was the oldest of Grandma's four children. Her real name was Angelina, but she much preferred being called Angie. Auntie was a heavyset woman with a very pretty face. She was a woman with great common sense whom everyone turned to for advice, and typical of her Neapolitan heritage, she had a terrific sense of humor coupled with a great laugh. She had an uncanny ability to create nicknames, and always hit a bull's eye, once she launched one of her descriptive missiles. She and Grandma basically ran the family.

Auntie Angie was married to Uncle Jim. They had three children:

Grace, Theresa and Vincenzo, who everyone called Vinny. The family lived above a small grocery store on Garden Court Street.

Mom's brother, Carmine, lived down the street with Aunt Loretta and their two children, Caterina and Edward. Loretta was a very attractive woman who everyone thought looked like the 1940s actress, Gene Tierney.

Uncle, for a while became a local hero, when one day a woman fell from her first-floor window while washing it. Lucky for her, Uncle happened to be in the right place at the right time and broke her fall. From then on, he could have dated any woman in the North End.

Our Mom, Carmela, was the youngest of Grandma's children and without doubt, the feistiest, she loved being with people. She was full of life, the spark plug of the family. She, like her two sisters and brother, never made it out of high school, something that Mom always regretted. This was so typical of the children in the North End of her era. Mom, who was only five foot one, was the shortest of the children, slightly heavyset and very pretty.

Grandma lived frugally but comfortably, on savings derived from the butcher shop Grandpa opened on Prince Street, just around the corner from Garden Court Street, in the 1920's. It was shortly after Uncle Carmine left the business, Grandpa decided to close-up shop. Grandpa was very tall for an Italian of his day, standing well over six feet. He had a serious case of asthma and in the end succumbed to a heart attack.

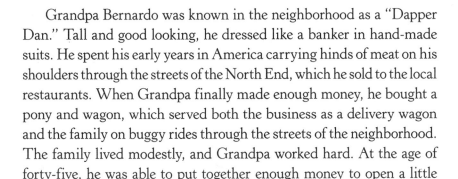

Grandpa Bernardo was known in the neighborhood as a "Dapper Dan." Tall and good looking, he dressed like a banker in hand-made suits. He spent his early years in America carrying hinds of meat on his shoulders through the streets of the North End, which he sold to the local restaurants. When Grandpa finally made enough money, he bought a pony and wagon, which served both the business as a delivery wagon and the family on buggy rides through the streets of the neighborhood. The family lived modestly, and Grandpa worked hard. At the age of forty-five, he was able to put together enough money to open a little butcher shop. Grandpa only worked in the morning, leaving the shop midday in the hands of Grandma and his children, while he served as ambassador to the coffee shops of Hanover Street, earning in his mind, the right to semi-retirement.

There was a little theatre named the Casino, located in Scollay Square, which often showcased traveling Italian plays and musicals. Grandpa loved these little reviews, and on the first day of their arrival, he would perform a certain ritual. At about 12:00 in the afternoon, he would walk to Garden Court Street, stand in the middle of the street and whistle, a whistle immediately recognized by Grandma. She would come to the window of their fourth-floor flat and signal to him, she'd be down in a minute. Whatever their situation, happy or sad, they would stroll together, her arm entwined in his, in a manner typically Italian. They made their way from Garden Court Street over to Hanover, up to the Casino, growing increasingly happy as they approached the theater. Two immigrants, if only for an hour or two, would come close to their homeland. When the Neapolitan *Sciantosa* (Diva), Gilda Mignonette, headlined the show, no power on earth could keep them from attending. Emotions, which for Italians are always near the surface, would flow from the audience the moment Gilda sang out, as she turned to a scene of the Bay of Naples, just behind her, *"Napoli, io vengo a te."* (Naples, I'm coming back to you). The all-Italian audience would cheer, applaud and toss flowers at the Diva, Grandpa enthusiastically shouting from the balcony, much to Grandma's embarrassment: "Bravo Gilda! Bravo Gilda!"

After Grandpa passed away, Grandma and Auntie Stella took a flat on the second floor of a bow front building, over a barber shop, on Garden Court Street, the same street Rose Kennedy once lived on when the neighborhood was Irish. Their building had a black, spiral, iron staircase, which everyone feared was too difficult for Grandma to climb, but she managed just fine.

Grandma had this black, French Bulldog, Blackie, that always sat at the entrance of her flat. She never closed the door, so the dog spent all his time sprawled across the threshold, peering down the spiral staircase. Blackie snored and farted all day long, making the entrance to Grandma's flat smell of whatever Blackie ate the night before and had trouble digesting. One steamy hot summer day, Grandma was trying to take a nap. Blackie's snoring, farting and occasional snort, prevented her from sleeping. Grandma was swearing at the dog in Italian, yelling out: *"Smetti di russare e scorggiare!"* (Stop snoring and farting!) When she couldn't stand it any longer, she threw her slipper at him, hitting Blackie on the head, bending his ear. Grandma spent the rest of the day massaging Blackie's ear, trying to make up with the dog, and get the ear to stand straight. She feared what Auntie Stella would say after seeing the ear bent, because this happened before, only it involved Blackie's other ear. The ear never straightened out, and Blackie continued to snore and fart, seemingly, to take revenge on Grandma for her burst of temper.

Grandma and Auntie Stella had these little skirmishes that didn't amount to much, but certainly enlivened each day. Although Grandma could speak English, her arguments with Auntie Stella were always punctuated with Italian, while Auntie Stella argued in both English and Italian. Grandma was at a disadvantage, she could not understand everything Auntie was saying, aggravating her. When arguing, every inch of her body was animated, she made hand gestures that didn't need translating. The arguments always ended with Grandma tossing one arm in the air and walking away, leaving Auntie Stella alone with Blackie, while Grandma proceeded down the stairs, muttering things in Italian.

There were times when Grandma would decide to go to church in the middle of an argument. She put on her little black, straw hat, fastened to her head by a long hat pin with a pearl at the end, make her way down the stairs muttering in Italian, with only the black veil and brim visible from the landing above. It all ended with Auntie Stella looking out the window, making certain Grandma made it safely across North Square to the church. Grandma invariably planned to spend some time cleaning the family shrine, dedicated to Our Lady of Pompeii, which she had erected in memory of Grandpa Bernardo when he passed away in 1940. There, she could be alone with her memories. Before she began cleaning, she would sit for a couple of minutes saying her rosary, and pull from her purse a little handkerchief fringed with lace. This was followed by her dusting the brass candleholders, flanking the picture of the Madonna, and white marble shelf they sat on. She was now totally calm and ready to return home.

CHAPTER 5
Our Neighbors

We shared our floor with one other flat that changed tenants constantly. For several months, there was Joe the Bookie and his wife, Vita. They were always entertaining friends who constantly spoke of horse races and betting. Mom and Dad went to just one of their parties, it was a New Year's Eve party. The flat was crowded with people waiting for midnight and the beginning of another year. For a while it was like any other New Year's Eve party, until there was a loud knock on the door just before midnight. Joe urged Vita, Mom and Dad to climb out the window and hide on the fire escape. That's when he let on, he was a bookie and never knew when he would be raided. It turned out to be just another guest; Mom and Dad climbed back in and rejoined the party. Needless to say, they never accepted another invitation from Joe and Vita.

After the Bookie came the "Clock Man." The Clock Man had fifteen clocks, set one minute behind each other. Each hour was welcomed in by fifteen minutes of chiming, followed by Mom screaming at him through our common wall. This went on for a year, until he finally left. Oddly enough, we never saw him leave, in fact, we rarely saw anyone leaving. Tenants seemed to go as mysteriously as they arrived, with never a sign of a moving truck. Next came the Marino family, consisting of an elderly mother and two spinster daughters. Like the Clock Man, they had aggravating habits. They argued a lot. The more heated the argument, the more often they would say, "Well!" It would go something like this: "So you don't want to do the cooking tonight,

Well!" "Well! I did the cooking yesterday, so now it's your turn." "Well! I'm going to tell Mama on you." Now, their Italian mother, Michelina, joined the chorus, "Rosina, Anna, *non discutete!*" (don't argue!) At this point, Mom would yell out from our side of the common wall, "Well! Well! Well!" All would go silent next door. The "Wells" would stop for the rest of the day, only to begin the next morning, followed by Mom shouting out, "Well! Well! Well!" once again.

Julia, our landlady, lived on the floor just above us with her sister and two bachelor brothers. She was widowed early in life and never had children. She practically adopted Bobby and Charlie as her children. Her house smelled of tomato sauce, brandied cherries and all the fruits and vegetables that she preserved in mason jars, stored in a large cupboard just off the kitchen. Julia had a cast iron stove that stood on four curved legs. There was a shelf built into the stove, just above the burners, where she kept food warm. Just off the kitchen was her living room.

It was filled with overstuffed furniture adorned with little lace dollies, antimacassars, she attached with pins to the backs and arms of the chairs. There was also a collection of stuffed animals that kept Julia company and fascinated us no end. They were collected by her late husband, Luigi, and for that reason, they remained close to her heart. The room was always dark. One of her stuffed animals, a pheasant, stood in the middle of the dining room table. Other stuffed animals decorated the living room with the same beady, glass eyes as the pheasant. Whatever the animal, the eyes were the same, all giving the impression they were constantly staring at you. One in particular, a bird of paradise, sat on a hat and was a constant source of fascination to us. What was this bird doing on a hat? We could not figure it out, so with some effort and the help of a pair of sharp scissors, we liberated it. Evidently, it was Julia's prized hat, for when Julia saw the bird sitting on an end table, the rest of the hat sitting on the kitchen table, she could not believe her eyes. She looked as though she was going to scream but didn't. She gathered the pieces and attempted to stitch the hat back together. Since one of the feathers of the bird was lost, the recreated hat looked lopsided, causing Julia to place the hat on a stand, that part of the bird facing a wall. We could not figure what the fuss was all about. The bird looked better on the end table. Why was it back on the hat?

CHAPTER 6
A Family Visitor

I t was the summer of 1949, when Grandma's nephew, Pietro Petruzelli, arrived from Italy to spend the summer with the family. Pietro was planning to enter the seminary in the fall, upon his return to Italy. His trip to America would be his last taste of a carefree life before beginning years of study in Rome. He was the youngest of two sons of Grandma's brother Gerardo, the one member of Grandma's family who became financially successful. Thanks to his good looks and his astute legal mind, he became one of Rome's most sought-after lawyers. He married Velia Conte, a member of an aristocratic Roman family, tracing its lineage back to the Renaissance. They were the social equal of any of the old Roman families. Velia and Gerardo lost their oldest son, Umberto, at Anzio during World War II. They managed to hold on to their villa, even though the rest of their possessions were looted as the Germans pulled out of Rome. They slowly returned to prominence by re-establishing the Contes' banking empire, through a long-established network of prominent Roman friends and politicians.

Pietro arrived in the North End in mid-June. Gossip immediately made him a local celebrity. Who is this good-looking young man so elegantly attired? Why has he come from Italy to visit our Villaggio? Is he an eligible bachelor? These are the questions that swirled through the coffee shops that summer. Pietro had an aristocratic bearing that both appealed to and put off North Enders. On the one hand, he carried a sense of mystery with him that was quite appealing, while on the other hand, North Enders were always suspicious of strangers who entered their Villaggio. The natural reaction of a tight-knit immigrant community.

As a future seminarian, Pietro was given duties at our parish church that occupied much of his time, taking him out of circulation, much to the dismay of over- anxious North End mothers, unaware of his vocational plan. They knew they had to move fast, if they were to catch him for one of their daughters. Not seeing him on the street as part of the North End summer scene frustrated these anxious mothers, provoking such comments as, "He thinks he's too good for us," or more to the point, "He's a stuck-up pain in the ass!" These bitter comments became a general refrain among disappointed mothers, who scoured the cafes along Hanover Street searching for him, plotting to make a match with their daughters. He became the talk of the neighborhood. Baseball and the Red Sox took a back seat to Pietro that summer of '49. We had Italian aristocracy living in our midst.

Pietro was to spend the summer at our flat. We were already cramped, five of us living in a tiny apartment with one and a half bedrooms, but we did have a cot that could be set up in the small alcove off the living room, sharing the room with Bobby and Charlie. To welcome Pietro, Mom decided to re-wallpaper the living room, something she had done every three to four years. She got in touch with Mr. Levine, the wallpaper hanger Mom used who lived in the West End, choosing a floral paper from among his samples. Mr. Levine returned a week later with rolls of wallpaper sticking out of an old baby carriage he used to transport his supplies. After stripping the old wallpaper, he filled the cracks and crevices of our damaged walls with newspaper, gluing it flat, before wallpapering. Once done, it was cup of coffee, a bit of conversation, and Mr. Levine, pushing his baby carriage, was off to his next job.

"Roberto and Carlo, I will be your guest this summer," Pietro said on the first night of his stay with us. We were happy to have him share our room, and we let it be known by tossing our pillows at him, the moment he jumped onto his cot. In time, Pietro became like another brother to us. Mom, who was full of fun, only separated in age from Pietro by little more than a decade, became more his sister than cousin.

CHAPTER 7

A Great Catch

Pietro was quite busy that first week. Since he was planning to enter seminary in the fall, he contacted Father Francesco, our pastor, as advised by his pastor in Rome, seeking his spiritual guidance while in Boston. Wanting to blend in, he found his way to Filene's Basement where he augmented his hand-made Italian clothes with khaki pants and sneakers. The change of dress almost, but not quite, pulled off the transformation. Pietro had the look and bearing a change of clothes can't disguise, and new money can't buy. He was an aristocrat with the bearing and manners of old money. His world was one of privilege. In Rome, you would seldom see his family on the street or have occasion to run into them in everyday life. He mixed in circles defined by class and his was one of the most exclusive. It was a world of walled villas and glittering salons, where a renowned family name opened doors that new money could never achieve. Pietro spent most of his early teen years at a Swiss boarding school where he rode out the war. It was there he learned to speak English with a charming Italian accent, and further refined his comportment to a classy demeanor, little concealed by his newly acquired American clothes.

There is a saying, if you sit at one of the outdoor cafes along Rome's Via Veneto, you will eventually see the entire world pass by. So it was with the North End's Hanover Street of 1949, where the favorite pastime was to pull up a chair at any of its sidewalk cafes, order an espresso, and watch the constant flow of North Enders interspersed with an occasional intrepid tourist. It would not be long before you were joined by a friend.

It was on his second weekend in the North End when Pietro was spotted at Café Roma having his morning shot of espresso, attired in sun glasses, white polo shirt, khaki pants and a copy of La Stampa. Pietro naturally oozed Italian class. There had been an earlier sighting of Pietro the day Monsignor Primo took him to Symphony Hall. Monsignor Primo was a friend of Father Francesco, who once was a house guest of the Conte Family while in Rome. Pietro was seated in the passenger's seat of the Monsignor's black Packard. The Packard was a huge sedan that was given to the Monsignor by his brother. The car was used for funerals and the rare occasion when the Monsignor went to Symphony. Driving that black beauty was the one great indulgence Monsignor Primo allowed himself, and he loved it. The Monsignor looked regal sitting behind the wheel, while Pietro, dark and handsome, dressed to kill, sat beside him. As the limousine passed, someone yelled out, "They think they're the Cat's Ass!" North Enders had this way about them, when we felt we were being put down, the best method of defense was to hurl the epithet, "Cat's Ass!" at the offender, generally followed by, "Who the hell do they think they are!" Glances of satisfaction and agreement would be exchanged among the onlookers, as happened in this case, though the Monsignor and Pietro were oblivious to it all.

The word went out over some hidden but highly efficient communication system, within minutes of Pietro's sighting at the Café Roma. Mothers with their daughters in tow, gradually began filling the seats surrounding him, while he remained engrossed in his newspaper. They flew in like migratory birds, silently alighting on wood and rattan perches, cooing and exchanging threatening glances at the competition, all without Pietro aware of the strategies taking place around him. It was at the moment of his near total encirclement, that something stirred in him, bringing him to his feet, something primordial that informs the hunted of the nearness of danger. He quickly surveyed the encampment nearly encircling him, spotted the only avenue of escape, the gap between the tables of Gina Romano and Angelina Marino, nodded and smiled at the ladies as he slipped away, deftly avoiding the snares that had been set out around him. The daughters of Caesar had been outmaneuvered.

In a display of defiance, Anna Delvecchio stood up, grabbed her bust and shouted out, "That stuck-up bastard!" The words were strong, but when accompanied by the bust grab, they were dangerous. This was a mother determined to marry off her daughter, and she drove the point home with drama and panache.

CHAPTER 8

A Saint Among Us

I t's hard to explain to an "outsider" the relationship we had with our church. As immigrants and children of immigrants, we relied heavily on the church and the community that naturally formed around it. We were a window into survival from the medieval past, living in a sort of walled city with the church at its center. The church provided spiritual refuge, continuity with the past, and at times much needed support. Its importance in our lives can't be overstated; it was central in our lives.

Grandma would often walk over to the church to light a candle to Our Lady of Pompeii. She then wandered the church speaking to each of the saints as she passed. To Saint Lucy, patroness of the eyes, she would ask for good vision. To Saint Jude, patron of hopeless cases, she would ask for a husband for Auntie Stella. When she passed Our Lady of Sorrows, she would offer up a prayer for her husband, Bernardo, who was very devoted to Our Lady, expressing her sorrow by uttering a slight mournful sigh. She would continue this way, praying and dusting as she walked the silent chapel, passed saints and sun-lit images in stained glass windows as familiar to her as the members of her family. For Grandma, as for most of us at the time, the church was not a separate place, but another room of our flat, that we wandered in and out of with a certain irreverence that comes with familiarity.

Friday was the day the women of the parish descended on the church with buckets, wash cloths and brooms to clean the shrines and benches of the church, alternating each week between the upper and lower church. Grandma would sit at the shrine she erected to Our Lady of Pompeii, dressed in black from head to toe, praying and reminiscing while Mom and Auntie Angie joined in the cleaning by polishing, arranging candlesticks, and washing the railing surrounding the shrine on three sides. The women were from different religious societies connected with the church. They cleaned their assigned shrines, taking a break and coming together in the small hall at the rear of the church, to exchange gossip and cookies, kept in their apron pockets. The scene was that of a picnic in the church, mothers and daughters, old and young, gossiping, laughing and munching, seemingly irreverent to an outsider, but perfectly natural to North Enders, who as we said earlier, tended to regard the church as another room in their flats.

It was during one of these cleaning sessions that Pietro was next spotted. It was a steamy morning in July when Sandra Rossi, Gina Bianchi and Carla Ricci, three members of the Saint Theresa Society, met up in the foyer of the church. The inner doors to the lower church were closed. Gina, who had just turned sixteen, peaked in to see if anyone was in the chapel, gasped, quickly shut the door and blurted out, "Pietro is in there!" It was a call to action. Sandra and Gina began tugging at their dresses trying to press the wrinkles out with their hands; they were arranging each other's hair, pinching their cheeks for color, and smoothing their eyebrows with spit. Carla, content with her appearance, entered the chapel before her friends. If Saint Theresa was looking forward to having her shrine cleaned, she would have to wait another day, or settle for a lick-and-a promise, for the girls were intent on finally meeting Pietro.

The lower chapel was far less formal than the upper church. The upper church was used on Sundays, holidays, and for marriages and funerals; the lower chapel was more intimate and regularly used during the week. To prepare him for seminary, Pietro had been advised by Father Primo to spend at least a half hour each day reading his breviary, preferably in church. He regularly took his seat at the front of the chapel by Grandma's shrine. Deeply engrossed in his reading, Pietro did not notice Sandra and Gina slipping along the side aisles until Gina Bianchi was standing directly in front of him. "You're Pietro Petruzelli, aren't you?" Gina asked. Pietro looked up from his breviary, somewhat groggy. He had begun to doze off in the stuffy chapel and was caught off guard. "I am Pietro," he replied and returned to his reading. "Are you becoming a priest?" Gina asked.

"I am considering the priesthood" replied Pietro, never looking up from his breviary. Standing at his side, Sandra Rossi pretended to dust Pietro's breviary to get his attention. "Are you ladies here to clean?" He asked in a tone, reflecting both his class and irritation. Carla stood apart from the group. She wanted to meet Pietro but did not think the moment was appropriate under the circumstances. "Girls, Saint Theresa's shrine is full of dead flowers," she announced, to draw Gina and Sandra away from Pietro.

Unaware of her presence, Pietro was startled by Carla's voice. Softly, she called to her friends once more, "Girls, we should be cleaning." Pietro turned just in time to see Carla sweep her hands through her thick, auburn hair. She was standing in front of the statue of Saint Theresa, caught by a shaft of light coming through a stained-glass window. Tall and thin, green eyes, the olive-colored skin of a southern Italian, and face and body by Botticelli; Carla was a knockout. Pietro caught himself starring at Carla. Hoping he wasn't noticed, he quickly resumed reading his breviary, but now totally distracted by thoughts of Carla. Accustomed to having girls flock around him, he anticipated Carla making a move on him, but it never happened. She simply turned and began dusting the statue of the Saint without ever glancing at Pietro, apparently uninterested, at least that's what he was led to believe, for she was immediately attracted to him. Pietro, unaccustomed to a cold shoulder, sat silently for a moment. He quickly cast a glance in Carla's direction, who by now was directing Gina and Sandra, motioning they should pick up the dead flowers gathered at the shrine. Pietro turned back to his breviary, but its words seemed devoid of meaning. He was far too distracted by Carla to continue reading. He closed the book and decided to leave. He made it a point to cross the sanctuary, going to the opposite side of the chapel, attempting to show his lack of interest in the ladies. Carla's apparent indifference toward him, managed to "get under his skin."

"Goodbye Pietro," whispered Gina, echoed by Sandra, but with never a word from Carla, who just kept dusting. Pietro glanced in their direction, half expecting Carla to be watching him leave. Once again, she reacted in a way unaccustomed by him, ignoring him, as she busily swept up leaves around the shrine. "Girls, help me sweep up the leaves," Carla spoke in a hushed tone, her voice soft and sensuous. Pietro hesitated for a moment, hoping she would bid him goodbye, but she never looked up from her dusting. He left the church without saying a word to the girls, somewhat disoriented by the experience.

CHAPTER 9

The Saint Theresa Society

The Saint Theresa Society was a women's Society, headquartered in a one-story building, tucked in a back street of the North End. The Society was dedicated to Saint Theresa of Lisieux, the Saint known as "The Little Flower", a Carmelite nun who passed away at 24 in 1897. Carla's mother once belonged to the Society, making it easy for Carla to join. The Shrine housed a statue of Saint Theresa, meticulously cared for by the women of the Society. Come September, the statue was carried through the streets of the North End. It was not unusual to see women in bare feet following the statue, a sign of a favor received from the Saint, or one requested. Carla's life seemed to revolve around the Society. The Saint was her patroness, the members her friends, and the chapel, a place to escape the tedium of her everyday life.

There was always a topic that captured the attention of the women of the Society. Talk of a person or a happening in the neighborhood would wrap around each of the members like a vine, joining them in gossip, sometimes dominating the conversation for days and weeks on end. Pietro's presence in the North End captured the attention and imagination of the ladies, like nothing in recent memory. The Shrine became a hot bed of intrigue and gossip. The women speculated on all aspects of his life. Does he have money? Is he a virgin? Will he become a priest? Is one of them a "good match" for him? Pietro was a sensation, demanding as much attention as Saint Theresa. He was young, rich, handsome and tantalizingly unapproachable, making him irresistible to the women. Saint Theresa was going to have serious competition.

Carla went about her duties at the Shrine seemingly indifferent to Pietro, determined to hold herself above the speculation. "Saint Theresa won't be abandoned by me," she vowed to herself, yet thoughts of Pietro kept working their way into her head, unleashing a flurry of cleaning in an attempt to drive the wanton thoughts away. She was torn by her emotions. Speculation over Pietro among the members had gone on for days till Carla could no longer contain herself. "How quickly you forget the Saint!" She scolded. "Pietro wants to become a priest, don't tempt him, it's a sin." "Don't tempt him, it's a sin!" Rosa Fiore said sarcastically. "He's a man and he's not a priest, so we can scheme and plan all we want. I bought a new red dress for The Saint Andrew Feast, and it's tight and silky and shows all my "assets." Get it Carla? All my ASSets!" Carla, boiling over, shot back, "Rosa, you have a dirty mind. Pietro is becoming a priest. Don't tempt him. All this talk is distracting us from our duties at the Shrine. This talk is turning the Shrine into a bordello. You are acting like a bunch of *puttane* (prostitutes)." "Bullshit!" Shot back Rosa. "Saint Carla is pretending she's not interested in Pietro. You want him just as much as the rest of us."

Walking over to Rosa, Carla shoved her cleaning cloth in her face. "Next time, I'll shove it up your assets, Rosa!" Carla snapped. "Saint Carla has a temper. I think she's got the "hots" for Pietro, but she just doesn't want to admit it," said Rosa, rubbing it in. Carla reached for Rosa's hair, but was stopped by Claudia Risoto, Carla's best friend. "Cut it out! Cut it out! What's going on in this place? A guy comes along and we're at each other's throats. Forget Pietro. He's snooty and he's planning to go into the priesthood. Carla and Rosa make up," she implored. The girls looked at each other, began to laugh, both hiked up their skirts and strutted around, pretending to be streetwalkers, then they burst into laughter, the crisis at the Shrine was over.

CHAPTER 10
Neapolitans

The Riccis were fishermen and close friends of our family. Egidio, Carla's father, was carrying on a family tradition hundreds of years old. Carla's five older brothers made up Egidio's entire crew. The Riccis lived in a three-story brick building occupied entirely by their family. Egidio Ricci lived on the first floor with Carla and his son Lorenzo. Frank, who was married, occupied the second floor with his  wife, Anna. On the third floor, Egidio's other sons, Alberto, Mario, and Roberto lived. It was unusual in the North End for one family to occupy an entire building, but the Riccis were successful fishermen and could afford to do so. There was once a bakery in the basement, but it was long gone, and the Riccis used the space to store their fishing equipment, old nets, fishing lines, buoys and all kinds of apparel for life at sea.

Carla's mother died giving birth to her, making Carla the woman of the house, while at the same time, imposing on her a sense of guilt she could not escape. As if to punish herself, she worked tirelessly around the house trying to be a mother, a sister and a daughter, seeming to forget herself and her needs, while constantly attending to the needs of her father and brothers. It was always assumed she would become a nun, given her religious fervor. Carla never commented on the speculation, content to express her religious calling through her devotion to Saint Theresa.

The men of Carla's family were hard working, rough, handsome, unattached, except for Frank, and thoroughly spoiled by Carla. One other thing, they were highly protective of their kid sister and daughter, so much so, guys were afraid to approach her for a date. The entire neighborhood knew what happened to Jerry Lombardo who grabbed her in her doorway. Carla screamed, the brothers stormed down their stairs and beat the crap out of him. Old man Ricci finished the job by waving a large fish hook in front of Jerry's face, promising to use his balls for fish bait. The brothers let him go, sending him on his way with a swift kick in the ass. From that moment on, Carla was "off limits" in the North End, a gorgeous woman no guy would approach. She was forbidden fruit.

The Riccis were from Naples and naturally settled on Garden Court Street with their fellow Neapolitans. To an outsider, the North End was simply an Italian neighborhood, but the residents knew better. You had to be Italian to understand the subtleties of the North End and the way it was settled. It was regionally populated, a microcosm of their native Italy. During the years in which the North End was almost entirely Italian, a period extending into the 1970's, it was a neighborhood divided into sub neighborhoods, determined by the region of Italy you came from. Genoese lived on upper Salem Street and Hull Street near the Old North Church. Business like and somewhat dower, they were known to be "tight with a buck." Neapolitans lived in the center of the North End along Hanover Street and the streets that ran from it. Gregarious, fun-loving and musical, they filled the streets of their neighborhood with laughter and noise. The Sicilians, who were mostly fishermen, lived by the sea, particularly on North and Fleet Streets. Their husbands and sons were often lost at sea, resulting in their neighborhood suffering a disproportionate amount of sadness. They possessed fierce family loyalty and a strong connection to their ancestral roots in Sicily. Salem and Endicott streets housed the Calabrese. Together, these groups made up the bulk of the North End's inhabitants. We, like most North Enders, tended to stay close to our regional neighborhood, straying into another section only when necessary.

Garden Court Street, where Mom's family lived and where Mom grew up, was part of the Neapolitan world. It announced itself as Neapolitan from a block away as you approached it. Family life seemed to spill out of the flats and onto the street. Nothing was so private it could not be shouted to the entire street. Births, deaths, infidelities, engagements, every occasion, every emotion was shared with the "street", binding residents together more like family than neighbors. Grandpa Bernardo would sit on his stoop for hours on end, playing his mandolin and serenading Grandma, his native Naples, and anyone who came along. Grandma didn't appreciate Grandpa's public show of affection, at least on the surface. During his frequent serenades, she would come to the window and gesture with her hands that he should stop singing. This was done more for the neighbors than for Grandpa. Privately, she was flattered and never said a word to discourage him. The Riccis were their neighbors and like so many Neapolitans, they were very proud of their once-illustrious city. A common Italian dialect created a natural bond between our families. Neapolitans are a spontaneous group, inclined to do whatever comes into their heads.

There was a little old lady by the name of Concetta, widowed for many years, who lived across the street from Grandpa and Grandma. She perched on her windowsill like a blackbird, watching the goings and comings of her neighbors and shouting insults in a thin, shrill voice to those who ignored her. She had a large, black mole on her face that added to her witchlike appearance. The kids thought she was a witch, and she did little to discourage their thoughts. She seemed to have a grudge against street vendors, cackling out Italian curses while placing her order from the window. Tomaso was a little old man who sold vegetables from a rickety old wagon drawn by Pepe, a rickety old horse. One summer day, she grabbed Tomaso by the throat and accused him of cheating her. He gave her the vegetables for nothing, vowing never to sell to her again. As if in revenge for Concetta's bad treatment of his master, Pepe would take a particularly long piss under her window, whenever they passed her way. Hot and steamy, the odor drifted into Concetta's flat, setting off a torrent of curses which delighted Tomaso, as he danced a little jig, indicating his delight and further angering Concetta.

It was a hot Wednesday in July when every window in the neighborhood was open. Concetta's was no different. It was into the third week of the pissing and dancing when the old lady decided she had enough. She waited for Tomaso at an open window, hidden from sight by a faded rose-colored curtain. Tomaso and Pepe slowly made their way down Garden Court, when as if on cue, Pepe stopped and began to relieve himself just under Concetta's window. In an instant, Concetta appeared at the window with a bucket of cold water, dumping it over the back of the horse, startling him and shutting off the piss as if she turned off a spigot with a monkey wrench. Pepe began to gallop down Garden Court Street with Tomaso running behind the cart screaming, "She tried to kill my horse!" As for Concetta, she stood at her open window, cackling and cursing, every bit "the witch" in her moment of triumph.

Stuff like that was happening all the time. Street vendors selling their produce, making their way slowly through the tangle of streets; statues of saints parading through the streets; old men making wine in their basements from age-old recipes; old women sitting on their stoops on hot summer evenings, talking and crocheting, reminiscing about Italy in broken English that slipped naturally into Italian. There were groups of kids buzzing through the narrow streets on homemade scooters made from a two by four found in the railroad yard, a discarded orange crate from Haymarket, and an old pair of skates; and always the church, the heartbeat of the neighborhood. Not apple pie but cannoli, not Coca Cola but Tamarindo. We hovered somewhere between the old and new world, never alighting on one or the other for very long, and never realizing how different and how lucky we were. We were not your typical American neighborhood.

CHAPTER 11
Zia Elena

Please permit me to say a few words about my daughter Elena. You might remember, I said at the beginning of this book, I would interrupt the story every so often, when I thought it was necessary to shed a bit more light and better explain the events in this story.

Elena is the second youngest of my five daughters. She was full of mischief as a child, always getting in trouble, while at the same time, possessing a heart of gold. She has a true Neapolitan soul, hardworking and full of fun. There is a saying, Italians can turn stone into bread in order to feed their families. It perfectly applies to Elena. Like me, she has eight children and like me, she is poor. The similarity ends there. Elena could rely on her wits to survive, whereas I needed the help of my wife, Philomena. Her little cantina helped put bread on our table, where as I said earlier, I worked for small wages as a sexton in our village church. In truth, it was the only place I felt at home. I guess, I never quite left the monastery. I have said enough.

It was on Saturday, roughly three weeks after Pietro's arrival in Boston, Grandma decided Pietro ought to meet her sister Elena and the relatives living in East Boston, just a five-cent ferry ride away. She asked Mom to accompany her. Since we loved the adventure of the ferry ride, we asked Mom if we could come along. Mom cautiously agreed, but warned Bobby, "I don't want you taking Charlie to the railing of the ferry. He might fall overboard. The two of you will sit with me."

The ferry ride over to East Boston was always a fun experience; for five cents, you got yourself a twenty-minute mini ocean voyage. The ferry pier was located on Atlantic Avenue. There were two ferry boats that made the crossing to East Boston. One was docked in the North End, while the other was docked in East Boston, allowing for a continuous flow of passengers and freight. The boats had a wooden super structure, painted dark green, that sat upon what looked like a large grey barge with a rounded bow, protected by rubber tires, acting as bumpers. When docking, the ferry would be nuzzled into a pier having the same rounded shape as the ferry's bow, receiving the ferry with a series of slams and bangs, as it came to a stop. Once stopped, a wooden gate would lift and automobiles, pushcarts, anything with wheels were pushed or driven off the lower deck as passengers disembarked, climbing down from the upper deck. Once emptied, the process was reversed, as carts, wagons and automobiles were pushed or driven onto the lower deck, and passengers climbed metal staircases, on either side of the ferry's superstructure, to the upper deck.

During the crossing, parents took time to socialize with neighbors while their kids played pirate, dangling off the side of the ferry, driving their parents and the skipper crazy. The idea was to make the skipper blast his horn, stand and yell from his cabin. We knew he had to remain at the wheel, so we could taunt him through the entire trip then run like crazy, leaping to the pier, just before docking. Often, making the crossing to markets on the opposite shore, were smelly trucks carrying chickens in wooden cages. The kids would slip between the parked cars till they reached the offending truck, and release as many chickens as possible from their cages. The truck driver would be frantic, torn between chasing after his chickens and wanting to grab us. Every so often, a chicken would run right off the deck straight into the ocean. This would set off curses from the truck driver as he watched his profits sink with the frantic chicken.

Pietro, standing by the railing, was both stunned and amused, as he watched the tangle of life arranging itself around him. There were mothers with carriages, old men and women struggling to find seats, vendors with their goods in leather carrying bags roaming the deck, and the smell of food drifting over the crowd mixing with the scent of the sea, stirring appetites. Mom, as usual, dashed up the flight of stairs leading to the upper deck and grabbed a space large enough to accommodate the five of us. She insisted Charlie and Bobby should not leave their seats, fearing they would join up with their friends who she knew would be dangling off the side of the ferry. Grandma seemed to take charge of Pietro. Knowing he was unfamiliar with the ferry, she urged him to sit with her through the twenty-minute crossing.

The moment we left the pier, shopping bags quickly opened, and food appeared: sandwiches, wine, cheese and fruit. The upper deck of the ferry was immediately transformed into an outdoor, floating trattoria. Passengers passed food from one to another, anxious to try the cuisine of the various regions of Italy represented on board. Salami seemed to be in every shopping bag, including Grandma's. The spicy meat was shoved in your face accompanied by, *"mangia, mangia."* You were urged to eat with an urgency, which seemed to suggest, your eating powered the ferry. We had twenty minutes before docking; twenty minutes to eat, share, drink and complement. Children and the elderly were always taken care of first. It was then a free-for-all that magically ended with a thud, as the ferry collided with the docking pier. All that remained of the frenzy, which had just taken place, were the food wrappers blowing around the deck and into the harbor.

Pietro had thoroughly enjoyed the food fest, sampling a bit of everything handed him. Unaccustomed to our form of dining at sea, he was splattered with food, from his neat white shirt to his tan linen trousers, wearing a sampling of the day's menu. Grandma, taking pity on him, tried to clean him up, but it was useless. Tomato sauce and sausage drippings would have to accompany him to Zia Elena's house, which was actually a good thing, for he would blend right in with the rest of her family. The fact we were also splattered seemed to make little difference to Grandma and Mom, this was our usual state at the end of these crossings.

East Boston in the 1940s was like the North End, a population totally made up of Italians. It was unlike the North End because of its rural quality. This was the result of the wooden houses as opposed to the red brick tenements found in the North End, and the amazing produce gardens that were a part of every double and triple decker house. The gardens often abutting each other, creating mini farms. Elena was an earthy woman, rough around the edges, with survival instincts honed out of a need to support her eight children. Her husband, Gaetano, loved tending their garden. He was never able to find a job that paid enough to support the family, leaving it up to resourceful Elena, a true daughter of Naples. The two sisters were opposite in every way. Grandma was petite, reserved in dress and manner. Elena was heavyset with a grease-splattered apron permanently wrapped around her waist. She had an outgoing personality that made her loved by the neighbors. She was courted by politicians who knew for a favor, they could count on Elena to swing neighborhood votes in their direction. She was a favorite of Boston's legendary Mayor Curly, making it a point to stand curbside with her eight children, whenever he paraded through the neighborhood. She would gesture and shout to the mayor, reassuring him that in an election, she could deliver votes.

Elena had a dog named Skipper, a German Shepherd that wandered into her backyard and never left. Elena never knew its former owner, she figured he must have been a crook because of a peculiar trick that Skipper performed. Whenever Elena took the dog into a grocery store, Skipper would gingerly open his mouth, quickly glance around, making certain he was not being observed, and scoop into his mouth whatever was available. He could even handle eggs without breaking them. At first, Elena scolded the dog and tried to break him of his habit, but he wouldn't obey, so she figured, what the hell, he could help feed the family.

Elena and Gaetano lived on Paris Street with their eight children in a rundown house, that seemed on the verge of collapse. The house was a hotbed of activity with people coming and going. Children, friends, and neighbors came and went throughout the day and into the night. It was the backyard that made the house so amazing. Every inch of their tiny yard was covered with plants. There was a section for tomatoes, another for green beans and peppers in the rear by the fence. You passed into the garden through an enormous arbor of grapes destined to become wine in the autumn. Under the arbor, stood a battered table covered with a checkered red oilcloth surrounded by four or five battered chairs. Food was constantly present. It seemed to magically appear, get devoured by someone or something and again reappear. Crockery pitchers filled with peaches soaked in homemade red wine never seemed to run dry. Old wooden wine barrels scented the garden from vintages of past years. They were piled up aside the house waiting to be filled once again in autumn.

CHAPTER 12
A Bit of Italy

As we wrote earlier, Zia Elena lived as if she never left the farm in Naples. Her door was always open, family, friends and strangers passing through her house, as naturally as walking down the street. There was a sampling of everything growing in her garden, growing in her house. The windowsills were crowded with cuttings from the garden, the kitchen table strewn with food in all stages of preparation. Garlands of garlic were hung everywhere, taralli, circles of cooked dough, looking something like misshapen donuts, were hung from strings by the window near the kitchen sink, constantly removed and replenished to serve the never-ending flow of people passing through her kitchen.

We arrived at Elena's, just in time to hear her telling her daughters Susie and Josie to clean off a space on the kitchen table for her guests. As Grandma entered the house, she made her usual comment, *"Elena, la tua casa e' sempre sporca."* After making her point in Italian, she repeated it in English, "Elena, your house is always dirty." She would then add, "I have to lift my skirt when I enter it." It was Grandma's way of saying hello. Elena would always respond, *"Puoi stare a casa tua"* (Then stay home.) Once they got through their greetings, they hugged, while Elena reached for a string of taralli and asked Susie to put on a pot of espresso. Grandma and Mom sat at the kitchen table, while the two of us ran into the garden to see what we could catch to bring home as a pet. Pietro appeared overwhelmed. Before he could say *buongiorno*, Elena was kissing him on both cheeks while shoving him into a chair to eat something, and onto several tomatoes that looked as if they were sitting there for ages. They squished as only over ripe tomatoes can squish, causing Grandma to scream. Pietro jumped to his feet, but it was too late, he now was stained on his backside with tomato skins clinging to his linen pants, then dropping to the floor.

"Take them off!" ordered Elena. "Susie will wash them and hang them in the garden to dry. By the time you leave, you will be nice and neat." Grandma was now half crazy. "Elena, *sei fuori di testa* (Elena, you are out of your mind)!" She screamed. "Pietro is a gentleman. He's becoming a priest and you want him running around in his underwear." "What underwear?" Elena screamed back! "He can wear my husband's pants." "But your husband is filthy, he's a *cafone* (boor)!" Screamed Grandma. Elena, hardly offended by Grandma calling her husband filthy and ignorant, began pulling on Pietro's belt, motioning to him to remove his trousers. Pietro appeared to be in shock, he seemed unable to speak or move. Grandma came to his rescue by taking him by the hand, bringing him into a little bedroom separated from the kitchen by an old red drape, that looked as if it was hanging there for 100 years. She then yelled out to Mom, "Carmela, find Pietro some clean pants, I will wash out his trousers."

Several minutes later, Pietro emerged wearing a pair of Zio Gaetano's pants, several inches too short and several sizes too large, held up with a rope tied around his waist. He also appeared in his undershirt, Grandma decided to wash out his badly soiled white linen shirt. In a matter of twenty minutes, Pietro was transformed from an Italian gentleman to an Italian peasant. Zia Elena had struck, Pietro was both her welcomed guest and her latest victim. Within minutes of his transformation, we all settled into a banquet that seemed to appear from out of nowhere, while Grandma was scrubbing Pietro's pants and shirt on a washboard at the kitchen sink. Pietro, for his part, seemed at ease. He was laughing and once again becoming splattered with tomato sauce. All his reserve was gone. He was digging in like the rest of us, nineteen years of fine Roman breeding, suspended in Elena's kitchen.

CHAPTER 13

Several Hours Later

I t was late afternoon when Grandma and Mom decided to return home. Elena wanted us to stay for supper, but Grandma insisted we had to leave. Mom asked Zia Elena where Bobby and Charlie were? Elena pointed to the garden, while at the same time pulling some lettuce leaves off a head of Romaine. "Bobby and Charlie, come in, we're leaving!" Mom cried out. We slipped into Elena's kitchen with a shoebox, she had given us for the new little pet, we planned to take home. Mom caught sight of the box we were trying to conceal under an old dishcloth. "Carmela, it's nothing, just *un coniglietto* (a baby rabbit)," Elena explained. She had several in a cage that she was fattening up for some future feast. "I don't want that rat in my house!" Mom shouted. To Mom, anything with a pointy face and fur was a rat. "Carmela, it's not a rat, it's a rabbit, when it gets big, you can eat it." Mom was beside herself. "Elena, you live on a farm. We have a three-room flat with six of us living in it, along with a dog and goldfish. Once that rabbit comes home, the kids will never give it up." Elena seemed to be deaf, without a hint of acknowledging Mom's complaint, she opened the box just enough to feed the rabbit the lettuce leaves she was holding in her hand. "Mangia, mangia," and as if it understood Italian, the rabbit began eating.

It was then Mom caught a glimpse of the gray furry ball, she melted, and we knew we could keep it. "It will have to remain in the kitchen. You can't take it to bed, and you have to make sure the dog doesn't kill it." We anxiously agreed to Mom's terms, as we have always agreed in the past, knowing Dad would ultimately take care of Peter. She then asked, "Did you name him after Pietro?" "No, after Peter Cottontail." Pietro, listening intently, joined in, "Who's Peter Cottontail?" We tried to explain, but quickly dropped the subject when Peter hopped out of the box and headed into the garden. Pietro took off after his namesake, got as far as the bean plants, where he tripped over a garden hose, landing face down in the mud surrounding them. Grandma caught sight of the entire incident and began screaming, "We have to leave *questa casa di pazzi* (this crazy house)!"

She called to Mom to help clean him up, while she went to the clothesline looking for Pietro's clothes which she had hung out to dry. When she couldn't find them, she panicked, thinking they were stolen. Grandma yelled out, "I should never have hung the clothes outdoors. Pietro's clothes are the clothes of a gentleman, a *cafone* in the neighborhood stole them!" Elena yelled from the kitchen, "What cafone! The big shot from the North End thinks we're all cafoni. I hung them over the stove so they would dry quickly." Grandma, sensing a disaster, ran past Elena to the stove arriving just in time to see Pietro's pants catch fire. Grandma panicked and began slapping at them with a wet towel. Elena, on the other hand, treated the incident as a routine occurrence. She simply grabbed a pan of water sitting on the stove, tossed the water in the direction of the pants, and walked away without seeing if the fire was extinguished. Miraculously, it was. The pants began to smolder, mimicking Grandma's mood. She was ready to burst with exasperation and embarrassment. Only Pietro was spared her wrath.

"Carmela, get the boys, we're leaving." By then, we had our rabbit back in the box sitting a-top of a shopping bag full of vegetables from Elena's garden, waiting by the entrance door. Pietro joined us, still wearing Gaetano's pants, only now his undershirt was filthy from his role in the mud. Mom had tried her best to clean it, but it was hopelessly soiled. Mom was still wiping him off while we were waiting for Grandma at the front entrance. We then caught sight of Grandma emerging from Elena's cellar, she was carrying a bottle of red wine, Elena following with a crock of vinegar peppers. It was obvious she was attempting to win over Grandma for the various disasters of our visit, and it worked. Grandma joined us at the doorway. She slipped the bottle of wine into the shopping bag containing Peter and the vegetables. She eyed the shoe box, gave us one of her looks, but said nothing, figuring, Peter was not her problem. She probably had Easter in mind, when rabbit is often served. Elena and Grandma embraced, they then kissed each other on both cheeks, setting off a torrent of kisses from Elena. She got each of us, saving her biggest and wettest for Pietro. He embraced her and kissed her on both cheeks; his eyes were glistening with tears, as he simply said, *"Ti amo Zia Elena"* (I love you Aunt Elena). You never left Zia Elena's empty handed, wine and vinegar peppers for Grandma, vegetables for Mom, and a rabbit for us. As for Pietro, he lost his fine clothes, but gained an aunt who made him laugh, fed him till he was about to burst, and most of all, loved him as one of the family.

CHAPTER 14
Visit to Fenway Park

It was about the fourth week of Pietro's visit, when Mom decided Pietro's stay in Boston would not be complete without a visit to Fenway Park. After all, summer in Boston is all about baseball. Boston in 1949 had two teams, the Red Sox over at Fenway, and the Boston Braves at Braves Field. We, like so many in the North End, were loyal Braves fans. They were the underdog team you "just had to love." The Red Sox, on the other hand, had Ted Williams and Dom DiMaggio, two local heroes who we all wanted to emulate. The Yankees were coming to town, which of course meant Joe DiMaggio, "The Yankee Clipper," would be playing. He was returning to the roster after being sidelined by a bone spur. He was a god. Even though he played for the arch enemy, we all rooted for him, we had no choice. Not only was he baseball's greatest hitter, he was Italian, which meant the entire North End would be at the game cheering for Joe and cursing the Yankees.

Our oldest brother, Anthony, was assigned the job of familiarizing Pietro with the rules of the game that seemed to totally confound him. Pietro spoke in soccer terms while Anthony was talking baseball. Mom kept saying, "Pietro, we don't kick the ball, we hit it with a bat." Anthony finally gave up trying to teach Pietro, telling Mom, "It's only a visit to Fenway that will get through to him." Dad, who worked the night shift at the newspaper, remained home getting ready for work. Mom warned, "Bobby and Charlie, you can come along, but you can't get into trouble."

We caught the subway at Park Street Station. It was a steamy hot

Saturday, the train was packed with people, all heading for the game. The train was a hotbox. An old fan in the ceiling was making a whirring sound; it did little to make things comfortable, its sole purpose seemed to be, to make a whirring sound. The windows of the train were open, filling the car with the dank smell of Boston's ancient subway system, while dust and grime swept up by the train clung to our sweaty skin. We swayed and lurched our way to Fenway, accompanied by the constant screech of the wheels, and passengers numb from the heat, dizzy with body odor that you could cut with a knife. Everyone was wet and sweaty, one older woman kept threatening to faint. When Pietro tried to help her, she called for the conductor, claiming she was being accosted. Anthony called her an old bag and told her to shut up, as for the passengers, they seemed too dazed from the heat to pay attention to her. Everyone just wanted to get out of the hotbox. One final lurch and we arrived at Kenmore Square. The doors opened, and a sea of humanity, heading for Fenway, pushed and shoved its way into the bright light, all instantly invigorated by the fresh air and the thought of the game about to begin.

We were headed for the bleachers, along with everyone else from the subway. People were coming from all directions. Mom bought our tickets; we then worked our way up to the bleachers where we were lucky enough to find five seats together. Fenway was filling to capacity. You could always count on a full house whenever the Yankees were in town. Pietro was totally captivated by Fenway, not only the look of the old Park, but by what was going on all around us. People were already in high spirits, shouting the usual insults at the players. Typical of the insults, "Yanks, you suck, we're going to kick your ass in!" One guy was holding up his shoe, yelling, "Hey Yanks, this is going up your ass!" The hot dog vendors were out in full force, while other vendors were selling pennants, hats and anything that could turn a buck. The atmosphere was electric, the sun broiling, and the crowd growing noisier as the game drew near.

Mom wanted to buy some peanuts from a vendor two sections away, so she took off in a flash wanting to be back for the National Anthem. It was then two teenage girls sitting behind us made their move. Betty, a strawberry blonde with a Veronica Lake look-alike hairdo and too much makeup, grabbed Anthony by the arm while shouting in his ear, "Hi

Doll, want to buy me a hot dog?" Cindy, a busty brunette done up like Jane Russell, was all over Pietro. "I heard you speaking. You're Italian, aren't you? I love your accent, it's so sexy." Anthony and Pietro looked at each other, shrugged their shoulders and decided to have some fun. Pietro stood on his seat, reached over to Cindy, and maneuvered her onto his seat and onto his lap. Anthony, who was younger and smaller, could not manage the same move, but liked what Pietro managed to accomplish. He improvised by asking Betty to step over the back of his seat, into his aisle, and onto his lap. Betty was obliging. All the while being the younger brothers, we kept yelling out, "When Mom returns and sees what you're doing, she's going to be really mad!"

Just as everyone was settling into their new seating arrangements, a voice could be heard above the crowd. It was Mom returning with the peanuts. "What the hell is going on?" She shouted, taking Cindy by the arm. She shouted again, "What's going on? Who are these floozies?" Cindy pulled away and quickly shouted back, "Who are you, their grandmother?" Now she was in for it. Cindy hit the wrong nerve, the age nerve. It was not going to be pretty. Mom dumped her peanuts on Cindy and tossed the box at Betty. Anthony and Pietro were up in a flash, leaving the girls in the seats they once occupied as couples. "Isn't this a pretty picture!" Yelled Mom. "Two floozies trying to tempt a priest and a young boy!"

The word priest hit Cindy like an electric shock. "You're a priest!" She shouted. "You're going to make me go to hell!" Pietro was now half out of his mind with Mom's insistence on calling him a priest. "I'm not a priest. Why does everyone keep calling me a priest?" By this time, Cindy and Betty were lifting their skirts to climb back into their seats. Cindy kept shaking her ass in Pietro's face driving Mom crazy. Mom yelled out, "You're tempting him again!" While she was saying this, Pietro was trying to steady Cindy by holding on to her ass. Anthony was attempting the same maneuver when Mom gave him a whack on the back of his head, cutting him short, while at the same time telling Pietro, "Priests don't act that way. Leave her rear end alone." Mom shouted out to Anthony, "You're going to get it when we return home!" He tried to put on a brave face, but he knew what Mom meant. She would tell Dad everything, and Dad who we sometimes called the Pilgrim because of his puritanical tendencies, was not going to like Anthony's latest antics. Even Pietro was looking a bit sheepish at Mom's threat.

While all this was going on, the National Anthem began. Gradually, we all settled down out of respect for the flag. While the anthem was playing, Mom kept looking at Pietro with a look that seemed to be saying, "What's going on with you?" The sight of Cindy sitting on his lap was setting off warning signals in her head, confirming an uneasy suspicion that was now identified (Is Pietro meant to be a priest?) As for Anthony, she figured sooner or later girls would be in his life. She would prefer a little later, but she knew Dad would straighten him out. Pietro, on the other hand, was planning to be a priest, so what was Cindy doing on his lap?

The umpire yelled out, "Play ball!" All our attention quickly turned to the game. The booing from the crowd clearly announced that the Yankees were at bat. Mom began booing. The incident was over, at least for the moment. When Joe DiMaggio finally came on deck, you could feel the electricity in the stands with every practice swing he took. The crowd erupted in cheers. Yankee or Red Sox fan, everyone cheered for "The Yankee Clipper." As the game proceeded, the Red Sox took a 7 to 1 lead which faded by the eighth inning when the game was tied 7-7, DiMaggio contributing 3 of the Yankees' runs. Once again, DiMaggio was at bat, it felt like the calm before the eruption. The pitcher fired one across the plate. "Strike one!" The umpire shouted. DiMaggio, stepped out of the batter's box, returned in a second, cocked his bat, and waited for the next pitch. The crowd was screaming. He swings, the unmistakable crack of the bat, announcing he was back for real. He knocked a two-run homer over the Green Monster, winning the game for the Yankees, 9-7, an all-too-familiar scenario that Boston fans had to once again suck up. Any goodwill generated by DiMaggio for the Yankees went down the toilet with that homer.

CHAPTER 15
Leaving Fenway Park

As we were leaving Fenway, a Yankee fan shouted to the man with the shoe, "Now you can shove the shoe up your ass!" In a flash, the shoe went flying at his head, prompting a small cheer from the immediate fans. Within seconds, the two guys were rolling on the ground punching each other. Then someone from the crowd yelled out, "Are there any other Yankee fans around here?" Someone in the crowd yelled back, "We really kicked your ass in!" At this point, Mom yelled out, "Let's get the hell out of here, they're going crazy!" We pushed our way to the exit. Pietro kept looking back to see the free-for-all that was erupting. Mom grabbed him by the hand and pulled him toward the exit ramp. Once we hit the street, Pietro, as if to disprove any doubt of his vocation, was on his best behavior. He kept his eyes cast down as we maneuvered our way through the dejected fans, and when we ran into Cindy, he seemed to have amnesia as he breezed right past her. Cindy, on the other hand, had no loss of memory, as she shouted out, "That stuck up little shit is a sneaky little bastard!" A comment returned by Mom with her usual, "Wash out your mouth, you little floozy!"

Now that the air was clear of doubt, we figured things would return to normal, but we figured wrong. Mom decided to take us to the Kenmore Sandwich Shop. We followed the crowd toward Kenmore Square, straight into the sandwich shop, where Mom decided to treat us all to banana splits. It would be a treat for all of us, and in particular Pietro, who was unfamiliar with this American classic. The place was crowded with disappointed fans who seemed to be turning to ice cream to lift their spirits. We waited for a table. When one opened, Mom made a dive for it. In no time, the five of us were seated around a table meant for two. Mom doing the motherly thing, cleared the table of empty frappe glasses, while complaining, "These people are a bunch of slobs," as she placed the empty glasses on a side cart meant for busboys.

Shortly, a waitress appeared. She took our order, five banana splits topped with marshmallow and chocolate sauce. The waitress was gone for just a moment when we were paid a visit by Cindy and Betty, only this time they were with their brothers, who were not in a good mood. Cindy's brother Joey, was built like a truck, and Betty's brother Carl, had a scar that ran down his left cheek, gaining him the nick name "Scar Face." It was Scar Face that got things going. "I heard you guys are too good for our sisters," he snarled. "Don't answer him," Mom cautioned. "He's looking for trouble." "I repeat, I heard you guys think you're too good for our sisters." "He's becoming a priest and Anthony is just a kid," replied Mom. "So, what were our sisters doing on their laps if they're so innocent," shot back Joey, adding, "I heard grandma over there, thinks our sisters are floozies." "Who the hell is their grandma!" Mom fired back. Cindy added to the raucous, "Don't like being called grandma, grandma?"

Mom was now in a real fighting mood. "Hey Cindy, you're no Betty Grable. Those gams of yours would look great on a piano." Mom's wisecrack caused Scar Face to laugh. "Hey Cindy, granny is calling you Piano Legs." "Enjoying yourself Carl? Why don't we tell the folks how you got your scary scar?" Carl backing off said, "Why don't you keep your trap shut, Piano Legs!" That did it. Cindy was pissed off, really pissed off. "Hey granny, take your kids and stand aside, I'm going to mop the floor with this asshole." "Carl, wasn't it Bridget Sullivan who cut you with a letter opener when you got fresh with her, and what did Carl do, big scary Carl? He fainted! He fainted like an old lady from the sight of his blood." Carl reaching for Cindy's offending mouth was stopped in his tracks by Joey. He caught Carl's hand in midair and twisted his arm behind his back. Betty seeing her brother in trouble, kicked Joey in the shins. It wasn't long until the four of them were punching each other, while Cindy was climbing all over Carl's back.

Someone yelled for the manager. Mom began shoving us, "Come on, let's get the hell out of here, the manager is going to call the cops!"

The moment we got out of the sandwich shop, we began running toward Kenmore Square and the subway. We were laughing as we ran. Mom was laughing like the rest of us. It was as if she was a kid again. Pietro ran like a gazelle. He would get out in front of us, turn, say something in Italian, then turn back and continue to run. He was having a great time. In fact, we were all having a great time. We just had to keep it all quiet so that Dad didn't find out about our great time.

CHAPTER 16

Cooking School

The great thing about the 1940s was that moms were still housewives and at home for the kids. Mom was no exception. She was always there waiting for us, only she usually had her coat on, and was ready to take us somewhere as soon as we came through the door. One of her favorite places was cooking class at the North End Trade School. The North End Trade School in the 1940s oriented itself to basic neighborhood needs that included a nursery, craft classes, summer camp and of course, cooking classes. The school was housed in an old three-story brick building. The cooking classes were held in a large kitchen on the main floor, where a dozen or more neighborhood women would gather twice a week to learn basic American cooking, but the classes seemed to be about anything but cooking.

Mom was a good cook and really didn't need lessons. In fact, most of the women who attended the classes were good cooks. Mom went to learn how to cook American style food, at least that's the explanation she gave Dad. She really went because she and her friends at the school enjoyed getting together, gossiping and just being out of the house for an hour or two. They would drive Mrs. Clark, their cooking teacher, crazy by sprinkling garlic liberally on every dish she taught them, from macaroni and cheese to southern fried chicken, nothing escaped a drenching with garlic powder. Toward the end of class, they would sit down to eat what they just learned to cook. Mrs. Clark would invariably be upset with the changes Mom and her friends made to her recipes.

Eventually, she would succumb, toss up her hands as if to say, "You're all incorrigible," then would sit and enjoy the gossip and the joking among her students who were actually her friends. A sea of carriages was parked outside the kitchen, their occupants kept calm with cookies, milk or anything that would keep the kids from crying. Laughter was always the main ingredient of the cooking lessons. The mothers had a blast. Mrs. Clark would try to keep a semblance of order, but it was always short lived. The mothers were young, the gossip plenty, and the neighborhood so close, the mothers were more like members of one family than neighbors.

It was in July that Carla Ricci decided to join the cooking classes. Like the other women, she was a good cook, but she offered the same reason for joining, she wanted to learn American style cooking. Carla arrived at the class greeted by a roar of laughter. One of the ladies told an off-color joke with a punch line that was being delivered as Carla walked through the door. She spotted Mom talking with Mrs. Clark and went over to her, greeting her with a kiss on the cheek. "Hi Carmela. I heard you like the cooking classes, so I thought I'd join to learn American style cooking." Mom was happy to see Carla and introduced her to Mrs. Clark. "Carla and her family are close friends of our family. They're from Garden Court Street," Mom explained. Mrs. Clark greeted Carla with her usual stiff handshake, then handed her an apron, pointed to the kitchen and shouted to the ladies, "Let's get cooking!" The women gathered in the kitchen to watch Mrs. Clark prepare brownies.

Class was just about to begin when one of the babies began crying, spreading from baby to baby until the entire makeshift parking lot erupted in tears. Mrs. Clark, familiar with these interruptions, placed her mixing bowl on the kitchen counter and gave out her usual, "Let's take five." Carla spotted a pot of coffee perking on the stove. It seemed about ready to drink, so she poured out two cups and followed Mom who was dragging two chairs to the far end of the kitchen, where they could talk and catch up on news. Bobby and Charlie were in a class on the second floor, learning how to weave gimp, so Mom was free to talk to Carla while the kids were being kept out of her hair. They were busy weaving together red and blue plastic strips to make a leash for Queenie, their latest pet; a black mongrel that spent her time chewing up the linoleum in the hallway, just outside our flat.

After the usual small talk about family and friends, Carla maneuvered the conversation to Pietro. Nervously, she asked, "I heard you have a guest from Italy living with you for the summer." "Yes," Mom replied. My mother's nephew, Pietro Petruzelli, my cousin. He will be entering the seminary in the fall. He was sent to America to see the rest of his family and enjoy the summer." "I've seen him in church reading his breviary. He seems very nice," Carla responded. Mom's antenna began rising slowly. She thought to herself, "Carla is a beautiful girl and Pietro very handsome." Carla is not blind. Mom figured, she might be interested in him, she figured right, but she wasn't going to let on about her suspicions, Mom was too foxy, she was hoping to sound Carla out.

Carla questioned, "Pietro is a young man. Do you believe he knows his mind?" "He's going to become a priest," Mom emphasized, trying to nip in the bud any possible situation. "As I've said, he will be entering seminary in September when he returns to Italy." Mom responded with a growing suspicion of Carla's intentions. Then Mom went for the juggler. "Have your brothers beaten up anyone lately? I heard about Jerry Lombardo." Carla got the message. She knew Mom was on to her, so she stopped fishing. Trying to dispel any suspicion from Mom's mind, Carla asked, "Do you have a lot of interruptions like this, you know, babies crying?" Mom wasn't buying it. "I remember your father threatening Jerry with a large fish hook. All this because Jerry made a pass at you." Carla, knowing she was getting nowhere with Mom, stood up. "I can't stay any longer. Please tell Mrs. Clark, I will return some other day."

Josie and Nora, two of Mom's closest friends, worked their way across the kitchen as Carla brushed by them on her way out. In her usual blunt manner, Nora asked, "What was going on between you and the Ricci girl?" Mom preferred not giving Nora a straight answer, knowing whatever she told her would be spread around the North End in a day. "We were just discussing cooking class. She wants to learn American style cooking." "It looked more serious than that," Nora replied, fishing for a good piece of gossip. "The girls of Saint Theresa Society think

Carla's got a "thing" for your cousin Pietro." "If it's true, Pietro better watch his step," chimed in Josie. "You know the stories about her brothers and father, Carla is definitely hands-off." "What are you girls talking about?" Mom shot back. "Carla wants to learn how to cook American style, you girls have dirty minds." "Then why did she leave? Whatever you said to her seemed to have pissed her off. I think you were talking about your cousin Pietro, not how to make hamburgers," Nora continued. "Maybe she wants to make hamburgers with Pietro," Josie said with a snicker. "I heard Carla likes hamburgers." Now it was Nora's turn to stir the pot. "If something's up and her brothers get wind of it, they'll make hamburger out of Pietro." "Pietro is becoming a priest. He's not interested in having a fling," Mom responded defensively. "You girls should wash out your mouths."

Mrs. Clark was now back in the kitchen, the babies had settled down, and it was time to get cooking. "OK girls, pay attention. Today we will be making brownies, everyone's favorite." "I think Carla was interested in hamburger," Nora whispered in Josie's ear, loud enough for Mom to hear. Mom sent off one of her most nasty looks, quickly shutting Nora up. "Ladies, I don't know what's going on but let's get cooking," insisted Mrs. Clark. "Do you put garlic in brownies?" Wisecracked Josie. Mrs. Clark with the patience of a saint, simply answered, "No," as a roar of laughter filled the room, and the women got cooking.

CHAPTER 17

Pasquale

Every family has its black sheep, for us it was Pasquale, at least for a while, for he was to undergo an amazing transformation, which will be explained later. He was a gambler and a very good one at that. He had an amazing memory that served him well in his gambling, particularly in playing Gin, his game of choice. Because of his effectiveness, many people lost to him, some could not cover their losses.

Pasquale was a brute of a man, the type you would never want to run into in a dark alley. He was related to us through Mom's side of the family, a fact that Dad never allowed Mom to forget. Pasquale went on for years gambling and occasionally threatening force to collect his debt, but never used, because of his size and powerful built. Every so often, he would leave for Florida for a few months. On his return, he could be spotted in his Cadillac cruising down Hanover Street with a big cigar in his mouth, sporting a deep tan. As far as Pasquale was concerned, he was living a great life.

Everything changed the day Pasquale paid a visit to one of his debtors in East Boston. It was a routine job. A man by the name of Vito owed him $3,000 and did not intend to pay. Pasquale knocked on Vito's door. When Vito didn't answer, Pasquale kicked the door in with such force that he knocked it off its hinges. Vito was waiting for Pasquale. The moment he stepped into his flat, Vito jumped up from behind a sofa, and got off two shots before taking off. The first missed, but the second hit Pasquale just below the heart. Pasquale dropped to the floor where he lay semi-conscious. He then, tentatively reached for the spot he was hit. There was no blood, only the bulge of a pocket Bible he carried with him since his First Communion. The bullet was lodged in the Bible. It hit with enough force to knock him off his feet, but it never penetrated the Bible. Pasquale knew the "Good Book" saved his life. He took it as a sign that he needed to change his ways, and so he did. He took an early retirement from his job. This all happened five years earlier. From then on, Pasquale was a fixture parked in his Caddy in front of our church, a cigar clenched firmly in his mouth and Frank Sinatra playing on the car radio at a respectable volume.

From his vantage point, Pasquale saw the goings and comings of visitors to the church. Older women afraid to be in the church alone, were comforted by the fact that Pasquale was just outside the door, a self-appointed Guardian Angel. He would sit there from 10:00 in the morning until 4:00 in the afternoon. He moved his Caddy every so often to take a brief spin down Hanover Street for a meatball sub, brought to him by one of the waiters at Nicolino's, or pass by Louisa's Pizzeria for a pepperoni pizza. His schedule was inflexible, allowing the restaurants to prepare for him, 12 noon at Nicolino's, 3:00 at Louisa's.

Pasquale was an easy guy to talk to. He would greet people from his Caddy as they passed him on their way to church. They would stop to have a chat. He was always willing to offer advice as he puffed on his cigar, while taking an occasional bite out of his sub or pizza, depending on the time of day. His advice generally was "on the money," but every so often he slipped into his old ways by offering, "I'll beat the shit out of him" as a solution to the problem. Invariably, he would catch himself and counter with some sign of remorse, anything from crossing himself to kissing his Communion Bible, still with the hole in it, as a reminder not to return to his old life.

Mom had a soft spot for Pasquale. He was the younger brother of her cousin Anita, who she played with as a child. Anita died young, leaving Pasquale alone with his very stern widowed father. Pasquale often turned to Mom for affection, and Mom was always there for him. Mom would often speak to him of his sister, Anita, who he barely remembered. One of her favorite stories was the time the two young cousins were frightened by a rat. Mom was visiting Anita and decided to spend the night. The two young girls shared a bed as they often did when Mom stayed over, talking and eating cookies until midnight. Anita was a sloppy eater, crumbs from her cookies were sprinkled all over the bed and floor. It was about two in the morning, when the girls were awakened by the sound of scratching under their bed. They knew it was a rat because it happened before. Both girls ducked under the covers and stood quiet, while the rat continued scratching and eating. Mom whispered to Anita, she was a slob, that her crumbs were attracting rats. Anita remained silent, she was munching on a cookie hidden under her pillow. Mom whispered, "Anita stop eating, I'm afraid the rat will come onto the bed." Anita began to giggle. Mom becoming increasingly irritated, shoved Anita off the bed onto the floor, with Anita screaming, the rat was going to bite her. Mom shouted, "You shouldn't be such a sloppy eater. While all this was happening, they could hear the rat scurrying out of the room. Anita quickly hopped back into bed and the two cousins fell asleep. Whenever Mom told one of these stories to Pasquale, he would laugh and cry at the same time, feeling grateful to Mom for recounting these little glimpses into the life of the sister he hardly knew.

Pasquale knew Dad worked the night shift at the newspaper, so he appointed himself our Guardian Angel. He circled our building in his Caddy at least twice during evenings Dad worked. He usually was accompanied by some bombshell snuggled up beside him. Come ten o'clock, our lights would go out, and Pasquale was on his way to the night spots of Park Square.

CHAPTER 18

The School Dance

F riday night was dance night in the North End. The best place to go dancing was the school hall that sat a-top our Grammar School. The hall was a massive wooden structure, a great place for rehearsing the school band. It was decorated with colored lights that circled the hall and posters made by school children. A wooden floor worn from decades of school band rehearsals and functions was interrupted at the center by a parquet inlay, laid for dancing. Usually present was one of our parish priests, their presence automatically reminded the younger people that they were not in a Scollay Square dance hall.

One of our priests, Father Paolo, had a particularly loud voice. Every so often during the night, he would let out a howl triggered by one of the kids acting up. One of the characters who appeared at every dance was Nick Russo, a seventh grader, known as "The Monkey." He would shimmy up one of the columns supporting the roof, getting high enough so no one could grab him. He then shouted insults at the dancers. Nick clung to the column as if he had suction cups attached to his fingers. Once, he began slipping down a column, approaching the grasping hands of Lucretia Galante, just called "Fat Ass" by Nick. Anxious to get her hands on him, she brought a window pole over to her older brother, Gregory, that he hooked on to Nick's belt, pulling him down right into the hands of Lucretia, who clobbered him over the head. Mario Ventre had a mirrored ball he picked up from a dance hall in Scollay Square. The owner had bought a larger ball, so he gave Mario the old one, which he hung off the rafters of the school hall just before the dance began. Mario insisted on taking it down after the dance and taking it home, knowing by possessing the ball, he was the most important guy at the dance after the band leader. Paul Bianco and his three-piece band played all the latest tunes and many "old standards." The kids wanted the jitter bug while their parents were asking for Big Band music.

Little, brown, metal chairs lined the walls of the hall where the "old people" sat, which meant anyone over thirty. If you were under thirty sitting on one of those chairs, you were considered a "beast" or a "dog." It made no difference if you were a girl or a guy, you never sat on one of those chairs. The old ladies sat together doing their knitting and gossiping, only getting up to do the tarantella Bianco would play early in the evening. It only took a couple of opening notes for grandmothers, mothers and daughters to be up on their feet, making their way to the dance floor, and the ever-widening circle of dancers. The women joined hands, then round and round they went, changing direction, collapsing the circle into the center then opening it again. Grandmothers seemed decades younger as they flashed smiles of joy, keeping up with their daughters who would often kick off their shoes, lift their skirts, shaking them briskly from left to right.

Mom was a great dancer and could not wait for Friday nights. We ate dinner in a flash. Mom had already sent Dad on his way to the late shift at the newspaper with a lunch made from whatever she was cooking up for us. Mom was determined to have Pietro come along with the four of us. This would be his first dance in America. She figured it would be nice for him to be with lots of young people his age. Pietro, at first seemed reluctant. He brought up his vocation and felt it would be inappropriate. Mom convinced him the dance was made up of people from the neighborhood who were familiar with his calling and would respect it.

The dance had already begun by the time we arrived. Paul Bianco was playing a tarantella. Mom couldn't wait to join the swirling circle of dancers. As she made her way to the dance floor, she shouted out, "Pietro, watch over Bobby and Charlie!" She cut into the circle and quickly joined hands with dancers to the right and left of her, immediately swept up into the swirl of the dance and the fun and laughter. Mom had a strong voice you could always hear above the crowd. We could clearly hear her laughing as the tempo picked up and the dancing became increasingly hectic. As she was dancing, Mom spotted Grandma sitting with Auntie Stella and shouted in Italian, *"Ma', vieni a ballare!"* (Ma, come and dance!) Grandma kept waving her arms as if to say, "Don't bother me," when finally, Auntie Stella stood up and yelled out, "Old lady let's dance!" This brought Grandma immediately to her feet. She gave Auntie Stella one of her dirty looks, and reluctantly followed her to the dance floor, where Mom grabbed hold of Grandma's hand who in turn grabbed hold of Auntie Stella's, and immediately they were swept up into the swirl of the dance. Grandma, instantly getting into the spirit of the dance, shot off her shoes while keeping pace with the rest of them, shouting out, *"Ora, di chi e' una vecchia signora* (Now, who's an old lady)?" More shoes were kicked off, and before you knew it, all the women were dancing in their bare feet as if they were back in their villages in Italy. The tarantella ended with shouts and laughter, accompanied by applause from the onlookers. The women then began searching for their shoes, which were all in a pile in the center of the dance floor. Auntie Stella kept bringing Grandma the wrong shoes, making her increasingly frustrated. Grandma then turned in the direction of Mom and yelled out, "The Little One did this to me!" Mom shot back, "Who told you to kick off your shoes?" This caused Grandma to laugh while taking one more spin in her bare feet. Mom knew she had a great time.

Pietro wanted to sit and watch the dancing. We told him not to sit on the little, brown, metal chairs lining the wall. He sat on one anyway. Anthony then shouted, "People will call you a dog!" Pietro shrugged his shoulders unconcerned.

Pietro noticed the girls from Saint Theresa Society were at the refreshment table. The crowd was shouting to Paul Bianco, "Play another tarantella!" Carla, who was standing amid the Saint Theresa girls, began glancing around the hall for Pietro, when she noticed he was looking at her. Not wanting to seem interested, she quickly turned her head and began talking to Gina Biaggi. The tarantella had begun. In a flash, Carla made her way to the dance floor, joining up with the other dancers. The tarantella was picking up speed, the women dropped their hands, lifted their skirts and shook them in tune with the music. Mom was having a blast dancing her second tarantella. Grandma and Auntie Stella were already back in their chairs. Mom was twirling and laughing while calling to us. She knew we loved to see her dance. She looked ten years younger. Carla was also ripping up the dance floor, but she was adding stuff to the tarantella. She kept bending her head and throwing her auburn hair back, while at the same time shaking her skirt wildly, her eyes flashing in the direction of Pietro. She seemed to become more beautiful as she danced. Everyone was staring at her, most of all, Pietro. He followed every move she made, seemingly mesmerized by Carla's dancing.

All this did not go unnoticed by her brothers. Finally, the women joined hands once again for a few more turns around the dance floor, with shouts of happiness and laughter, the tarantella was over. Pietro sprung to his feet and began to applaud enthusiastically. He was shouting, "Bravo! Bravo!" as if he was at La Scala in Milan. This led to an epidemic of applause and bravos, prompting the dancers to take an impromptu bow. Carla was the spark that generated Pietro's enthusiasm, and it showed in his eyes. They were firmly fixed on her, as Mom's were fixed on Pietro. She could spot trouble and knew she had to do something.

Once again, Mom decided not to confront Pietro, afraid that any confrontation would drive him away from the family and into Carla's arms. Mom decided she would take the matter up with Grandma the next day, and have Pasquale watch the both of them, since he spent most of his time outside the church frequented by both.

Pietro was back up on his feet and heading in the direction of Carla, who was making her way out of the hall. "Carla, Carla," he anxiously called out to her. Mom, spotting his intention, made her move. She cut across his path and stopped in front of him. "Pietro, do you know how to dance the Charleston?" Mom asked. Pietro was caught off guard and stopped short. He seemed flushed and obviously disturbed. "No, no cousin, I do not know that dance." His eyes never leaving Carla. "Then I will teach you." "Not now cousin", Pietro impatiently replied. Mom continued as if she did not hear him.

Mom loved to dance the Charleston, in fact, she would often dance it by herself in our kitchen. She could dance the shoes off any partner. Mom called out to Bianco to play the Charleston, he obliged her with a sizzling version of the dance. "Pietro, move your legs like this and grab your knees as you do it." Mom was now in full flight, arms and legs moving in tune with the music. Pietro seemed uncoordinated. He was still watching Carla while trying to figure out the dance. Mom, on the other hand, seemed ready to take off. It was then Pietro, who was ready to burst with frustration, in desperation blurted out, "I can't dance this crazy American dance!"

Everyone around him stopped dancing in response to Pietro's outburst. Mom seemed embarrassed, but just for a moment. She noticed Carla was making her way out of the dance hall, so did Pietro, who was torn between running after her and apologizing to Mom. He settled for the latter, and once again trouble was averted, or so we thought.

CHAPTER 19

Storm Warning

You would think, now that Carla left the hall, things would calm down. The band began playing Sentimental Journey, and everything seemed to be returning to normal, but normal was not to be. As Mom was observing Pietro, and Pietro observing Carla as she departed, the five Ricci brothers were observing all of us from the opposite side of the hall, and they weren't happy. The five brothers made what appeared to be a huddle, formed a circle as if to say, "World keep out!" The moment Carla left the hall, Frank Ricci, the oldest of the Ricci brothers, made his move. Slowly, he made his way across the dance floor, Pietro clearly in his sights. Just under six feet and powerfully built, his weathered features added to his menacing approach.

Pietro was busy trying to make things right with Mom for his sudden outburst, when suddenly he felt the tight grip of Frank's powerful hand squeezing his shoulder. "Are you Pietro Petruzclli?" Frank asked, already knowing the answer. Pietro kept trying unsuccessfully to break the grip Frank had on his shoulder, but the fisherman's hardened hand was too powerful. "I'm Frank Ricci, Carla's brother, and I've been watching you. In fact, all Carla's brothers are watching you," he said ominously while gesturing to the other brothers, who as if on cue, began waving to Pietro. Pietro, somewhat panicked by the sight of the five tough looking fishermen and unable to break away from Frank, called out to Mom for help. "Cousin Carmela, do you know this man? Tell him I don't know what he wants from me." Mom grabbed Frank's hand

and pulled it off Pietro, then let Frank "have it." "What's wrong with you Riccis? My cousin Pietro is going to become a priest. He's a man of refinement, and not a roughneck like you and the rest of your family. He's not interested in Carla the way you think." Frank responded, "My sister Carla is a beautiful woman. Any man would want her. Pietro is no different. We've been watching the way he looks at Carla. He can't keep his eyes off her." Mom shot back, "You saw how your sister was dancing. Everyone was looking at her. Someone called her a temptress."

Frank was incensed at Mom's words. "My sister is not a temptress. She's not a loose woman." Mom shot back, "Then she should keep her dress down, and what was she doing with her hair? I thought we were at a burlesque house." Ricci was boiling. "You and your sisters all have big nasty mouths. Never talk about Carla that way again." Pietro was caught in the middle, he was sandwiched between Mom and Frank and couldn't break away. "You Riccis think every man wants to attack your sister. You all have dirty minds." Mom was pissed off and was just getting started. "Let me repeat myself, Pietro is a gentleman. He's going to become a priest. He doesn't think like you Frank." Angrily, Frank responded, "Pietro is a man with blood in his veins. He wants what every man wants out of a woman, and if he tries to get it, we will turn him into a soprano." Pietro, incensed by the way Frank spoke to Mom and what he was being accused of, took a swing at Frank. Frank caught his hand in midair and began squeezing it, causing Pietro to recoil in anguish.

Mom had it with Frank. At the top of her lungs, she called him a (*cafone*), then she included his brothers and finally the father, driving home the fact she thought of them all as acting boorish. Grabbing Frank's hand, she shamed him into releasing Pietro who dropped to the floor like a limp rag. Mom, helping Pietro to his feet, tried to comfort him, but Pietro was shamed in public. He appeared to be less than a man in his mind, the worst thing that can happen to a man and particularly to an Italian man. He broke away from Mom and quickly made his way out of the dance hall, while Mom and the rest of us looked on.

CHAPTER 20

The Bakery

Mom was preparing breakfast the following morning. She was in the kitchen singing. One by one, we made our way to the kitchen and gathered round the kitchen table, all except Pietro. Mom pointed to Pietro's chair and asked Anthony, "Where is he?" Anthony gestured in the direction of the living room. Mom concerned over the events of the night before, decided to see what was going on with him. Cautiously, she walked into the living room to find Pietro sitting by the window, seemingly staring into space. Mom placed her hand on his shoulder, Pietro barely responded.

"What's wrong Pietro? You can tell me," Mom asked softly. There was no response. Mom asked again, this time she stroked his hair. The immediacy of her touch seemed to pierce Pietro's wall of silence and pent up emotions. Turning toward Mom, she could see the pain on his face. "Carmela, please forgive me. I know you were trying to help, but Frank Ricci shamed me, and he did it in front of your friends. I'm an embarrassment to you." Pulling up a chair, Mom sat as close to Pietro as she could. "Pietro, you're a student, Frank Ricci is a fisherman, hardened by the sea. You're a mere boy by comparison, no match for Frank, but you stood up to him and I'm proud of you. The whole family is proud of you. Pietro, I knew Frank would never hit a woman when I stepped in to help you. The Ricci brothers are tough, very tough. As I've said, you're a boy beside them, yet you tried to defend me, which took courage." Mom stood up, took Pietro by the hand, softly said, "Let's have breakfast."

Then pausing a moment, looking directly at him, she asked, "Pietro, do you have feelings for Carla Ricci?" Emotionally, Pietro responded, "I don't know cousin, I'm very confused." The earnestness of his response was enough to convince Mom of his sincerity. She then led him to the kitchen. Pietro took his seat at the breakfast table. We had already eaten everything Mom prepared and were waiting for toast. It was then Mom noticed we were out of bread and asked Anthony to run to Giovanni's, our favorite bakery, for a loaf of Scala. Anthony was getting ready to go, when Mom suddenly turned to Pietro and asked if he would go. She wanted him to get out in public as quickly as possible, and Giovanni's was as good a place as any to make an appearance, since the bakery was always busy in the morning.

Giovanni's was famous for its crusty Italian bread. Mornings were always busy at the bakery, when the aroma of bread, still hot from the oven, filled the shop and drifted out to the street. We always wanted to get there while the bread was still steaming, break off an end piece, and eat it on the way home. Nothing is more delicious. Often in winter, Mom would slice bread into several thick pieces, drizzle it with leftover tomato sauce and sprinkle on grated cheese, "instant pizza." Walking into the bakery, you were greeted by lit showcases filled with Italian cookies. The walls, covered with tin sheeting, were banked with shelves displaying loaves of bread in all shapes and sizes: round *bustone*, baguettes, and miniature loaves, ideal for making an Italian cold cut sandwich. We always bought the *Scala* loaf, which derives its name from its shape, an oval loaf of bread formed in sections reminiscent of steps in a staircase, hence the name *scala* (stairs).

Pietro arrived several minutes before the bread was fully baked. Deciding to hang around the shop, he purchased a fig square, found a copy of La Stampa, took a seat near the window and settled in for the ten-minute wait. He was deeply engrossed in a story of a strike in Rome when he heard his name called, spoken just above a whisper. Carla had come for her morning Scala. Her hair was pulled back into a ponytail, looking just washed. She was wearing a white linen skirt and blouse that clung to her body like the crust on the soft Scala bread. Her olive skin was shiny with perspiration from the humid summer morning, adding to her sensuality. "Pietro, I am happy I've run into you," her voice reflecting her concern. "I want to apologize for Frank and my brothers. They are overly protective of me. Sometimes it makes them act crazy." Pietro dropped the newspaper, hardly realizing it slipped out of his hands. His heart was racing at the sight of her. He was thinking, how anyone could look so beautiful so early in the morning. When he tried to speak, he could only manage a whisper. "Carla, it was nothing, I know your brother was looking out for you. I'm a stranger to him. I understand." As he spoke, Carla moved closer to him. Pietro was now standing. He could feel his body trembling as she drew closer. The scent of sandalwood drifted from her wet hair. Slowly, Carla caressed his cheek. *"Pietro, mi dispiace."* Her apology, now expressed in Italian, stirred Pietro to his core, as Carla gently stroked his cheek, both increasingly unaware of their surroundings, until the blunt voice of Giovanni announced the bread was ready. Carla drew her hand back, responding to the announcement, leaving Pietro standing with his eyes closed, still wrapped in the moment. "Hey Pietro, the bread is ready," insisted Giovanni. Pietro opened his eyes just in time to see Carla leaving the bakery, casting a final glance in his direction as she departed, all closely observed by Signora Ferderico.

"Carla is a beautiful woman, is she not? I know her family very well," announced Mrs. Federico. Pietro was not listening. He bolted after Carla, Giovanni shouting to him, "You forgot your Scala." Pietro caught up with Carla just outside the bakery. "Please let me walk with you," his voice filled with emotion. "Pietro, please, Signora Federico is watching. She knows my family. I don't want to make things worse for you with my brothers," Carla warned. She continued walking up Prince Street in the direction of her home. "I don't care about your brothers, I must see you again," insisted Pietro, keeping pace alongside of her." Pietro, there is your priestly vocation, please, I forgot myself for a moment. I'm so sorry. I must get home to make breakfast for my family, I know they will be looking for me. "I must see you again Carla, please tell me where and when?" Pietro implored. To calm Pietro, Carla suggested, "I will meet you at School Street Diner next Monday at twelve noon. Is it a good time for you? It's only five minutes from the North End on School Street, near City Hall. Anyone can give you directions. We will be safe from people who know us." Pietro agreed without hesitation. "Please, Pietro, we can't be seen together. Go back and get your bread. I must rush home to prepare breakfast." Pietro did not move, his eyes were fixed on Carla as she made her way up Prince Street, turning the block onto Garden Court. Only then, did he return to the bakery.

The weekend passed uneventfully. There was some talk at the church coffee following Sunday Mass about the events at the Friday night dance concerning Carla, Pietro and the Ricci brothers, but everyone thought it had blown over. Mom knew better and was watching Pietro, knowing he could not get Carla out of his mind.

CHAPTER 21
School Street Diner

School Street Diner was located in an alley very close to Scollay Square. It had the reputation for making some of the best éclairs in the city. When Grandpa was alive, he would often send Mom to the Diner to purchase pastry, always éclairs, which Grandma loved. You entered the Diner through a narrow doorway that led to a brightly lit basement cafeteria. The most prominent feature of its rather bland environment was the school chairs that filled the room. They were arranged in rows on a black and white tile floor. Each simple brown, wooden chair had an attached writing table, identifying it as a school desk, but instead of using the attachment for writing, it was used as a snack table.

Pietro arrived early and took a seat at the rear of the restaurant. Several days had gone by since he saw Carla, and he was feeling anxious about her arrival, if indeed she would come at all. Several minutes passed. He was feeling increasingly anxious when he heard the sound of footsteps rushing down the stairs. Carla, out of breath, tried to apologize to Pietro for being late, but before she could get the words out, Pietro took her hand and kissed it. Carla stroked his brown, wavy hair, lifted his head, and motioned him to sit, while she took a seat beside him.

"Carla, would you like an espresso?" Pietro offered. Laughing, Carla responded, "Pietro, this is an American cafeteria, they don't serve espresso, but I will have a cup of American coffee." Embarrassed by his mistake, Pietro agreed to try a cup. It was only a minute or two later when he returned with two steaming cups of coffee and two éclairs, all on a brown, wooden tray, which he set down on Carla's snack table.

Pietro sipped the coffee, grimaced, and reluctantly choked it down. "Carla, how can you drink this American coffee? It has no flavor." Carla began to laugh, imitating Pietro's expression after tasting the coffee. "Carla, I didn't look like that." Carla responded, "Oh yes you did Pietro. You wrinkled your face up like a prune." Pietro took another sip as if to prove she was wrong. Once again, he couldn't help making the same expression, causing Carla to burst into laughter. Catching her breath, she teased Pietro by repeating in Italian, *"Si guardi come una prugna,"* as she once again compared his expression to a prune. Pietro began to laugh, made the face once again, this time without sipping the coffee. Pietro then tried the éclair which he thoroughly enjoyed. After taking a large bite, whipped cream gathered at the side of his mouth and chocolate was on the tip of his nose. Once again, Carla began to laugh. "Now, what are you laughing at Carla?" Pietro asked searchingly. "Pietro, you're a mess. You have whipped cream on your cheek and chocolate on your nose." She dipped her napkin into a glass of water and began cleaning his face. With each stroke of her hand, Pietro felt an unfamiliar excitement gathering within him. His emotions kept building as she continued to wipe his face, until he could no longer contain himself.

"Carla, I love you!" Pietro blurted out. Reacting to Pietro's confession, Carla drew her hand back and stood up. "Pietro, you mustn't say such a thing. We hardly know each other. I believe I love you also, but the situation is impossible." I 'm not free to fall in love, my family needs me, and shortly you will be entering the seminary." "I need you Carla. I need you *cara mia.*" Pietro 's voice desperate, as he reacted to Carla's words of caution.

"Pietro, we must not be foolish, we hardly know each other." Carla repeated. "Your life will be as a priest, a beautiful life in the service of God. You are confused and I'm not helping the situation." "Carla, I love you!" Pietro repeated. There are many ways to serve God. God wants us to be happy. If we love each other and live good lives, will we not be serving God?" Pietro's voice began to tremble as his eyes weld up with tears, melting Carla's resolve. Suddenly, Carla repeated in a voice slightly above a whisper, "Pietro, I do love you. How can this be?

We hardly know each other, yet, I know I love you. This is impossible. Please, I must go." "Carla, please don't go. You just arrived. Please stay a little longer." Pietro implored.

Anxiously, Carla responded, "I will be missed" as she began mounting the stairs. "I must see you again," cried out Pietro. In desperation, Carla offered, "I will send you a note that will tell you where and when we can meet." Continuing up the stairs, she could hear Pietro following her and quickly turned. "Pietro, for the love of heaven, let me go. I will send you a note, we can't be seen together, wait five minutes before leaving." Pietro returned to his seat and watched as Carla exited the Diner. Her words were racing through his head, his thoughts fixed on their next encounter.

As you may recall, I said I would have something to say from time to time as you read this story of my family, so please, have patience with an old man, especially one who is now in heaven. As you can see, love can be very powerful. I loved my wife, Philomena, and because of her, never returned to religious life after my monastery burned to the ground. Thank God, I was never professed. My daughter Lucia loved Bernardo and never became a nun, and now my grandson Pietro is in danger of walking away from his calling to the priesthood, all because of the power of love. Sometimes, I think my family must anger God. He seems to call us to religious life, and yet for some reason, something always stops us. Yet, we have lived good lives, always close to the church. Perhaps, that is the way He meant it to be for *la mia famiglia* (my family). You will serve Me in the world rather than religious life. I guess I've done the right thing, for look at where I am. Please forgive me for thinking out loud, but it helps. Enough of me. Back to the story.

Just a word about School Street Diner's éclairs. They were huge with melt-in-your-mouth chocolate running the full length of the top, and a delicious yellow cream filling packed into their center. The body of the éclair was a soft yellow cake that perfectly complimented the filling and chocolate topping. Eclairs were a luxury we would have on special occasions, otherwise it was Mom's icebox cake, she would knock off at least once a week. Icebox cake was "tailor made" for Mom: layers of graham crackers crust with cooked pudding sandwiched between, find a spot in the refrigerator to let it set, then eat. No sifting, stirring or baking, a match made in heaven for Mom.

Dad was the cake maker. His work as a typesetter demanded that he be precise, that every character on the news sheet he laid out be counted. His precision showed itself in his cake making. He mixed them completely by hand in an old crockery bowl, stored in a tiny pantry beside the kitchen sink. He stirred the batter precisely 300 times; one tiny example of his precision in contrast to Mom's slam bang approach to things.

Since we didn't own a car, Dad always wanted to live within walking distance of his job. Dad faithfully walked the route from our home in the North End to the newspaper and back, five times a week, no matter the weather; it was a round trip distance of about three miles. Before leaving for work, he always wanted to be certain we had dessert for supper. If one of Mom's icebox cakes wasn't in the refrigerator, he would bake a cake or make pudding, it was always one or the other. Dad's cakes always came out of the oven sunken in the middle, so we called them volcano cakes. He would try to cover the depression with frosting, but the crater would always reemerge; they tasted good, and that was all that mattered.

CHAPTER 22

Sunday Dinner at Grandma's

The following Sunday, as usual, we went to Grandma's for dinner. It was always the same, 12 o'clock Mass, followed by a walk across North Square to Grandma's second story flat that looked onto the square and the church. Dinner at Grandma's was a time for the entire family to get together, an all-day affair. It would begin at about 2 o'clock in the afternoon. The adults sat at the dining table, while the children sat at a card table, Grandma set up in the kitchen. The entire family gathered at her table to discuss family activities of the week, as Grandma nodded her approval or disapproval. She shuffled back and forth to the kitchen, always returning with another platter of food, you knew you were expected to sample, even if it meant bursting. Grandma had a pair of salt and pepper shakers, she always placed on the children's table, that for some reason amused us. They were pale blue ceramic, tall, and curved in on the sides, each with a little button on the top, one was white for salt, the other grey for pepper, releasing a quick burst of their contents when pressed. The fact you did not have to shake them to get the contents out, but simply press a button, captivated us as children.

She served a classic Italian Sunday dinner, beginning with an antipasto made up of salami, prosciutto, provolone cheese and black shiny olives. A bottle of homemade red wine, Grandma just brought up from the cellar, sat in a straw basket on the table. Everyone drank the wine including the children whose wine was diluted with water. This was followed by an enormous serving of macaroni with meatballs, sausages and *braciole*. At this point, most non-Italians would think the meal was finished, but not so for Italians of Grandma's era. In the oven was a huge capon stuffed with scrambled eggs and ham, ready to make its appearance followed by roasted potatoes, stuffed mushrooms and eggplant parmesan. The dinner had to be spread over several hours, otherwise you were in danger of exploding. Each course was separated by discussions of family matters, gossip and whatever was going on at church. At about 5 o'clock in the afternoon, Grandma appeared with Italian pastries and cookies.

Everyone recounted their activities for the week. Auntie Angie, Auntie Stella, and Mom would usually speak of a movie they had seen together at the Lancaster Theater on Causeway Street, while Uncle Jimmy and Dad spoke of work. Uncle Carmine seldom attended these gatherings, irritating Grandma who felt all her children should come together at least once a week.

On this Sunday, just after serving the pastries and several minutes after Pietro and the kids left for a Bocce game, Grandma took a seat at the head of the table, sitting ominously quiet. Everyone knew something was up. Finally, Grandma slammed the table while shouting out, *"Silenzio"* (silence)! Then came the dreaded words, "There is talk about Pietro." Auntie Angie and Auntie Stella seemed unaware of any reason for gossip concerning Pietro, but Mom continued eating her piece of ricotta pie, as if she heard nothing. Mom then looked up and asked for the recipe. "Carmela, do you know what they are saying about Pietro?" Mom, ignoring the question, said "Mama, give me your recipe. My ricotta pie is soggy compared to yours." Grandma, with her eyes fixed on Mom, responded, "Carmela, forget the ricotta pie. Pietro is in your care and people are talking about him. The Little One is foxy and doesn't want to answer me." Whenever Grandma was angry with Mom and felt Mom was putting something over her, she always called her the "Little One". We could never figure if it was because Mom was her youngest or because Mom was the shortest of the sisters, whatever the reason, it was a signal that Mom was on Grandma's frying pan and definitely in trouble with her. "Mama, Pietro is fine. He's having a good time with my boys. They go everywhere together." "Carmela, why then did Angelina Rosato tell me that Pietro *a fatte le corna con Carla?*" Loosely translated, Pietro is making out with Carla.

"Carmela, the relatives in Italy will never forgive us if Pietro gets a girl in trouble. He is their pride and joy, and he is meant to be a priest." Now the "Little One" demonstrated why Grandma called her "foxy." "Mama, Angelina is old, she imagines things. She thinks that her husband, Giuseppe, who is *mezzo morto* (half dead), is two timing her." "Carmela, *basta*" (enough). "Angelina saw the two of them at *la pasticceria* (the pastry shop), the one where your Papa once bought me éclairs, now your sister Stella gets them for me. They were in each other's arms. Pietro was kissing her hand. Carmela, *io non sono uno stupido* (I am not a fool). You must do something about this."

Mom knew that Grandma was concerned, so she came clean. "Mama, Pietro has little experience with women, he's infatuated with Carla. It will pass." "Carmela, he is straw, and she is the match. If she makes a fire, the relatives will blame me, not you. Speak to Pietro, remind him of his calling to God. *Portalo al cimitero* (Take him to the cemetery)." Grandma's last suggestion was her most ominous, for when she suggested a visit to the cemetery, everyone knew she meant business. For Grandma, a visit to the cemetery was a wake-up call, a reminder to do the right thing with your life. She knew the life story behind many of its inhabitants, therefore, guided by the message she intended to convey, she stirred you to the appropriate grave site.

For infidelity, she would guide you to the grave of Giovanna and Giovanni. They ran a bakery in the North End. It seems that Giovanni did more than bake bread in his little shop. He used the back room for encounters with several of his customers, in particular, Claudia, a buxom beauty from Calabria. It was during one of their more intimate encounters, Giovanna unexpectedly came to the bakery, catching them together. She crowned Giovanni with a rolling pin, sending him to the hospital. It took eighteen stitches to close the wound in his head, Giovanni never fooled around again.

For what she termed loose morals, it was the grave of Bettina for women, marked with an angel playing a harp, and not far from it, the grave of Gaetano for men, marked with a statue of Saint Anthony. She would grab your wrist with one hand while pointing to the grave with the other. In her most solemn voice, announce, *"Questa e' la puttana"* (This is a loose woman) or *"Questo e' uno gigolo"* (This is a gigolo), driving home the point that even in death, your reputation follows you.

If you were too fat and she believed you should lose weight, there was Johnny Fat, who cashed in his chips while eating a lamb chop. If you were too thin, she would encourage you to eat by taking you to Skinny Matilda, who was hit by a car at night. According to Grandma, she was too thin to see.

Grandma used the graves to make a point. With this in mind, she informed Mom of the graves she should visit with Pietro. "Carmela, listen to me. Take him to Luigi the shoemaker. It is the grave with the statue of Our Lady of Sorrows. He left the seminary over a woman and broke the Madonna's heart. Tell him the story, Carmela." Grandma then stood up and went into the kitchen to get an espresso. It was at this point, Dad and Uncle Jimmy got up and announced they wanted no part of what was going on. They called it women's business, and both went out for a smoke. Auntie Stella and Auntie Angie, who were taking it all in at the end of the table, went over to Mom. Auntie Angie asked, "What's going on with Mama? She's talking about you taking Pietro to the cemetery, which means there's trouble." Mom was now attacking the ricotta pie, wanting to polish it off before Grandma returned. "Angie eat the ricotta pie, it's delicious." Auntie Stella was becoming more and more annoyed. "You're eating and choking on the ricotta pie, then you'll go home, leaving me with her. She wants you to take Pietro to the cemetery, that means something is really wrong." Mom looked up, swallowed the last piece of ricotta pie, and dropped the bomb, "Carla and Pietro have the hots for one another, they can't keep their hands off each other." Auntie Angie looking shocked, said, "Carla is a saint, she belongs to the Saint Theresa Society, everyone believes she will become a nun." Mom fired back, "If Mama knew everything, she would kill me!"

Auntie Stella ran to the kitchen to make certain Grandma didn't hear what was just said. She then came back to the table and reminded Mom of Carla's brothers and father, that they would kill Pietro if they found out what was going on. Grandma returned to the table and everyone went quiet. "You can't fool me. I know what's going on." Looking Mom straight in the eye, Grandma continued, *"Porta Pietro al cimitero*

(Take Pietro to the cemetery) and take him to Luigi the shoemaker. Tell him the story about the Madonna and how he broke her heart." Mom nodded, didn't say a word, but knew she had to do something. She would take Grandma's advice and take Pietro to the cemetery.

CHAPTER 23
The Cemetery

O ur family cemetery looks like an outdoor museum, beautiful gravestones, sculptures and mausoleums sprinkled throughout the grounds, reminiscent of cemeteries in Italy. When Grandpa Bernardo passed away in 1940, Grandma wanted to demonstrate her love for him by building a mausoleum for his final resting place. Grandpa left Grandma financially comfortable, but not so comfortable, she could spend a bundle on a mausoleum. The family had a hard time convincing her that she could not afford it. When it was apparent, she would not change her mind, Auntie Stella called in the big gun. She asked Auntie Angie to speak to her. Auntie Angie was a realist. She repeatedly demonstrated her practical nature by making a simple statement that went right to the heart of the matter. Grandma was firm in her decision to build a mausoleum. She could not be persuaded to drop the idea as being impractical, until Auntie Angie arrived on the scene. Auntie listened quietly to Grandma, as she described the mausoleum.

It was to be made of granite with two Corinthian columns at its front, a marble floor with a fresco of the Madonna in the rear, and accommodations for eight people. There would be Cypress trees flanking it, and ornate bronze doors to complete the structure. A cement walk would take you to its front doors, flanked to the left and right with flagstones, where Grandma could set up her lawn chair to greet visitors who came to the cemetery, virtually every Saturday during the summer. Behind the mausoleum would be a small patch of land where she could plant tomatoes. When Grandma finished describing her building project, Auntie Angie, who was listening intently, nodding her head as if agreeing with her, then informed Grandma, after the mausoleum was built and she ran out of money, she could move in with her husband.

This didn't go over lightly. When Grandma was mad, she became agitated, making quick gestures causing the small pug she wore on the top of her head to come undone, resulting in her looking somewhat comical. She would then slip from English into Italian, using expressions that no one could figure out, but by the tone of her voice, were obviously not flattering. Auntie Angie, on the other hand, would simply rest her knee on a chair, a signal that she was about to speak, stare directly at her, or whoever else she was confronting, and make some pithy remark that always went straight to the heart of the matter. Grandma was not going to have her mausoleum. Auntie Angie could do in a few words what no one in the family could do in endless arguments with Grandma. Auntie brought Grandma to her senses. Reluctantly, Grandma finally settled for a life-size white marble statue of Christ passing through a granite arch.

Once Grandma acquired a plot at the cemetery, she entered a whole new world, the world of cemetery society, and she adapted to it very quickly. At least once a week during the summer, Grandma, like so many of her friends and neighbors, would plan to spend the better part of a Saturday afternoon sitting on a lawn chair in front of the family plot, visiting loved ones and tending her small tomato patch behind Grandpa's stone. If you were rich enough to have a mausoleum, you would open its doors as if you were about to do spring cleaning, sit at the entrance welcoming neighbors and occasionally offering a visitor a cool drink and a cold cut sandwich. It was a somewhat macabre picnic that they treated as being quite normal. To a stranger, this cemetery society might seem a bit peculiar, but it all made perfect sense to the society members.

Grandma always packed enough food for a day's stay at the cemetery. She filled a wicker hamper with sandwiches, fruit and wine, coke for the kids, and we were off by subway to the cemetery in Roslindale. It took two of us to carry the basket. The weight of the basket gave a clue to the length of time Grandma planned to be at the cemetery, they were almost always three-hour baskets. Grandma packed enough for everyone who accompanied her with some left over for her guests. As the day progressed, Grandma alternated from being hostess to being a guest. All her friends from church were doing pretty much the same thing. The ladies would wander in small groups down the paths of headstones, checking out who was recently buried and commenting on them. They talked and gestured in Italian as they slowly made their way around the cemetery, rosary in hand, stopping for a glass of wine or cookie at one of the lawn parties, and then continuing on their way. While Grandma was socializing, we would be watering the grass on Grandpa's grave, planting geraniums in the pots that flanked the stone, and scrubbing the statue to remove the oak mold that had gathered on it during the preceding autumn and winter. Grandma's turn around the cemetery would take about an hour and a half. By the time she returned, we had forgotten we were in a cemetery; it had become a picnic ground with holy statues, and we were ready to eat.

It was on the following Monday that Mom took Pietro to the cemetery, supposedly to visit Grandpa's grave, but she was really carrying out Grandma's suggestion of taking him to the cemetery with the hope of cooling off his infatuation with Carla. They stopped to visit Grandpa's grave then slowly walked along the aisles of headstones, stopping every so often at the grave of a friend or relative of the family, Mom felt might be of interest to Pietro. Carrying out Grandma's wish, she took him to the grave of Luigi the shoemaker. Although she intended to tell Pietro the story of Luigi breaking the Madonna's heart by not going into the priesthood, she said nothing, feeling Pietro was already too attached to Carla and Grandma's suggestion would have no effect. Mom simply said he was a friend. Pietro remained silent as they strolled through the cemetery. It was on their return to Grandpa's grave when he began to speak. "Cousin, I know you are concerned. I know there is talk about me. I can't help myself, I love Carla." Pietro's confession and earnestness caught Mom by surprise. They continued to walk without exchanging a word. Finally, Mom stopped and turned to him.

"Pietro, do you know your mind? You are so young, please give the matter some time. You will be with us till September, it is only July, please go slowly and think about what you are doing."

"Cousin, I love Carla. I know I'm to go to seminary school in September. If I've changed my mind, God understands. I must follow what is in my heart." Mom, for a moment was going to bring Pietro back to Luigi's grave to tell Grandma's story, but once again, thought better of it.

"Pietro, God wants only what is best for you. When you do His Will, you are doing what is best for you, but is marrying Carla, God's Will? You must give this time. Please consider what you're saying. You have your entire life ahead of you." Pietro listened carefully to Mom's advice, then in a whisper, said reassuringly, "I will go slowly, don't worry cousin Carmela." Tears of relief were in Mom's eyes as she kissed him on the cheek, then both knelt at Grandpa's grave before leaving for home.

CHAPTER 24

Smells, Sounds and Sights of the Seasons

L ife in the North End has always been a highly sensory experience. The seasons of the year separated one from the other by distinct smells, sounds and sights unique to each. Autumn in the North End was a special time, the experience of a very old culture preparing for winter, making its way in a new world. There was the distinct, acrid smell of discarded crushed grapes, rising from bushel baskets piled high on every corner. The discarded grapes waiting for trash pickup, the by-product of the many regional wines being prepared from recipes centuries old, in cellars scattered throughout the North End. Although Grandpa Bernardo passed away several years ago, Grandma deeply sentimental, could never part with the three enormous wine barrels used to make his version of a Southern Italian wine. Grandpa had asthma and no sense of smell. He was unable to taste the wine to determine if it was ready to be bottled. Mom and Auntie Stella became his wine tasters.

The story goes, Grandpa would send them down into the cellar to test the wine by siphoning off a bit of wine from each of the three barrels. The fresh wine was both delicious and strong. On one occasion, the two young girls siphoned and re-siphoned the wine, swallowing more than usual, wanting to make certain it was ready to serve, becoming somewhat inebriated. They surfaced from the cellar holding a half empty bottle of wine, declaring, "It's ready!" Grandpa caught sight of his daughters, who obviously had one too many, and said to Grandma, *"E' questo che insegni alle tue figlie? (Is this what you teach your daughters)?"* Grandma, never to be put down, shot back, *"Sono anche le tue figlie* (They are also your daughters).*"* Grabbing the bottle out of Auntie Stella's hands, she told the two girls to go to bed, which they did, giggling all the way to their room. Just before closing the door, Auntie Stella turned and said, "Papa, you make delicious wine." With that, he tossed a dish towel at her, while yelling, *"Va' a letto!"* (Go to bed!) After closing the door behind them, the two girls could be heard giggling until they fell asleep.

Autumn was also the time when the red and green peppers, bought at Haymarket from street produce stalls, were being preserved in jars filled with vinegar and spiced with garlic cloves. For reasons of space, the filled jars were stored under beds throughout the North End like buried treasure. Their contents would be used to spice up a salad or add a delicious flavor to fried pork chops, prepared for dinner on the chilly evenings that lay ahead. Tomato sauce was set aside in sealed jars that lined shelves bowed from the weight of previous seasons. Resourceful North Enders were preparing for winter. The sight of children playing in the streets after school, the sound of church bells filling the brisk air beckoning the faithful to morning Mass and later to Mass at day's end, contributed to an atmosphere distinctly Italian. It was a time in which the North End felt more like an Italian village than a neighborhood in a big American city.

The smell of winter was a mixture of the pungent odor of range oil, used to heat our flats, with mysterious odors rising from mounds of snow and ice that sat for weeks, clogging the narrow streets, not quite revealing whatever was trapped beneath them. In winter, we ate heavily spiced foods, the scent of which filled our flats with the aromas of Italy. Garlic, used for flavoring, was sprinkled over everything. Heads of garlic, formed into garlands, sometimes worn as necklaces to ward off sickness, hung from hooks in our kitchens. One winter, Grandma tried to make us wear garlic necklaces to school to protect us from an outbreak of flu. We thought it was a good idea, figuring that the Irish nuns would go nuts when they saw the crazy Italians wearing their smelly necklaces. Mom told Grandma, we were not in Italy, and she should stop making her garlic necklaces. Grandma began shouting in Italian, something about pneumonia, so they compromised, and we ate garlic cloves that made our breath stink. Mom reasoned, with our strong garlic breath, none of the kids would come near us, therefore, we would avoid their germs, and she reasoned right. For the most part, it worked.

Spring was the time to open our windows and air out our flats. The clothes hung to dry in bathrooms and over stoves during the freezing months of winter, took flight over the North End on clotheslines, lacing the buildings together like spider webs. The clotheslines were not only used for drying clothes, but also as a means of conveyance. Bundles of food, secured by clothespins, were passed from apartment to apartment along with anything the clothesline could support, and clothespins securely grip. Jugs of wine were sent in leatherette shopping bags, sometimes traveling too fast and smashing against the building of its destination. This would invariably lead to the recipient cursing the sender, calling him, *"stupido!"* (no translation needed), and the sender cursing the recipient, also calling him "stupido!"

The kids used the clotheslines to send messages from flat to flat, a kind of telegraph system that could summon gangs of kids to come out to play within minutes. A clothespin was attached to the end of a string that we pulled, causing the pin to drum on the receiver's window, informing him that a message was waiting. The telegraph system was very active just after school, when we knew our friends were home to receive a message.

It was during spring when Grandma performed the age-old ritual of airing out the mattresses. Grandma insisted on making her own mattresses as her mother, grandmother and countless generations made them in the past. She stuffed large durable cotton sacks with bundles of clean wool arranged side by side to form the mattress. Every spring, we would help her drag the mattresses to the roof to air them out. Grandma would open them and expose them to the cool spring breezes She would substitute bundles of clean wool for the worn wool, firming up the compressed mattresses, stitch them closed, and have them back on the beds by evening.

The smell of tomato sauce permeated the North End in summer. It drifted through open windows creating pools of recognition, revealing to a North Ender, the region of Italy the cook came from. A spicy aroma from south of Rome, an herbal aroma from north of Rome. The summer also smelled of Sulphur Naphthol. All the restaurants used it to wash their sidewalks. Every morning, waiters would splash buckets of water containing the smelly liquid in front of their restaurants and coffee shops, scrubbing it into the pavement with a straw broom. Even the waiters smelled of Sulphur Naphthol from liquid splashed on their pants. We used Sulphur Naphthol to clean the bathroom, and sometimes we diluted it to wash our flea-infested dog, Queenie, making her smell like the sidewalk. Queenie was really a dirty dog. She was given to us by some old lady who never said a word about the fact Queenie could not be house broken. After a month or two, she was only partially house broken, whenever she made a mess, we used Sulphur Naphthol to clean it up. Occasionally, Queenie messed in our dimly lit corridor where an unsuspecting milkman, once stepped in it and began yelling at us through the door. Queenie lasted about six months before Mom finally sent her to a farm, where she knew Queenie would be right at home.

CHAPTER 25

Pets, Pets and more Pets

North End families were still large in the 1940s and 50s. Kids tumbled out of the two and three-story brick buildings that lined our narrow streets, filling the neighborhood with the sounds of children at play. Mini neighborhoods within our tiny Italian enclave were formed by the residents of the narrow alleyways lacing our streets together, adding further complexity to the buzz of life that filled the streets. Despite the crowded conditions, many of us kept pets that were in every way part of the family. Favorites were Canaries and Parakeets that brightened flats with their chirps and color. Some of our neighbors raised Homing Pigeons. They were kept on roofs in ramshackle wooden coops. Some of the pigeons were pure white, others brown and white calico, and others simply looked like street pigeons. One species called the Nun was everyone's favorite. It was black and white with an outcrop on its neck, reminiscent of a veil, hence the name "Nun". The owners of the birds raced them once or twice a year against the pigeons of other neighborhoods, bets of all sizes were made on the outcome of the race. Our next-door neighbor, Mario, kept his bird coop on his roof adjacent to our roof. He had about 30 or 40 birds. We helped build the coop, therefore, had open access to it. The coop was filled with feathers, had a strong smell of bird crap, particularly smelly on hot summer days.

Many dogs and cats in the North End were abandoned. The dogs ran in packs through the streets and often got into fights among themselves, while the cats moved like shadows from building to building, under cars and sometimes seen precariously walking along the parapet of a roof looking for mice, or anything they could sink their teeth into. There was one dog named Red, a Chow that had grown particularly vicious and terrorized the neighborhood, until he was killed by a car. He once fought a German Shepherd in the middle of North Square and was about to kill it, until the neighbors began pelting Red with stones, managing to drive him off.

Queenie was just one of the many pets we had. Others came in quick succession. There was Pudgy, a mixed breed with little personality and not very friendly. She was gone within three months. We traded her for a huge sun turtle we kept on our roof in a big, black metal tub. When summer was over, our brother Anthony said it was smelly, he tossed it into the ocean at the end of our street, to set it free, never realizing the difference between a fresh and a salt water turtle. Then there were the six chicks given to us one Easter that we gave to a local farm after a month. They were followed by Donald, a yellow duckling, purchased by Dad from a local pet shop and brought home in a shoebox. The moment we opened the box, Donald made a beeline for Dad, from that day on, Donald was never more than three steps behind him. Donald was a lot more fun than the chickens because he was very playful. Mom loved the quacks and amusing sounds he made as he ran through the house. As he got bigger, Mom insisted we keep him on the roof where he took up residence in our former chicken coop. There was no way Donald was going to stay in that coop. He would hop down the roof stairs, wait at our door quacking, until one of us opened it to let him in. He was looking for Dad.

Donald's favorite food was spaghetti with marinara sauce that he could smell from up on the roof. He came bouncing down the stairs quacking wildly at the door until one of us let him in. He would then rush up to Mom demanding his share. Mom would serve it in a bowl, swearing at the duck as she put tomato sauce over the spaghetti; he wouldn't eat it any other way. She would serve it hot, which seemed to aggravate the duck and delight Mom, but that didn't prevent Donald from eating. Mom claimed his beak was made of asbestos. Donald would break out into a frenzy of activity, twirling spaghetti in the air as he snatched it from the dish. His white feathers turned bright red with tomato sauce, splashing him, as he twirled the spaghetti in the air. By the time the last strand of spaghetti was plucked from the dish, Donald, splattered with tomato sauce, was a sight to see. Dad would then pick him up and wash him in a tub of warm water in the bathroom, which Donald seemed to love, while Mom was in the kitchen cursing the duck. Sometimes, she would open the door to the oven, threatening to bake Donald, claiming he would make a great Sunday dinner. Donald just kept quacking, enjoying his bubble bath. When Donald got too large, we had to give him up. We gave him to a farm, where within weeks, Donald began laying eggs to the delight of the farmer. Mom joked, the damn duck switched sex to please the farmer.

It was within weeks of Donald's departure, we decided to visit the pet shop in a small department store on Washington Street. We only had our allowance, which was fifty cents between us, and figured there was nothing we could buy except for a goldfish, which really wasn't much fun, we couldn't play with a goldfish. Much to our delight, we discovered fifty cents would purchase two white mice. Quickly, we purchased them. The mice were placed in a white cardboard box, resembling a takeout food container. Figuring the mice needed something to eat, we took them over to the sandwich bar and asked for some lettuce. We were given one leaf, which we shredded and tossed into the box containing our two mice. We couldn't wait to get home to open the box and begin playing with our new pets.

As we entered the apartment, Mom spotted the box and asked, "What's in the box?" She followed with, "There better not be a mouse in there. You know how frighten I am of mice." For some reason, the shape of the box suggested a mouse to Mom. Little did she know, we had two. Her questioning reminded us that she was afraid of mice. So, we told her it was a turtle. We brought the box into the parlor, in an instant, one mouse escaped and ran out into the kitchen. It was only a minute later when Mom began to scream. She opened the door, letting the mouse run out of the flat and into the hallway. Then she slammed the door and came after us. We were trying to hide the other mouse, but she spotted what we were doing and screamed out, "Do you have another rat in that box?" Suddenly, the mouse jumped out of the box and frantically headed toward Mom. It began running in circles in front of her, causing Mom to scream as she ran out of the room, slamming the door behind her. Through the door, she screamed, "Wait till your father comes home. He's going to kill the two of you!" Quickly, we grabbed the mouse, putting it back in the box, figuring, if it was out of sight, everything would be fine. We opened the door and told Mom, we put the mouse back in the box and would make certain we wouldn't let it run loose again. She then told us to get the mouse out of the flat and get rid of it.

After searching the building for the other mouse and unable to find it, we took our mouse to the doorway where we sat on our front steps, trying to figure out what we would do with it. If we released it, one of the neighborhood cats would surely get it. We couldn't bring the mouse back to the flat, and we didn't want to give it away. It was then, we noticed our mailbox, nailed to the wall just inside the front door. We figured it would be a good place to keep the mouse just for overnight. It was long, and deep enough so the mouse could not jump out. There was some newspaper just under the mailbox. We shredded a sheet, put it at the bottom of the mailbox, and placed the mouse in its temporary home. Closing the lid, feeling he would be safe till morning, we returned to our flat. When we returned home, we found Mom standing in the middle of the kitchen, keeping her distance from the two of us. Immediately, she asked, "Where's the rat?" We told her, we gave it away and couldn't find the other one. At that point, she asked us to turn, and managed with one swing to whack the both of us on the ass with her wooden macaroni spoon. She then yelled out, "Don't ever bring another rat into this house!"

The following morning, we were off to school, figuring, we would find a home for the mouse when we returned home at 3 o'clock. On our way out of the building, we checked on our mouse. It seemed to be happy at the bottom of the mailbox. We gave it a couple of pieces of bread from our lunchbox plus a tiny bowl of water, closed the lid and were off to school. The stage was set for a disaster. It happened that afternoon when Mom returned from shopping and decided to check the mailbox for mail. It was seconds after reaching into the mailbox that she began to scream. Unwittingly, she grabbed hold of the mouse, which began to squirm in her fingers. The mouse ran up her sleeve, and revealed itself, causing Mom to scream even louder. She shook the mouse back into the mailbox and slammed it shut. Mom bolted up the stairs, threw open the door where she found Dad getting ready to go to work. She screamed out, "I'm going to kill the two of them!" Followed by, "They almost gave me a heart attack!" She explained what happened.

Dad began to laugh, which infuriated Mom. She accused him of spoiling us and told him that she was going to take the two of us to Sister Francine in the morning, letting her know how fresh we are. Mom told Anthony to get rid of the mouse before we came home, and wash out the mailbox, which Anthony did with delight, knowing we were in a lot of trouble. It was only a half hour later when we returned home from school. We entered the building and quickly checked the mailbox finding it empty. We figured, our new pet jumped out and ran away. We ran up the stairs, threw open the door as usual, and found Mom standing in the middle of the kitchen. She seemed to be waiting for us.

Looking at us, she said, "Guess what happened to me today?" She was standing with her hands behind her back, which we found a little frightening. We stood our ground and quietly asked, "What happened?" She then said, "She almost had a heart attack when she went to get the mail." She followed with an ominous, "Guess why?" We were frozen with fear and couldn't speak. Mom, then took her hands from behind her back. She was holding a macaroni spoon in each hand. We ran for our lives into the bedroom and tried to hide under the bed. She managed to pull us out and began to whack both of us on the ass with the spoons. In the middle of it all, she yelled out, "Tomorrow, I'm taking the both of you to see Sister Francine. I'm going to tell her the whole story and let her know how fresh the two of you are!" Later that night, Anthony came to our bed and said, "You guys are in trouble. I heard Mom is taking you to Sister Francine in the morning." He seemed to be enjoying the fact that we were in so much trouble. He then told us that he set the mouse free. Needless to say, we didn't sleep much that night.

It was at lunch time, the following day, when we were called into

Sister Francine's office. Mom was standing at Sister's desk. Both were looking directly at us as we entered the office. The sight of Mom in that office revealed to us, we were really in trouble. Sister asked us to sit in two chairs placed directly in front of her desk. Mom was standing at Sister's side. Sister began, "I heard you boys frightened your mother. Whatever possessed you to put a mouse in your mailbox, and why did you do it after your Mom told you to give it away?" Haltingly, we replied, "It was late in the day and none of our friends were around to take it. So, we put it in the mailbox to keep it safe." "Didn't you realize that someone would be putting their hand in the mailbox to check for mail?" Sister asked. At that point, Mom jumped in and described how the mouse ran up her sleeve, when she reached into the mailbox for mail. For just a moment, Sister Francine seemed ready to laugh but she quickly composed herself, reached under her desk and brought up a bucket with two large scrub brushes inside. Mom looked at the bucket, and then looked at us with a menacing grin on her face. Sister looked directly at us and said the dreaded words, "Guess who will be helping the girls from the Saint Theresa Society to clean the church on Friday?" Mom shot out, "For a month!" But Sister replied, "No Carmela, just for one week." Sister handed each of us a scrub brush, with that said, "I want you boys to promise never to do anything like that again." We took the brushes and agreed to be good. The menacing look returned to Mom's face as she said, "Next time, Sister will make you do it for a month!" Sister didn't say a word but seemed to nod in agreement. As we left the office with Mom and our bucket and brushes, Sister quietly repeated, "You will be doing God's work, and you will be better boys for it."

Our favorite pet was Terri, a little Fox Terrier that made the greatest impression. Dad purchased Terri for us when she was about 2 months old. Mom and Dad figured by having a dog, we wouldn't be tempted to bring home anything slimy, web footed, or most of all, pink tailed. Terri was very bright and extremely high strung, becoming part of our family more completely than the other pets. She was an affectionate dog, sharing in all our family's activities. Over the years, she gravitated toward Dad, becoming more his dog than ours. He responded to her in a way different from the other pets, quietly showing his affection for her by preparing her meals each day and taking her for daily walks. Their affection for each other expressed in the kindness Dad showed to Terri and her loyal companionship. When Dad was home, she could always be found on his lap, mimicking him in mood and expression. When Dad was happy, she looked happy. When Dad was mad, she looked mad.

Terri loved ice cream and whenever Dad brought it home, she ran wildly through the house letting him know, she wanted her share. Dad would dole out ice cream in scoops, giving Terri a small scoop of her own, serving her last. Now the race was on. Terri would quickly gobble hers down and begin begging for more. She would keep glancing at Dad and then at us, as if to say, "Get them to share." Never wanting to share with Terri, we ate our ice cream quickly, knowing she would be begging for ours the moment she polished off her scoop. Problem, we would get brain freeze and had to stop, while Terri never stopped, causing Mom to speculate, she didn't have a brain.

She would then pick us off one by one, each of us succumbing to her begging and sharing a bit of our ice cream with her. At the end the race, she became glassy eyed and seemed to be in a stupor. She would then jump back on Dad's lap, fall asleep, making little twitches and sounds from the sugar high she was obviously on.

CHAPTER 26
The H

The old adage, you don't appreciate what you have until it's gone, perfectly applies to the pier at the North End Park, we dubbed The H. The H got its name from its shape, a wooden pier with upper and lower decks, connected in the center by a staircase, giving the entire structure the appearance of a horizontal H when seen from a distance. There was a small beach that fronted The H, frequented by North Enders. A swim in the ocean involved dodging the clumps of oil that drifted in from the nearby Navy Yard on incoming tide, deposited on the beach, as the tide retreated. The place smelled of fuel oil and whatever was being dumped into the harbor on that day. Debris tended to accumulate on either end of the beach, just about 100 yards apart.

The H was the North End's "hot spot" during the summer. All the young people gathered on the sun-drenched upper deck of the double decker. Music could always be heard in the distance from an old radio playing in the nearby bathhouse. The Andrews Sisters were red hot the summer of '49. Their songs were on everyone's lips, and blended perfectly with the relaxed atmosphere on the pier. Old people sat in the shade of the lower deck. They seemed to never go home. Day after day, the same people would be in the same places. Mothers with baby carriages, arranged themselves in a line along both sides of the upper deck. Bathing beauties took up the middle of the upper deck, where they spread their towels everywhere, especially near the end of the pier where the guys gathered. It was where the water was deepest at high tide, ideal for diving. A diver would stand on the guardrail, wait for the girls to look at him, make the sign of the cross and dive. Most guys did something close to a belly-flop, but the girls were impressed, that was all that mattered.

Then there was Bobby C. Bobby C was a god. He acted as if he owned the pier because he could dive better than everyone else. He was well-built, always tanned, and always wore a white bathing suit to show off his tan. He had black shiny hair that he slicked down with Vaseline, so it wouldn't get mussed up by the water. When Bobby C started his assent to the highest point of the pier, everyone stopped what they were doing to watch him dive. He could do a perfect jackknife, for which he would receive a thunderous applause every time he completed one. When Bobby C was ready to dive, the girls would flock to the end of the pier and shout out, "Bobby C, you're a doll!" They would be waiting for him to make the magic gesture which occurred just before diving. He would point to one of them and say, "This one's for you doll!" That would drive the girls crazy. They were both happy and envious of the lucky bathing beauty he chose. His showstopper was the swan dive which he kept for the very end of his performance. Standing on his toes, on a beam that extended out from the pier, Bobby C would cross himself and leap. Arms spread, he would glide through the air, every muscle in his body taut and glistening in the sun. He drove the girls crazy. The moment he surfaced from his dive, the girls would scream out, "Bobby C, I love you! Bobby C, marry me!" On the other hand, the guys both hated and envied him, for when he was on The H, they didn't have a chance with the great-looking girls.

The girls of the Saint Theresa Society would go to The H as a group, at least once a week during the summer. Carla loved the feeling of freedom the rickety old pier gave her, the sense of escape from the monotony of life, and the watchful eyes of her brothers. The girls sat together, creating an island of chatter and gossip. Carla, invariably sat apart from her friends. She would stretch out her towel, drop her sun dress, revealing a form-fitting bathing suit and her tanned graceful body. She would then take a slow walk along the perimeter of the pier, enjoying her temporary freedom, while driving the guys crazy. She threw off sparks of tension and desire, both dangerous and inviting. Carla was forbidden fruit. She knew it and the guys knew it. When Carla showed her stuff, there were no takers, and no one could figure if that's how Carla wanted it.

CHAPTER 27

The Encounter

July in the Boston of our youth, the Boston of the late 1940s, was always hot and oppressive, with clouds of smoke and pollution trapped in a suffocating blanket of humidity. We were crammed into tiny flats stacked like packing crates on top of each other; flats packed with kids, parents and grandparents, all living together, everyone coated with sweat and grime, and a public Bathhouse on North Bennet Street, our main source of bathing.

In the evenings, we were driven to the streets or to the rooftops, any place out of our steamy flats. Most of all, we flocked to The H for relief from the incessant heat. Summer evenings on The H were wondrous. Warm gentle breezes blowing in from the harbor, music always in the air, the soft sound of a guitar or mandolin blending with the murmur of voices; voices speaking of family life, work, and always love. Soft voices speaking in Italian, mingling with the foreign sounds of English, while cheap perfume drifted on sultry breezes. We sang and danced to the strains of Benny Goodman and Artie Shaw. That summer, Hoagy Carmichael's Stardust, was having a revival, at least in the North End, and was on everyone's lips. The evenings were soft and sensuous, laced with an element of mystery and romance.

The H was the North Enders' escape from the harsh reality and grind of everyday life. Like the rest of our neighbors, our family often headed to The H for several hours to escape the heat trapped in our flat. It was late Sunday afternoon, the July heat was unbearable, and

Mom decided we should have an outing on The H, anything to get us out of our steamy flat. "Charlie and Bobby, I don't want you running around the pier like wild kids," Mom cautioned. "When we arrive at The H, look for your cousin Pietro, who went ahead of us and asked us to join him."

That evening, the Saint Theresa Society also came to the pier. Like the rest of us, they were trying to escape the heat. Once again, Carla sat slightly apart from her friends. Glancing around the pier, she spotted Pietro leaning over a guardrail staring into the dark waters of the inner harbor. His fine clothes separated him from the rest of us, yet he was present in every whisper, quietly observed under the cover of night.

Somewhere on the lower pier, a little combo of local musicians was playing Stardust, soft and lovely; it was the perfect song for the perfect evening. Carla's heart began to race at the sight of Pietro. As if in a dream, she rose to her feet, caution giving way to passion. She slowly worked her way along the guardrail, gradually moving toward Pietro. Caught up in the moment, as she approached Pietro, she abandoned her reserve and began to sway to the rhythm of the Carmichael classic. Her entire body was in motion, rhythmically turning and swaying in the heat of the sultry evening, her arms reaching out to him, adding to her sensuous allure.

Pietro turned in her direction. He felt captured by the vision of Carla shimmering in the moonlight, her dress clinging to her body. They locked eyes. He wanted to embrace her, but remained fixed to the spot. Carla's movements were smooth and undulating as she drew closer to Pietro. The scent of her perfume reached him, and he reacted by reaching out to her. Carla beckoned to him, slowly they locked hands, moving separately at first then drawing closer as one, while Carla softly sang a word or two of Stardust. She went silent as her eyes cast up and down Pietro's lean body. Putting his arm around her waist, Pietro drew Carla closer. Pent up instincts were coming alive in him, instincts that aroused unfamiliar passion. Wrapping his arms around her, he backed her toward the guardrail, shielding her from view with his body. "Carla," Pietro whispered, as she rested her head on his shoulder; they remained motionless. The world had fallen away as they abandoned themselves to the moment, melting into the sultry summer evening.

"Carissima," he whispered. He could feel himself losing control and it frightened him. Still reacting instinctively, he took her by the hips, drew her closer to him. Suddenly, remembering his calling and coming to his senses, he pushed her away, knowing many eyes were watching them. "No! No! I can't do this!" Carla was pushed into the guardrail. The force of the blow seemed to wake her, as if from a spell. She looked around embarrassingly, hoping that her encounter with Pietro went unnoticed, but it didn't. All eyes were locked on them, especially Mom's, who had just come up to the second level of the pier, to hear the words Mom most dreaded hearing, spoken by Marina Vinci, North End's biggest gossip. "She's a disgrace. She's tempting him and he likes it. What kind of a seminarian will he make ?"

Hearing the words, Carla reacted by turning her back to her taunter. Facing the ink black sea, she began to cry, visibly shaken by Pietro's rejection, and the scathing remarks of her neighbor. Pietro's caution melted at the sight of her. Her distress became his distress. As he approached Carla to comfort her, she pulled away, crouched down to the wooden pier, sobbing with her hands to her face. Pietro tried to reach out to her, but the damage was done. With tears in her eyes, she muttered, "What have I done?" She rose to her feet, turned from Pietro, then ran the length of the pier crying. All eyes were on her. Pietro was about to chase after her when Mom caught him by the arm. "Pietro, what's going on here?" Mom demanded. Pietro tried to shake loose from Mom's grip, desperately wanting to chase after Carla, but Mom's grip was too firm. "Cousin, for the love of God, let me go!" He yanked himself free from Mom's grip with a force that drove Mom to her knees, scraping them on the wooden pier, causing them to bleed, a sight bringing Pietro to his senses. Helping Mom to her feet, torn with emotion, he asked Mom to forgive him while blotting her knees with his fine linen handkerchief. Mom reached down to Pietro, lifted his face only to see his eyes filled with distress. She pulled him up to his full height, held him for a moment, and advised, "Pietro, let's leave. Everyone is watching." Pietro put his arm around Mom's waist as if to steady himself, together they walked the length of the pier; Mom knowing what just happened would be the talk of the North End in the morning.

CHAPTER 28
The Rebuke

The North End coffee shops on Monday buzzed with the encounter of Carla and Pietro the night before. It happened less than 24 hours ago, and already was the subject on everyone's lips. Only a raid on a bookie parlor would move this juicy piece of gossip to a back burner. Marina Vinci had done her job well.

Gossip of what had been described as Carla's seduction, spread quickly through the neighborhood. When finally it reached Grandma, she was embarrassed and afraid of what her brother in Italy, his wife, and his aristocratic in-laws would think of her. Pietro was placed in her care. She was to watch over him, and now he had become seriously involved with a woman. And what was to become of his religious vocation? Grandma put on her little black, straw hat, but instead of heading to church, her usual destination, her little hat was moving at unaccustomed speed down North Square to her daughter Carmela's flat, our flat on Richmond Street. As she approached our building, Nick the butcher, surprised at seeing Grandma so early in the morning, greeted her with a, *"Buongiorno signora Lucia."* Grandma was in no mood for such pleasantries. She simply replied with a brusque wave of her hand, Italian sign language for, "Don't bother me now!"

Grandma arrived at our door disheveled and out of breath. The black veil of her little hat had come unpinned, and was dangling off to the side, hanging on precariously by a hat pin. Mom, having heard her mounting the stairs, opened the door just before Grandma burst in.

Standing as erect as her arthritis would allow, Grandma greeted Mom with the one word that summed up all the gossip over Pietro and Carla, "*Scandalo!*" She repeated it again, this time pulling herself up to her full four feet eleven inches, "*Scandalo!*" as she dramatically scratched her face, the sign of ultimate distress.

Mom was stunned at the sight of Grandma and her ominous greeting. She attempted to straighten Grandma's veil, only to have her hand brushed aside. Grandma took the veil, ripped it off her hat and stuffed it into her little black pocketbook. Mom sat down, apprehensively waiting to hear the news that Grandma was bursting to let out. "Carmela, what is going on with Pietro? He confides in you, *figlia mia.* Do you know what the neighbors are saying? There is a romance taking place between a priest and a nun." Mom was beside herself. "What priest and nun, Mama?" "Pietro and Carla. She is tempting him!" Grandma replied angrily. "Mama, Pietro is not a priest and Carla is not a nun." Mom's reasoning did not calm Grandma. She erupted, "Carla is supposed to be a good girl, and everyone believed she would become a nun. Now, everyone is calling her *una tentatrice* (a temptress) and what next? They will be calling Pietro, a womanizer, and what about her father and brothers, you know how the Riccis are, they are possessive of Carla, they will hurt him." Mom, growing increasingly concerned both for Grandma and the situation, responded, "Mama, please calm down. Carla is not *una tentatrice*. She's from the family of our closest friends, and Pietro is not a womanizer." "Carmela, we need to separate them. She's tempting him. Men are weak. He will give into her, and the family will never forgive us. They sent him to us a virgin, and he will go home a sinner." Mom shot back, "Mama, calm down. Let me make you some espresso." Grandma was now completely exasperated. "Carmela, you're making coffee, and *una tentatrice* is tempting a priest."

Mom was now half crazy with Grandma's insistence on calling Pietro a priest. "Mama, stop saying that. What do you want me to do? I took him to the grave of Luigi the shoemaker who left the seminary for a woman, as you wished." Mom left out the fact, she never told him the story of Luigi as Grandma wanted. "Speak to him, tell him she has turned his head from God. She has the ways of *una sirena*," Grandma blurted out. "Mama stop calling her a siren. Let's speak to Angie. She always knows what to do. Let's speak to Angie before we both go crazy."

CHAPTER 29
The Plan

E veryone turned to Auntie Angie when a problem came up. She always seemed to have an answer, or at least a wise saying that seemed to be an answer.

Auntie was having one of her Tuesday migraines, only it was happening on Monday, when Grandma, Mom with Charlie in tow, arrived at her Garden Court Street flat. Auntie greeted them with a wet cloth around her head, that automatically appeared whenever she had a migraine. She would soak the cloth in cold water, wring it out and line it with potato peels, skin side down. She then wrapped the cloth around her head, keeping it there till the headache broke. Supposedly, the potato skins were a poultice that would draw the migraine out. It was a remedy given to Auntie by her friend Annunziata, who everyone called *"La Strega"* because she was filled with old-world potions that seemed to be concocted by a witch.

Mom once had a headache that lasted three days. Out of desperation, she took Auntie Angie's advice, and called for Annunziata. She arrived at the flat with a worn leather bag filled with her tools of the trade: a little glass bowl, a small bottle of olive oil, and another small bottle of water. Annunziata was a tall, thin woman with coal black hair and sharp features, who always dressed in black, mourning the death of her husband. The overall effect, combined with her mysterious old-world remedies, made her seemed vaguely frightening, contributing to her reputation of being a witch. Upon seeing Mom, she declared, someone had given her the evil eye. Annunziata then pulled from her bag, the little glass bowl and a small bottle of olive oil placing them on the table in front of Mom. She filled the bowl with a cup of water, poured out a drop of oil which floated on the water and did not disperse, a sign to Annunziata that someone definitely gave Mom the evil eye. She went over to Mom and really got down to business. She began pulling at Mom's hair and spitting on it. It was pull, spit, pull, spit, with Mom complaining how disgusting it was, while Annunciata was telling her to be silent. Annunziata then asked Mom for a knife.

Auntie Stella, who was with Mom, pulled a knife out of the kitchen cabinet drawer and handed it to her with a slight grin on her face. She seemed to be enjoying the entire procedure. Mom on the other hand, becoming increasingly frightened, looked at Auntie Stella while she handed Annunziata the knife and said to her, "This witch is going to kill me!" Chanting some incantation, Annunziata took the knife, waved it over Mom's head, plunged it into the bowl of water, and dramatically threw it into the far corner of the kitchen while screaming out, "No one touch the knife until the oil in the bowl separates!" At this point, Mom looked like she was ready to collapse, while Annunziata appeared exhausted from battling with the evil eye. When she went to the bathroom to wash up, Auntie Stella decided to make Annunziata a cup of coffee. Mom screamed at Auntie Stella, "Forget the coffee! Throw that witch out! My head is ready to explode. I'm going to kill your sister Angie for having her come to the house." When Annunziata emerged from the bathroom, she looked at the oil which still had not dispersed, and asked Mom, "How do you feel?" Mom gestured, "A little better." While putting on her coat, Annunciata cautioned Mom not to move the knife until the oil dispersed, otherwise the headache would grow worse. She then grabbed her leather bag and left in a whoosh. When Mom knew she was safely out of the building, she turned to Auntie Stella and said, "I'm going to kill your sister for sending that witch here. I still have the headache, but now my hair is full of spit, and I'm afraid to remove the knife from the corner of the kitchen."

When Auntie Angie was having one of her migraines, she could barely talk. Seeing Grandma looking distressed, she asked, "Mama, what's going on, you all look disturbed? Carmela, why is Mama so upset? Give the boy a cookie." "Carla is tempting Pietro and the North End is talking about our family!" Grandma shouted. "She's tempting a priest!" "Mama, he's not a priest," Mom insisted. "Stop saying that." Auntie grabbing her head, shouted louder, "You're going to make my head burst! Why are you saying these things and in front of the boy?" Grandma shot back, "He doesn't know what we're talking about, he's still messing his pants." Charlie then ran out of the kitchen, crying at all the shouting. "You made the boy cry!" Auntie shouted to Grandma and Mom. Auntie called to Charlie, offered him a cookie, quieting him down. Auntie Angie then asked, "What makes you think Carla is tempting Pietro?" Grandma responded, "Did you hear what happened on The H last night? Carmela was there. Let her tell you how Carla was tempting Pietro. How she threw herself at him. The whole North End is talking about it. If we don't stop this, Pietro will lose his head and he will do a "job" on her, and if Carla's brothers find out what's going on, *l' uccideranno* (they will kill him). The relatives in Italy sent him to us a good young man, someone who was going to become a priest, and now he's playing with a temptress and he could get himself killed. They will never forgive us in Italy."

Auntie Angie turned to Mom who was sitting quietly at the kitchen table. Auntie pulled the cloth from her head, the peels clinging to her forehead as if they were glued, tossed the cloth on the kitchen table, then deliberately removed the peels from her head, one by one, with her eyes fixed on Mom. She then asked Mom, "What did you do? You were supposed to be watching Pietro." Mom trying to change the subject, cleverly asked Auntie, why she was removing the cloth from her head. Annunziata said it should stay there till the migraine broke. Grandma, spotting what Mom was up to, shouted out, "Forget Annunziata! *Lei e'una Strega* (She's a witch)! The Little One is being tricky. She won't tell you the story. Pietro is losing his mind over Carla." Auntie Angie took a seat at the kitchen table beside Mom and Grandma. She had a certain look on her face that appeared whenever she was about to make an important announcement, a half grin with her mouth slightly crooked. It was a signal she had hatched an idea and was about to spring it.

"Ma, we're all going to Kingston in five days for our family vacation." Grandma shot back, "Angie, what are you talking about? The priest has lost his mind over a woman and you're talking about vacation." Auntie Angie stood up, put her right knee on her chair, always a sign that she was asserting her authority as the oldest child, and repeated, "Ma, we're all going on vacation." The look on Auntie's face had changed to the look she displayed when she hatched a great idea. Grandma immediately recognized it. Looking up at Auntie, she asked, "Angie, *cosa stai dicendo? (Angie, what are you saying)?"* Mom, from her side of the table, figured it out and said, "You can always count on Angie. She wants to separate them." Grandma looked at Auntie Angie and shouted out, *"Brava figlia mia.* Now I know you're my daughter. We will take Pietro to Kingston where he will return to his senses and forget Carla."

Mom began to have second thoughts about the plan. "Angie, what makes you think he'll come with us to Kingston? Carla has gotten under his skin, and he wants to be with her." Auntie Angie turned in the direction of Mom, her mouth once again slightly crooked, this time signaling she was about to drop a bomb. "Carmela, you made those two get together, now it's up to you to break them up." Mom shot back, "Angie, I told you, she has gotten under his skin, he's got the hots for her." Grandma now sided with Auntie Angie against Mom. "Carmela, Angie has a good idea. We're going to separate them. You made the flame touch the straw, now it's up to you to do or say whatever it takes to make Pietro come with us to Kingston. Think of the relatives in Italy. They will never forgive us if Pietro loses his head over this woman. Pietro must come with us, and Carmela, the Madonna will put the right words in your mouth. She will tell you what to say. We leave in five days for Kingston."

Auntie Angie then grabbed the cloth from the table and ran it under cold water at the kitchen sink. Ringing it out, she placed the potato peels, skin side down, along the length of the cloth, lifted it up gingerly and tied it around her head. She turned to Grandma and gave her one of her winks, a signal to Grandma she did it again, she solved the family problem. She then exited the kitchen triumphantly, heading to her bedroom where she would spend the rest of the afternoon in bed tending to her migraine, while Grandma cooked for her kids and Uncle Jimmy.

Mom got up from the table, her head was spinning. Auntie Angie "put the finger" on her. As she was ready to leave, she called to Charlie,

"We're leaving." She pushed him out the door ahead of her, then said, "Ma, I don't know what to say to Pietro to make him come along with us. He loves Carla." Grandma reached into her apron pocket and pulled out her rosary. Holding it up, she said solemnly, "Carmela, the Madonna will put the words in your mouth." Mom fired back, "Then let the Madonna talk to him." Grandma sternly said, "Carmela, don't make fun of the Madonna. She will punish you." Grandma turned and walked away, she had enough. Frustrated, Mom went to the door and began shouting at Charlie who was halfway down the two flights of stairs leading to the street. "Don't run out onto the street, you're going to get hit by a car."

CHAPTER 30
Vacation Bound

G randma and the family were planning to leave for Kingston in five days for a two-week vacation, so Mom had to work quickly. She had to convince Pietro to come along with us, aware of the fact, it was the last thing he wanted. His thoughts were of Carla, his love for her and the terrible incident on The H. Mom knew she had to speak to Pietro and she had to do it alone. It was Thursday morning when Mom headed over to the church, knowing Pietro would be there reading his breviary. Before entering the church, she decided to speak with Pasquale, who as usual, was sitting in his Caddy outside the church, puffing on a Cuban cigar. Pasquale, anticipating mom's question, removed the cigar from his mouth, pointed to the church, cigar in hand, and said, "Pietro is in the church alone and has been there for twenty minutes."

Mom thanked Pasquale, quickly walked over to the church, opened the door, and could see Pietro sitting at the shrine of Our Lady of Pompeii, eyes cast down as if in a trance.

Without saying a word, Mom took a seat beside him. He hardly acknowledged her presence. Mom asked, "Pietro, how do you feel?" Pietro, without looking up, murmured, "Cousin Carmela, I feel terrible. I lost Carla." Mom reached over to Pietro, took his face in her hands and turned him in her direction. She noticed there were tears on his cheeks. "Pietro, you've been crying. I feel terrible for you." Pietro whispered, "Cousin, I don't know what to do." Still holding his face in her hands, Mom offered, "Pietro, let me make a suggestion. The family is planning to go to Kingston for a two-week vacation. Come along with us and allow things to cool down. When you are away from here, things will seem different. You need time to think." Pietro responded, "What is there to think about, I love Carla." "Pietro," Mom insisted, "I'm older than you, and I know what I'm talking about. Mama wants you to come with us to Kingston. Carla will be here when you return, and by then, things may seem clearer to you."

Pietro was about to say no, when Mom pleaded with him to come along with the family for two weeks. "If not for me, do it for Mama. I'm afraid she will become sick worrying about you." Once again, Pietro was about to refuse when Mom said, "Please, do it for Mama." Pietro, seeing Mom so distressed, answered, "Cousin, I will come, but I won't promise to stay for two weeks." Mom stood, wiped the tears from his face with her handkerchief, kissed Pietro on the forehead, and left the church. Waving to Pasquale, she walked home to prepare dinner.

Early Saturday morning, the family gathered at Grandma's flat for the departure to Kingston. Grandma had been cooking for two days in preparation for the trip. She had prepared enough food to fill two large hampers. We were to travel to Kingston, as usual, in two cars, Uncle Jimmy's Plymouth and Uncle Tino's Buick. Uncle Tino was Grandma's younger brother. He was a guy who liked to play the field, had many girlfriends but never settled down. He enjoyed gambling and fast living. They signaled their arrival on Garden Court Street with a blast of their horns, setting in motion the family's departure. Gradually, the cars filled with food, suitcases and shopping bags stuffed with clothing and enough first aid material to stock a small clinic. Uncle Tino, noticing the car was gradually filling, stood in the middle of the street with a cigar firmly planted in the corner of his mouth, shouted up to Grandma, "Lucia, there's going to be no room for the family. Stop sending things down!" When Auntie Stella appeared in the doorway carrying Grandma's canary and cage, Uncle Tino shouted, "What the hell is this? Do you have to take the canary?" Grandma popped her head out the window, shouting, "If we leave the canary, *morira'* (it will die)." Uncle Tino shouted back, *"Lascialo morire* (Let it die)! All it does is eat and shit!" "The canary sings and makes me happy", Grandma responded. She then directed Mom, "Put the canary in the car. I will carry the cage on my lap." Uncle Tino then shouted, "If you take the canary, you're going to have to leave one of your grandchildren behind!" Grandma responded by slamming her window closed, a signal the argument was over, the canary was coming, and none of us would be left behind.

While all this was going on, the street gradually filled with neighbors, drawn by the commotion taking place under their windows. Mom, never missing an opportunity, enlisted the DeStefano brothers, who were watching our street scene, while sitting on their stoop. She asked them to lift the larger trunks and place them on top of both cars, tie them down, and secure them with rope for the 40-mile journey ahead of us. Finally, the family made its way to the cars. Dad was to remain behind for a week, because of work, and would be joining us the following week. The rest of us piled into Uncle Jimmy's Plymouth. Mom ordered Anthony and Bobby to get into the back seat with Auntie Stella. Charlie sat on a child's chair jammed sideways between the front and back seats. Auntie Stella had one of Grandma's food hampers on her lap. Auntie Angie took her place in the front seat beside our driver, Uncle Jimmy, with Grandma sitting by the window. We were all holding packages of food or clothing on our laps. In Uncle Tino's car, Grace and Theresa took the front seat, also holding packages on their laps. Pietro and Mom were in the backseat surrounded by bundles, small pieces of furniture, and the canary Pietro volunteered to carry for Grandma, chirping excitedly on his lap. Uncle Tino was always the last to enter the car. Before entering the car, he checked the tires, commented on the fact that both cars were riding very low, and one would probably break an axle before the journey was over. He then, as he did in the past, cursed the canary sitting on Pietro's lap, still chirping excitedly in its cage, making certain Grandma could hear him. Grandma waved her hand in front of her face, in a gesture of defiance that translates, "Shut up and let's get started."

Uncle Tino banged the roof of his car in frustration, squeezed himself into the front seat, slammed the door and we were off to Kingston. Before leaving, Grandma insisted on a blessing from our beloved church, so we drove down Garden Court Street, on to Fleet Street, circled the block, and came up North Square. As we approached the church, both cars slowed down. Grandma put her hand outside the window, made the sign of the cross, and invoked God's blessings on our little convoy. We all shouted goodbye to Pasquale, knowing he would be watching over the church. He reassured us by tooting the horn of his black Caddy, and we were on our way to Kingston.

CHAPTER 31

Kingston

In recollection, vacations in the 1940s were far simpler than today. If indeed you took a vacation, it was generally to a place close by. For North Enders, an effort was always made to go to a place with a big Italian community, for many of us, that place was Kingston. Lying just 40 miles south of Boston and north of Plymouth, it is a jumping off town to Cape Cod. Kingston is a coastal community. During the 1940s, the beach area was made up of mostly run-down cottages that were rented on a weekly basis. We don't know how Grandpa discovered Kingston, but he liked it, and would take the entire family there for two weeks in August. It was a tradition he started sometime in the mid-1930s. He rented the same cottage every year from one of the locals, a widow by the name of Mrs. Johnson.

Mrs. Johnson was a large, buxom, good-looking woman with a prominent rear end, who lived off the land. Grandpa was fascinated by her size. When Mrs. Johnson went for her morning swim, Grandpa made it a point to take his morning walk by the seashore, just to get a glimpse of her. Grandma knew what he was up to. One day, she asked him, *"Bernardo, ti piacciono le donne grandi?"* (Bernardo, do you like big women?) Grandpa never admitted to his casual interest until one day, Mrs. Johnson came to the cottage and told Grandma, "Lucia, keep your husband home when I'm on the beach." Mrs. Johnson was a very private woman and was well-aware that Grandpa was checking her out.

One morning, when Grandpa was making his way out the door, he found Grandma sitting on the porch waiting for him. *"Bernardo, dove stai andando* (Bernardo, where are you going)?" She asked. He quickly responded, *"Lucia, vado a fare una passeggiata, come sempre* (I'm going for a walk, as always)." Grandma quickly shot back, *"Guarderai la signora Johnson sulla spiaggia* (You're going to check out Mrs. Johnson on the beach). *Mi ha detto che la guardi mentre cammini* (She told me that you watch her as you walk)." Grandpa slyly responded, *"Lei ha un culo grande come la luna. Perche' dovrei guardarla? (She has a rear end as big as the moon. Why would I watch her)?"* Grandma turning his words on him, said, *"Ti piace la luna ma la luna non ti piace.* You like the moon, but the moon doesn't like you.) *Alla luna non piace che tu la guardi* (The moon doesn't like you watching her). Go! Go! Look at the moon! When the moon yells at you, don't call me." Grandpa knew Grandma had the goods on him. Trying to maintain his dignity as he headed back into the cottage, he asked her to make him a pot of espresso and to put out a couple of taralli. Five minutes later, Grandma invited Grandpa to the table. He noticed it was set with three cups and a plate of taralli sitting in the center. Grandpa sat, then asked Grandma, *"Chi e' la terza tazza per? (Who's the third cup for)?"* Grandma replied, "It's for *la bella luna."*(the beautiful moon). A remark that caused Grandpa to shake his head from left to right, a gesture to an Italian which means, "you got the best of me." With that, Grandma poured the espresso, leaving the third cup empty, and Grandpa never again went to the beach early in the morning.

Just down the road from Grandpa's cottage was a little old man who lived in a run-down shanty. It was a real dump and an eyesore. There was as much junk strewn around the lawn as there was stacked up within the house. The owner of the house was simply known to everyone as Mr. O'Hare. He seemed to be naturally dirty and enjoyed it. He had this ratty old dog named, Hound, that looked like him and was just as dirty. The dog seemed to spend all his time smelling the junk in the front yard and making piles of crap that were everywhere. Mr. O'Hare considered Hound's piles surrounding his shack to be a mind-field, a natural deterrent to his neighbors and did nothing to discourage it. It was impossible to enter his front yard without stepping into Hound's crap. He was aware everyone considered his house a dump and would like nothing better than to see it blow down in one of the summer storms. Knowing this, Mr. O'Hare would sit on a rickety rocking chair on his front porch in his soiled Union suit, seeming to take great delight in the nasty remarks often directed toward him, Hound and his shack by passersby. Wanting to make a point and to make known his feelings toward his neighbors and passersby, Mr. O'Hare, in a stroke of genius, decided to name his shack. Up to that time, it was the only cottage without a name. Everyone simply knew it as "The Dump." It was Saturday morning and Mr. O' Hare was busy working on his porch. Some people thought he was fixing it up, no such luck. He was working on a sign. Pounding the sign onto the front of his cottage, he announced to the world in crude lettering his disdain for his neighbors, naming his home, "SUITS ME." From that time on, Mr. O'Hare could be seen sitting under his sign in his Union suit reading his newspaper, oblivious to the world, with Hound busily strengthening the mind field with new piles of crap. Mr. O'Hare had the last laugh.

CHAPTER 32

The Arrival

The trip to Kingston was a slow and bumpy one, Uncle Jimmy and Uncle Tino cursing every bump we hit, afraid they would break an axle due to the overloaded cars. Depending on which car you were in, the trip was a totally different experience. If you were traveling with Grandma, in Uncle Jimmy's car, you would be eating from the moment you left Garden Court Street to the arrival at Kingston. It was a traveling feast of meatball sandwiches, fruit, cheese, and glasses of lemonade.

Traveling in Uncle Tino's car was a whole other story. Mom and Uncle Tino were both live wires. From the moment they left Garden Court Street, songs and jokes filled the car. Mom would be singing "By the Beautiful Sea" and "Shine on Harvest Moon", while Uncle Tino's repertoire was salty and right out of the barrooms he frequented. Pietro started the trip sad. His thoughts were of Carla and not wanting to leave her, but by the time we arrived in Kingston, he was singing along with Mom, Uncle Tino, Theresa and Grace.

Grandma had been renting a cottage named Erin Go Bragh since the mid-1930s. It was an old, cedar shingled Cape that hadn't seen repairs for years. Within minutes after our arrival, our luggage and belongings were sitting on the porch, ready to be carried in various directions. Grandma's copper pots and pans, along with Grandma, and all the food she prepared in Boston, headed straight to the kitchen. The clothes were distributed throughout the four bedrooms, and the canary wound up in the living room, beside a bay window. We performed like a well-drilled troop, but Pietro, unfamiliar with the drill, seemed lost in the blur of activity happening all around him. He sat on a large rock outside the front steps, staring down the road we had just traveled. Mom spotted Pietro sitting by himself, and quickly recruited him to carry bundles and packages up to the second floor. Pietro was to share a room with Anthony, Bobby and Charlie. There were two sets of bunks in the room; Anthony and Pietro took the bottom beds, Charlie and Bobby took the top.

The hot weather beckoned us to the beach, as it was just 3 o'clock in the afternoon, Mom decided we could unpack later. She was anxious to get into the water. Mom loved the beach, and wanted to give Pietro and the rest of us time to enjoy the ocean before the sun set. We tore through our bags, found our bathing suits, and within minutes were walking down the road heading toward the beach singing "By the Sea."

The moment we spotted the ocean, we began to run, found a clear spot on the beach where we could spread our towels, and dashed toward the water yelling and screaming at the top of our lungs. Pietro's spirits seem to immediately pick up. His Italian accent drew the attention of several bathing beauties, who seemed to find him irresistible. One tossed a beach ball in his direction, which Pietro caught, and shot right back to her. Another paraded by him, showing her stuff, and she was definitely checked out by Pietro. None of this went unnoticed by Mom, who was slowly getting the idea, Pietro's calling might not be to the priesthood.

To break up the girly show taking place around Pietro, Mom got us to drag him into the water where we had a free-for-all, with Mom laughing at the shoreline. Charlie found a horseshoe crab and yanked it out of the water by its tail. Pietro, who had never seen one, seemed to be frightened of it. Once Charlie noticed he was frightened, he tossed it in Pietro's direction, causing him to dive into the water. He surfaced right into the arms of one of the bathing beauties. Mom was watching the whole thing, wanting to see how Pietro would react. Pietro reacted by picking her up and dumping her into the water. Anthony, spotting Pietro was making out pretty good with the girls, grabbed a horseshoe crab out of the ocean and began to chase a little blonde standing near him, threatening to shove it down her bathing suit. Now, Mom swung into action. She wasn't going to have a repeat of what happened at Fenway Park. She waded into the water, grabbed Anthony by the hair, pulling him in the direction of the beach. Mom then made her way to Pietro, who by this time had two girls clinging to him. She yelled out, "Your cousin Stella just came with a basket of sandwiches. Your friends can join us."

We sat in a circle on the sand joined by Pietro's two bathing beauties. Auntie Stella turned toward Mom and asked, "Who are those two floozies?" She said it loud enough for them to hear. The girls, knowing they were getting under Mom's and Auntie Stella's skin, began teasing Pietro by tossing sand on him. Mom was getting ready to break it up when a good-looking guy came down the beach and sized her up. That stopped Mom in her tracks, and she seemed to be enjoying the attention. She smiled and struck a Betty Grable pose.

Auntie Stella yelled out, "What are you doing?. The beach is making everyone go crazy!" Mom quickly jumped to her feet and turned her back to the guy, but not before Anthony and Pietro spotted what was going on. Pietro shouted out, *"Cugina Carmela, penso che piaccia a te"* (Cousin Carmela, I think the man likes you!) Mom embarrassed, threw sand at Pietro who in turn threw sand at Mom. This of course erupted into a sand fight, and we all began throwing sand at each other. Someone got the bright idea that mud would be more fun than sand. Bobby came back from the ocean with two buckets of mud and Charlie had another horseshoe crab, planning to throw it at anyone who appeared to be frightened of it. He tossed it at one of the bathing beauties who caught it and screamed. At the same time, Bobby tossed a bucket of mud at the other bathing beauty; mud was flying everywhere. Our neighbors on the beach began yelling, "Get off the beach or we'll call the cops." Mom began running toward the water, yelling out, "Everyone into the water, we have to clean up!" Anthony and Pietro grabbed Mom, picked her up and dumped her into the water. Mom, then spotted Auntie Stella standing on the beach, still wearing her travel dress. Mischievously, Mom got the four boys to drag her into the water, Auntie Stella screaming all the way. Once she was soaked, she joined in the fun, and we all began splashing each other all over again. We were only in Kingston for an hour and already the place was in an uproar.

CHAPTER 33
Back at the Cottage

W e left the beach running along the road leading back to the cottage. We were laughing, joking and horsing around with each other, and for a while, age distinction seemed to melt away, we were all kids having a good time, including Mom and Auntie Stella. As we approached the Erin Go Bragh, Grandma was standing on the porch. She was wearing an apron and slippers, holding a mixing bowl in her hands, stirring slowly and deliberately. She called out to Auntie Stella and Mom, "*Ti stai divertendo e stai giocando* (You're having a good time and playing). Your sister and I are working, putting all the groceries away and preparing dinner for tonight." Auntie Stella, who never gave anything a second thought, quickly answered, "We're having a great time." On the other hand, Mom realizing she and Auntie Stella needed to share in the chores, grabbed the bowl from Grandma's hands and began to stir the contents vigorously, as she entered the cottage. All three disappeared into the kitchen where they were greeted by Auntie Angie, who had assumed her classic pissed off pose, standing with one knee on the chair and her mouth slightly twisted. All three became immediately frightened, including Grandma, whose side she was on.

There was a brief and terrifying silence, then Auntie Angie spoke, "Jimmy and Uncle Tino were walking near the beach and saw the trouble you caused. Carmela and Stella, I can understand the boys acting up, but you two were just as bad. Carmela, you were supposed to be keeping an eye on Pietro, instead, the girls were all over him. We left the North

End to bring him to his senses, but within an hour of being here, he is playing with the girls." Grandma kept urging Auntie Angie to say more. "Tell them what the relatives in Italy will say." Auntie Angie was just about ready to say more when Mom shouted out, "He's never going to be a priest! The women like him, and he likes the women!" Grandma was ready to have a fit. Excitedly, she exclaimed, *"Carmela, cosa stai dicendo* (Carmela, what are you saying)? While he is in America, he has to remain pure." Auntie Stella, always the real bomb thrower, shouted out, "Mama, Pietro will never be a priest! He was grabbing the girls and enjoying it. Gerardo and Velia are crazy. *Gli piacciono le donne* (He likes the women)."

Mom then began laughing and broke out into song. Provocatively strutting around the kitchen with her hands on her hips, she began to sing the Neapolitan love song *"Femmina"* (Female). This caused a riot. Auntie Angie, with her knee still on the chair, shouted back, "The two of you are wise guys! See how smart you are when the relatives in Italy find out Pietro knocked up Carla!" This frighten Grandma, who turned to Auntie Angie and said, *"Mio Dio, non dirlo!* (My God, don't say that)!"

From outside the cottage, we could hear the battle that erupted in the kitchen. Theresa and Grace slipped out of the cottage through a back door, grabbed all the guys, and began pushing us in the direction of the beach. They began running ahead of us, yelling out, "The last one on the beach gets buried in the sand!" Pietro took off like a gazelle, running after them as we followed, knowing Mom and Grandma would be pissed off when we returned, but for now, it was too much fun. We would face the music when we returned. We charged down to the beach yelling and screaming. As we jumped into the water, immediately, Charlie began searching for a horseshoe crab, while Bobby filled up a bucket with mud and tossed it at Theresa and Grace. At the same time, Anthony, who had managed to climb up on Pietro's shoulders, threatened to cannonball anyone who came near them. All this, prompting a guy on the beach to shout out, "Those little shits are back again, and now they brought their sisters!" This prompted Theresa to shout out, "We're not their sisters, we're their cousins and who the hell are you?" The situation was about to get out of hand when Uncle Jimmy, standing on the beach, called to us to get out of the water, and come over to him. Without saying a word, he just pointed in the direction of the cottage while Uncle Tino, speaking through his stogie, growled out, "Get back to the cottage, and you on the beach with the big mouth who called my nieces and nephews little shits, one more word, and this cigar is going up your ass!" It was supper time and we were already up to our ears in trouble. That night, we sat at the table in an eerie silence, Grandma and Auntie Angie staring at Pietro with concern, while Mom, Auntie Stella and the rest of us were eating spaghetti with clam sauce, tasting even better in the salty air. We would all be heading to bed shortly with blueberry picking planned for the next day.

CHAPTER 34
Blueberry Picking

We woke up to a typical early August morning, damp and steamy with the promise of uncomfortable heat in the afternoon. By the time we got downstairs, Grandma was already dressed for Sunday Mass and was anxious to get going. The eleven of us jammed ourselves into two cars, we were off to church in Plymouth.

The church was a white, shingled wooden church that looked more Protestant than Catholic, totally unlike the baroque churches we were familiar with in the North End, yet it was the church so many Italians from the North End attended while vacationing in Kingston. The Italian visitors tended to sit in a group, standing out like a hot pizza pie in a Boston Brahmin's dining room. We sat together on one bench amidst our Italian neighbors. The chatter of Italian voices from North Enders, accustomed to talking in church, stood out in sharp contrast to the silent local parishioners. Grandma sat next to Pietro, insisting he say his prayers in Italian, not wanting him to become anymore accustom to English and our American ways. Pietro, knowing Grandma's concern, dutifully went along with her wishes, quieting Grandma, while Auntie Angie, always a skeptic, remained unconvinced of Pietro's return to his religious vocation.

With the completion of Mass, we were back in the cars and hurried to the cottage, where Grandma put together a breakfast of a prosciutto and mozzarella frittata, taralli, juice and coffee. It was a strongly Italian breakfast in response to the non-Italian church. While having breakfast,

Grandma commented, she missed sitting at her shrine of Our Lady of Pompeii during Mass. It was her custom to clean the shrine after Mass. She seemed uneasy with the thought, petals from roses, she placed at the shrine just before leaving for Kingston, would be dropping on the white marble making the shrine look untidy, at least in her mind. She then reminded her daughters to get out of their church clothes and into aprons to go blueberry picking.

The blueberry patch was located just down the road from our cottage. It was hidden from the occasional passerby by a screen of tall bushes but was well-known to the locals. We stumbled onto it several years ago, quite by chance, much to the chagrin of Mr. Baker, whose land was adjacent to the public field, but acted as if he owned it. The field was about three acres in size. Mr. Baker ignored "locals" picking the blueberries but was thoroughly unfriendly to outsiders, like us. Every so often, to show his displeasure to some pickers he didn't recognize, Mr. Baker would fire his BB Gun into the air to frighten them off. At first, he succeeded in driving us off, but after a couple of years, we had grown accustomed to his tactics and simply ignored his warnings.

Within minutes after Grandma reminded her daughters to pick blueberries, we were on our way. Mom with Anthony, Charlie and Bobby carrying empty buckets for the blueberries, Auntie Angie with Grace and Theresa carrying larger buckets, and Auntie Stella with Pietro carrying a hamper of sandwiches, quickly thrown together, with wine for the adults and lemonade for the kids. We were quite a sight heading into the field, for in minutes, we had transformed ourselves from Americans to Neapolitan field workers. Mom, Auntie Stella and Auntie Angie were wearing long dresses to protect them from poison ivy with white aprons cinched at the waist. Colorful kerchiefs covered their hair. Mom always wore red, Auntie Angie favored blue and Auntie Stella, yellow. Grace and Theresa wore pretty much the same outfits, but their dresses were shorter. The boys all wore old overalls, cut off at the knees, and different color polo shirts, making them look like the *Scugnizzi* of Naples, known for their mischievous antics. Pietro, taller than the rest of us, wore a pair of Dad's old pants, much too large for him. Mom simply cinched them at his waist with a rope and rolled up the cuffs, making him look like a pirate. Pietro, delighting in his new swashbuckling image, began jumping around with an old branch pretending it was a sword, as we walked into the blueberry field.

Once we got into the field, we began singing. Because of the bright sunny day, Pietro wanted to sing the Neapolitan classic "O Sole Mio," but Mom would have no part of it, as she went into a rendition of, "By The Beautiful Sea" with Auntie Angie and Auntie Stella joining in. Pietro liked the sound of the song and began singing it in broken English, which was fun to hear, prompting all of us to sing in broken English. As we sang, Mom, Auntie Stella and Auntie Angie continued to gather blueberries in their aprons, as they would have done in Avellino, just a generation ago, while the rest of us ran from bush to bush picking them clean, eating as many blueberries as we placed in our buckets. We were cutting through the field like locusts, within an hour, our buckets were filled.

Mom decided we should take a break, so we spread out a blanket under an old Maple tree, growing at the edge of the field near Mr. Baker's house. While Mom was spreading out the blanket, we were to have lunch on, she began doing her imitation of Patty Andrews, singing the "Boogie Woogie Bugle Boy." Auntie Angie and Auntie Stella quickly joined in, together they began singing and dancing like the Andrews Sisters, standing shoulder to shoulder, clapping their hands and swinging their hips to the Jive Rhythm. Pietro grabbed Grace and began dancing with her, while the rest of us jumped up and down making a lot of noise. The raucous we were making attracted Mr. Baker's attention, who first began to shout at us, and then set off a blast from his BB Gun. None of us were frightened, but we decided we should clear out, for we picked the place clean. So, we pretended to be frightened, shouting, "Mr. Baker don't shoot, we're leaving!" As we got back on the road, Pietro turned toward Mom and jokingly said, "I guess he didn't like your singing." Mom threw a fistful of blueberries at Pietro, some of which he snatched from the air and stuffed in his mouth, causing Mom to laugh. She turned to Pietro and said, "I know a monkey back in Boston that does the same trick." So, she threw another fistful at Pietro, once again, he snatched some out of the air and stuffed them in his mouth. This caused Auntie Angie to shout, "Stop! Mama will kill us if we don't bring home enough blueberries to make her pies and preserves!" Mom stopped horsing around, and Pietro began to sing, "By the sea, by the sea, by the beautiful sea," setting off a chain reaction that ended at Grandma's porch.

Grandma was on the porch and greeted us in her apron, mixing bowl in hand. When she caught sight of us, she began to laugh, shouting out, "You look like Neapolitan *Scugnizzi!*" Pietro jumped up on to the porch, twirled Grandma in a circle while singing his American song. The sadness that had accompanied him from Boston seemed to have slipped away, if only for a while, in the relaxed setting of sun and beach. Grandma continued to do a little dance on her own. After a few quick steps, she stopped, reassumed her position as matriarch of the family, and said, *"Tutti in cucina* (Everyone into the kitchen.) We're making blueberry pies and preserves."

CHAPTER 35
Clam Bake Italian Style

Several days passed rather uneventfully. We were all having a good time. On the surface, all seemed to be going well, but it was obvious that Pietro was thinking of Carla. We all did our best to distract him, but something about his demeanor betrayed his yearning for Carla, which was obvious to Mom and Grandma.

On Friday evening of our first week in Kingston, Dad arrived by train, as he always did, to spend the following week with us. On Saturday morning, Dad suggested we should go quahogging on the flats in the bay. We all knew this would be followed by a dinner of spaghetti with crab sauce, made up of Alaskan King Crab legs, Dad always bought in Plymouth. Just before heading to the flats, Dad pulled Mom aside to tell her he heard the Ricci brothers were coming to Kingston to visit their Uncle Seymour, who was renting a cottage just down the road from us. Mom anxiously asked Dad if Carla would be coming along with them. When Dad responded he didn't know, Mom began to worry, for if Carla came, it could mean trouble.

It was about 10 o'clock in the morning when the guys all gathered on the beach to wade out to the flats. The tide was dead low, we had two hours of quahogging ahead of us before the returning tide would terminate our hunt for the delicious mollusk. We waded out to the flats in our bathing suits, and began the process of searching for quahogs by plodding through the mud in our bare feet. Quickly, we were all knee-high in mud, hoping with each step, to feel the subject of our search beneath our feet. Every time one of us hit a quahog, he would yell, "quahog!" Everyone cheered. Pietro, seemed to be frozen in place, finding the whole process amusing and foreign to him. Dad kept urging Pietro to wade through the mud. Finally, he got moving, and before long he found his first quahog. About an hour into the hunt, Charlie reached into the mud and pulled a horseshoe crab out by its tail. He threw it into his bucket with the quahogs, planning to take it back to shore to terrify the women. Dad spotted him, knew what he was up to, and told him to get the crab and throw it in the water, which of course Charlie didn't obey. Instead, he put it at the bottom of his bucket and covered it over with quahogs, figuring one of the women while preparing supper, would uncover it and begin screaming. With our buckets filled with quahogs, and the one special bucket containing the stowaway horseshoe crab, we headed back to the beach. The tide was returning, and the flats were already submerging under the incoming waves.

Back at the cottage, the women were speculating if Carla would be coming with her brothers to Kingston. As they talked, they were preparing for the evening's feast, a clambake Italian style. The King Crab legs, Dad purchased earlier in the day, were protruding from the huge pots of tomato sauce they flavored, looking as if they were attempting to escape. "Carmela, do you think *la sirena* (the siren), Carla will be coming from Boston with her brothers?" Grandma asked, as she sprinkled the tomato sauce with red pepper flakes. "Mama, do I know?" Mom replied, as she turned to Auntie Angie and repeated Grandma's question. "Angie, do you think she's coming?" Before Auntie Angie could reply, Auntie Stella let fly one of her juicy comments. "If *la sirena* comes here, I'll take care of her." Finally, Auntie Angie could get a word in. "Carmela, if you were keeping a better eye on him, this wouldn't have happened." Mom, feeling the pressure from Auntie Angie, was in no mood to take a scolding. "Angie, supposedly, he's becoming a priest. How could I know he would fall head over heels for Carla?"

Full of frustration, Grandma shouted from the other side of the kitchen, "*La sirena, la sirena,* stop with *la sirena.* He's going to disgrace us. We will never be able to face the family in Italy and our friends in the North End. The "Little One" made this happen, now the "Little One" has to fix it." Auntie Angie then blurted out, "What about the

Ricci brothers? They will beat him up if they think he's fooling around with their sister."

The kitchen was filling with steam from all the kettles boiling on the stove. From the midst of the billowing steam and heat which Auntie Stella couldn't stand any longer, she exploded, "It's as hot as hell in this kitchen! The old lady had to cook all this crap in the middle of summer. We're supposed to be on vacation. Only the men are on vacation, we women are slaving away in the kitchen!" Auntie Stella's wisecracks made Grandma furious. Pulling a King Crab leg out of the pot, she waved it in Auntie Stella's direction and said, "I can throw this at you!" Another puff of steam rose from the stove, temporarily concealing Auntie Stella. From somewhere in the steamy kitchen, Auntie Angie, trying to calm things down, pleaded, "Mama, put the crab leg back in the pot, and Stella shut up!" While Mom was in the process of adding water to the boiling pot, without thinking, she asked, "Why shouldn't Pietro go out with Carla, if he really loves her?" Steam from the pot immediately enveloping her. Mom's comment was too much for Grandma, who ran to the pot of tomato sauce, pulled out a crab leg, threw it at Mom, piercing the fog and hitting her in the back of the head. Mom spun around and screamed, "Mama, are you going crazy?" Before Grandma could answer, Auntie Stella, somewhere in the steam-filled kitchen, yelled out, "The heat in this damn kitchen is making everyone crazy!" Auntie Angie, trying to calm the situation, shouted out, "Everyone out of the kitchen and on to the porch! We can talk out there."

The four women, one by one, emerged from the fog of steam that filled the kitchen, with sweat dripping from their foreheads, and aprons stuck to their bodies. No sooner did they settle down on the rocking chairs, lined up on the porch, Auntie Stella spotted the men returning from the beach with buckets of quahogs. Auntie Stella, wiping the sweat from her face, shouted loud enough for them to hear, "Here they come with more crap!" "Stella shut up. You have a big mouth!" Shouted Auntie Angie. Grandma, more irritated than ever, turned to her and scolded, "Stella, you always have something nasty to say."

The men began coming up the steps onto the porch. Uncle Tino, always wanting to tease Auntie Stella, grumbled, "While you ladies were sitting on the porch fanning your asses, the men were up to their knees in mud digging for quahogs." With that, Auntie Stella stood up, and began nervously tugging at her apron, still stuck to her body from sweat. She turned to Grandma and her sisters and complained, "Did you hear what he said, we're fanning our asses." She reached into one of the buckets of quahogs, grabbed one, and threw it at Uncle Tino, hitting him in the back. "Who's fanning their ass? Shouted Auntie Stella. I sweated so much in the kitchen, my apron is stuck to my ass!" Wiping the sweat from her arms, Grandma scolded, "Stella, *non parlare cosi* (don't talk like that), it's disgusting." Auntie Stella, more agitated than ever, turned on Grandma and said, "You like all this crap! They had fun in the sun, digging up all this stuff, now we have to clean and cook it in that hot kitchen!"

From somewhere in the steam-filled kitchen, Uncle Tino entered to deposit his buckets, he shouted out, "I would like a cold beer!" Knowing Uncle Tino was rubbing it in, Dad turned to Uncle Jimmy and said, "We better give the women a hand or we're going to have a war down here." Uncle agreed. Leaving the women on the porch to cool off, the men began shucking quahogs in the steamy, hot kitchen, attempting to make peace. After shucking quahogs for a half hour, the women having cooled down a bit, went back into the kitchen and began dropping the spaghetti into pans of boiling water, sending more steam into the air as they prepared for the evening feast.

Just when everything had calmed down and tempers were subsiding, the little time bomb Charlie placed in the bucket was about ready to go off. Charlie had placed his special bucket of quahogs, containing the horseshoe crab, under the kitchen table. It was very close to where Auntie Stella was standing. Maliciously, Charlie called the hidden bucket to Auntie Stella's attention, causing her to reach under the table for the bucket. Placing it on the table, she peered into the bucket and came face to face with the horseshoe crab that had worked its way to the top of the bucket, attempting to escape. She screamed at the top of her lungs and threw the bucket into the air, causing the quahogs and the horseshoe crab to be scattered across the kitchen floor. Now at the end of her rope, she screamed out, "That little brat did it!" Uncle Tino began to laugh, but Mom would have none of it. Turning to Auntie Stella, Mom asked, "What little brat are you talking about?" Auntie Stella yelled out, "It was one of your little brats! I bet it was

Charlie! He's the only one that does this shit!" Charlie ran for his life out of the kitchen, while Mom turned on Auntie Stella, prepared to defend him. Annoyed and ready to attack, she yelled, "You always blame my kids for stuff like this." Auntie responded, "They're the only ones who pull off this shit." Uncle Tino, always wanting to make a bad situation worse, once again asked Auntie Stella "Where's my cold beer?" She then screamed out, "I could scald you with this pan of hot water!"

Grandma stepped in, just before the situation was ready to explode. She screamed out, *"Tutti ziti!"* (Everyone shut up!) Retreating to Italian to establish her authority. This was a sign she was furious, and everyone immediately quieted down. All went silent and motionless. It was the opportunity for Auntie Angie to restore order, as she always did in these situations. Speaking quietly and deliberately, she began issuing directives in the kitchen, everyone went about their jobs without speaking a word.

Mom noticed Dad had picked up the horseshoe crab and was making his way out of the kitchen. He placed the crab in one of the empty buckets just outside the kitchen. Quietly, Mom went over to him and asked, "Joe, what are you doing with that thing?" In measured tones, Dad responded sternly, "With this, I'm going to teach Charlie a lesson he will never forget." Mom knew Dad was mad. She didn't say anything, but trusted whatever Dad planned to do, it would be for Charlie's good.

It was about six in the evening when the clambake got underway. The women had laid out plates on an old wooden table in the backyard. The men carried out large steaming pots of spaghetti with crab sauce and buckets of steaming quahogs, placing them in the center of the table covered with a red checkered, plastic tablecloth. Tempers had cooled, and we were all back to normal. Once everything was set, Grandma called everyone to the table to begin our American clambake, Italian style. A jug of homemade red wine was quickly passed around the table, with small amounts, diluted in water, given to the kids. A quick prayer was said, then Grandma began plating the spaghetti from a huge bowl. Each plate she passed to Auntie Angie, who ladled crab sauce from a large pot placed on the table. As Dad instructed earlier, everyone got a plate except Charlie, who asked anxiously, "Where's my spaghetti?" Dad reached under the table, took the bucket containing the horseshoe crab, and placed it by Charlie. He told Charlie, he could play with the horseshoe crab, while the rest of us ate. Charlie began to fill up with tears, for he really loved spaghetti with crab sauce. Grandma, feeling badly for Charlie, shot a look at Dad as if to say, "Let the boy eat." Dad responded with a reassuring wink to Grandma, conveying the fact Charlie would get his spaghetti. He asked Charlie to apologize to Auntie Stella and promise never to do such a thing again. With a voice barely audible, but clearly heard by Auntie Stella, sitting across the wooden table from him, he apologized and promised never to do it again. This prompted Auntie Stella to kiss the tips of her fingers and place them on Charlie's forehead, a signal for Grandma to dish a plate of spaghetti for Charlie, that Auntie Angie loaded with extra crab sauce.

The feast was in full swing with everyone stuffed and having a good time. The homemade wine flowing liberally helped brighten spirits, angry just hours ago. Grandma was ready to go into her version of "O Sole Mio", when Auntie Angie looked up, gave an ominous, "Oh, Oh," followed by, "Here comes trouble," while kicking Mom's leg under the table to draw her attention. Mom, responding to Auntie Angie, glanced at her as Auntie Angie gestured in the direction of the road. The Riccis had come to spend time at their uncle's cottage in Kingston, and were about to pay a visit.

CHAPTER 36
Stormy Waters

The Riccis came into the backyard in order of seniority, Egidio leading the group. Frank, the oldest brother, came next, followed by Alberto and Roberto. Mario and Lorenzo remained in Boston to mend fishing nets, their specialty, for an upcoming trip. Carla remained to cook and keep house for them. Egidio greeted Grandma with a kiss, while Frank, Alberto and Roberto stood back, waiting to see how Grandma and the family would receive them and their father. After Grandma kissed Egidio on the cheek, she beckoned to the three brothers to join our clam bake, a signal that all was forgiven, particularly what had happened at the school dance a couple of weeks ago. They responded immediately, headed to the table where each of them took a heaping plate of Grandma's delicious spaghetti. The brothers sat on the steps leading down to the garden, while Egidio took a chair next to Grandma at the head of the table. From their position on the steps, the brothers were able to size up Pietro sitting beside Mom. Tension kept building in Pietro, who could feel their eyes sizing him up. Spotting what was going on, Dad decided to walk over to the brothers and asked them if they would like to play a game of bocce. The brothers declined, preferring to remain on the steps where they could intimidate Pietro.

Feeling more and more uncomfortable and wanting to break the tension, after completing supper, Pietro motioned to Anthony, Bobby and Charlie to join him for a walk. Once Pietro and the brothers left for their walk, Auntie Stella let loose with one of her bombs. She asked

Egidio, "Where's Carla and why isn't she with you?" Auntie Angie turned beet red. Daggers were jumping from her eyes as she motioned to Mom to shut her up. "She remained in Boston to keep house for her brothers, Mario and Lorenzo," Egidio replied. Auntie Stella quickly shot back, "Why didn't they all come with you?" The table began to shutter, as Auntie Angie was boiling mad and ready to leap at Auntie Stella. Normally, she would have screamed out, "Stella shut up!" Restraining herself in front of company, she simply asked Auntie Stella to go to the kitchen and bring out more spaghetti. Seconds later, Auntie Angie followed Auntie Stella into the kitchen. Once the door closed behind her, muffled sounds of what appeared to be an argument between the sisters could be heard. Grandma, trying to distract Egidio from what was taking place in the kitchen, struck up another chorus of "O Sole Mio."

The brothers, knowing something was going on in the kitchen between Pietro's cousins, didn't utter a sound. Mom, sizing up the situation, ran into the kitchen to warn her sisters that the Riccis were sitting on the steps, straining to hear everything being said. Entering the kitchen, she gestured to Angie and Stella to be quiet, the brothers were listening. Auntie Angie, needing to express her anger, resorted to Italian sign language. She called Stella by name. The moment Auntie Stella turned in her direction, Auntie Angie began to bite her hand, a Neapolitan gesture that means, I can kill you. From that point on, not a word was spoken for the Riccis to hear, but Auntie Angie made it quite clear that Auntie Stella should shut up.

The three sisters emerged from the kitchen pretending to be laughing for the benefit of the Riccis, carrying fresh bowls of spaghetti to the table, leaving the Riccis puzzling as to what just took place in the kitchen. As the three sisters sat at their places, Egidio, once again responded to Auntie Stella's question. "Lorenzo and Mario remained in Boston to repair the family's fishing nets. Carla remained to tend house and prepare meals for them. Fishing nets require constant maintenance, Mario and Lorenzo are experts in this regard." Auntie Stella unable to contain herself, reiterated, "It doesn't seem fair they should be left in Boston, while the rest of you are enjoying yourselves." Auntie Angie seemed ready to jump out of her skin after Auntie's last remark. Once again, she kicked Mom under the table to get her to say something to quiet Auntie Stella. Before Mom could get a word out, Egidio offered, "I agree, next time, we will all come together."

The families spent the rest of the evening at the dinner table, talking about mutual family friends, church, Saint Theresa Society, and everything else they had in common. They talked about everything but Carla, preferring to keep that subject untouched, yet she was ever present in the words that were never spoken.

CHAPTER 37

An Unexpected Arrival

Sunday morning broke hot and humid. It was the type of day that would be unbearable in the North End, driving its residents to the street for relief, but in Kingston there was relief, the ocean beckoned invitingly to overheated vacationers. We returned from Mass and planned to head to the beach, where we would remain until sunset. Before Mass, Grandma prepared what she considered to be beach food, consisting of sausage and meatball sandwiches, leftovers from the previous day, reconstituted with fresh tomato sauce, and whatever else she could stick between two slices of bread. We would only be gone for an afternoon at the beach, but she seemed to prepare for a week's stay. Auntie Angie, exasperated at Grandma's version of beach food, knowing better than to say anything, kept making motions in Mom's direction, expressing with her hands, we were going to look like *cafoni* at the beach. Auntie Stella, picking up on Auntie Angie's sign language, shot out, "She's always concerned with what other people think. I don't give a crap!" Mom could care less, she was planning to have a good time on the beach and was determined Pietro and the kids should also have a good time. We made a beeline to the beach, staked out a spot near the water, safe from the incoming tide, where we could remain undisturbed for the day while Dad, Uncle Jimmy and Uncle Tino roamed slowly behind, bringing up the rear of our little march to the sea.

Within minutes after arriving, old army blankets, left over from Uncle Jimmy's military days, were spread over the sand. These thread-bare blankets, that survived the trenches of France during World War I, were a constant fixture at picnics and beach outings for well over three decades. Grandma, in some uncanny way, was able to turn our little encampment on the beach into her dining room, with bags of food strategically placed at various corners of the blankets, holding them in place from the refreshing sea breeze. We had these old collapsible, wooden beach chairs, made of red and blue striped canvas, strung between unfinished wooden frames. They were placed on either side of the blankets, not to obstruct the view of the water. It would be minutes until Uncle Tino and Uncle Jimmy took up permanent residence on the chairs, while Dad headed to the ocean where he would float for hours on end, eliciting the same remarks from Auntie Angie to Mom, "Carmela, aren't you nervous your husband might float out to sea?" This would be followed by Mom's familiar response, she would jokingly say, "Let him float away."

Mom, Auntie Stella and Auntie Angie, for a while, sat in a huddle deeply engrossed in conversation. Auntie Angie was wearing her typical swimsuit, black and white with a little skirt. Auntie Stella and Mom were more daring, both wore more fashionable one-piece bathing suits, Auntie Angie frowned on. As for Grandma, she just wore a short apron that came just below her knees, about as far as she would go in beachwear. Grandma continued to fuss with the food on the army blankets until Mom, concerned she was not having a good time, took her by the arm, together they walked to the water's edge, where Grandma waded into the water up to her ankles. She moved a little deeper into the water, where she began splashing, rotating her hands one over the other, like the paddle wheel of a riverboat. This was her version of swimming. She then wiped salt water on her legs and arms, believing it was good for arthritis. Mom agreed, responding by rubbing salt water on the back of Grandma's neck and then on herself, to hopefully fend off the possibility of any arthritis entering her body. The moment we grandchildren spotted Grandma in the water, we flocked around her and began teasing her, pretending to splash her. Grandma, knowing we would never splash her, but going along with the charade, uttered some angry sounding words in Italian, laughing all the time she said them. Charlie, predictably, searched out some sea creature, preferably multi-legged, and pretended to toss it in Grandma's direction, prompting Grandma to yell out, "Carmela, make Charlie stop!" Mom shouted to Charlie, "Don't frighten your Grandma!" Charlie dropped the creature back into the sea, and Grandma returned to her paddle wheel.

Whenever the girls got in the water, they wanted to play volleyball. It would usually break down to Grace and Mom on one side, Theresa and Auntie Stella on the other. The game would never take place. The moment the girls began playing, one of the boys would invariably grab the beach ball to play a competing game of volleyball, driving the girls crazy. All this, while Grandma stood making her paddle wheels, and Dad floating on by. Every so often, a crab would take flight, and one of the girls would scream, as Charlie couldn't resist tossing them at the women. Ideally, it would be a horseshoe crab, but because they were few and far between, any old crab would do or a blob of seaweed, when nothing else was available. In the meantime, Uncle Jimmy and Uncle Tino remained on their canvas beach chairs, talking and dozing off in the heat of the day.

While all this activity was taking place, Pietro tended to stay aloof, stretching himself out on the beach to get sun, attracting the local bathing beauties with his good looks, lean body and Italian accent. Just like in the North End, Pietro became immediately sought after by the girls. All of this, under Mom's watchful eye, wondering to herself, "Will he ever become a priest?" It was late afternoon, Grandma was busy laying out food on the old army blankets, she and Auntie Angie had shaken clean of sand, arranging the four blankets into one large square. From out of the wicker baskets emerged meatball and sausage sandwiches, stuffed peppers, eggplant parmesan and pizza along with an assortment of cold cuts and fruit. Grandma placed the food in the center of the square as we gathered at the edges, choosing whatever we desired from the selections she had prepared. Auntie Angie, always fastidious, took great care to keep the blankets clear of anything that decided to crawl or alight onto them. While waving her arms over the food, she looked up, gasped for a moment, and let out one of her ominous, "Oh Ohs!" Mom and Auntie Stella, instinctively knowing trouble was on its way, simultaneously turned in the direction Auntie Angie was staring, and could hardly believe their eyes. Carla was walking along the beach, coming in our direction, and she looked like a million bucks. She was wearing a white floral skirt, cut just below her knees, tied at the waist. It was split up the front, revealing tanned shapely legs. A white scoop blouse, peasant style, rested just off her tanned shoulders, tantalizingly giving the impression, it was about to slip off at any second. Her long auburn hair kept blowing across her face and over her shoulders, and of course, there were those beautiful green eyes. She appeared more goddess than human, a creature of the Aegean, a Circe from the island of the sirens.

Pietro, who had rejoined the guys, was horsing around in the water, unaware of the earthquake about to take place. Pietro was the first of the guys to catch sight of Carla. He reacted as if hit by an electric shock. Seeming to lose all control, he rushed out of the water in her direction, in full view of Mom, Auntie Stella and Auntie Angie, with Grandma looking startled. Carla had arrived unexpectedly, the Ricci brothers and father were close by, and Pietro head over heels in love. Dark clouds had blown in from the sea, we were in for a summer storm.

CHAPTER 38

Trouble on the Beach

Pietro sprinted toward Carla. His lean, muscular body wet with sea water, glistened in the sunlight. Reaching her, they embraced. The curves of their bodies seem to complement each other perfectly. They were god and goddess on a white sandy beach, under a timeless sun. Incomplete on their own, they completed each other as a single organism, not to be separated. "Carla, I missed you." Pietro, barely able to get the words out. He repeated his words, "Carla, I missed you," as they stood in each other's embrace, slowly turning in the sand without thoughts of overly meddling families, just the two of them in each other's arms. "I also missed you, Pietro," confessed Carla. Her words tearful, full of the same uncertainty faced through the ages by young star-crossed lovers, meant to be together, but kept apart. "I love you Pietro. I needed to say these words to you." Together, they dropped to their knees burying their faces in each other's arms.

The sound of a pan dropped by Grandma, crashing into the dishes below, seemed to shatter the moment taking place only yards away. Grandma appeared stunned, as she witnessed the scene unfolding before her eyes. Uncle Tino, sitting on his striped canvas beach chair, was strangely amused by what was going on, for he knew it could only mean trouble, and trouble is what Uncle Tino delighted in. Glancing up to Grandma from his prone position, he said in somber tones to his sister, "Hey Lucia, I think we're going to have a new niece in the family." When the meaning of Uncle Tino's words finally registered on Grandma, she reached down for the pan she had dropped seconds before, pulled herself up to her entire 4 feet 11", lifted the pan high in the air, and said, *"Potrei colpirti con questa padella! (*I could hit you with this pan)!"* Uncle Tino, seeing the sight of this tiny woman looking so angry, couldn't help laughing, for no matter how hard she tried, her small stature and angelic face countered any show of anger Grandma could muster. Auntie Angie, taking in the entire scene, shouted out, "Carmela, grab the pan from Mama, she wants to hit Uncle Tino!" At the same time, Auntie Stella kept urging Grandma to bash her nemesis, the guy who made it a point to call her "Skinny Stella", every time he saw her. Auntie Angie shouted out, "Stella, are you going crazy, don't encourage her! Carmela, grab the pan before she swings it!" Uncle Tino was laughing uncontrollably, driving Auntie Stella crazy. She now made a play for the pan Mom wrestled away from Grandma. Auntie Angie shouted out, "We're making a disgrace of ourselves!"

All this, while Carla and Pietro remained lost in each other's arms. When Carla finally looked up to see what was happening around them, she burst into tears. "Pietro, can you see this will never work? Your family hates me. They will never let us be together. They think I'm a temptress who took you away from God and becoming a priest." When it seemed that things could not get worst, they managed to. The Ricci brothers and their father were moving toward the lovers like a Roman regiment, ready to do battle. Egidio made the first move, grabbing Pietro by the shoulder, while Lorenzo separated the lovers by inserting his body between them, causing Carla to shout, "Leave him alone! Don't hurt him! I promise I will never see him again!" Egidio, becoming even more incensed, seemed ready to strike Pietro, bringing Uncle Tino to his feet. "Leave them alone!" Uncle Tino shouted. "He's family, if you strike him, it will be too bad for you!" Egidio, knowing Uncle Tino's reputation for being a tough guy, let go of Pietro. His sons then made an attempt at grabbing Uncle Tino. Egidio shouted at them, "Stay back, this is between him and me and doesn't involve you!"

Carla screamed out, "This has nothing to do with any of you! It's between Pietro and me!" Pietro joined in, "Why don't you people leave us alone?" Reaching out to comfort Carla, he was immediately pulled away by Lorenzo, while Egidio grabbed Carla by the arm and scolded, "We're going back to Boston. You should have never come."

The rumpus on the beach brought Dad in from the water. As he approached Mom and the rest of the family, he asked, "What's going on?" Grandma, looking incredulously at Dad, repeated his words, shouting out, "What's going on? What's going on? *Stiamo in disgrazia!* (We are disgraced)! There are a thousand eyes on this beach, they have seen everything that has happened. Before the night is over, the relatives in Italy will know everything, and we will be the talk of the North End." Egidio then ushered Carla off the beach, Frank and Lorenzo trailing behind, looking back, casting threatening glances and making threatening gestures at Pietro to keep him away.

We spent the rest of the day secluded within the walls of our cottage, knowing the events on the beach would have a profound effect on our family, while Pietro, shaken to his core, remained at the beach, preferring to be alone. Grandma was particularly agitated. She turned to the sanctuary of her kitchen, where she began preparing Sunday night's dinner. She waved off any help, even that of Auntie Angie, wanting to do it alone. She seemed to do her best thinking while cooking, and now more than ever, she needed a clear mind to formulate the next move for not only herself, but the entire family. Grandma was the matriarch, and she took her role quite seriously. Finally, somewhere between the minestrone and the chicken parmigiana, Grandma had her revelation, and with that, she summoned her daughters into the kitchen, announcing with the deepest solemnity, "We must restore harmony to the family. Tonight, is for making things right with our family, putting what happened on the beach behind us."

CHAPTER 39

The Morning After

Mornings in Kingston were always filled with activity. Everyone was under one roof: Grandma and her daughters, their husbands, children and of course Uncle Tino, unpredictable as a late summer storm. Now there was Pietro, quiet and brokenhearted, trying to recover from the events of Sunday. Carla had returned to Boston with her brothers and father, who were more determined than ever to keep her apart from Pietro. The women were in the kitchen preparing breakfast. Slowly, everyone emerged from their rooms, gathering around the table for breakfast. When Grandma noticed Pietro wasn't among us, she sent Mom to inform him, breakfast was ready. It was more a summons than a request. Grandma was determined to have her way. We were all to be at the breakfast table and continue our vacation as if nothing had happened. It would be Grandma and Grandma alone, who would come up with the plan to solve the family crisis.

Mom climbed the steps to the room we shared with Pietro. She knocked on the door, with no response, waited a moment, knocked again, still no response. Finally, nervously, Mom opened the door to find Pietro lying on his lower bunk, staring at the sagging mattress over his head. "Pietro, what are you doing? Mama would like you to join us for breakfast." Still there was no response. "Pietro, you are not responding, are you sick? Mama wants you down for breakfast." Mom repeated. Finally, Pietro responded, "Cousin Carmela, I should never have come to America. My life has been turned upside down. I feel my insides twisted into knots. I want to cry, but I can't. I am so confused. I don't want to live anymore."

Mom, with both concern and passion in her voice, responded, "Pietro, what do you mean, not wanting to live anymore? You are a young man and have your entire life ahead of you." Before Mom could speak another word, Pietro turned on his side in the direction of Mom, looking straight into her eyes, said, "Cousin Carmela, I love Carla. I discovered a love I've never known, and that love has been ripped away from me. My family is against us, her family is against us, and when my parents in Italy discover what has happened, they will never forgive me. What is there to live for?" Mom, seeing the depths of his despair, became increasingly concerned. She knew she must say something but could not find the words. Quietly, she shut the door behind her and sat at the foot of Pietro's bed, where he had returned to lying on his back, staring at the mattress above him. "Pietro, I am going to speak to you like a cousin, like a sister, and most of all like your friend. You must listen to me. I know everything has grown dark for you. Love can be a wonderful thing and a terrible thing. When everything is going right, it fills your heart with joy like nothing else can, but when things go wrong, when love is ignored and torn from you, it's like a death, leaving you empty and in despair." Pietro remained unresponsive, acting as if he didn't hear Mom's words, yet Mom continued.

"Pietro, you must listen to me. You and Carla love each other. I don't know how to solve this problem, what words to say, what action to perform, but the love that you and Carla have for each other cannot be denied and will not be denied. You must trust me. I pray to God that He will guide us as we try to make right this impossible situation." Pietro, sensing the sincerity of Mom's words, once again turned in her direction. Reaching up to Mom, he grasped her hands. With a voice filled with emotion, he said, "Thank you cousin. I know you want to help, but the situation is impossible. I feel I am being torn in two, as if God and my family are pulling me in one direction, and Carla is pulling in the opposite." Mom, squeezing Pietro's hands as hard as she could, quietly whispered, "Pietro, God wants only the best for you and so does your family, if it is Carla that you are meant to be with, in one way or another, it will happen. I promise you, it will come to be. Clean yourself up, come down to breakfast, the family is waiting for you. We won't say a word to anyone about what we spoke of." "Not even to your mother and sisters," Pietro whispered. "Only to God" was Mom's response. With that, Mom left the room, Pietro following several minutes later. Mom's words seem to comfort Pietro, offering the reassurance, someone was on his side.

"I promised I would speak to you every so often. Seeing my grandson so unhappy, I guess it is time for his Grandfather, Antonio to say a few words. Pietro and Carla have a deep love for each other, the question is: Will their parents recognize and accept the reality of their love, and no longer stand in the way of what appears to be God's plan for their children? Italian parents can be very strong willed. It is time for me to pray that in this matter, as in all matters, they will allow God's Will to be done. I have said enough. It is time to return to the affairs of my family."

CHAPTER 40
The Telephone Call

It was Thursday morning, we had begun to pack for our return to Boston on Saturday. Grandma was busy at the stove, which by now had become her stove, when she looked up to see Mrs. Johnson hurrying across the lawn from her house, shouting out, "Lucia, there is a phone call for you from Boston. It sounds important!" Grandma's heart began pounding. Why should anyone be calling her from Boston? It had never happened, it must mean some tragedy had befallen a member of our family. Wiping her hands on her apron, Grandma without further thought, headed for the door ready to follow Mrs. Johnson back to her house. A sense of panic had enveloped her. She quickly came to her senses, called for Auntie Angie, who she always turned to in a crisis, to immediately come down and accompany her.

Grandma and Auntie Angie, half running and half walking, followed Mrs. Johnson back to her house. Entering the house, they both eyed the standup phone with the receiver off the hook. Grandma motioned to Auntie Angie, who instinctively knew she was to pick up the receiver and speak to whoever was on the other end of the line. She approached the receiver as if it was a live snake, ready to bite. With an uncharacteristic quivering voice, she asked, "Who's calling?" "Lucia is that you?" The snake responded. "This is your sister Elena." Grandma, overhearing the voice on the phone, knowing it was Elena, who only called when there was trouble or a tragedy, became increasingly frightened. Auntie Angie, after casting an eye on Grandma to see if she was okay, nervously barked into the phone, "Aunt Elena, this is your niece Angie. What do you want? Mama is standing beside me and she is frightened to death. She knows you only call when there is trouble or death in the family." Annoyed at Auntie Angie's critique, Elena quickly shot back, "This is about trouble in the family. Let me speak to my sister." Grandma, who was standing quietly by the telephone, didn't seem to breathe for the entire time Auntie Angie was speaking to Elena. "Ma, she wants to speak to you. Elena said there is trouble." Mustering up all her courage, Grandma snatched the phone from Auntie's hand. Holding the receiver to her angelic face, she demanded, "Elena, what is the trouble in the family? Whenever you call, I know it's about trouble or death."

"Lucia, our brother Gerardo sent me a telegram from Italy, he is not happy. He heard rumors from someone in the North End, Pietro is flirting with a girl by the name of Carla Ricci, and Velia is very disturbed." *"Basta!"* Grandma shouted into the receiver. "Elena, you are like *la civetta* (the owl) that always brings bad news." For some Italians, the owl was considered a harbinger of bad news. "Why should Gerardo contact you about this? Why didn't he send the telegram to me? Why is he accusing me?" *"Lucia, conosci Velia, quella ricca stronza di Roma, lei e'una piantagrane* (Lucia, you know Velia, that rich bitch from Rome, she is a trouble maker.) Gerardo is afraid of her and her rich family." Once again, Grandma asked, "Elena, why didn't he send it to me?" She was as equally disturbed by the message as she was that he chose Elena rather than her, since she was the matriarch of the family. "Lucia, you forget, you are on vacation. He did send a telegram to you, but it never reached you, so he turned to me. You should be happy you gave me Signora Johnson's phone number for emergencies. He and Velia are very concerned and want you to call or send them a telegram to explain what's going on with Pietro." Grandma, half frightened and half angry by Elena's tone of voice, turned to Auntie Angie. *"La civetta* said that Gerardo and Velia know." "They know what, Ma? What do they know?" *"Loro lo sanno, lo sanno!* (They know, they know!)" Grandma repeated in a thin shrill voice. "Do you mean they know about Pietro and Carla?" Auntie Angie said hesitantly. "Sì!" Elena shouted out from the other end of the telephone. *"Loro conoscono l'intera storia.* (They know the whole story.)"

Grandma went from ready to faint to ready to strike back. She shouted out, *"La civetta! La civetta!* She is gloating."* Then Elena began shouting out on her end of the line, "I am not *la civetta!*" Auntie Angie, grabbing the receiver from Grandma, asked in a panicked voice, "Are you sure they know what is going on?" Elena, in a tone that seemed somewhat amused, responded, "The rich bitches know everything, and they want to hear from you, if they don't hear from you, they will come to America." Then, with a gloating voice, Elena shouted into the receiver, "Lucia, if they come to America, you can introduce them to Carla, Pietro's *fidanzata* (girlfriend)!" At this point, Grandma went wild. She grabbed the telephone and yelled, *"Mi odi, sei sempre stato geloso di me!* (You hate me, you have always been jealous of me!)" Auntie Angie snatching the phone from Grandma's hand, gaining composure, asked, "Aunt, are you sure they know?" "Si, and they want to know how the family could allow Pietro to get into trouble. They think there is a scandal brewing."

When Grandma heard the word scandal, it was as if her worst fear came true. Not only would scandal make her family the talk of the North End, it would also reverberate in Rome, where such things would not be tolerated in the noble circles the Contes travelled. It would be devastating to them, for it was a time when extramarital relations were not tolerated, or at least not acknowledged, especially within their rarified world. Auntie Angie hung up the receiver without saying another word to Elena. She turned to Grandma and their eyes locked. Not a word was spoken. Mrs. Johnson, who had been standing in the other room, overheard the entire conversation. Walking over to Grandma, she stooped and stared into her eyes. "Is everything alright with you Lucia?" She asked, to calm her. "No, everything is not alright, and it's going to get worse," Grandma replied. Mrs. Johnson hugged Grandma reassuringly. Grandma and Auntie Angie left Mrs. Johnson's house and headed back to the cottage. They walked the walk of the condemned. They neither spoke nor looked at each other, for their worse fear had come true.

CHAPTER 41

The Clam Bake

It had become a tradition, the Thursday before leaving for Boston, we would have a clambake on the beach. Through the years, Grandma learned what constitutes a great American clambake: lobsters, clams, sweet corn, and pizza. Yes, pizza, for with Grandma, no meal was complete without something covered with tomato sauce. She decided pizza was perfect because it would travel well, and could easily be served on the beach. It was about 4 o'clock in the afternoon, the men were out on the flats digging for quahogs, while the women were in the kitchen preparing food for the evening's clambake.

Auntie Angie decided to let lose the bomb. She motioned to Grandma to take a seat at the table. Mom immediately knew something was in the wind. "Angie, what's going on? Mama never sits while we're preparing food." "Carmela, sit beside Mama, Stella stop cooking and sit at the table for a couple of minutes. I have something to tell you." When everyone was seated, Auntie Angie pulled up a chair and placed her knee on it, assuming her classic pose, this time telegraphing, "I have something important to say." Auntie Stella, reading her sister's body language, looked up at the ceiling and exclaimed, "Oh boy, here comes trouble." Auntie Stella's remark was expected by Auntie Angie, so she remained quiet, determined to drop her bomb with its greatest effect. Looking at Mom with her mouth slightly twisted, the bomb dropped. "Your aunt and uncle know everything about Pietro and Carla." "Which aunt and uncle?" Mom questioned, somewhat apprehensively. Auntie

Angie, once again said, "Your aunt and uncle know everything." Auntie Stella, thoroughly exasperated, shouted out, "She always does this! Whenever she has a bomb to drop, she acts this way!" Auntie Angie returned her classic remark, "Stella shut up and let me talk." Grandma, exercising her authority, stepped in and continued, "Gerardo and Velia know everything about Pietro and Carla, and it's a scandal in their eyes." If anyone was going to drop one of the biggest bombs of the decade, Grandma was determined it would be her, aggravating Auntie Angie.

Mom recognizing big trouble was on the way, piped up, "Angie, you've got to be kidding. How do they know?" Auntie Angie, still annoyed over the fact that Grandma dropped the bomb and she didn't, angrily shot back, "Carmela, don't act foolish. How do I know the way they found out? What's important is they know everything. It must have been some big mouth from the North End who telephoned them." Auntie Stella, not wanting to be kept out of the conversation, chimed in, "Mama, you better call them or else they will come to America, and there really will be trouble. If the rich bitches in Italy think they're going to cause trouble with us, because of what's going on between Pietro and Carla, they're crazy." Grandma responded, "We need to speak to Pietro, but the time has to be right. We need to let him know his parents have found out what's going on between him and Carla. When we return to Boston, I will send a telegram to Gerardo and Velia to calm them. The worst thing we can do is to remain silent. When I write the telegram, I want all my daughters around me." Auntie Angie, still smarting from the fact she didn't drop the bomb, approved, and the four women, after talking it over for a while agreed, the best time to speak with Pietro would be Friday morning. Grandma and Mom could take him for a walk around the neighborhood and inform him, his parents know everything, and unless they can be assured, all is well, and there is nothing serious going on between him and Carla, they will be coming to America.

The beach we frequented was little more than an oversized cove, hemmed in on three sides by large boulders stacked one on another. The site of our clambake was to be where it always was, by the boulders, right side of the beach. Because of the narrowness of the beach, we planned the clambake for low tide, eliminating the need to protect ourselves against an over-aggressive incoming tide. Small tide pools were scattered in wells among the rocks, their residents stranded by the outgoing tide. They provided great places to find all sorts of sea life, ranging from small schools of minnows to hermit crabs and an occasional horseshoe crab, which Charlie would immediately seize with the idea of causing mischief, always with the girls. Cedar trees flanked the upper reaches of the cove, scenting the beach with their distinct fragrance. On hot sultry nights, much like the one we were having for our clambake, the scent of the cedars grew even stronger, mixing with the smell of the sea and the newly exposed beach. It was the scent of Kingston, so familiar to all of us, helping to provide a wonderful atmosphere for our family clambake. We were at the end of our vacation, and as usual, there was a bittersweet feeling, one of enjoying the time we spent together at the beach, but now coming to an end, for tomorrow, we would be packing for our return trip to Boston and the uncertainties that lie ahead.

Uncle Tino, Dad and Uncle Jimmy built a roaring fire by the rocks, over which they had placed a large kettle suspended on a tripod stand. They filled the kettle with water, brought it to a boil, and began tossing into it their catch of the day: quahogs, clams, and of course lobsters. Everything was to be cooked by boiling. Uncle Tino stood by the pot with a long-crooked branch, cut from a tree near our cottage, stripped of its bark, he used to stir the pot. Charlie kept threatening to throw a horse shoe crab, he had just found in a tide pool, into the pot. When Charlie approached the pot with the horseshoe crab, Uncle Tino turned to him and threatened, "You put that crab in the pot kid, and you're going in after it." Charlie yelled out, "Mom, Uncle Tino wants to throw me into the pot!" Charlie kept yelling out, "He wants to throw me into the pot!" Mom told him, "Get rid of the crab and he won't throw you into the pot." Charlie brought the crab back to the tide pool where he found it, and left it there for safekeeping, planning to remove it once again during the evening. The salt air made everyone ravenously hungry. Grandma, seeing the pot had just begun to boil and had a way to go before its contents were cooked, decided to serve the pizza early. She called her daughters together, and like a well-drilled troop, the pizza was cut, put onto paper plates, and placed along the edge of the blankets, delineating our space on the beach.

From a house just across the road, the sound of music drifted on faint breezes through the steamy night. It was "Sentimental Journey," creating a mood at once, magical and melancholy. The sisters stood and began dancing, first with each other, then with their husbands. Auntie Stella danced with Uncle Tino, who approached her with his arms wide open as a sign of truce, while Theresa danced with Anthony, and Pietro danced with Grace. Charlie and Bobby were off looking for more horseshoe crabs, while Grandma looked on lovingly at the scene unfolding before her eyes, weighed down by the problems concerning Pietro that troubled her. Yet, it was a beautiful night, there was happiness on the beach, and the problems of life could be put off for a few more hours.

CHAPTER 42

A Change of Heart

Friday morning dawned, steamy and hot, typical August weather. Once again, it was a morning that would have been oppressive in the North End, but in Kingston, it was a morning extending a welcome invitation for fun in the sea. This would be our last full day of vacation. Had it been like any other vacation in the past, it would have followed a certain pattern, the kids spending the entire day at the beach, in an effort to make the most of it, the men on the flats picking a load of quahogs to bring back to Boston, and the women repacking the leatherette shopping bags, old duffle bags, and suitcases that originally carried our belongings from Boston. This would have been the pattern of the day, had it not been for Elena's phone call, and the meeting planned for that morning with Grandma, Mom and Pietro.

It was a little after 10 o'clock in the morning, when Mom called to Pietro and asked him to join her and Grandma for a walk. Pietro first refused, wanting to spend the day alone at the beach, but he could see something was on Mom's mind, something serious, suggested by the tone in her voice; he reluctantly agreed. Mom assured Pietro she was on his side, but for now, he must allow Grandma to speak to him. The three set out, heading down Cole Street, in the direction of the old recreation hall with its attached worn tennis court, that hadn't seen use or repair in years. A torn tennis net sagged between two silver metal posts, standing half upright on the black worn pavement. It has been this way, year in and year out, for as long as we've been vacationing in Kingston. Mom and Grandma planned to walk around the neighborhood, returning to our cottage approximately in an hour's time.

Grandma got the conversation going, reminding Pietro, within a month, he would be returning to Italy and entering seminary school. Pietro didn't respond. He acted as if he didn't hear what Grandma said. Mom, picking up on the threads of Grandma's observation and wanting to lead the conversation toward her point of view, carried it one step further and asked, "Pietro, what will you be studying in your first school year?" Pietro remained silent. His silence concerned Grandma. She reached behind Pietro, who was walking between them, and pulled on Mom's pocketbook as if to say, "Carmela, ask him again." Mom knew all Grandma's tricks and sign language. Responding to Grandma's nudge, she repeated the question, "Pietro, what will you be studying in your first school year?"

"Cousin, what type of bird is that hopping on the road in front of us?" Pietro asked. "I have never seen one in Italy." Mom having no idea of the species, simply responded, "It's a blue bird." Grandma, quick to become exasperated, asked, "Pietro, we would like to know what you will be studying in your first year of seminary school. Why don't you answer your cousin?" Pietro, trying to avoid the subject, once again questioned the species of the bird hopping just in front of them. Grandma blew her top. Without mincing words and no longer able to contain herself, she finally let Pietro have it. "Pietro, yesterday I received a very disturbing call from your Aunt, my sister Elena. Everyone is talking about your affair with Carla. It has spread throughout the North End and has reached your parents' ears in Italy. You were sent here and placed in my care. You were to be a priest, a man of God, and now you seem willing to throw everything away for a summer romance with a girl you just met." Pietro, finally addressed the subject. "Aunt Lucia, you call it a summer romance, and it isn't fair. I love Carla and I know she loves me, but for some reason, everything has gone wrong. What should have been something beautiful, has turned out to be something dirty and scandalous in the eyes of my family and friends."

Pietro's words touched Mom deeply, reassuring her, siding with Pietro was the correct thing to do. Instead of joining with Grandma, she took pity on him, knowing how unfairly Pietro and Carla have been treated. She thought to herself, she and Angie were allowed to marry the men they loved, why should Pietro not be allowed to marry the woman he loves? Why should he be forced into a life that appears he no longer wants to pursue? He and Carla met, fell in love, and now want to be together. It's all they desire but seems to be the last thing anyone wants for them. Yet, it's Pietro and Carla's lives, and they should be allowed to live them.

Mom stopped walking, turned Pietro toward her and softly asked, "Pietro, how can I help you?" Then casting a menacingly look at Grandma, she restated her question, "How can we help you?" Grandma caught the look she knew so well and knew Mom was not kidding. Mom had taken pity on Pietro and Carla and openly came over to their side. Grandma, using the method she always used when she wanted to say something only for the ears of her family, questioned Mom in Italian, "*Carmela, cosa hai detto?* (Carmela, what did you say)?" Remembering Pietro is Italian and understood everything she said in questioning Mom to silence her, Grandma became embarrassed, instantly realizing her embarrassment stemmed from the shame she unconsciously felt, meddling in Pietro's and Carla's lives. It was a moment of clarity that secretly changed Grandma's mind concerning the lovers, but she would not let on what had just occurred, wanting to bring her daughters together and discuss what was to be the new plan, and more carefully consider her feelings. For now, she was convinced that Carla and Pietro should be together even though his parents wanted him to be a priest. If marriage was to be his way of life and their love for each other true, would not God bless them as He would if Pietro became a priest? All this came to Grandma's realization in a split second, but it was all that was necessary to move her to action. Still, she kept it to herself, wanting first to speak to her daughters. They continued walking, with very few words spoken among them. The change of heart Grandma experienced would be revealed the following day. For now, Grandma preferred saying nothing.

CHAPTER 43

Grandma Speaks

"I guess it's time for me to interrupt the story once again. Finally, my daughter Lucia, and my granddaughter Carmela, have come to the realization Pietro and Carla should be together. It will not be easy. Not only will they have to convince Carla's family they should be together, but also convince Pietro's family in Italy, which will be far more difficult, for they have their hearts set on having a priest in the family. Perhaps, they see him as a future bishop or cardinal or even pope. If Lucia and Carmela have their way, there will be one less priest in the church. I must admit, there are a few up here who don't believe he should become a priest, but, as we say in Italian, "Quello che sara sara (What will be will be)." I am certain God knows what He is doing, and it will all turn out for the best. I've noticed Lucia has brought her daughters together in the kitchen, so let's get back to the story."

It was early Friday afternoon when Grandma planned to meet with her three daughters in the cottage kitchen. She had brewed a pot of espresso and set taralli on the table, around which they would all gather as Grandma revealed her new plan, which was to bring Pietro and Carla together and make it right in the eyes of her family and friends. "Ma, what's going on?" Auntie Angie asked. "Angie, come into the kitchen. Your sisters are coming. We have something to discuss." Auntie Angie noticed Grandma's eyes were bright and full of mischief. Rather than question her any further, she decided to remain quiet, anxious to hear what her mother was planning. Mom arrived next, somewhat anticipating Grandma's change of heart stemming from her unexpected silence earlier that day. They both took their places at the table, waiting for Auntie Stella to arrive. Finally, she could be heard coming toward the kitchen. As she entered, she let out one of her wise cracks. "The witches are all together, something is up. The old lady is full of tricks." Before she could say another word, Auntie Angie blurted out, "Stella sit down and shut up, but first close the door behind you. Mama has something to say." Auntie Stella was just about ready to utter another sharp remark, when she caught a look from Grandma which shut her down, causing her to take a seat.

When all were seated, Grandma poured the espresso into the cups and motioned in the direction of the taralli, indicating they should try them. When everyone had been served, there was a momentary silence in expectation of what Grandma had to say. Finally, she spoke. "What are we going to do about Pietro and Carla?" Before she could get out another word, Auntie Stella shouted out, "Oh Madonna! We're going to talk about those two?" With that, Auntie Angie sternly responded, "Stella shut up! Listen to Mama!" Grandma continued. "What are we going to do about Pietro and Carla? Is it right two people so much in love should be kept apart by their families?" Grandma then answered her own question. "No, it isn't right." As Grandma spoke, Auntie Stella nervously kept stirring her espresso. The clink clanking against the sides of her cup was annoying Grandma. Reaching over, she pulled the spoon away from her, slamming it on the table. "Stella, you got to listen to me. We have to do something about this." Auntie Stella quickly retorted, "Why do we have to do something about it?" Grandma responded, "Because what's happening to them isn't right." Auntie Stella, always ready to throw kerosene on the fire, shot back, "We wouldn't be in this fix if it wasn't for Carmela. She was supposed to keep an eye on him. She allowed Carla to tempt Pietro and now he wants to marry her."

Mom counted, "Stella, Carla is a good girl, she loves Pietro." Auntie Stella responded, "You're always reading those romance novels. You love this kind of thing." Auntie Angie once again demanded, "Stella shut up! Let Carmela speak." Mom was ready to go on, suddenly, Uncle Tino burst through the door, holding a bucket of quahogs he wanted the women to cook for dinner that evening. He looked around, seeing the women all sitting at the table, immediately knew something was up. He asked, "What's going on in here?" Auntie Stella, just rebuked by Grandma, was more edgy than usual. She knew what Uncle Tino wanted, and before he could get the words out, she shouted out, "Get that bucket of crap out of here!" Uncle Tino shot back, "What crap. These are quahogs. We want to eat them tonight." Auntie Angie gave Auntie Stella a look, silencing her, then told Uncle Tino, "We're talking. Come back later with the quahogs." Auntie Stella responded, "When he brings that bucket of crap back, you clean them. We all stink of fish from cleaning those damn things for the last two weeks."

Grandma becoming more and more frustrated by what was going on in the kitchen, and wanting to discuss her plan instead of quahogs, asked Uncle Tino to come back later. Uncle Tino was ready to leave the quahogs in the kitchen sink, when Auntie Stella shouted out, "Get that crap out of here! I'm tired of the stink of fish!" Uncle Tino exited the kitchen with the bucket of quahogs, but not before reaching into the bucket and tossing a quahog on Auntie Stella's lap, igniting the bomb. She jumped to her feet, ready to chase after him, when Grandma shouted, "*Stella smettila! Hai l'umore di tuo padre* (Stella stop! You have your father's temper). We have things to discuss." Auntie Stella stopped chasing him, but before coming back to the table, she let fly the quahog hitting Uncle Tino's back as he was exiting the cottage, laughing and yelling out, "Skinny Stella, I really pissed you off." Auntie Stella yelled out, "I could kill him! He always calls me Skinny Stella." She turned to Mom and said, "You're closest to him, tell him to stop calling me names."

Grandma, who was sitting quietly, stood up. With a taralli still in her hand, she pointed to Auntie Stella and then to her chair. The expression on her face let Auntie Stella know she wasn't messing around. She wanted silence, so Mom could continue talking. Auntie Stella took her seat, grabbed the spoon Grandma slammed to the table, and began stirring the espresso. Clink, clank, clink, clank, letting everyone know she was still very annoyed but had decided to remain silent.

Auntie Stella was still fuming when Mom began to talk. "Mama and I were talking with Pietro. He really loves Carla, and Carla loves him. "What are we going to do to help them?" If they are meant to be with each other, that's how it should be. The hell with what people think."

Grandma then waved one hand in the air, a gesture indicating it was her time to speak. The three daughters went silent, knowing Grandma was dead serious. Auntie Stella even put down her spoon temporarily, knowing it wasn't the time to continue to demonstrate her anger at Uncle Tino. Grandma began speaking in soft measured tones. *"Questa e' una questione molto seria* (This is a very serious matter)." Whenever Grandma opened her remarks in Italian, it was understood she wanted everyone's undivided attention.

Yes, this is about Pietro and Carla and whether they should come together in marriage, but it is also about their souls and doing the Will of God. *Io sono una donna anziana* (I am an old woman), and supposedly with age comes wisdom. I am wise enough to know it is necessary to speak to a priest in this matter. We cannot do this alone. Some say, let them get together, some say, keep them apart. This is not a game. As I said, it's about their lives and about their souls. When we get back to Boston, we must immediately speak with Padre Francesco." Auntie Stella then shot out, "Here she goes again with the pastor. Whenever something goes wrong, her answer is go and see Father Francesco." Grandma cast a look at Auntie Stella, immediately silencing her. Auntie knew her snippy remarks were not welcomed; Grandma considered the matter too serious. Auntie Angie reached over and grabbed Grandma's hand. "Mama, what are you saying? Are you saying you want Father Francesco to bless their relationship?" Grandma, drawing her hand back, simply replied, "By going to Padre Francesco, we are placing the matter in God's Hands. For if Pietro is to be a priest of God, take the matter to a priest to discover what we should do." Mom nodded her approval. "Mama, it's exactly what we should do. We should have thought of this earlier."

The clink clanking began once again. This time it was with greater agitation, leading to one of Auntie Stella's sarcastic remarks. "Oh, here we go. The two saints are going to be running to Father Francesco. Good! Now the Riccis will kill Pietro and Father Francesco." That last remark triggered Grandma. Picking up a taralli from the table, pointing it at Auntie Stella, she said in her most caustic voice, "You always have a nasty remark. You take after your father with your tongue and your temper." Auntie Angie, seeing the way the wind was blowing, knowing nothing would change Grandma's mind, agreed to the plan. "Mama, I want to go with you when you see Father Francesco." "We will all go together", replied Grandma. Mom then asked, "Even Stella?" Grandma casting a menacing look directly at Auntie Stella, "Si, *soprattutto Stella* (Yes, especially Stella)." That set off a volley of clink clanks, as Auntie Stella nervously stirred her coffee, not daring to say another word. The old lady was going to have her way, and nothing was going to stop her. It was time to see Father Francesco.

"Here I am again. I thought it was necessary to once more speak up for I knew in the end, my daughter Lucia would bring this matter of Pietro and Carla to a priest. She has always been a woman with a deep and fervent faith, and it was only a matter of time, she would seek the council of the Church to help in this matter. We are all watching from up here and are as curious as you to hear what Father Francesco has to say."

CHAPTER 44

Packing Up

Leaving Kingston was never easy, for it was the one time of year we vacationed as a family, everyone enjoying the outdoors. Our departure from Kingston seemed to bring our summer to a close, even though another month of summer lay ahead. Shortly, we would be looking toward autumn, when the children return to school, and Grandma performing her many chores preparing for winter. Within a week of our return, she would pull out the large jars meant to contain her vinegar peppers. Smaller jars scrubbed out and made ready for preserving tomatoes and sweet-smelling basil, Grandma grew in containers on her roof. When Grandpa was alive, he and his daughters would clean out old wine barrels, making them ready for the next batch of wine he prepared in the early fall. Now those barrels lay idle, stacked in the corner of a cellar on Garden Court Street, his secrets of wine-making taken with him into the next world.

It was mid-morning when Uncle Tino and Uncle Jimmy brought their cars to the front of the cottage, signaling it was time for us to depart. We began by packing Uncle Tino's car. The shopping bags and old suitcases that carried our belongings from the North End were already packed and made ready for the return. The canary sat in its cage on the porch, chirping excitedly, getting its last whiff of country air. Uncle Tino, on seeing the canary, was already yelling out, "Where the hell are we going to put that thing?"

Grandma, as always, made certain her treasured copper pots and pans were the first items placed in the car. They went deep into the back of the trunk. She padded them with the old army blankets (our beach blankets), protecting them from the bumpy ride that lay ahead. Next, our clothing was squeezed in, filling the tiny trunk beyond its capacity. Uncle Tino, Dad and Uncle Jimmy tied the trunk lids down, lashing them to the bumper, while Uncle Tino emitted non-stop, the expected barrage of curses. The stand for the canary cage was tied to the top of Uncle Tino's car. Now the curses were really flying. When Grandma placed the cage on the back seat of the car, that would eventually ride back to Boston on her lap, Uncle Tino's comment was always the same, "If that bird shits on my upholstery, I will ring its neck." Always, there would be jars of blueberries Grandma planned to turn into preserves upon our return to Boston.

Once the cars were packed and ready to go, the next trick was to round up the kids who were determined to get the last swim in before their return to Boston. It always worked out the same way, Grandma and Auntie Angie be in the cottage supervising the operation, while Dad, Uncle Jimmy and Uncle Tino would be squeezing our belongings into every nook and cranny of the cars, leaving just enough room for all of us. Mom and Auntie Stella would always be on the beach with the children, just as determined as the kids to get in the last swim, always complaining that we were leaving too early. Pietro seemed particularly sad, perhaps for reasons different than ours, for he was aware our return to Boston would signal his departure from a family he had grown to love, but most of all, from Carla, who had stolen his heart. He would be asked by his family to enter religious life, a life he no longer felt called to.

We all ran into the water for one last swim, but it was different, for now there was a sense of melancholy, knowing these carefree days would be behind us. Auntie Angie came down to the beach, yelling out, as she approached us, "Come out of the water! We must go! I can hear Uncle Tino cursing from here!" This brought us out of the water, dripping wet, as we hurriedly made our way up the road back to the cottage, where Uncle Tino was standing by the car with the door wide open, shouting out, "You're not coming into my car with those wet bathing suits!" An invitation for one of us, usually Mom, to dive into the car, sit on the front seat creating a huge damp stain, driving Uncle Tino wild. Mom, as always, ducked out the other side of the car, leaving Uncle Tino to mop up the water, cursing all the time. Once we were in our dry clothes, we returned to the places in the cars we occupied on our trip down, only now, we all had souvenirs further adding to our cramped quarters.

When we were all in our places, Uncle Tino in the lead car with Uncle Jimmy following and Dad beside him co-piloting, Auntie Angie spotted Mrs. Johnson hurriedly making her way across the lawn calling to Grandma, "Lucia, Lucia, wait!" Grandma motioned for Uncle Tino to stop the engine, which he reluctantly did, cursing under his breath. "Lucia, I made some preserves for you." Handing Grandma the preserves through the window of the car, she looked straight into her eyes and asked, "Lucia, is everything going to be alright?" The two women were from different worlds, but united in the care they had for each other. Grandma knew Mrs. Johnson was concerned for Pietro, whom she came to care for, but most of all, she was concerned for Grandma, who had become very close to her over the years. Grandma stepped out of the car, put the canary cage that was on her lap on the seat, and gave Mrs. Johnson a big hug. The two women stood motionless for a moment, rocking in each other's arms. Grandma then pulled back and kissed her on both cheeks, Italian style.

She re-entered the car, took the canary cage off the seat, and placed it back on her lap. The touching seen was interrupted by Uncle Tino, his stogie clinched tightly between his teeth, shouting out, "Can we go now?" As the two cars rolled down the gravel road with hands stuck out every window waving to Mrs. Johnson, Mom shouted out to Uncle Tino, "Drive by the beach! I have something to do!" Uncle Tino, fit to be tied, shouted back, "What the hell is it now?" When the little convoy finally reached the beach road, Mom signaled, Uncle Tino should stop the car. She flung open the door, stepped out of the car holding a blue bucket Charlie smuggled into the car. Sticking the bucket under Uncle Tino's nose, she said, "He was bringing a horseshoe crab back to Boston." "That little shit brought that stinking crab into my car!" he snarled. He continued to sputter as Mom made her way to the water releasing Charlie's new pet. As she came back to the car, Uncle Tino shouted, "Can we finally leave?" Grandma replied, *"Andate,"* and we were on our way back to Boston.

CHAPTER 45

Father Francesco

W e arrived back in Boston just in time to catch the full brunt
of an August heat wave. Hot sultry air sat over the city like
a steamy, wet blanket, and a milky white sky added to the oppressive
atmosphere. It was only a day since our return, and each of us slipped
back into the groove of everyday life, almost as if we had never been
away. The two exceptions were Pietro and Grandma. Pietro grew quiet
and distant. He returned to his favorite bench at the church, near the
shrine of Our Lady of Pompeii. Being so close to Carla, and yet unable
to see her, seemed to drive him into himself, as he sat beside the shrine
in deep thought. Grandma, who normally would have spent her time
washing and scrubbing everything that accompanied us on our trip to
Kingston, performed none of these chores. She did not even try to clean
Grandpa's shrine at the church, which she always felt needed tidying up
after being on vacation. It never failed, when she was preoccupied with
the affairs of the family, the affairs took center stage. Pietro and Carla
were on her mind, she had to see Padre Francesco. She needed to speak
with him, lay the matter before him and seek his advice.

Grandma always turned to the church in troubled times, and Father
Francesco had always offered her good advice. He was a dignified
looking man in his late sixties and had been pastor of our church for
nine years, an unusual length of time for his Order, who never kept their
priests in the same parish for more than six years. We never knew why
his Order did this but assumed it was not to have their priests become

attached to any one place. In Father Francesco's case, he was very much loved by the people of the parish; since he was approaching retirement age, it seemed prudent to leave him at the church.

It was early Monday morning when Grandma came to our flat on Richmond Street. We had just finished breakfast when she knocked on the door and pushed it open. Before Mom could say a word, Grandma spoke, "Carmela are you ready to see Padre Francesco? Your two sisters are already at the church waiting for us." Mom was still doing the breakfast dishes and was not yet prepared to go off with Grandma. She asked Grandma to sit while she finished the dishes and made the beds, so she could feel the house was in order before leaving. She reminded Grandma, it was only 9:30 in the morning. This did not sit well with Grandma who was anxious to speak with Father Francesco, but she took her seat while Mom darted around the apartment to get things done. "Ma, help yourself to a cup of coffee. It's on the stove." "Is it espresso or Americano?" "Ma, it's Americano. The espresso is like mud, nobody drinks it." "Carmela, you don't know what good coffee tastes like." "Ma, just have a cup of coffee. You always do this. Americano coffee will not kill you." Reluctantly, Grandma poured out a cup of coffee, sipped it and then made her customary face, wrinkled her nose, a facial expression to convey her message of disapproval. Mom from the other room, anticipating Grandma's reaction, shouted out, "Ma, stop wrinkling your nose, the coffee is good!" Grandma did not respond. She simply pushed the cup aside.

"Carmela, are you ready? We have to go and see Padre Francesco." "Ma, do you know what you plan to say to him?" "I want to speak to him of Pietro and Carla. We need his advice. Are they making a sin? Have we made a sin letting their affair go this far?" "Ma, how could you say that? Pietro's loving Carla is not a sin. He's not a priest. What would be wrong is forcing him to become a priest." "Carmela, what do you think we should say to Padre Francesco?" "Ma, let's just explain to him the whole story. How the relatives in Rome expect him to become a priest and sent him here for a brief vacation before entering the seminary. How he met Carla and fell in love with her. How the Riccis are against Carla marrying him. How possessive they are of her." Grandma kept nodding her head in approval, agreeing with everything Mom had to say. Then Grandma spoke up, "What about the scandal? What the neighbors will think, and the relatives in Italy, how they will blame us for allowing Pietro to fall in love with Carla. We have to explain this to Padre Francesco." "Ma, there's nothing we can do about it," replied Mom in an irritated voice. "This is not a scandal. You can't stand in the way of two people who love each other and want to get married." "Carmela, I know you're right but let's get going. I want to speak with Padre Francesco." Mom grabbed Anthony and told him to take care of Bobby and Charlie, and not to wake up Dad, who had to be at the newspaper for the 3 o'clock shift. Grandma and Mom were heading to the door when Grandma turned, remembering her duty as matriarch and Grandmother, made a little gesture to us as if blessing us. She then grabbed Mom under the arm, and they were off to see Father Francesco.

Mom and Grandma made their way up North Square. Pasquale was already sitting in his Cadillac in front of the church, puffing on his cigar. Grandma approached the car, stuck her head in the window, asked Pasquale how he was doing, and had he seen anything interesting in the past day. Grandma was obviously pumping Pasquale for anything he might have seen concerning Pietro and Carla. Pasquale took a deep puff on his cigar, blew the smoke out of the driver's window, turned to Grandma and said, "Angie and Stella are in the church." "Is Pietro there?" Grandma asked. "Yes, he was. He came earlier, but when Angie and Stella arrived, he left." Grandma was relieved. She motioned to Mom to bring Stella and Angie over to the rectory. The three sisters came out of the church. Auntie Angie called to Grandma, still talking to Pasquale. Auntie Stella, seeing Grandma's head stuck in the open window of Pasquale's Caddy, yelled out, "She's looking for gossip! Pasquale sits there all day long watching everything that goes on in the Square. He knows everyone's business."

Grandma pulled her head out from the window, made a threatening gesture with her hand in the direction of Auntie Stella, immediately silencing her but not before Auntie Stella made one more remark of disapproval. Mom then piped up, "Let's knock on the door. We have to speak with Father Francesco." Mom knocked on the door, as the four women gathered in front of the rectory door waiting for Father Francesco to answer. A moment or two passed, someone could be heard walking toward the door. The door swung open and Father Francesco was standing there. Always formal, he was dressed impeccably in clerical garb. Surprised at the sight of the four women gathered at the door so early in the morning, and the look of anxiety on their faces, he immediately surmised something was wrong. "Has someone died?" He asked in a very concerned voice. "No, Padre Francesco. No one has died in the family, thank God. We are here to speak of a serious matter," replied Grandma. *"Grazia Dio!"* Father Francesco exclaimed, thanking God, with a sigh of relief. "Come in ladies, come into my office and we will talk."

The women followed their pastor down a long wood paneled corridor to a dimly lit office. Though the day was still young, the rectory looked as if it was twilight. It was always dimly lit by lamps that were on continuously. Father Francesco's office was particularly dark because its only windows opened to a narrow alley, sunlight never entered. The women took their seats in front of his battered mahogany desk. There was a statue of Jesus in the corner, and what appeared to be official documents piled on the desk just in front of him. Sliding the pile off to the right, he quietly asked, "How can I help you?"

Grandma opened the conversation. "You know my nephew Pietro. He was sent by my brother and sister-in-law to spend his summer vacation with us in America. He's a wonderful *giovanotto* (young man), and as you know, in September he is meant to go into the seminary in Rome." "Si, Lucia, I am aware of this. I have him doing little duties around the church as an introduction to religious life, but lately he doesn't seem as enthusiastic." "Si, Padre, he has become distracted by a woman." Auntie Stella jumped in, offering, "Carla tempted him; she won't leave him alone." Father Francesco could not let her remark stand. "Stella, I know of this situation. You are speaking of Carla Ricci, you should not be saying such things about another person." Auntie Stella was just about ready to counter with another remark when Grandma grabbed her hand, silencing her. Grandma continued, "Padre Francesco, I am afraid for their souls. Pietro is meant to be a priest, and he is giving up everything for the love of a woman." Father Francesco then spoke. "Lucia, you can't force a person to be a priest. It is a special calling to individuals known only to God. I know your brother and sister-in-law desire that Pietro be a priest, but in the end, it is God who makes that determination."

Mom, who was silent till this point, finally spoke up. "Father Francesco, Pietro and Carla love each other, and they should be left alone. Isn't it better Pietro found Carla before becoming a priest, avoiding an impossible situation?" Auntie Angie, anxious to get in some words, added, "What do we say to the millionaires in Italy? They sent their son to us for a summer vacation; he was all set to go into the seminary in September. Within a couple of weeks after arriving, he's romantically involved with Carla Ricci, and what makes it worse, she has a very possessive family. The Ricci father and brothers are very protective of Carla. Who knows what they will do to Pietro if they think he fooled around with her?" Auntie Stella then chimed in, "The father has a fisherman's hook, he threatens to stick it into anyone who fools around with Carla and use their balls for fish bait." Grandma had enough. *"Silenzio, Silenzio,* Stella, have respect for the priest!" She said in her most stern voice. Auntie Stella, about to ignore Grandma's command, felt Grandma's fingers digging into her hand, accompanied by one more command, "Stella, *silenzio!"* Finally shutting her up.

Grandma turned to Father Francesco. "Padre, forgive my daughter for her words. She is hot headed the way her father was. What should we do?" Father Francesco, pushing away from his desk, leaned back in his chair, his countenance becoming quite grave as he began to speak. "I will speak to Pietro alone. Lucia, tell Pietro I would like to see him this afternoon. I must find out what's in his heart. Depending on what he says, I will then take further action. But first, it is important for me to speak with Pietro. Once I have spoken to him, I will speak to you and your daughters, but Pietro will know all I am doing. I will not go behind his back." "Si, Padre, we would never ask you to say or do things behind his back." "I know Lucia, but I want to make it clear, this is how I intend to act." He then stood, blessed the women, a signal the meeting was over, and the women were on their way.

CHAPTER 46
Priestly Advice

It was 4 o'clock in the afternoon when Pietro arrived at the rectory. He rang the bell, Father Francesco quickly appeared at the door. "Pietro, you are here, how are you doing my son?" "Padre, I know why you called me here. You want to know what is happening between Carla and me, and what my intentions are concerning the seminary." "Pietro, your aunt and cousins are very concerned for you. They want only the best for you." "Padre, I arrived in America with the intention of becoming a priest, and yes, I met a woman who I love, and she loves me, but everything has gone wrong. My family is against it, the Ricci family hates me, only cousin Carmela would like to see us together." "Pietro, are you sure you know your mind?" Father Francesco questioned. "You are very young and inexperienced in matters of the heart. Are you in love with Carla, or is it simply infatuation? You should give this more thought, before walking away from your possible calling to religious life."

"Padre Francesco, I don't love God any less for loving Carla, and I know He does not love me any less for loving her. Should I be asked to enter religious life when I feel this way?" Father Francesco reached over and clasped Pietro's hands between his hands. "Pietro, my son, you are young. I would like you to give this matter some thought and pray over it. God will help you, but you must trust in Him. I know everything seems very confused right now, but I am here to help you. If you still feel the way you do in a day or two, return with Carla and we can continue our talk. Meanwhile, I would suggest you go to your aunt's shrine and pray. Pray the rosary and ask Our Lady to lead you."

Pietro stood up, bent over, brushed his cheek against Father Francesco's hand as a sign of friendship and respect. Taking Father Francesco's advice, he went to the shrine of Our Lady of Pompeii, and there he sat praying for guidance.

CHAPTER 47

The Telegram

"Angie, we have to write to Velia and Gerardo in Italy, it's time to let Pietro's parents hear from us directly. Go and get Carmela and I'll get Stella, we can work on the telegram together; we must say the right words." Within ten minutes, Mom and Auntie Angie could be heard climbing the metal stairs to Grandma's flat. They entered to find Auntie Stella and Grandma sitting at the table waiting for them. Even before Mom and Auntie Angie reached the table, Auntie Stella let out her first salvo, "The old lady is going to write to those snobs in Italy about their son. Who asked them to send him to us to cause all this trouble?"

Grandma was in no mood for Auntie Stella's comments. Turning to her, she simply said, "Stella, *basta* (enough). It's time for Velia and Gerardo to hear from us directly. As soon as we write the words, Angie, you will take it to, *come si chiama quel posto* (what do you call that place) for telegrams?" "Western Union, Mom." "Si, si," Grandma affirmed. "You will take it to Western Union. Now let us write the words. Angie *scrivi* (write). Angie, how do we begin?" "How do we begin; how do we begin?" Auntie Stella interjected nervously, "Dear Velia and Gerardo, your son Pietro is in love with a woman, he will never be a priest." "Enough Stella, this is serious," Grandma scolded. Turning to Auntie Angie, she began, "Angie we will begin by saying, Caro Velia and Gerardo, it has been a while since I have written. Pietro is fine. He is a wonderful young man. We know you have heard about his infatuation with a young woman, Carla Ricci. We have sought the help of our pastor, Padre Francesco." Grandma then looked toward her daughters for assistance. Mom piped up, "Mama, tell them we are putting the matter in God's Hands." "Si, si, Carmela, you're right." Grandma continued, "We are placing the matter in God's Hands with the help of Padre Francesco. Know I love you both and we will all do our best to help Pietro make the right decision. Your loving *sorella* (sister), Lucia."

At the completion of her dictation, Grandma became aware the table they were sitting at was rocking back and forth. Knowing exactly what was happening, she turned to Auntie Stella. "Stella, when the table rocks, I know you are nervously moving your leg back and forth. Why are you nervous?" Seizing the invitation, Auntie Stella snapped back, "Why didn't you write the Ricci brothers want to beat him up and the father wants to use his balls for fish bait!" *"Stella, ma sei pazza"* (Stella, but you're crazy). "What I said is true. We will write to them again, once Padre Francesco gives his advice." "Stella," Mom said nervously, "Why do you say these things to Mama? You know it works her up." "Oh, now we are hearing from the other saint," Auntie Stella sarcastically commented. "Ma, are you satisfied with what you wrote? It sounds good." Auntie Angie said reassuringly, ignoring Auntie Stella's comments, "I'll take it to Western Union." *"Grazie, grazie,"* Grandma responded. Auntie Angie was off to send the telegram.

Here I am again. It has been a while since I commented on what my family is up to. Finally, my daughter Lucia is doing the right thing, placing the matter of Pietro and Carla in God's Hands, and letting my son Gerardo and his wife know exactly what she has done.

Years ago, when my daughter Lucia was sick with scarlet fever, I climbed a steep hill in my bare feet to the shrine of Our Lady of Monte Virgine near my home town of Pratola Serra. I did this as a sign of my faith in the Blessed Mother, asking her assistance in helping to cure my daughter. Through her, I placed the matter in God's Hands, and all worked out well. Lucia is following in her father's footsteps.

CHAPTER 48

Setting up for a Feast

It was now mid-August, time for the Saint Andrew Feast. The feast was one of many held in the North End commemorating different saints. This feast was dedicated to Saint Andrew the Apostle, who before being called to be an Apostle was a fisherman. It was Tuesday, just before the opening of the feast. The men of the Society were busy erecting the bandstand and ornamental backdrop, made up of cardboard, crepe paper and bright lights. The Society was based in a small building located on the waterfront, and it was there they enshrined a statue of Saint Andrew. He was kept in a chapel on the main floor. The basement of the building was where meetings of the Society took place. It housed a small kitchen and dining area where the men, who would never go near a stove in their homes, took turns doing the cooking for the Society members, and as usual, the fare consisted of spaghetti and meatballs. It was Tuesday afternoon, Ernesto, one of the members of the Society, had set up a table and chairs on the street, at the rear of the shrine, which had been cordoned off for the upcoming feast. He was serving spaghetti with calamari sauce, a specialty he cooked every year at Feast time. Ernesto kept his recipe for calamari sauce to himself, and everyone agreed his sauce was the best. It was 4 o'clock in the afternoon, the heat of the mid-August day was just subsiding.

"Hey knuckleheads, it's time to eat," said Ernesto. It was his way of summoning the guys who were working on the bandstand. Minutes later, the banquet was in full swing with ten guys sitting around the table, while Ernesto made trips back and forth to the basement of the Shrine as he dished out the spaghetti. He refused to bring the pot of spaghetti to the table, saying it would cool down and lose much of its flavor, so he made the extra effort of plating in the basement, taking dish by dish to each of the members. With his mouth full of spaghetti, Vito declared, "This will be the best feast ever. The guy that we got to entertain, Jerry De Rosa, sings like Frankie Lane. We will get him to sing a lot of Italian songs. We have a six-piece band to back him up that plays at the Totem Pole. Nancy Conley, who sings with the band, doesn't have much of a voice, but she has Jane Russell's ass." "What good is her ass!" shouted out Phil Risoli, "if she doesn't have a good voice." Ernesto responded, "Phil, now I know you're an old guy. Who cares about the voice if the singer has Jane Russell's ass? You just proved to me you're over the hill." "Who's over the hill, you little shit?" Phil responded, his mouth full of spaghetti. "If she stinks, the crowd will go crazy."

Vito, wanting to add his two cents to the conversation said, "Hey Phil, not only does she have Jane Russell's ass, she also has Jane Russell's knockers." "Quit it Vito, my friend Carmela is coming, you don't want her to hear the way we're talking." Mom knew all the guys at the table. She walked over to see what they were eating. "Why were you talking about Jane Russell?" "Who was talking about Jane Russell?" Vito replied. "We were saying, she's a good cook." Mom began to laugh. "Yeah, yeah, she's a good cook. I'm going to tell your wives. All you do is sit around eating spaghetti and talking about Jane Russell." "Carmela, grab a seat and have a plate of spaghetti." Vito pulled out a chair and Mom took her seat at the table. As soon as Mom sat down, Ernesto emerged from the basement carrying a steamy plate of spaghetti with calamari sauce. "Carmela, would you like a glass of wine?" "No thanks Ernesto, a glass of water with lemon will be fine." Quickly, he made up a glass, brought it up from the basement, and took a seat at the table. "Carmela, how's the family?" Vito asked. "We're fine. We just came back from Kingston. We took my cousin Pietro Petruzelli with us." When Mom mentioned Pietro's name, it caught Vito's attention. "I heard about your cousin. He's the one who wants to become a priest, so what is he doing chasing after Carla Ricci?" "How do you know about that?" Mom asked angrily. "Carmela, calm down. The whole North

End knows about it. You know how it is down here, everyone knows everyone's business."

Mom, still smarting from Vito's remark, quickly replied, "It's just an infatuation. It will fade away once Pietro enters the seminary. Stop making more of it than you should." "Carmela, your cousin better be careful. You know how the Ricci brothers are with their sister. You remember what they did to Jerry Lombardo. They frightened the crap out of him." "Vito, I told you, it's just a summer infatuation. Once he gets back to Italy, it will all settle down." Vito knew he struck a nerve, so he rubbed it in all the more. "Carmela, that Carla is quite a dish. She's enough to turn any guy's head." Mom stood up. "I had enough of this crap. You guys are like a bunch of old ladies!" Mom said angrily, as she readied to leave. Trying to calm her, Ernesto urged, "Carmela, sit down and finish your spaghetti." "No, Ernesto, I told you I had enough." Ernesto trying to appease Mom, extended to her a special invitation and privilege of the Society. "Carmela, why don't you bring your entire family, including Pietro, to the feast Sunday night. You will be guests of the Society, sit inside the Shrine with the statue of the Saint and have a front row seat." "Ernesto, first you give me poison with your talk, now you're offering this special honor. What's wrong with you?" "No, Carmela, I mean it. You can be our guests. We will reserve seats for you and the family in the Shrine."

Mom responded, "Alright Ernesto, I will mention it to Mom and my sisters, and I will speak with Pietro." Mom began walking away, turned on her heels, with a grin, shouted out, "Yeah Ernesto, Jane Russell does have a good set of knockers! I have half a mind to tell your wives what you guys talk about." "Carmela, is this the way to talk after we offered you such an honor?" responded Ernesto. "Yeah, yeah," Mom responded. "You're all afraid of your wives." Mom continued down the street, then turned a second time. The guys were still watching her, she repeated, "She does have good knockers." She began to laugh, shouted out, "I never heard a thing!" and continued on her way to Grandma's house.

CHAPTER 49

A Family Honor

When Mom arrived at Grandma's building, she could hear a lot of yelling coming from her flat. Mom ran up the stairs, entered the apartment and found Auntie Stella and Grandma arguing. "What's going on with you two?" Mom asked anxiously. "The old lady wants me to marry James Cataldo!" Auntie Stella replied angrily. "James Cataldo is a good catch," said Grandma. "He owns his own cleaning business. He's been standing across the street, waiting for your sister to call him up to the flat. She's going to become una vecchia zitella (an old maid)." "Ma, you know I don't like short men," retorted Auntie Stella. "He's not short," Grandma fired back. "He's got a good business and can take care of you."

Auntie Stella was eating a sweet corn just before the argument broke out. Picking it up from the table, she walked over to the window, looked at James who was looking up at her, gave him a brief smile, then turned to Grandma, who for a moment lit up, seeing Auntie Stella smiling at her love-struck suitor. Auntie Stella turned back to Grandma, holding the sweet corn vertically in one hand, sarcastically said, "He's as big as this sweet corn." Grandma's smile quickly turned to anger. "What do you mean! He's as big as the sweet corn? That's why you're going to be an old maid. You don't have a good word for anyone." Mom was roaring laughing. She turned to Stella and said, "Stella, hold up the corn, say it again." Mom could hardly get the words out, she was laughing so hard. Auntie Stella was just about ready to do it when Grandma grabbed the corn out of her hand and threw it in the barrel. "I told you, she doesn't have a good word for anyone. Carmela, you're laughing at her, you're just encouraging her." "Okay, Ma, calm down. I have something important to tell you."

Grandma and Mom took their seats at the kitchen table. Mom called Auntie Stella over to sit with them. Before she came, she went to the window, gave one last look at James, and pulled down the shade. Grandma totally exasperated, shouted out, "That's it Stella, pull down the shade. *Sarai una vecchia zitella* (You're going to be an old maid!)"

Then she demanded, Auntie Stella come sit at the table. Mom recounted the conversation she just had with the members of The Saint Andrew Society. "Ma, they invited the entire family, not only to the feast, but to sit in the Shrine." Grandma realizing this was an honor being bestowed on her family, asked, "Why are they doing this? We're not from their *paese* (town) in Italy." "Mom, the guys were teasing me. They were talking about Carla and Pietro. Ernesto Mucci knew it disturbed me and wanted to make amends by inviting us." "Including Pietro?" Grandma asked cautiously. "Yes, Ma, including Pietro." Auntie Stella, failing to see the honor bestowed on the family, sharply remarked, "Who wants to sit in there with all the old farts? I'd rather be on the street dancing and singing."

Grandma, still smarting from Auntie Stella's sweet corn performance, slammed her hand on the table and said, "Stella, you're not going to insult our friends by refusing this honor!" Auntie Stella sharply remarked, "You're making me an old maid. How am I ever going to find a man sitting in a shrine with a statue of a saint and all old farts? You're turning me into a nun." Grandma had enough. She once again slammed her hand on the table, shot a look at Auntie Stella that immediately quieted her. Mom turned to Auntie Stella and joked, "Why don't you have another sweet corn?" Auntie Stella, knowing Mom was "digging it in", caustically responded, "Don't you start up Carmela. You're already married; she's going to make a nun out of me."

Now Grandma was exasperated at both her daughters. She grabbed Auntie Stella's hand to silence her once and for all, then turned to Mom and said, "Carmela, tell me the complete story and stop teasing your sister." "Ma, that's the story. They want us at the feast, and they want us to sit in the Shrine of the Saint." Grandma responded, "Carmela, we will go on Sunday night when they have entertainment. Do you know who will be performing?" "Some man who sings like Frankie Lane." Grandma, not knowing who Frankie Lane was, asked, "Is he an opera singer?" "No, Ma, he sings popular American music." "Good, we will go Sunday night, my three daughters, Pietro and the family." Mom rolled her sweet corn in the direction of Auntie Stella who quickly got the message. "That's it, tease me Carmela. We're all going to be in there with all those old farts. The old lady loves that." Grandma, knowing she laid down the law, sat at the table with a complacent look on her face, looked at Auntie Stella, and took a large bite out of the sweet corn on her plate.

CHAPTER 50

Preparing for the Feast

The Saint Andrew Feast began on Thursday, with a candlelight procession in the early evening to the waterfront, led by Father Francesco. He was to bless the fishing boats, anchored at the wharves along Atlantic Avenue. With the procession still hours away, Mom entered the church wanting to speak with Pietro, who was sitting by the shrine of Our Lady of Pompeii. "Pietro, how long have you been here?" "About an hour," Pietro responded, blurry-eyed. "Pietro, Mama would like you to come to the feast with us on Sunday night. We've been invited by the Society to spend the evening in the Shrine. It's considered a great honor." "Cousin Carmela, please don't ask me to do this. I'm in no mood to face crowds of people."

"Pietro," Mom insisted, "You must come. Mama would like you to be there, and furthermore, it would be good to show yourself to the people of the North End. They know you're still in Boston, why make them think you're hiding from them?" "Cousin Carmela, I don't care what they think. Let them think what they want." "Pietro, you will be returning to Italy, but we have to live with these people. You must show you have nothing to be ashamed of and nothing to hide." "I have nothing to hide," snapped Pietro. "Pietro, I know that's true, but by being there you will prove it." "Cousin Carmela, let me consider it. I don't want to do anything further that would make the family's life uncomfortable. So please, let me give this a little thought," Pietro conceded.

Mom squeezed Pietro's hand affectionately, left the bench, genuflected, and slowly walked out of the church, leaving Pietro to make his own decision, which Mom felt certain would be to join the family on Sunday evening.

There was a religious feast in the North End virtually every weekend of the summer during the late 1940's. The Saint Andrew Feast came toward the end of the festival season. Next came the Feast of Saint Francis of Assisi. Pride in one's origin, reflected in how many bright lights, food vendors and how big a bandstand was erected. The object of the feast is to honor a saint associated with a town or region of Italy, sharing the same spirit with their Italian counterparts. The feasts generally culminate with a procession of the honored saint, carried by members of the Society through the streets of the North End. Long ribbon streamers, radiating from the statue, are held by members of the Society, on which offerings to the saint are pinned, as the procession proceeds through the streets. A band generally precedes the saint, playing a variety of Italian songs, some of them real tear jerkers like "Mama" and for the Neapolitans, "O Sole Mio." Devotees continue to join the procession as the saint wends its way through the narrow streets of the North End. Church bells ring, greeting the oncoming saint, as a blizzard of confetti is let loose from the windows of the crowded tenements, heralding the coming of the saint.

Every so often, the procession stops beneath a window, where a garland of dollar bills, attached to a ribbon, is lowered to the outstretched hands of a Society member. It's greeted by an abbreviated rendition of the Italian National Anthem, in gratitude for the donation. People cheer, the procession moves on, accompanied by young girls handing out prayer cards and buttons bearing the image of the honored saint. The religious societies that maintain private chapels, will open their doors in a gesture of honor to the saint being celebrated that weekend. The honored saint will be brought to the doorstep of the chapel, where a garland of dollar bills will be placed over the head of the saint by a member of the Society. The feasts are a time of merriment, but there are rituals to be observed and customs to be honored. Things that might escape the casual onlooker, are carefully observed by the various societies of the North End.

"Mama, Pietro will be joining us on Sunday night." "Are you sure Carmela. Did he say he would?" Grandma asked anxiously. "Yes, Ma, I know Pietro, he knows how important this is to our family, and I know he will not disappoint us."

CHAPTER 51

Good News

I t was 2 o'clock in the afternoon on Thursday, the day the fishing fleet
was to be blessed, when Father Francesco walked into the chapel of
the church and found Pietro saying the rosary. "Pietro, I see you are
deep in prayer. That is very good my son," said Father Francesco. "Yes,
Padre, I am praying for a very special intention." "That is good my son.
I'm certain that Our Lord will hear you and answer your prayers in the
best way. Pietro, tonight is the blessing of the fishing fleet. I would like
you to carry the thurible. You will walk just in front of me with a candle
bearer on either side."

"Yes, Padre," Pietro responded dutifully. "I will be happy to carry
the incense burner, and I will get my cousins, Bobby and Charlie, to
carry the processional candles." Father Francesco was delighted Pietro
was going to accompany him and he even managed to find candle
bearers. "Pietro, we will all meet in the lower chapel at 5:30 this evening
and prepare to receive the Saint at the door of the church." "Will there
be a crowd, Padre?" "Yes, Pietro. This is one of the biggest feasts of the
North End. Members of the Saint Andrew Society and all their relatives
will be in the procession." "Padre, I will go to my cousin Carmela's
house and let her know Charlie and Bobby will be in the procession. I
know she will be delighted. We will return at 5:30."

Pietro rushed home and could not wait to inform Mom, Charlie and
Bobby would be in the procession with him. Mom was delighted with
the news. She was also happy, Pietro decided to be part of the procession.

As thurifer, he would lead the procession and be noticed by everyone in the North End, a sure sign that he has nothing to hide. "Pietro, go find the boys, they are on the street playing tops with their friends. Tell them to come home and wash up. I 'm heading over to Mama's flat to let her know the procession will be headed by our family. This will make her very happy."

Mom rushed over to Grandma's. Grandma, Auntie Stella and Auntie Angie were making cookies in the kitchen. They were planning to bring them to the members of the Society, as a thank you gift for allowing our family in the chapel. Grandma was overjoyed by the news but somewhat worried for Pietro, afraid someone would make an insulting remark concerning Carla. Auntie Angie quieted her fears, delighted over the fact the family would be playing a prominent role in the feast. On the other hand, Auntie Stella couldn't care less. She was chewing gum and snapping it while making cookies, aggravating Grandma. When she completely ignored Mom's news, it became all too much for Grandma. "Stella, stop snapping the gum, be happy for your family." Auntie Stella did not respond and kept snapping her gum while stirring the macaroon batter, a specialty of Grandma's. Grandma turned to Auntie Angie and shouted out, "What's wrong with your sister?" Auntie Angie, equally aggravated, asked Auntie Stella to stop snapping her gum, she was upsetting Grandma, and to be happy the family was being honored at this year's Saint Andrew's Feast.

Auntie Stella responded, "Why should I be happy? No one in our family is a member of that Society." Grandma then snatched the bowl containing the macaroon batter from Auntie Stella. This prompted Mom to yell out, "This is a crazy house. You people fight over everything." It was Mom's referring to her family as "you people" that got to Auntie Angie. "Who are you referring to as, 'you people'?" She asked, as she pulled out a chair to rest her knee, a sign that she was ready for battle. "Angie, I didn't mean it that way, but every time I come here, everyone is fighting." "Oh, Saint Carmela has spoken," Auntie Stella remarked, in a caustic voice, from the back of the kitchen. "Stella, I'm not a saint, but you can really be bitchy and make Mama nervous." "Who's a bitch?" responded Auntie Stella, punctuating her remark with a snap of her gum. "Stella, *Madonna mia*, throw the gum away. I can't stand it any longer," once again demanded Grandma. Auntie Stella threw the gum into the drain of the kitchen sink, while Auntie Angie removed her knee from the chair, a sign the argument was coming to an end, and she would go no further.

Mom shouted out, "I gave you the news, now I'm heading home." Auntie Angie tossing a sweater over her shoulders also headed home, anxious to tell Theresa and Grace the boys will be in the feast procession. Before leaving Grandma's, Auntie Angie was emphatic, declaring, "Our family has to make a good showing in the procession." Grandma nodded in agreement while Auntie Stella simply shrugged her shoulders, indicating her indifference.

CHAPTER 52

The Blessing of the Fishing Boats

W e all gathered at Grandma's flat at 5 o'clock in the evening. Grandma was agitated and was anxious to get to church before the bells began to chime, signaling the Saint was on the way to the church. Charlie, Bobby and Pietro were in their surplices and cassocks, they had put on at the church. They wore them to Grandma's, knowing she would get tremendous pleasure, seeing them dressed for the procession. Grandma noticed the hem on Pietro's cassock had torn lose. Immediately, she took out her needle and thread and basted a new hem without Pietro having to remove it. Charlie somehow managed to get his surplice soiled, somewhere between the church and Grandma's. Once again, she swung into action. She had Charlie take off the surplice, washed the spot gently on her wash board in the kitchen sink, and blotted it dry with kitchen towels; the surplice was good as new, and the emergency was over. Once all repairs were completed and she felt we were properly representing the family, Grandma gave the signal for the family to leave for church. It was now 5:20 and the Saint was expected in ten minutes. Even Auntie Stella seemed excited. She helped Grandma straighten her hat, anchoring it with the large hat pin with the artificial pearl at one end, fastening it to Grandma's pug. Quickly, we made it down the stairs and onto the street with Charlie, Bobby and Pietro running ahead of everyone to be at Father Francesco's side, who was waiting at the entrance to the church. The rest of the family joined the crowd already gathered at the front of the church, awaiting the arrival of the Saint.

Meanwhile, back at the Saint Andrew Shrine, the procession was getting ready to depart. The Saint had been removed from his pedestal, carefully placed on the litter, to be carried through the streets of the North End by members of the Society. The procession would make its way to the waterfront, where fishermen and their boats had congregated between Commercial Wharf and Long Wharf, gingerly working their boats forward, to get as close to the shoreline as possible.

"One, two, three, lift!" Sonny, the lead litter bearer, called out to his team. The eight burly men hoisted the litter now bearing the Saint onto their shoulders. The statue lurched first to the left, then to the right, steadied by the men moving in a counter direction. When he felt the statue was ready to travel, Sonny gave the word to Sam, the director of the band. Sam waved his hand and the band began to play. A second wave, and the band moved out. The ten men, who made up the band, moved in unison, rocking to the left, then to the right, as they made their way to North Square, the litter bearers following just behind. The crowd instinctively separated, allowing the band and the litter bearers to pass through their midst.

The litter was set on a low platform erected in front of the church, just for the purpose. The bells of the church were ringing from a bell tower, that in the nineteenth century, once called Methodist worshipers to this former Seamen's Bethel, where it is said, Herman Melville visited while writing Moby Dick. The ringing of the bells added pageantry and a momentous feeling to the occasion. The band and the Saint were greeted by Father Francesco, who was dressed in a spectacular gold embroidered chasuble that shimmered in the late afternoon sun. Beside him stood Pietro, holding a brass urn of holy water and a sprinkler, meant to be used by Father Francesco to bless the fleet of boats and their crews. Just to the right of Pietro, on a brass stand, was the thurible sending up puffs of incense scented smoke. Just behind Pietro, dressed as altar boys, stood Bobby and Charlie on either side of him, carrying processional candles. Mom, Grandma, Auntie Angie and Auntie Stella worked their way to the front of the crowd, standing just behind the Saint, as the crowd continued to gather in North Square.

Father Francesco, taking the sprinkler from the urn of holy water held by Pietro, took the opportunity to bless the crowd. He shot droplets of holy water first to the left, then to the right, and finally to the center of the crowd. With each sprinkle, there arose from the crowd a roar of appreciation. After completing his blessing, Father Francesco gave Sonny the signal to depart, who in turn motioned to the litter bearers, who once again lifted the Saint onto their shoulders. The band struck up "Isle of Capri" while walking and swaying, this time in the direction of the waterfront. Pietro handed the holy water urn to Father Francesco, detached the thurible from its stand and began swinging it from left to right, with Bobby and Charlie flanking him, candles lit, and Father Francesco following, carrying the urn of holy water. The celebrants took their places in front of the Saint, with a crowd of many hundreds following behind, as they made their way to the waterfront for the blessing of the fishing fleet. to the waterfront for the blessing of the fishing fleet. All of this accompanied, once again, by the ringing of the church bells in tribute to the Saint. The litter bearers took a slightly different route on their way to the waterfront. They headed down Moon Street, took a right onto Fleet Street, and finally across Atlantic Avenue to the waterfront and a clearing between the many sheds that lined the fish pier.

The fishing boats were packed tightly between Long Wharf and Commercial Wharf, so tight, the fishermen were able to pass from one wharf to the other by simply jumping from boat to boat. Horns began to blare from the harbor at the first sight of the Saint, while relatives of the fishermen, marching in the procession, let out a roar not to be outdone. It was a spectacular moment of both pageantry and religious fervor. Once the Saint was seated safely on the pedestal, earlier placed on Commercial Wharf, Father Francesco moved to the edge of the wharf where he motioned for quiet.

Instantly, all went silent, both on land and sea. He handed the holy water urn he was carrying to Pietro, then stretched out his hands in the direction of the fishing boats and delivered a short prayer. Pietro was standing beside him holding both the urn of holy water and thurible with Charlie and Bobby flanking him, holding their lit processional candles. Pietro then noticed Carla on the Ricci's fishing boat, anchored close to the wharf. The brothers were all on deck looking in the direction of Father Francesco, while Carla's father, Egidio, was positioned at the wheel. Carla was standing just behind a fishing net, stretching from the bow of the boat onto its cabin. She was wearing a yellow dress that hung off her tanned shoulders, gathered tightly at her waist, falling softly just below her knees. Her auburn hair, caught in the breeze, gently blowing over the harbor, first flowing in front of her face, then tossed gracefully back onto her shoulders. She was looking directly at Pietro who seemed to become increasingly mesmerized by the sight of her; the sounds of the crowd falling away. For a moment, Pietro was aware only of Carla, as she swayed in graceful response to the waves just beneath the boat. Auntie Stella became aware of the encounter.

After gaining Mom's attention by nudging her with her elbow, she nodded in their direction. Mom, recognizing the potential for trouble, nudged Auntie Angie, drawing her attention to the lovers. Auntie Angie let out an audible gasp that drew Grandma's attention. Now all were looking in the direction of Carla and Pietro. Auntie Angie instinctively grabbed Mom by the arm and began nervously squeezing it, causing Mom to pull away. Auntie Stella, spotting what was going on between her sisters, displayed a slight grin, as if to say, "I told you so," which Grandma caught. Narrowing her eyes in the direction of Auntie Stella, she was able to wipe the grin off her face without saying a word. Not a word was spoken among them as they communicated by familiar gestures, while cautiously looking at the lovers.

Suddenly, their silence was interrupted by Father Francesco, who had come to the end of his prayer and gestured to Pietro for the holy water. Pietro, entranced by Carla, was totally unaware of Father Francesco's request. Once again, Father Francesco looked in the direction of Pietro and motioned for the sprinkler. Finally, Bobby nudged Pietro, breaking his trance. It was then, Pietro heard Father Francesco beckoning to him. He quickly dunked the sprinkler into the holy water and slammed it directly into Father Francesco's hand, who let out an audible sound of pain, while scowling in his direction. Father Francesco turned his head toward the fishing fleet. He blessed the fleet, sprinkling first to the left, then to the right, spotting Carla, his hand froze for a moment in midair, as he recognized the drama playing out around him. Grandma, noticing Father Francesco's hesitation, became aware he knew what was happening. Auntie Stella then whispered, "He knows." Auntie Angie quickly shut her up.

Father Francesco continued the blessing of the fleet, now sprinkling to the center. He turned back to Pietro and handed him the sprinkler. The look on Father Francesco's face was one of displeasure, but he quickly erased it, trying not to draw attention to the little drama taking place in their midst. The horns blasted, and the crowd cheered, "*Viva Sant 'Andrea.*" The fleet had been blessed for another year, in the hope God, through the intercession of Saint Andrew, would grant them abundant fishing and safe passage.

CHAPTER 53

Dining Out

Life in the North End during festival season spilled out of the apartments and onto the streets, particularly affecting those whose saint was being honored from their region of Italy. Families set tables of food and drink on sidewalks in front of their buildings, where members sat from early afternoon till late in the evening, conversing with one another. Food offered to a never-ending stream of visitors, honoring the family, and sharing in their regional dishes.

Every year, the Ricci family set up several card tables in front of their doorway on Garden Court Street. Being one of the leading families of fishermen in the North End, they were expected to put out quite a spread and they never disappointed their neighbors. It would take Carla a week to prepare the food for the feast. The tables were covered with red and white checkered tablecloths that she loaded with platters of salami, cheese and all variety of Italian cold cuts, fried calamari, baked sausages, spaghetti and meatballs and calzone, all served in abundance. Large pitchers of chilled wine, peach halves floating in them, were scattered along the tables and refilled as soon as emptied. Papa Egido would play his mandolin throughout the early evening hours, as if to serenade the guests who visited his tables.

The sultry August evenings were magical with the sound of mandolin music and clinking glasses, as guests toasted each other and their patron saint, and always, the laughter drifting on evening breezes. Evenings imbued the feasts with a special magic, shrouding the foreign surroundings of their adopted land for both North Enders and immigrants alike, bringing to life the sounds and smells of Italy. People who came ashore in successive waves over decades, worn down from their everyday labor, seemed to be reignited like a flame given life through the strike of a match. The colorful lights that hung from the flats in tribute to the saint, cast their warm and familiar glow over worn tired faces.

"Carla, we are running out of Sangria. Bring more pitchers of wine for our guests," Egidio demanded, as he put down his mandolin to embrace two of his amici (friends), Roberto and Anna Gallo. *"Carla vieni subito"* (Carla come quickly), he once again demanded, as the click clack of Carla's sandals could be heard quickly descending the stairs in response to her father's request. "Papa, I'm coming, I'm coming," she reassuringly called out, as she descended the worn wooden flight of stairs leading to the street. Egidio reached out for the wine pitchers, and quickly filled the glasses of his friends. It was late in the evening and many of the platters had been emptied. Egidio slightly embarrassed, asked Carla to bring more cold cuts for the late arrivals. Swiftly, she rushed upstairs to fill two platters with salami, prosciutto and provolone. Minutes later, the click clack of her sandals could once again be heard, as she descended the stairs, a platter in each hand, much to Egidio's delight. While waiting for Carla, Anna and Roberto took their seats at Egidio's table. They filled their glasses with wine and toasted their host, took a sip and placed the glasses on the table.

Roberto then turned to Egidio and said, "Egidio, I heard your neighbors, Lucia and her family, will be given the honor of having seats in the Saint's shrine Sunday evening." Egidio, aware that the honor had been extended to his old friends, but also wary of the fact everyone knew of the romance that had sprung up between Pietro and Carla, did not respond. Cautiously, after collecting his thoughts, he looked at his guests and finally said, "Yes, it is quite an honor, especially since Lucia's family is not a family of fishermen." Egidio said these words in an unguarded moment as Carla was standing right beside him. Roberto further pressing the matter, asked, "Will the entire family be there?" Egidio, looking at his guest in a somewhat threatening way, angrily responded, "Roberto, what are you trying to say? Are you trying to tell me something?" The strain in his voice, apparent to his guests. Carla, quite aware of the undercurrent of Roberto's question, snatched the pitcher of wine from her father's hand and slammed it on the table, without saying a word. Her eyes flashing at Roberto. A smoldering fury seemed to surround her as she turned and stormed up the stairs to the apartment. "Forgive my daughter, Roberto, it's been a long day and she's tired, in fact, so am I. It's late in the evening and tomorrow will be an even longer day, for it's the evening of entertainment. We will be at the feast till the end of the evening."

Roberto and Anna took the hint, drank the last of their Sangria, kissed Egidio from cheek to cheek, expressed their *buonanotte* (good night) and left. As they turned, one could see a slight grin on their faces, for Sunday night, the main night of the feast, would be filled with singing and dancing as families gathered around the bandstand and the shrine of the Saint. Thoughts of Carla and Pietro were in their heads, the same thoughts they never expressed to Egidio.

CHAPTER 54

All Dressed Up

It was mid-Sunday afternoon, and the family was getting ready for the big night of the feast. "Stella, which hat do you like best?" Grandma asked, holding up two straw hats for Auntie Stella to judge. "Ma, all your hats look the same; they are all black, they are all straw, and they have a black veil." "Stella, you never have anything good to say. You would even talk about those who are *morti* (dead)." "Ma, your hats are all alike; you must have ten, and they all look the same." Auntie Angie and Mom were also at Grandma's flat, where the family was gathering before going to the feast. Mom was wearing a little black and white dress with white earrings and a white bead necklace. She looked like she was ready to dance and have a good time. On the other hand, Auntie Angie was wearing one of her Kate Smith specials, only it was summer weight. Mom always called Auntie Angie's dresses, Kate Smith dresses, after the singer made famous singing God Bless America, like Kate Smith's dresses, she didn't consider them stylish. She thought of them as looking like something from out of Victorian times. They were considerably below the knee, a high neckline and long sleeves, very much the way Kate Smith dressed.

"Angie, I see you got a new Kate Smith dress for the summer," cracked Mom. "Carmela, this is a beautiful dress. It has a beaded neckline. What do you know about clothes?" Auntie Angie responded. "Kate always wears a beaded neckline," Mom shot back. "Carmela don't aggravate me, it's too hot," Auntie Angie returned.

Auntie Stella walked in from the bedroom after helping Grandma select the hat she would wear for the evening. "That's it! She bought another Kate Smith dress," observed Auntie Stella. "Stella, now you're starting." "Angie, you have beautiful legs. Why do you cover them up with those damn long dresses?" "Give it to her Stella," Mom joined in. "I tell her all the time, come with me to Lerner's, where the dresses are up to date."

"Carmela, if Papa was alive and caught you with those short dresses, you wear to show off your nice legs, he would whack you in the back of the head, the way he did when you cut your long hair. Remember what he said, years ago, when you came out of the water at Kingston, "You look like a drowned rat." Auntie Stella joined in, "He gave you a good one, Carmela." "Yes, Stella, but I also remember you cut your hair a week later." "You have nice wavy hair, but you had it all pinned up in the back of your neck, like an old spinster."

At this point, Grandma came into the living room where her daughters had gathered. She was now wearing her little black hat and wanted to know what Auntie Angie and Mom thought of it. She was arranging the veil at the top of her hat, looking at her daughters, she asked, *"Ti piace* (Do you like)?" Mom looked at the hat and said, *"Piace* what? What is there to like? All your hats look alike." Now Grandma took offense. "This hat has a black feather in the back. It makes it look pretty." This brought a response from Auntie Angie, "Ma, who's going to see the feather? All your hats look alike."

Grandma was really frustrated, she thought the hat was quite festive. When Auntie Angie criticized the hat, it was the last straw. "Angie, you should talk. All your dresses look like Kate Smith." "Give it to her Mama," Mom cried out. "I tell her that all the time." Auntie Angie was fit to be tied because Grandma never criticized her. "Ma, what are you saying? Now the two of them will never stop." "Angie, you have beautiful legs. Look at your sister Carmela, she wears her dresses up to her knees, not halfway down to her ankles, like you." Auntie Stella, who had disappeared into Grandma's bedroom, returned carrying two of Grandma's hats, one in each hand, both looked exactly like the one Grandma had on her head. "Ma, do you see? All your hats look alike." Now Grandma was completely burned up. "Stella, leave her alone. She just said that Angie dresses like Kate Smith. Don't get her more frustrated," cautioned Mom. Auntie Stella turned toward her sister Angie and shouted out, "I'm glad, even the old lady said you dress like Kate Smith." Auntie Angie had enough. She caught both Auntie Stella and Grandma in her gaze, in her most caustic tone said, "What do you two hillbillies know?" Auntie Stella, who prided herself on her wardrobe, was now furious. "You're calling us hillbillies? I buy all my clothes at Filene's. You go to that Kate Smith store at North Station." Grandma kept asking, *"Cos'e un hillbilly* (What is a hillbilly)?" She knew it was possibly unflattering, but didn't know what it meant. "Angie, are you calling your mother a name?" Auntie Angie calmed down. "No, Ma, I didn't mean anything."

Grandma took the hat off her head and placed it beside the other two hats on the table. She began studying them carefully, as she walked around the table. She then looked up at Auntie Angie and began laughing. "Stella is right. My hats do all look alike." This was an invitation for the sisters to each take a hat and put it on her head. They began parading around the living room, with Grandma laughing uncontrollably at their antics, setting off gales of laughter from the sisters. Taking the hats off, they placed them back on the table, where Grandma once again chose the black hat with the black feather to wear to the feast, fixing it to head with the long hat pin with the pearl at the end. It was now 5 o'clock in the afternoon, shortly, they would be on their way to the feast and their place of honor in the Shrine.

CHAPTER 55

The Walk to The Feast

"Stella, *fretta* (hurry)! It's not polite to be late!" Grandma shouted to Auntie Stella, as she made her way down the curved metal flight of stairs, leading to the street. Mom and Auntie Angie were already on the sidewalk waiting for them. "Why is everyone in a hurry?" Auntie Stella could be heard shouting from the apartment. Grandma was just about to call out again when she heard the door to her apartment close, signaling Auntie Stella was on her way. Finally, all four women were on the street, and began to make their way to the Shrine where they would take their seats among the honored guests for the evening.

Charlie, Bobby, Anthony and Pietro who were waiting in front of the church, joined them. They made their way down North Square, continuing on to the Shrine. "Where are cousins Theresa and Grace?" Pietro asked Auntie Angie. She quickly replied, "They wanted to go off to The H, but they will meet us later at the Shrine." Auntie Stella was fit to be tied. "Why do I have to be there, and Theresa and Grace don't?" She shouted out, revisiting her complaint. Grandma responded, "Stella, you have to be there because I want you to be there. The Society invited our family which means all my daughters must be there. They will ignore nieces and nephews, but they will feel insulted if the four of us are not present." "That's all. She's always concerned what others will think!" Auntie Stella shouted out. Her voice filled North Square, bouncing off the buildings that ringed the square. Auntie Stella's complaints continued as they approached the feast, increasingly muffled by the music.

In the distance, a brightly lit bandstand could be seen, garishly colored in red, blue, gold fabric and foil, and lit in every color of the rainbow. The floor of the bandstand was painted midnight blue with faded stars along its perimeter. Twelve-foot wooden poles painted red, standing on end, surrounded the bandstand. They were supported by wires attached to fire escapes, flanking the street. Garlands of lights were strung between the poles, arching over the street, forming a pathway for visitors to the feast. As Mom and the family passed under each set of lights, they assumed the color of the lights. They turned red, blue and green for a second, then they were back under natural light, only to turn colors again when they passed under the next set of lights.

On the bandstand, dressed in a shiny blue suit, an old guy was trying his best to sing "O Sole Mio" accompanied by a five-piece band that barely knew the music. They seemed to be all out of tune, but in some strange way, they managed to make their music sound like "O Sole Mio." It didn't make any difference, no one was listening, the main performers would be singing much later in the evening.

"Why do I have to be here?" Auntie Stella shouted out once again. "That old guy can't sing, and he looks like he's messing his pants, and the people in the band look half dead." "Ma, tell her to shut up," Auntie Angie cautioned. "We're getting close to the Shrine; the members will hear her." Grandma, squeezing Auntie Stella's hand, said emphatically, "*Stella, silenzio* (Stella, silence)!"

When we arrived, the Saint had already been taken from the Shrine and was being paraded through the streets. People were seated in the Shrine; ten seats were left empty, obviously reserved for our family. On the sidewalk, in front of the Shrine, raffle tickets were being sold by members of the Society and their wives for a trip to Italy. People were sitting on collapsible chairs fronting the Shrine. Grandma paused a minute before entering the Shrine. Ernesto Mucci greeted her with a kiss on both cheeks while extending a *"Buona festa"* to the rest of the family. Grandma returned, *"Buona festa"* to Ernesto which was followed by a chorus of *"Buona festa"* from the rest of the family.

Listening intently for Auntie Stella's voice and never hearing it,

Grandma cast a sour look in her direction, forcing out a *"Buona festa"*. Confident the family made its proper greetings, Grandma followed Ernesto, who had already made his way into the Shrine, and was standing at the ten chairs reserved for the family. Grandma stood at the first chair as we filed passed her, taking our seats on the folded chairs arranged in a row. Charlie, Bobby and Anthony went first, followed by Pietro. When Auntie Stella tried to take her seat as the next in line, Grandma grabbed her by the wrist and held her by her side, allowing Mom and Auntie Angie to pass in front of her. Grandma was taking no chances. She was keeping Auntie Stella right beside her, preventing her from making any further wisecracks during the evening. Grandma was determined not to insult her friends. It was now 6:30, and we were all in place in the Shrine with a long evening ahead of us.

CHAPTER 56

The Escape

It was now 7:00 in the evening, the heat of the day continued relentlessly. Auntie Stella stood up, and began pulling on her dress, first her back, then her sleeves, and finally, she opened the top two buttons of her dress, and began fanning her chest. Grandma grabbed her wrist and said, "Stella, stop! You're going to disgrace us." From the row just behind Grandma, Auntie Angie whispered, "Stella, what are you doing?" "I'm hot. Everything is stuck to me," Auntie Stella responded. Grandma pulled Auntie Stella back onto her seat.

The band began to play the tarantella. Mom, seeing an opportunity to calm Auntie Stella down and knowing how much she loved to dance, grabbed her by the arm and said, "Stella, let's dance." Auntie Stella was up on her feet. All thoughts of stuck clothes were out of her mind. She grabbed Mom by the arm, and together, the two sisters raced out of the Shrine to a clearing beneath the bandstand, where they joined a circle of women who were turning one way, and then the opposite, to the rhythm of the tarantella. Auntie Stella was like a different woman, dancing and laughing as the circle of women continued to grow. Grandma and Auntie Angie were enjoying the sight, clapping their hands to the rhythm of the music.

Pietro also began clapping his hands, as he delighted seeing his cousins dancing to the music, so familiar to his ears. Bobby, Charlie and Anthony, who had slipped out of the Shrine minutes earlier, were standing with the bystanders, urging Auntie Stella and Mom to dance faster. Round and round the women danced, shaking their skirts, then grabbing each other's hands to maintain the circle. Colors of red, blue and green glistened on their sweaty shoulders and faces as they danced under the garish lights. The feast was now in full swing, and dancing would continue throughout the night. "Bobby and Charlie, let's go down to the Italian lemonade stand!" Anthony yelled out, trying to make himself heard above the sounds of the crowd and music. "Dad gave us a quarter each to spend at the feast, just enough to buy three lemonades." From the swirl of the dance, Mom spotted her boys making their way from the bandstand and shouted out, "Where are you going?" Anthony shouted back, "We're going to buy Italian slush!" That seemed to satisfy Mom, she continued to dance with Auntie Stella, both having the time of their lives.

Turning to Pietro, Grandma asked, *"Pietro, ti stai divertendo* (Pietro, are you having a good time)?" *"Aunt Lucia, si, sono felice di essere qui con te e la famiglia* (Aunt Lucia, yes, I am happy to be here with you and the family)." "Where are the boys?" Grandma asked. "They slipped out ten minutes ago," Auntie Angie replied. "They thought I didn't notice them." Pietro then added, "I heard Anthony say, they wanted to buy Italian slush." "That sounds good," Grandma replied. "Why not get some for all of us?" She opened her black pocketbook, that looked exactly like all her other black pocketbooks, removed a dollar and some coins from a tiny purse buried deep in her bag, and handed the money to Pietro. "Aunt, I will be right back with slush for all of us," assured Pietro. "Don't forget to get one for yourself," responded Grandma.

Pietro left the Shrine and turned in the direction of the bandstand. His attention was drawn to the colorful lights overhead and the overstuffed cherubs, attached to the gold and blue crepe paper, that formed the backdrop of the bandstand. As he searched for a way through the crowd, his eyes suddenly fell upon Carla, standing just ten feet away from him. She was wearing a white floral dress. Her shoulders glistened with perspiration, reflecting the colorful lights from above, a low scoop neckline revealed generous breasts hidden just out of sight. Carla's auburn hair was held off her face with a white headband. Once again, the crowd seemed to disappear around them, falling away like shifting shadows, silence enveloping them, for a moment, all that existed were the two lovers. They remained motionless, until Carla became aware the band had begun to play the beautiful strands of "Stardust."

The music seemed to drift over and around them, creating a spell, drawing the two lovers closer and closer together, until they were in each other's arms, dancing slowly, ever so slowly, in the heat and under the colorful lights. The evening guest singer, Nancy Conley, began to sing. Her sultry voice adding to the moment. As they danced, passions began to rise as Pietro gently stroked Carla's hair. Carla, in turn began to run her fingers through Pietro's hair, their eyes never parting from each other. The crowd surrounding the lovers, becoming aware of the magic of the moment, parted around them, leaving Pietro and Carla to quietly drift in each other's arms, on the haunting waves of a melody that seemed to capture their love. *"Carla, ti amo"* (Carla, I love you), whispered Pietro, his eyes captured by Carla's. *"Anche io ti amo, Pietro"* (I love you also, Pietro), whispered Carla as her body continued to sway in his arms.

Grandma, suddenly becoming aware of the lovers, cried out, *"Angie, cosa stanno facendo* (Angie, what are they doing)? Pietro and Carla are dancing like lovers in front of everyone. I saw the Ricci brothers earlier. They are at the feast. There's going to be bloodshed." "Mama don't get excited," replied Auntie Angie. "They won't do anything in front of a crowd." "Where is the Little One?" Grandma anxiously cried out. "She got us into this, we should never have come to the feast." She's with Stella and the boys, getting slush," Auntie Angie replied. "That's all we need, Stella and her mouth. She will get us all killed." Grandma continued, "Look at the two of them, they are dancing like lovers. I can't believe this is happening before my eyes."

Mom, Auntie Stella, Bobby, Anthony and Charlie were returning to the Shrine, each with a cup of slush, they were thoroughly enjoying. Mom, noticing Pietro and Carla, turned toward Auntie Stella, and was about to call them to her attention, but Auntie had also become aware of them. "Carmela, look at what's going on. They are practically making love with the crowd all around them." "Stella, shut your mouth. If the Ricci brothers hear you or see what's going on, there's going to be trouble here," Mom responded anxiously. "Trouble my ass," replied Auntie

Stella. "Those two are a disgrace." "Stella, they are in love. We need to help them."

Mom then glanced up at Grandma, who was anxiously staring down at her, Pietro and Carla dancing between them. Mom did a double take as she tried to interpret Grandma's frantic gesturing. Grandma was moving her hands in the direction of Pietro and Carla, indicating that she do something about it.

As Pietro continued to dance with Carla, it was obvious, they were in love with each other. Their movements became slower and slower as they gazed deeply into each other's eyes. The area designated for dancing grew crowded, as feast goers, caught up in the magic of "Stardust", continued to make their way to the dance floor. Pietro and Carla, oblivious to everything going on around them, each being ignited and aroused by the touch and feel of the other.

Carla put her arms around Pietro's neck, slowly swaying to the music, as she gazed into his eyes. Pietro remained almost motionless, in response to Carla's slow seductive swaying. He then reached out to her, capturing her by the waist, drew her closer to him, and as their bodies touched, they began to sway as one, abandoning themselves to the moment. Slow movements that conjured up a depth of passion each had never known, finally declaring to everyone around them their love. Grandma watching from the Shrine, grew more and more agitated. She could see what was happening in front of her eyes and knew the neighbors could see it also, which meant, sooner or later the Riccis would be informed, and all hell would break loose.

The evening darkness quickly enveloped the lovers as they danced under the colorful lights of the feast, continuing to abandon all caution; Carla resting her head on Pietro's chest as he softly stroked her hair. This prompted Grandma to call out Mom's name, while anxiously gesturing for her to do something. Before Mom could make her move, she noticed two of the Ricci brothers beginning to wade through the crowd of dancing bodies. "Stella, the Riccis are here, and they spotted Pietro and Carla. There's going to be bloodshed." Grandma, aware of the approaching brothers, moved to the entrance of the Shrine. Pietro, becoming aware of the two Ricci brothers, separated from Carla, taking her by the hand, they began swiftly walking through the crowd of swaying bodies. "Pietro, what are you doing?" Carla cried out. "Carla, we got to get out of here, your brothers are on the way." While Pietro and Carla were making their way across the dance floor, Mom quickly swung into action, instructing Auntie Stella to intercept the Ricci brothers, slowing them down so the lovers could get away. Auntie Stella stood in the path of the advancing Riccis. Grasping at straws, she yelled out, "Boys, where is your father and the rest of your brothers?" Catching the Riccis by surprise, they stopped for an instant to respond, giving Carla and Pietro enough time to slip away. Mom gestured to Grandma, she would do something. Quickly, she chased after the lovers catching up with them, as they were about to cross Atlantic Avenue and onto the fish piers. "Carla, Pietro, stop! I've got to talk to you," cried out Mom. "Listen to me. Don't go any further. Carla, two of your brothers are coming in this direction. Stella has distracted them, slowing them down. Go down to The H and hide under the pier. I will come to you the moment I know it's safe and we can talk."

Taking their hands, she pressed them reassuringly and urged them to make their way to The H as quickly as possible. She then raced back to the Shrine, to inform Grandma and Auntie Angie of what she had done.

CHAPTER 57

Desire under The H

"Pietro come this way." Carla leading Pietro through a forest of pilings supporting the pier. Finally, when she felt they were sufficiently concealed, she stopped, turned to Pietro, threw her arms around him and began to cry. "Pietro, what are we going to do, what are we going to do? Our lives are not our own." Pietro put his arms around her waist, drew Carla to himself. The touch of their bodies once again ignited inner passions. "Carla, I love you. I've loved you from the first moment I saw you," Pietro confessed passionately. He kissed Carla first on her shoulders, then on her cheeks, and finally his lips met hers and in the silence of their long embrace, the two became as one.

Pietro backed Carla up to one of the pilings. Bracing herself against the piling, Carla raised her right leg, hooked it around Pietro's left leg, and breathlessly drew him against her body, releasing pent-up passions as they began to lose control. Gradually, they slipped down into the cool, soft sand beneath the pier. Shadows created by a full moon that hung directly overhead, danced across the couple's bodies, as they dropped to their knees beneath the pier. A tapestry of seaweed given up by past tides, surrounded the couple. Breathlessly, Pietro began undoing the buttons of Carla's dress, while Carla ran her fingers through his thick brown hair. Their bodies began to move instinctively as if responding to some ancient call, the call of the sea, the cradle of life. Carla then began undoing the buttons of Pietro's shirt, eagerly aided by him. Before the buttons were completely undone, Pietro pulled the rest of the shirt from his trousers and tore off whatever buttons remained fastened. Carla, her passions rising, slipped the shirt off Pietro and tossed it onto the wet sand, his lean, sweaty body glistening in the moonlight. Excitedly, the couple rose to their feet. Carla threw her arms around Pietro and began kissing his chest. Pietro in turn, slipped Carla's dress off her shoulders where it hung precariously, ready to drop to her waist. The lovers, once again, slumped down into the sand as their passions continued to rise.

"Pietro, Carla, where are you?" It was Mom searching for the couple amidst the pilings. Her voice seemed to lift the fog of passion that surrounded the couple, reluctantly bringing them to their senses. "We're over here, Cousin Carmela," Pietro cried out as he and Carla quickly dressed themselves, pulling themselves together as best they could. As Mom approached the lovers, they were now standing, but the hot look of passion was still on their faces and could not be concealed. Mom could easily read the signs. Hoping she arrived before things went too far, she anxiously asked, "What are you two doing? Carla, you know the danger if your brothers find you. If I can find you, so can they, and if they catch the two of you making love, God help us all." "Carmela," Carla said quietly, "What are we to do? We love each other, all we want is to be together."

Mom, growing increasingly anxious for their safety, knew they couldn't return to the feast or to their homes. She needed to send them to a place where they would be safe for at least a day or two, or at least until she spoke with Grandma and the Ricci father and brothers. Mom then spoke with a renewed confidence in herself. "Pietro, I want you to take Carla to Zia Elena's house in East Boston. I want you to stay there until you hear from me. Elena knows about you, remain there until we come up with a solution."

Pietro looked anxiously at Carla as if to say, "Are you willing to do this?" Reading his thoughts, Carla simply nodded her approval. Mom blew a kiss to both, then urged them to hurry, the last ferry of the evening was about to leave. "Thank you, thank you Cousin Carmela," Pietro said excitedly, grabbing Mom by the hand. Mom reached over, embraced him then Carla, and urged them to go. As Pietro turned in the direction of the ferry, Mom called his name. When Pietro turned back to her, Mom simply said, "Pietro, button your shirt correctly. You look half undressed." Pietro looked down at his half-buttoned shirt then back up at Mom, for a minute a smile shot across his face as he recalled, Mom was known to the family as the Foxy One, he realized Mom thoroughly understood what was going on under the pier.

CHAPTER 58
The Ferry Ride

The ferry was just ready to pull away from the pier, when Pietro and Carla showed up. Holding hands, they both made a slight leap onto the ferry. Looking into Pietro's eyes, uttering a sigh of relief, Carla softly said, "Now I feel safe." Pietro bent over and brushed his cheek against Carla's, taking her by the hand, they walked slowly to the round bow of the old ferry, and there they stood, as the ferry quietly made its way through the inky black waters of Boston Harbor to East Boston. In the distance, music from the feast could be heard, fading into the night as the lovers made their way to East Boston and the safety of Elena's house. Silently, the couple stood with their arms around each other, staring into the night. Not a word was spoken between them, they had each other.

CHAPTER 59

Back at the Feast

B y the time Mom made it back to the feast, Grandma was standing outside the Shrine anxiously looking for any sign of Carla and Pietro. "Carmela, you've returned. Where are they?" Grandma asked anxiously. "Ma, I sent them to Zia Elena's house where they will be safe. No one will ever think of looking for them there." "Carmela, I don't think that was a good idea. You know your aunt; her house is *una casa pazza* (a crazy house). She will never keep them apart." "Ma, they are not going to be there long. Don't worry about it," Mom, trying to reassure Grandma she made a good decision. Grandma would have no part of it. "I know my sister, she will let Carla and Pietro do what they want, and it doesn't take too long for a match to set the hay on fire."

Auntie Stella, who was listening to the entire conversation, decided to throw some kerosene onto the fire. "That's it," she said jokingly. "You sent them to that crazy house. Before they leave, Carla will be knocked up." "Stella, keep your mouth shut! Don't worry Mama. Pietro is a gentleman, and he won't touch Carla." Auntie Stella, knowing she hit a nerve, continued to pour it on. "They are all gentlemen until they have their chance, then they turn into beasts," she said tartly. "Stella, why do you want to worry Mama? Keep your mouth shut!" Mom scolded.

Auntie Angie, who had been quietly listening to the entire conversation, decided to speak. "Carmela, you did the right thing. Carla and Pietro will be safe at Elena's, and nothing is going to happen between them. Stella, I don't know what's wrong with you. You're always trying to stir up the situation, you're frightening Mama, so shut your mouth." Grandma, turning to Auntie Angie, implored, "Angie, you believe they will be OK?" "Yes, Mama, they'll be fine at Elena's. We need to find someone to speak to the Riccis about Carla and Pietro. Someone they will listen to." Grandma's face then lit up. "We will speak with Padre Francesco. He is our priest, our pastor and Pietro's spiritual advisor. He is the one man everyone will listen to." "That's a wonderful idea," Auntie Angie affirmed. From the look on Mom's and Auntie Stella's faces, they also agreed. With that, they returned to the Shrine of the Saint and took their seats, determined to carry on despite all that took place. Grandma and Auntie Angie in the front row with Mom and Auntie Stella just behind.

"Carmela, go and get us some Italian Ice. It's time to enjoy ourselves. *Dobbiamo fare una buona impressione* (We must make a good impression)," Grandma said with a look of relief on her face, for she was convinced Father Francesco would come up with a solution to the problem.

CHAPTER 60

Hiding out at Zia Elena's

I t was 10:30 in the evening when Pietro and Carla arrived at Elena's house. They arrived to find the front door wide open, the sound of music and singing coming from the backyard. Carla and Pietro passed through the house and into the backyard where they were greeted by a surprised Zia Elena. "Pietro, you came to our party and you brought *questa bella signorina con te* (this beautiful girl with you)." "Aunt Elena, *la signorina* is Carla Ricci," Pietro explained. "Bravo, bravo, she's very pretty, Pietro. The two of you make a beautiful couple," Elena said with a twinkle in her eye. Pietro began to blush as he bent over to give Elena a kiss on the cheek. Elena responded by opening her arms, grabbing both Carla and Pietro by the waists, and shaking them back and forth. Elena's exuberance was contagious, causing Carla to laugh. Turning to Pietro, she said, "I love your aunt. She's full of life."

Elena broke away for only a second, returning with two plates of spaghetti piled high. Handing one to Pietro, the spaghetti sauce splashed onto his shirt. "Now I know I am at your house, Zia Elena" Pietro said laughingly. "I'm already splashed with food." Carla took the plate from Elena carefully, not wanting to be Elena's next victim. Once she had the plate of spaghetti firmly in her hand, she looked back at Pietro and burst into laughter, for now even his trousers were splashed with tomato sauce. Pietro looked down at his trousers then at Carla, shrugged his shoulders as if to say, welcome to Zia Elena's, and began laughing. Elena grabbed both by their hands and pulled them deeper into the garden where her children and grandchildren were celebrating a birthday party. When Carla shouted out, "Elena, whose birthday is it?" Elena uncertain, simply responded, "I don't know, but sit down, have a glass of wine and enjoy yourselves."

Pietro and Carla sat under an arbor, heavily laden with grapes, Elena would be turning into wine in just a few weeks, for now, they served as wonderful decorations for a birthday party. Elena pulled up a chair, sat beside the couple, and curiously asked, "Why did you come at such a late hour? *C'e' qualcosa di sbagliato in mia sorella, Lucia* (Is something wrong with my sister, Lucia)?" Looking at Carla, Pietro responded cautiously, "No, Zia Elena. Cousin Carmela suggested we come to stay with you for a while. Is it possible for us to be here for a few days?" Without a moment's hesitation, Elena responded, *"Certo, che puoi restare qui* (Of course, you can stay here). I know of your troubles." Then, mischievously she continued, "But you must stay in separate rooms." The last remark caused Carla to blush as Pietro responded wholeheartedly, "Of course Zia Elena, we will stay in separate rooms." "Pietro, you will sleep with Giovanni, my oldest son. Carla, you will be with Suzie and Josie, my youngest daughters." Pietro breathed a sigh of relief, knowing Elena would be putting them up for a few days, but was there ever a doubt? The word "no", was simply not in her vocabulary. Elena never asked Pietro why it was necessary for the couple to be at her house. It was enough that Mom sent them to her, and she trusted Mom's judgment.

CHAPTER 61
Later that Evening

It was at 2 o'clock in the morning, Pietro, unable to sleep because of Giovanni's heavy snoring, left his room, went downstairs to the kitchen where he found Carla standing at the back door that led into the garden. She was still dressed in street clothes, her shapely silhouette merging with the shadows from the garden. "Carla, couldn't you sleep?" Pietro whispered. "No, Pietro. I was too caught up in my thoughts, I came downstairs to get a breath of air. But why are you up?" "I also couldn't sleep. Cousin Giovanni snores very loudly, and I was thinking of you. Pietro gestured to the garden, gently took Carla by the hand, and led her to the table under the arbor where they sat earlier in the evening. Before siting, Carla backed up against the arbor, turned toward Pietro, her eyes glistening in the moonlight. "Pietro, I love you," she said in a whisper. "I love you Carla," Pietro repeated. Gently taking Carla by the shoulders, he drew her to himself, softly he touched his lips to hers and they kissed.

Pulling away from her, he took a seat under the arbor and gently pulled Carla to his side. Taking a seat beside him, she placed her head on his shoulder, there they sat until dawn.

CHAPTER 62
The Threat

Monday morning broke hot and steamy. The North End, after a major feast, was always littered with confetti and strips of paper tossed from tenement windows and off roofs. Shopkeepers and street cleaners were busy sweeping up the debris from the day before. The sound of hammering could be heard in the distance, as members of the Saint Andrew Society were busy dismantling the bandstand and other remnants of the feast. In several days, the Saint Francis Feast would take place, followed by the Feast of Saint Theresa.

"Carmela," Grandma said anxiously. It's time to see Padre Francesco. Only he can speak to the Riccis and bring them to their senses. They will listen to him. If they should find Pietro before he can speak with them, *Dio non voglia* (God forbid). Carla is with him, you know how protective they are of her. Carmela, go to Padre Francesco immediately, and make an appointment for all of us to meet with him. Once he gives us a time, go to your Aunt's in East Boston and bring Pietro and Carla back."

Suddenly, the door swung open and Auntie Angie walked in. "Ma, have you heard from Pietro and Carla?" "No, Angie, I haven't heard a word, but if they left Elena's house, she would have let me know." "Yah, they're at Zia Elena's house," Auntie Stella offered, walking in from her bedroom. "That means anything can happen." Mom, ignoring Auntie Stella's remark, said, "Mama has a good idea. I'm going to the rectory to see Father Francesco and make an appointment for all of us to meet with him. Once he gives me the hour, I will go to East Boston and bring Carla and Pietro back, as Mama wants."

Mom was just about ready to leave for Father Francesco's office, when there was a loud knock on the door. Grandma, startled by the sharpness of the knock, turned to Auntie Angie with a deep look of concern in her eyes. Mom walked over to Grandma, looking for direction, then came a second knock on the door, followed by the angry sound of a man's voice, "Lucia, this is Egidio Ricci. I need to speak with you." When Egidio knocked for a third time, Grandma motioned to Auntie Angie to let him in, cautioning her to be calm. While Auntie Angie slowly made her way to the door, Grandma positioned herself at the kitchen table, motioning to Auntie Stella and Mom to sit on either side of her. *"Buongiorno,* Egidio," Auntie Angie said quietly and calmly as if she was greeting an old expected friend. "Where's Lucia? I need to speak with Lucia," Egidio demanded. Auntie opened the door wider, cautiously welcoming Egidio into the house. She then noticed, his oldest son Frank was standing off to the side. Together, the two men entered Grandma's kitchen. Before they made it half way across the kitchen floor, Grandma stopped them in their tracks by standing and greeting each by name. *"Buongiorno* Egidio, *Buongiorno* Francesco." "Where's my daughter?" Egidio fired out angrily. "I know she's with your nephew Pietro."

Grandma motioned to the two men to sit at the kitchen table. When they refused, she ordered them to sit, sternly reminding them, they were in her house. Grandma then sat, and the two men sat facing her. "Egidio, Carla is safe. You know she is in love with Pietro and Pietro loves her." "Carla is my daughter and she will do what I want her to do!" Egidio responded, pounding his fist on the table. Egidio's temper and fiery words seemed to steal Grandma's resolve. Firmly, she responded, "My nephew is a good man and he loves your daughter. I'm sending Carmela to speak with Padre Francesco. It's time that we all meet and discuss this matter." "I won't speak with that priest. She's my daughter, I demand you tell me where she is!" Egidio snapped.

Frank, who was sitting beside his father, was becoming increasingly agitated. Auntie Stella kept an eye on him, as she drew closer to Grandma, a gesture of protection. "This will come to no good," Grandma scolded.

"We will meet with Padre Francesco. Carmela will set the appointment, and I will make certain Carla and Pietro are there." Egidio, seeing he was getting nowhere with Grandma, stood up and motioned for Frank to stand beside him. "Lucia, you will have your way in this. I will wait for Carmela's call. In the meantime, Pietro better keep his distance from my daughter."

Frank, who had not said a word since he entered Grandma's flat, leaned over the table and sternly said, "He better not harm my sister. I warn you now Lucia, he better not harm her." Grandma stood facing him, never blinking an eye. The two men turned, quickly made their way across the kitchen, slamming the door behind them. The four women grew closer together, in response to the Riccis' threats. Grandma, turning to Mom, said in a voice just above a whisper," Carmela, go now and make the appointment with Padre Francesco. He must meet with us as soon as possible.

CHAPTER 63

Father Francesco Speaks

Mom quickly made her way down the stairs and across North Square to the church rectory. After ringing the bell two or three times, Brother Nino opened the door and greeted Mom with a *"Buongiorno,* Carmela." *"Buongiorno,"* Mom responded anxiously. "Is Father Francesco here?" "Yes, Carmela. Is he expecting you?" responded Brother Nino. "No, he is not expecting me, but I must speak with him for just a minute." "Only for a minute," responded Brother Nino sternly. "Father Francesco is a very busy man."

Without saying another word, he motioned to Mom to follow him, and took her into a small, wood paneled room adjacent to Father Francesco's office. Brother Nino led Mom to an arm chair in the waiting room, where she took a seat. He exited the room without saying a word, leaving Mom anxiously awaiting Father Francesco's arrival. Five minutes later, the rustling sound of Father Francesco's robe could be heard just outside the tiny room. Mom looked up nervously, as Father Francesco entered the waiting room. He greeted Mom and took his seat just opposite her. *"Buongiorno,* Carmela. You are anxious to see me. Is it about Pietro and Carla?" Mom, somewhat startled by Father Francesco's insight, responded nervously. "Yes, Father Francesco. I'm here representing my family. It's important that you meet with Pietro and Carla, my family and the Ricci family." There is so much trouble between us, and we are afraid that someone is going to get hurt. Pietro and Carla are staying at my Aunt Elena's house in East Boston. The

Riccis don't know this. If they find out, they will certainly go to East Boston, and who knows what can happen. Pietro is just a boy; he is no match for the Riccis. It's important that you see us immediately; this is a very dangerous situation."

Father Francesco, grasping the gravity of the situation, reached over, took Mom's hand, clasped it between his hands and said, "I will meet with all of you, tomorrow morning at 11 o'clock. I have to say a Mass at 12 noon, but I will ask Father Ralph to take my place, so I can give this serious matter my full attention without interruption. Carmela, go to the Riccis and inform them of this meeting." Mom, somewhat concerned, looked straight into Father Francesco's eyes, "Father Francesco, they are extremely angry, and they frighten me." "Then go with Brother Nino and your husband Joseph." Mom responded, "Thank you Father Francesco, it's a wonderful idea. I will do as you direct."

Father Francesco then rose to his feet. "Carmela, return in an hour with Joseph, and I will have Brother Nino waiting for you. Now, go and tell Lucia and your sisters what we discussed. Get a message to your Aunt Elena, asking her to keep Pietro and Carla out of sight." "I understand Father Francesco. Angie has a telephone, and I will call Elena." "Your aunt has a telephone?" Father Francesco questioned. "Yes, Father. It was given to her by some politician, she helped in his campaign." "Call her as soon as possible. I will see all of you in my office tomorrow at 11 a.m." Mom stood up, kissed the ring on Father Francesco's hand, as a sign of respect, and quickly left the rectory.

CHAPTER 64

The Arrangement

M om rushed across the square to Grandma's flat where Grandma, Auntie Angie and Auntie Stella were anxiously awaiting her return. She informed them of Father Francesco's plan, and the fact, he was willing to meet with all parties the next day. Grandma was elated, but when Mom indicated she had to go to the Riccis to inform them of the meeting, Grandma became concerned, even though Mom said she would be accompanied by Brother Nino and Dad. "Carmela, *i Riccis sono molto difficile* (the Riccis are very difficult). You don't know what they might do once you give them this news." Mom, picking up a stain of fear in Grandma's voice, trying to sooth her, responded, "Ma, remember, I will be with Brother Nino and Joe. They will never do anything, especially when one is a religious."

Grandma calmed down, still noticeably concerned. Auntie Stella then spoke up, "I'll go with Carmela and the men. If the old man acts up, I'll kick him in the balls!" Auntie Stella warned. Sternly, Grandma responded, "Stella, go with them but no violence."

Mom then filled Grandma in with the rest of the plan. "Ma, you must go to Angie's house and call Aunt Elena. Father Francesco wants you to do this. Tell her to inform Pietro and Carla that they must be here tomorrow for the 11 o'clock meeting at the rectory and be certain they remain out of sight. Mom then rushed home to speak to Dad. It was noon, Dad was having lunch, part of his daily routine before leaving for work at 3 o'clock. Mom burst into the house just as Dad was beginning to eat.

"Joe, put the fork down. You have to come with me to the church rectory where we will be meeting with Brother Nino." Dad loved to eat, nothing disturbed him more than interrupting a meal. "Carmela, what's going on? You see I'm getting ready to eat." This aggravated Mom. "Joe, put down the fork and come with me now. It's a matter of life and death." Dad could see Mom was very agitated, almost fearful.

Without saying another word, he put down his fork, went to the sink, washed his hands, then put on his shirt. Dad always had lunch in his tee shirt. Mom and Dad rushed to the church where the bent figure of old, Brother Nino was waiting outside the rectory.

"Carmela, Giuseppe, you know what Father Francesco wants us to do. We'll go now to the Riccis' house and inform them of tomorrow's meeting." Mom had failed to tell dad this part of the plan. Being caught off guard, he stopped, took Mom by the hand and asked, "Where are we going?" "We're going to the Riccis' flat, to inform them of a meeting Father Francesco has arranged between the Riccis and our family along with Pietro and Carla. On our way, we will pick up Stella, who will join us." "Carmela, the Riccis are difficult. That old man is tough. You know the stories told about him," Dad warned alarmingly. "Joe, we will all be there together, they won't do a thing."

Dad then cautioned, "Let's call him down to the street, and not go to his flat, it will be safer." Mom and Brother Nino agreed, and together they left to pick up Auntie Stella, and make the short walk diagonally across the street to the Riccis' building. Rather than entering the building, Mom called Egidio from the street. After two to three calls, Egidio popped his head out of the second-floor window. "Carmela, what do you want?" Seeing Mom accompanied by Brother Nino, Dad and Auntie Stella, he spoke in measured terms, before Mom could respond, he once again asked impatiently, "Carmela, what do you want?" Mom responded, "Egidio come down and speak with us. I have a message from Father Francesco you will want to hear." "Carmela, you can say it to me without my coming down the stairs," Egidio responded sharply. "No, Egidio," Mom countered. "Come down, you will understand once you hear what I have to say."

Egidio pulled back from the window, shutting it with a thud. In a minute, he could be heard coming down the wooden stairs, and finally a short flight of stairs leading to the street. "I see you are accompanied by friends. Are you afraid of me?" Egidio asked sarcastically. "No, Egidio, I'm not afraid of you, but I know you're a man with a hot temper, I believe my friends, as you call them, will help keep you calm." "Okay Carmela, I'm calm. What is it?" Nervously, Mom informed Egidio of Father Francesco's plan, to meet with the Riccis, our family, Pietro and Carla at the rectory, the next day at 11 o'clock. "Carmela, I'm not going to attend such a meeting. I want my daughter back, and I won't stand for this any longer." "Egidio," Mom responded, "for the love of God, and the sake of your daughter, do what Father Francesco asks. Bring your sons with you. He is a wise man, and he is a man of peace. By meeting with him, for the sake of Carla and Pietro, we will find a solution." "Carmela, the solution is Carla returns to my house, and leave that son-of-a-bitch cousin of yours." "Watch your tongue," Dad cautioned in a stern voice. "There is no need to talk that way. Have respect for my wife, Stella and Brother Nino."

Egidio turned to Dad with fire in his eyes. He was spoiling for a fight, but Dad simply kept staring at him and held his ground; Egidio backed off. "Your family thinks they are the pillars of the church. You think Father Francesco will solve this problem? Well you're wrong. When Carla returns to my house, then you will see what Egidio Ricci will do. Dad was about to respond, but Mom, to diffuse the situation, stepped forward and shot back, "That's all you Riccis do, bully and fight. If you love your daughter, you won't go any further, and you will come to the rectory tomorrow." "Who are you to tell me what to do?" Egidio snapped. "If harm comes to my daughter in any way, I will hold you all responsible, and I'll get even with you, starting with your cousin Pietro." "I'll be there tomorrow with my sons, and Carla better be there with that holy cousin of yours," Egidio said sarcastically.

He turned and headed back to his building, but before mounting the stairs, he turned, pointed at Mom, in his most threatening voice warned, "Remember my words, if anything happens to my daughter, I will get even with you." Auntie Stella, who had been uncharacteristically quiet, could no longer contain herself. "That's all you Riccis are good for. You like to threaten people. You are all a bunch of *cafoni*." Her calling Egidio a *cafone* didn't bother him, instead, he seemed to pride himself in being a boor. He shouted back, "This *cafone* will have the last word." With that, he mounted the stairs, a few seconds later, slammed the door shut to his flat, in a final act of defiance.

Mom and Auntie Stella quickly ran back to Grandma's, to report what had just transpired. Once Grandma knew the Riccis would be at the meeting planned by Father Francesco, she asked Auntie Angie to call Elena and inform Pietro and Carla of the meeting planned for the next day. Auntie did as Grandma asked, and Elena passed on the information to Pietro who then informed Carla. Carla, knowing her father's temper and that of her brothers, was immediately seized with fear and apprehension at the thought of Pietro meeting with her family. "Pietro, I beg you, don't take part in the meeting tomorrow. It's no use, let me return to my father's house." "No, Carla." Pietro, taking Carla by the hand, his touch seemed to calm her. "Carla, what choice do we have? Yes, you could return to your family and we could go our separate ways, but we love each other. We could run away together, but we would always live in fear of your family finding us. We can't stay at Aunt Elena's any longer, for sooner or later, we will be found out. Our only choice is to do what Father Francesco asks, to meet with your family and mine, and place our destiny in the Hands of God."

"Pietro, I understand what you're saying. I believe God will help us, but I also know my father's temper and my brothers' anger, and what they are capable of doing. You were brought up in a different world. You never experienced such things; therefore, I believe you could be going into this like a lamb to slaughter."

Carla at this point was crying, caught up in the emotions of her words. Pietro drew closer to Carla and began stroking her hair. He gently kissed her on her lips and in a whisper quietly said, "Carla, I am a man not a boy, and I am not afraid to do this. I will place my trust in God and in the wisdom of Father Francesco, I ask you to do so as well. My family would never put us in danger."

Carla began to smile. Looking straight into Pietro's eyes, she whispered in return, "Pietro, I love you and I don't want to see you hurt. I will go with you tomorrow, but tonight, I will pray to Saint

Theresa, who I always turn to, and ask her to guide us tomorrow." Pietro, drawing Carla closer to himself, quietly whispered, "Tonight, we will pray to Saint Theresa together, and together we will place our trust in the Holy Saint." Carla then returned to the chores that Elena had given her, and Pietro went into the garden, where he was busy repairing the grape arbor. Aunt Elena remained at a distance, picking tomatoes while watching the couple, knowing they were in love and trying not to disturb them. As for Pietro and Carla, they would meet that evening in the garden under the arbor. As promised, they would pray to Saint Theresa for guidance and protection.

CHAPTER 65
Pre-Meeting

Mom was up bright and early Tuesday morning. She couldn't sleep, thoughts of the meeting with Father Francesco kept her up, as dawn broke, she was feeling quite anxious. What will the Riccis do when Carla appears with Pietro in Father Francesco's office? What could Father Francesco possibly say to make peace, in a situation seemingly impossible to solve? Finally, how will Grandma react, knowing the entire North End is aware of the love affair between Carla and Pietro, and the family in Italy was counting on Grandma to make things right?

Mom quickly made breakfast, got the flat in order, told us not to wake up Dad, and just after 9 o'clock, she was on her way to Grandma's. "Carmela, you're early. We are not meeting with Padre Francesco until 11 o'clock." "I couldn't sleep Ma," Mom responded. "I'm very worried about Pietro and Carla, especially Pietro. Who knows how the Riccis will act when they see them together?" "Carmela, you are here early," Auntie Stella observed, as she exited her bedroom. "Stella, I know, I couldn't sleep." "You can't sleep. What's wrong with you? Are you afraid of the Riccis?" Auntie Stella said tartly. "Stella, you know they have a bad reputation, we don't know how that old man will react when he sees Carla with Pietro, and if the brothers lay their hands on him, who will stop them?"

Grandma then spoke up, "Carmela, *tutto andra' bene* (everything will be fine), they will do nothing in front of Padre Francesco. Let's sit, have a cup of coffee and wait for Angie. She will be here before 10 o'clock." Grandma took out her espresso pot, ground up an extra measure of coffee beans, feeling they needed to be as alert as possible for the meeting, filled the pot with water and set it on the stove to brew. From a string of taralli hung on a hook by the kitchen window, she removed four, anticipating the arrival of Auntie Angie. "Oh, there she goes, she's taking down those taralli. They are as hard as rocks. One day I'm going to break a tooth on them." "Stella, you always have something to say. You know you're supposed to dunk the taralli in coffee to soften them," Grandma responded nervously. "They have no taste. Why can't we have English muffins?" Auntie Stella replied. Grandma tossed a taralli in front of Auntie Stella. It hit the table with a clunk. She then responded, "Perche'siamo italiani non inglesi (Because we're Italian and not English)." "Stella, eat the taralli and be quiet. You know Mama makes them just for us." "Carmela, why should I eat this taralli? It's as hard as a rock." "Stella, eat the taralli. You are making Mama nervous. Angie will be here in a few minutes, then we can talk."

Auntie Stella, crossing one leg over the other, began nervously swinging it back and forth, as the three sat quietly awaiting the arrival of Auntie Angie. Fifteen minutes passed when clank, clank sounds could be heard, signaling Auntie Angie was climbing the worn iron steps leading to Grandma's flat. "You're all here," she exclaimed, as she walked through the door. "Angie sit down." Grandma, beckoned with a wave of her hand, to join them at the small table in the alcove, created by the bow front window, overlooking North Square. "We're having taralli and espresso."

"She always serves those rocks. Why can't we have English muffins?" Auntie Stella complained. Auntie Angie came back with the standard reply: "Stella, you're supposed to dunk them. You say that all the time. Why make Mama nervous?" Mom had enough. "Forget the taralli and coffee. We're here to talk about Pietro and Carla, Father Francesco, and the Riccis." Auntie Stella, having to get in the last word, sent out one more wise crack, "Go ahead, eat those rocks and you can forget about the toilet for a week." With that, Grandma shouted out, "Stella, forget the taralli, we got to talk about the meeting." A momentary silence fell over the table. Grandma then nodded to Auntie Angie, signaling it was her time to speak, she being the oldest daughter. "Ma, I think we should listen to what Father Francesco has to say. He's a wise and learned man and knows Pietro has to enter the seminary this September."

Before Auntie Angie could say another word, Mom spoke up, "Angie, the Riccis are going to be there, and who knows what they will do when they see Pietro and Carla together. They have been together for two days. You know what they'll be thinking. Who knows what the brothers and that old man will do?" Grandma then implored the Madonna. Raising her hands in the air, she quickly offered a prayer, "Mother of God, please help us." She then turned to Auntie Angie and asked, "Angie, what are we going to do if they become violent?" "Ma, we will be in the rectory with Father Francesco. They won't do anything. We know Pietro has been a gentleman, Carla will be fine.

It was 10:15 and the four women had 45 minutes to prepare themselves and Father Francesco for the meeting about to take place. Auntie Stella walked to the bedroom and brought out a little black straw hat for Grandma to wear to the meeting. "Ma, I brought you your hat, the one that you always wear to church." "Stella, we're not going to the church, we're going to the rectory. Bring me the hat that is on my bureau." Auntie Stella went back to Grandma's room, in a minute emerged with another black straw hat, almost identical to the first. "Ma, why do you make me do this extra work? The two hats look alike." "No, Stella, one hat has a black veil for church, the other hat has no veil for visiting." Auntie Stella was "fit to be tied." Handing the hat without the veil to Grandma, she responded, "What difference does it make? The hats are the same."

Without saying a word, Grandma placed the hat on her head and fastened it with a large hat pin, the one with the pearl at the end, while never taking her eyes off Auntie Stella. "Now, Stella, I'm ready to see Padre Francesco." Never one to let an opportunity go by, she decided to turn the knife a little. "Stella, put a few taralli in a bag, we will take them to Padre Francesco. He likes my rocks." Auntie Stella gave Grandma one of her twisted little smiles, knowing Grandma had the last word. Placing three taralli in a bag, she handed the bag to Grandma and responded, "You carry the rocks." With that, the four women left for their meeting with Father Francesco.

CHAPTER 66

The Meeting

"*B*uongiorno, Lucia." "*Buongiorno*, Brother Nino," Grandma replied. "*Buongiorno*, Angelina, Stella and Carmela." Brother Nino speaking with a thick accent. "Padre Francesco is waiting for you, follow me." Brother Nino ushered the four women into a large paneled library, where Father Francesco was waiting for them. "Lucia, you and your daughters take a seat on the couch where we can talk." Father Francesco sat on a large comfortable armchair facing them. The women took their seats, casting anxious looks at Father Francesco and one another. They sat for a moment in silence, before they could speak, there came a voice from just behind them, in the far corner of the room. "Good morning aunt, good morning cousins." It was Pietro, he had arrived earlier with Carla. Both had an air about them, one that suggested they were on vacation, but they were betrayed by the look of anxiety on both their faces. Grandma, immediately rushed over to the couple, embracing first Pietro, then Carla.

"It's so good to see both of you. I'm happy you're here. Come sit with your cousins and Padre Francesco so we can talk." Without saying a word, the couple walked over to the three sisters. They exchanged kisses, cheek to cheek, but the sense of joy that usually accompanies such unexpected encounters was absent, replaced by feelings of anxiety coupled with a sense of foreboding. "Aren't you a beautiful family," Father Francesco began.

"Carla, Pietro, I assume my sister made you comfortable while you

224

were at her home?" Grandma asked. "Yes, Aunt Elena made us very comfortable," Pietro replied. "Carla was your stay with Elena pleasant?" "Yes, Lucia. Your sister is very kind." "Yes, she is kind," Grandma replied. "You must have noticed her house is not well kept." Carla smiled. "She has a charming house, and she's a wonderful woman."

Mom, happy to see Pietro, took him by the hand. "Pietro, I'm so happy to see you. Angie, Stella, aren't we happy to see Pietro?" They responded in unison, they were happy to see him. Once again, a silence fell over the room, broken by Father Francesco when he announced, "We should await the arrival of the Riccis before we begin our discussion." Father Francesco's simple statement set in motion an explosion of glances from sister to sister, mother to daughters and finally, Carla to Pietro, ricocheting back to the cousins and Grandma.

"Please help yourself to coffee," Father Francesco offered, gesturing to the espresso pot placed on the coffee table between them. Grandma placed the bag of taralli, clutched in her hands till now, on the table beside the coffee pot. "Padre Francesco, I brought you some taralli," she said while grinning in the direction of Auntie Stella, knowing Auntie Stella wouldn't say a word in the presence of Father Francesco. Realizing Grandma was still retaliating for her earlier remarks, Auntie began to roll her eyes, muttered some little song under breath, and cast a glance at the ceiling.

Grandma seizing her advantage, which were few and far between with Auntie Stella, opened the bag and placed the taralli on a plate on the far end of the coffee table. After arranging the taralli neatly, she picked one up and handed it to Auntie Stella. "Mangia Stella. They go well with espresso." Auntie Stella crossed her legs and began rocking her leg back and forth. She was obviously mad. All this drama taking place under the nose of Father Francesco, who was totally unaware of what was going on, but obvious to Mom and Auntie Angie, who exchanged quick glances of amusement at one another, knowing Grandma had gotten the best of Auntie Stella. In a sign of defiance, Auntie Stella took the taralli and began tapping it on the table, causing the china to rattle. "Stella, stop! Dunk the taralli in the espresso and enjoy it." Mom couldn't contain herself any longer and began to snicker, knowing an old battle was raging on in front of Father Francesco. That set off snickering from

Auntie Angie, while Father Francesco looked in bewilderment, not fully understanding the little drama that was taking place before his eyes.

Father Francesco picked up a taralli, broke off a piece and was about to dunk it into his espresso, when a loud knock was heard at the front door. Immediately, a sense of foreboding filled the room. Carla and Pietro exchanged glances and turned to Father Francesco almost as if pleading for help. Father Francesco, reaching over, clasped both Pietro and Carla's hands in his hands, giving them a look of reassurance. Grandma in turn, looked anxiously at her daughters. Immediately, they came together as one, sensing danger might be at the door. "Go to the door, Brother Nino," Father Francesco requested. "I believe the Riccis have arrived." Brother Nino, who was seated at the far corner of the room away from the group, responded by slowly exiting the room, making his way to the entry hall.

CHAPTER 67

Enter the Riccis

"*Buongiorno, Signor* Ricci, *Buongiorno*, Francesco and Lorenzo." Brother Nino said in measured tones, greeting the Riccis at the door. Egidio decided to come with only his two eldest sons. "Where's my daughter?" Egidio demanded, his eyes fixed directly on Brother Nino. "Follow me, Signor Ricci, I will take you to her now." He followed directly behind Brother Nino, Frank and Lorenzo trailing behind their father. Brother Nino led them into the library. "You are all here!" Egidio barked out. "Carla, you decided to show your face to your Papa." "I have nothing to hide," Carla quickly responded. "I love Pietro, and he loves me; we have a right to our own lives." "Enough of this," Father Francesco interrupted. "Egidio, Lorenzo, Frank, sit down on the couch facing Carla and Pietro." The trio took their seats on the couch as Father Francesco requested.

"Good morning Egidio and your handsome sons," Grandma said softly. "Lucia, I don't want to hear from you!" Shouted Egidio. "You and your daughters are at the bottom of this. Before your nephew Pietro arrived, my Carla was a happy woman, devoted to her family and the church." "I was a dead woman!" Carla interjected angrily. "I never knew what love was, until I met Pietro." "Are you saying, I don't love you?" Egidio responded to his daughter's outburst. Before Carla could say another word, Father Francesco interrupted once again. "We are here to talk and come to a solution to this problem, not to argue." "There is no need to talk. The solution is, Carla is coming home with me and her brothers!" Egidio responding angrily. Auntie Stella, who had been quiet up to this point, had enough. Seeing Egidio had spoken harshly to Grandma, she stood up, pointed in the direction of the Ricci family and angrily said, "That's all your family is good for, threatening people. You are a bunch of *cafoni*", bringing the three Riccis to their feet. "We don't have to take this!" Shouted Frank. "Stella, be quiet," Auntie Angie spoke up. Mom was just about to back up Auntie Angie when Father Francesco barked, "Everyone take your seats. Enough is enough! We're here to talk, not argue."

An uneasy calm fell over the room, everyone took their seats, waiting for Father Francesco to speak. Pietro, who had said nothing up to this point, was about to put his arms around Carla to comfort her, but thought better of it, and the couple sat awkwardly side by side, waiting to hear what Father Francesco had to say. Once the room achieved the proper level of silence Father Francesco was seeking, he began to speak softly in measured tones. "This situation has gone far enough. The feelings that are being expressed in this room are not Christian, this situation must be resolved." Everyone remained silent. Every word spoken by Father Francesco seemed to carry enormous weight. "You've come to me for direction in this matter, and I have given it much thought. I believe Pietro should return to Italy and go through with his plan of entering the seminary this September. Carla should return home to her family."

Before Father Francesco could say another word, Carla blurted out, "You are sending me back to prison!" "My home is a prison to you!" Egidio shouted angrily. "Yes, Papa. Now that I know Pietro's love, anyplace without him would be a prison." Pietro was about to embrace Carla who was now crying, but Father Francesco once again began speaking. He called Pietro by name, interrupting the embrace that surely would have meant trouble. "Pietro, you must listen to me. Allow me to complete my thoughts. Enter the seminary, as I suggested, and complete your first year of studies. Carla, return to your father's house and the life lived before you met Pietro." "Impossible Father," Carla interjected. "It's impossible to return to my life, a life without Pietro." "Enough of this," Egidio demanded. "You will listen to Father Francesco and come home with us." "One moment, Egidio. You didn't let me finish my thoughts," insisted Father Francesco. "Carla should return to your home for one year and the life she lived before Pietro. Pietro should spend one year in the seminary. Both should regard this as a time of trial, a time when their love will be tested. If, at the end of the year, their love remains strong, they should be allowed to marry." Father Francesco's last words struck a nerve; Egidio stood bolt straight. "Your plan is insane Father Francesco. Carla, you are coming home with me," he insisted.

Finally, Grandma spoke. "Who are you Egidio, that you should act this way? Your words are those of a tyrant." "I will hear no more of this Lucia!" Egidio shouted, silencing her with a threatening wave of his hand, bringing the three sisters to their feet. Auntie Angie spoke first. "You are a tyrant, Egidio. You cannot treat this affair in such a manner." Egidio was about to respond but was cut short by Auntie Stella. "No, Angie, he's not a tyrant but a *cafone*." Mom was just about ready to put her two cents in, when Father Francesco slammed his fist on the coffee table, silencing them. "Enough of this! Everyone back in your seats. You came for my advice, and you must hear me out!"

Egidio could barely contain himself, his anger was so great. Grabbing Carla by one hand, he pulled her to her feet, as if to rip her away from Pietro. This brought Pietro to his feet. Egidio's treatment of Carla was too much for him to bear. "Leave her alone, Signor Ricci. Stop treating Carla in this manner!" Pietro blurted out, his anguish apparent in his voice. Frank then made his move. "You're the cause of all of this, Pietro Petruzelli. You have torn our family apart. We have taken enough from you and now I'm going to do something about it."

Mom, sensing something was about to happen, advanced toward Pietro. Frank, at the same time, pushed his father aside and lunged toward Pietro, but not before Mom put herself between them, absorbing the full force of Frank's charge. Auntie Stella instinctively rushed toward Frank but was deflected by a quick wave of his hand. "You dirty bastard!" she screamed out. Auntie Angie turned to Father Francesco, but he needed no words. Furious with what was happening in front of him, he shouted, "You are in the presence of a priest, a servant of God! I demand that you stop! I demand your respect, if not for me but for whom I represent!"

Egidio would hear none of it, as he pulled Carla away from the group, attempting to exit. "You are coming home with me. I heard enough from this priest!" He shouted contemptuously. As the Riccis exited the rectory, Pietro attempting to go after Carla, broke away from Mom, still shaken from Frank's charge. Before he could reach Carla, Frank turned, confronted Pietro, punched him in the stomach, causing him to drop to the floor. Frank slammed the door behind him, leaving Pietro in a heap, sobbing uncontrollably. Carla's voice could be heard in the distance calling to Pietro, as Egidio dragged her away. Grandma, frantic at what just happened, rushed to Father Francesco imploring him, "Padre Francesco, cosa dobbiamo fare (what are we to do?)"

Auntie Angie, alarmed at the sight of Grandma's anxiety, reached for a glass of wine, holding it in front of Grandma, calmly said, "Mama drink the wine, then we will talk." Father Francesco, aware of the possible danger to Grandma's well-being from the raw emotions displayed by all sides, took Grandma by the hand and calmly counselled, "Listen to Angie and sit." He then motioned to Auntie Angie to go to Pietro and comfort him. "Mom and Auntie Stella took their seats on the couch, left and right of Grandma, but only after Auntie Stella made certain Mom was feeling okay. Slowly, Auntie Angie brought Pietro over to the couch he occupied with Carla just minutes before, but this time she sat in Carla's place, wanting to remain close to Pietro to comfort him. Father Francesco returned to his seat, and a blessed silence fell over the room. The storm had passed.

Father Francesco began, "Now we must speak. Pietro, life teaches us many lessons, one is, we don't always know our minds. As a young man, it's natural for you to think you know what is best for yourself, that an old man like me simply doesn't understand you. The reality is, I do understand you, I experienced these things myself and know others who also have. I'm asking you to benefit from my experience, accept my words in faith, to trust my judgment."

Grandma then spoke. "Pietro listen to Padre Francesco, he's giving you good advice. For the sake of my brother and your mother, you must at least attempt to follow their wishes and trust the judgment of Padre Francesco." Mom was listening and uneasy with the advice being given by Father Francesco, knowing the depth of love that existed between Carla and Pietro. She was about to say something, but Grandma grabbed her hand, anticipating her thoughts, silencing her. Feeling Father Francesco was giving good advice, she did not want Mom saying anything to the contrary that might confuse Pietro even more. Pietro, seeing the interaction between Mom and Grandma, turned to Mom and implored, "Cousin Carmela, what do you believe I should do?" Mom, aware Grandma wanted Pietro to follow Father Francesco's advice, simply advised, "Listen to Father Francesco, but also listen to your heart." Grandma then gave Mom one of her looks, knowing Mom's words could be an encouragement to Pietro. "Carmela," Grandma speaking softly, "His heart tells him to see the wisdom in Padre Francesco's words." "Yes, Mama," aware Grandma was diplomatically silencing her, Mom reluctantly responded. "Yes, Mama, Pietro should listen to Father Francesco, he is a wise man."

Auntie Angie, taking Pietro by the hand, advised him to listen to Father Francesco. Pietro, finally turned toward Auntie Stella and heard a different message. "Why are you allowing those *cafoni* to come between you and Carla? You love each other." Grandma spun around and blurted out, "Stella *silenzioso, hai detto abbastanza* (Stella silent, you said enough)!" Auntie Stella turned toward the window and went silent. It was obvious that she was steaming mad. She made her point and did not want to further aggravate Grandma. "Aunt Lucia," Pietro once again implored. "Isn't cousin Stella, right? Don't we have a right to our own lives?" He turned to Father Francesco and repeated his question, "Don't we have a right to our own lives, Padre Francesco?" "Yes, Pietro," Father Francesco responded. "God created each of us as individuals, and as individuals, we must discover what He desires of us, but that takes time to discern, and part of that discernment is often separation, where time and distance allows passions to cool. If your love for Carla is true, it will live on beyond momentary passions. It will live on as a steady flame, rather than a hot burning fire which can be most deceptive."

Before Father could say another word, Pietro stood, obviously shaken with emotion. "I must leave, everyone. I know you are trying to help me, but I must leave. I will keep your words in mind and I value them, now I need time alone." "Pietro, dove stai andando (Pietro, where are you going)?" Grandma asked anxiously. "Aunt, I'm simply going for a walk along the docks. Don't worry about me. I will be home in a few hours."

Pietro left, and a momentary silence descended over the group. Father Francesco had given the advice everyone sought. Would Pietro accept it? Father motioned to the group the visit was over. Grandma stood and thanked Father Francesco for his time and advice and asked for his prayers on behalf of Pietro and Carla. The little group departed the rectory, sharing in silence the events that had just occurred.

CHAPTER 68

Back at Grandma's, the Telegram

W hile making the short walk across North Square to Grandma's flat, Auntie Angie swung into action. "We need to talk," she announced to the little group. "Once we get to Mama's, we must discuss what just happened." "That's all, the commander in chief gave the orders," Auntie Stella said sarcastically. "Now, she will talk for another hour. She loves to hear herself talk." As usual with these sudden outbursts from Auntie Stella, Grandma silenced her with a look. Auntie Angie, caught sight of the look, and knew Grandma was backing her up. They headed toward Grandma's flat with Mom trailing behind. She was deep in thought, obviously thinking about what Father Francesco had said.

As soon as they stepped into the apartment, Grandma headed to the stove and got a pot of espresso brewing. When Auntie Stella stepped into the kitchen to set the table for four, Grandma called out to her, and asked her to remove taralli from the garland Grandma kept constantly replenished. Auntie Stella, knowing Grandma's concern, did not make her usual sarcastic remarks. Dutifully, she cut the taralli from the string, and one by one tossed them onto the table, clunk, clunk, clunk, clunk. She had made her point, the taralli were hard. Grandma, well aware of what Auntie Stella was saying with her gesture, asserted herself by asking her to take down one more. Auntie Angie came in the kitchen, gathered the taralli and placed them on a plate. Auntie Stella then dropped the fifth one onto the plate. Auntie turning to Auntie Stella said, "Stella don't make her nervous." The two of them took their seats at the table. Shortly after, Mom entered the kitchen. "Sit here Carmela, beside us. Mama is making espresso."

Within minutes, Grandma brought the steaming pot of espresso to the table and poured out four cups. Taking her seat, she finally spoke. "Now, what are we going to do?" Instinctively, Grandma turned toward Auntie Angie whom she counted on for advice, but before Auntie could speak, Mom spoke up. "This is not right. Pietro and Carla love each other, and everyone is interfering in their lives. Angie, they are not much younger than you or me when we got married. So, what is this all about? Why is there so much trouble? Why can't everyone leave them alone?"

Auntie Angie then spoke. "Carmela, you know the answer. The relatives are expecting him to return to Italy and enter the seminary. You think they sent him here to get married, and to marry the daughter of a fisherman?" "What's wrong with fishermen?" Mom shot back. "They are honest people." "Carmela, if he was not going to become a priest, they would want him to marry someone in his class, someone rich like themselves and from a prominent family. Don't ask foolish questions. What about the Riccis? The father and the sons are a bunch of *cafoni*. They will never let Carla go." "You think this is right Angie?" Mom responded. "Who are we to sit here and decide their future?" Turning to Grandma, Auntie Angie asked, "Ma, what do you think is best? I know you are very concerned about the relatives in Italy.

Grandma, without saying a word, stepped out of the kitchen for a moment, and returned with her black handbag. Opening it, she took out a telegram and placed it on the table for all to see. It was immediately understood by the three sisters, it was from the relatives in Italy. "Ma, how long have you had this telegram?" Auntie Angie asked. "Only a day Angie, but it's serious." Grandma managed to grab the attention of everyone, and a pall of concern descended upon the table. Unfolding the telegram, Grandma began to read. "It's from my brother, Gerardo. I will read it in English. Dear Sister, I am writing to you to express the concern of our family for the future of Pietro. We sent him to you for a brief vacation before entering the seminary, knowing he would be safe in your hands. We have become aware of a relationship he has with one, Carla Ricci. We trust this matter will go no further, and you will represent our interests in America, my sister, and have him return to Italy as we sent him to you, a young man ready to enter the seminary. Your loving brother, Gerardo."

Grandma folded the telegram and ceremoniously placed it back in its envelope. Once she had it safely tucked inside, she placed it on the table and quietly said, "Now, what are we going to do? The relatives in Italy have spoken, and you know what they expect of us." "Carmela," Auntie Angie spoke up. "You are the closest to Pietro. You're closer to him in age and personality. He's staying with you and your family, the boys get along well with him, and Joe likes him. You know Pietro best, and you can influence him. I know at heart, we would love to see him and Carla together, but the relatives in Italy don't want it. He is their son. They expect us to do the right thing. You heard the telegram, we have no choice. Pietro must return as he came to us."

"Angie, that's impossible. He has fallen in love with Carla, things have changed, and they will never be the same. How can you say he could go back to Italy as if nothing happened?" "Carmela is right," Auntie Stella spoke up. "If the couple love each other, why should anyone stand in their way?" "Stella, shut your mouth," Auntie Angie reprimanded with frustration, evident in her voice. "You always say the opposite thing." "Angie, I mean it," Auntie Stella replied. "I'm still single and know how much I would love to find someone who cares for me," Auntie Stella revealed. "If the couple love each other, no one should stand in their way."

Grandma looked up and directly into Auntie Stella's eyes. She seemed both startled and surprised at her daughter's revelation. Her eyes became teary as she said, "Stella, *non sapevo* (I didn't know). Why did you keep this to yourself all these years?" "Ma," Auntie Stella responded. "You know I love being with you, but like Angie and Carmela, I would love to have had a family of my own, and because I know how I feel, I believe I can speak for Carla and Pietro when I say, no one should stand in their way if they truly love each other." Grandma, reached across the table for Auntie Stella's hand, grasped it, and quietly said, *"Figlia mia"* (My daughter.) With that gesture and simple words, she was able to convey her wishes to her daughters, and the little group came to a common decision, they would not stand in the way of Pietro and Carla.

The unexpected consensus was a relief to all. Before another word was spoken, Grandma spoke up. "We must send a telegram to Gerardo and Velia and ask them to call us at Angie's house on Friday at 11 o'clock in the morning. It's the only way we can explain to them the seriousness of the situation and how difficult it is."

Finally, the tension was broken, and a decision made. The four women began kissing each other from cheek to cheek in relief. Mom then spoke up, "How are we going to bring Carla and Pietro together? No one wants this relationship to continue, neither his parents nor hers. It's going to take a miracle." Grandma turned toward Auntie Angie, as she always did in moments of anxiety. Reading her mind, Auntie immediately spoke out, "Mama, we will pray for a miracle and place everything in God's Hands." Her words calmed Grandma. She repeated them, "*Si, metteremo tutto nelle Mani di Dio* (Yes, we will place everything in God's Hands). He'll show us what to do." The women began composing the telegram expressing their sentiments, which Mom later took to Western Union.

CHAPTER 69
Simple Chores

At the end of August, Mom would always take the three of us to Gilchrist department store to buy clothes for the upcoming school year. Starting at the beginning of summer, Dad would put money aside for this annual event. It took about $100 to clothe the three of us. After deciding on the hand-me-downs that would work, separating them from the clothes that were not wearable or no longer fit any of us, Mom would march the three of us up to Gilchrist to see Miss Rooney, who made her career stationed in the boy's department. Gilchrist was located on the corner of Winter and Washington Streets in downtown Boston. There were three department stores that faced each other at that location: Jordan Marsh, Filene's and Gilchrist. Gilchrist was the smallest and least expensive of the three. Entering Gilchrist, you would pass through a small cosmetic department leading to a short flight of stairs, taking you to the boy's department. The moment we entered the department, Miss Rooney would greet Mom and then each of us by name. Miss Rooney was a short woman, well proportioned, in her mid-fifties. Once we got through our annual greetings, she sized up Charlie, and as usual, would say he had to go to the husky boy's department. It never bothered Charlie, because the free lollipops offered to children were kept in that department, prompting him to fill his pockets before they were offered to the rest of us.

Mom had a thing for brown pants and green sweaters. The sweaters would invariably have animals on them, bears and reindeer, the animals most commonly offered. Our shopping spree never got beyond $85. Mom always planned to hold $15 aside, from the $100 Dad provided, for what she referred to as our good time money. It was always the same. We would go to the Adams House for lunch, where we would invariably have chicken croquettes. The croquettes were shaped pointy, a thick yellow cream sauce covering each of them. They served two to a plate along with mashed potatoes and peas. We called this American food, and enjoyed the taste, which was very different from our everyday fare. They were delicious, helping to make this annual event into a special treat. Following lunch, we would go to a movie. Movie Houses were located up and down Washington Street. Our favorite was the RKO Keith's. Not only did it have the best movies in town, it was also the most beautiful of the Movie Houses. It looked like a palace.

This year, things were different, Mom invited Pietro to come along with us. Pietro didn't need any clothes for he arrived from Italy with lots of fine things, far finer than our own. He looked forward to our little shopping spree and the distraction it would provide him. As soon as purchases were completed at Gilchrist, we were off to the Adams House with our bags in hand. Pietro, who had barely strayed out of the North End and our Italian world since he arrived in Boston, except for our vacation to Kingston, seemed fascinated by the Colonial atmosphere of the Adams House.

We all ordered croquettes which appeared just minutes after ordered. Everyone was hungry, and the croquettes were always a treat. It was in the few minutes before the croquettes arrived that Mom began to talk to Pietro, asking him how he was feeling. "Pietro, you have said very little about Carla since we left Father Francesco. What are your feelings?" "Cousin Carmela, I miss her terribly," Pietro replied sadly. "I don't know what is going to become of me." "Pietro, this is not the place to talk," Mom replied. "But let me tell you, Mama and your cousins are all behind you. You must be certain in your mind you truly love Carla and not meant to be a priest." "Cousin Carmela, you know we love each other. What else can I say to you, but I'm happy to know you and the family are on our side." Before Pietro could say another word, the croquettes arrived and were placed on the table in front of us, steaming hot and great smelling, we couldn't wait to dig in. Charlie began to dig in, but Mom stopped him. "Husky Boy, stop, we have to say a prayer." Charlie's mouth was full of croquette. He couldn't figure if he should spit it out or swallow the mouthful. Mom spotted it and said, "Swallow it, then put your fork down and we'll say a quick prayer." Charlie swallowed the croquette, then made it a point to indicate how delicious they were by smiling in our direction, as if to say, "I got to taste them first and you have to wait for the prayer." Mom knew what he was doing and told him to stop. Charlie put his fork down, and we all said a quick Hail Mary, followed by an explosion of forks, as the five of us demolished the croquettes and everything else on our plates.

Because Pietro was with us, Mom decided an extra treat was in order, for the first time ever, she ordered Indian pudding. Mom loved it, but the rest of us had never tasted it. Because of the name, Charlie began whooping, imitating Indians he had seen in Westerns, attracting the attention of other patrons in the restaurant. Mom, noticing we were attracting attention to ourselves, shouted at Charlie to stop, but not before one of the patrons, sitting adjacent to our table, made a remark. "Those Guineas are all alike," making certain he said it loud enough for us to hear.

That was all Mom needed, she was up like a shot and over to the table. Standing over the offender, Mom responded, "You jerk, this Guinea would like to shove those croquettes in your face." "I'm going to call the manager," the man countered. "Leave us alone." Mom warned him to never say that word again. With that, she returned to the table, and we began to discuss what movie we were going to see. "I want to see Gilda!" Anthony shouted out. "They brought it back to the Pilgrim Movie House, and I want to see it." Mom, always the fox, knew exactly what Anthony was up to. "You know about Gilda and Rita Hayworth." "What do you mean?" Anthony replied. "You know what I'm talking about," Mom shot back. "You want to see her do her little dance. Your brothers are too young for that movie, and we're not going to see it." "How will I ever grow up?" Anthony asked. Mom got up from her chair, leaned over the table, staring straight into Anthony's eyes and said, "You will grow up when you are ready, but not today. Your brothers are too young for that movie. Out of desperation, Anthony turned to Pietro and asked, "Pietro, do you want to see Gilda?" "Who's Gilda?" Pietro asked. Now Mom was really frustrated. "We are going to see Red River and forget Gilda. Pietro would be more interested in a cowboy movie along with your brothers." Pietro, not being aware of Gilda and Rita Hayworth, agreed with Mom, to Anthony's dismay. The decision was made, it would be Red River at the RKO Keith's; Pietro and Anthony would have to wait to see Gilda.

Leaving the table, Mom made it a point to bang into the chair of the jerk, causing him to spill water on his shirt. Bending slightly over him, Mom whispered, "Just a little reminder from a Guinea." With that, she paraded all of us out of the Adams House in triumph. We were off to see Red River.

CHAPTER 70

Preparing for the Saint Francis Feast

B ack then, one of the most popular feasts of the season was the Saint Francis Feast, the Saint who is everyone's favorite. For the Ricci family, it was no different, although they were fishermen and should have belonged to the Saint Andrew Feast, they were part of the Saint Francis Society because of Egidio's long time devotion to the Saint.

Three days had gone by since their meeting with Father Francesco. Carla had returned to her duties around the house, but an unnatural silence had come over her which made both Egidio and his sons anxious for her well-being. "Will you be marching with us in the Saint Francis Feast?" Egidio asked inquisitively of his daughter. "No, Papa. I will be participating in the Saint Theresa Feast, and as always, I imagine you and my brothers will be following Saint Francis to show your devotion to him." "Carla forget about me and your brothers. How are things going for you in the Saint Theresa Society?" "Very well Papa. We will be parading the Saint through the North End on Monday. We have been decorating the litter that will hold the Saint." "Do you plan to walk in the procession in your bare feet as your mother did for years?" "Yes, Papa, but I will be wearing white socks." "Very good Carla. I'm certain the Saint will be pleased." "Will you be walking for any special person?" "Yes, Papa, for Gemma Cataldo. She's a member of the Society, we just found out she has diabetes."

Wanting to change the subject, Carla asked Egidio, "Papa, what would you like to eat tonight?" "Carla, it's feast time, I know you're busy. Your spaghetti and meatballs are always good and easy to prepare." "Fine Papa, tonight I will make spaghetti and meatballs with marinara sauce." Feeling he must say something, Egidio turned toward Carla and asked, "Carla, what are your thoughts about Pietro?" "Papa, I don't want to discuss Pietro." "Carla, I need to know if you still have feelings for him." "Papa, do you think my feelings for Pietro will disappear because you want them to go?"

"Listen to me, daughter. You and Pietro are still children, you don't know your minds. You are a beautiful girl, any man would want you, and many men would try to take advantage of you. If I'm strict with you, it's because I'm your father. Not only do I love you, I must protect you." "And what about my brothers, Papa? They have managed to frighten away any man who has ever been interested in me." "Again Carla, they love you and they want to protect you." "Then Papa, what should I do with my life? I cook and clean and keep your house. Is that what you want of your daughter? You want me to be your servant?" "Carla, watch your mouth," Egidio snapped. "You are my daughter, not my servant. You're only 18 years old and you're ready to become serious with a man." "Papa, I have never known the affections of a man outside of you and my brothers, and that's not the same. If you shield me from all men, how will I ever know about men?"

"Carla, it's at times like this I wish your mother was alive. She could speak to you as mother to daughter, one woman to another. As your father, I can only speak to you as a man, knowing what a man desires of a woman. It's for that reason I'm strict with you and your brothers so protective of you." "Papa, you must trust me. You must trust the way you brought me up. Mama could not have done any more for me. You brought me up close to the church with good moral values. Don't you trust in the upbringing you gave me?" "Carla, of course I trust you and hope I have done a good job in bringing you up, but I don't trust the passions of men." "Papa, you must trust me. Don't you think I understand these things? Women talk to other women. In the Saint Theresa Society, we not only pray and clean the church, we also talk about men and the affairs of the heart." "So, you make dirty talk in the Saint Theresa Society, Carla," Egidio responded with a slight smile on his face. Carla was happy her father's mood had lightened, seeing he was joking with her. She tossed the dish towel in her hand at him, continuing with the joke. "No, Papa, we don't make dirty talk in the Saint Theresa Society," she said with a slight indignant tone in her voice. Egidio grabbed the cloth and looked at his daughter, happy to see a lightening in her spirit. "Carla, I'm going to the boat to see your brothers and we will be back in about two hours." Carla responded, "Papa, I will be going to the Saint Theresa Society while you're gone to finish decorating, then return home and prepare dinner." Egidio headed to the door, opened it, turning to his daughter for a moment, blew her a kiss and left.

CHAPTER 71
A Faithful Meeting

A minute or two after Egidio left his apartment, he was on his way down Garden Court Street to the wharf to meet up with his sons. On his way, he met Grandma, who was heading to Auntie Angie's flat, where Mom and Auntie Stella already arrived, awaiting the call from Rome. An hour ago, he might have avoided her, seeing Grandma as part of the problem between him and Carla, but now, after speaking with Carla, he stopped and greeted Grandma by name. *"Buongiorno,* Lucia." *"Buongiorno,* Egidio," Grandma responded cautiously. She then followed with the plea, "Please Egidio, don't make a scene. We're in public, and eyes are watching us." Taken aback by Grandma's plea, Egidio quickly retorted, "Lucia, what kind of a man do you think I am? Our families have known each other for years, I have a deep respect for you and your family."

Egidio's response caught Grandma completely by surprise, knowing his reputation and the situation existing between Carla and Pietro, she expected a sharp remark. Immediately, she sensed he must be softening in his position toward the lovers. She seized the moment by asking Egidio, "Are you having a good day, and where are you going?" Egidio responded, "Yes", somewhat impatiently, for he wanted to speak to Grandma about Carla and Pietro but didn't know how to get to the subject. Grandma, sensing Egidio's quandary and wanting to see what was on his mind, asked, "Will you and your sons be taking part in the Saint Francis Feast?" Grandma already knew the answer, for members of the Ricci Family were among the founders of the Society, and the family has always taken a very active interest in it. "Yes, Lucia, we will be there, and of course Carla will be walking in the Saint Theresa procession several days later." "Egidio, I as a woman, find the Saint Theresa Feast to be very meaningful. I have prayed to her often in times of family difficulty, she has always heard my prayers." "Yes, Lucia, it is a beautiful feast, and Carla is very close to Saint Theresa. Will you and your family be participating in the Saint Francis procession?" Egidio questioned. "Yes, Egidio. The people who sponsor the feast come from a village close to mine, Pratola Serra. We consider it our feast."

Both Grandma and Egidio were dancing around the subject of Carla and Pietro, but what was important, they were not arguing. There seemed to be an understanding between the two, something new had entered the situation. Neither of them would go any further for fear of insulting the other, but it was obvious his position toward Carla and Pietro had possibly softened, and he was making it known to Grandma. Knowing how proud a man Egidio is, Grandma would press the subject no further, sensing they had gone far enough. Very few words were spoken, but as so often among Italians, it is gestures, body language and the unspoken word that conveys the deeper message and understanding between them.

Before leaving for his boat to meet his sons, Egidio, wanting to reassure Grandma of his family's continued affection and friendship, uncharacteristically reached over for Grandma's hand, took it into his hands and gently kissed it. It was an act of unexpected gallantry, causing Grandma to blush. Slightly flustered, Grandma drew her hand back and jokingly said, *"Egidio vai alla tua barca* (Egidio go to your boat)." She said this while glancing at the flats surrounding them, anxious to see if anyone had caught the gesture. Egidio, sensing Grandma's embarrassment, quietly said, "Lucia, are you afraid the neighbors will talk?", Grandma tossed her hand in the air, turned, and simply said, *"Arrivederci,* Egidio." They parted with a deeper understanding of the situation that had divided their families.

CHAPTER 72
The Phone Call

S lowly, Grandma made her way up the stairs to Auntie Angie's third floor flat. She didn't have to enter the flat to know Mom and Auntie Stella had arrived. Their voices could clearly be heard as Grandma started up the second flight. She entered the apartment and quickly asked, "Angie, what time is it?" "Ma, relax. It's twenty minutes to eleven. The relatives should be calling in twenty minutes." Auntie Angie, Auntie Stella and Mom were already hard at work preparing food for the Saint Francis Feast, and as always, were in serious need of Grandma to get things just right.

"Angie, Stella, Carmela, you will never believe what just happened. I met Egidio Ricci on my way here and he was friendly," Grandma said excitedly. "When I saw him, I expected him to make a scene in public, instead, he was very reasonable." Grandma was so excited, she said these words before removing her little black hat, as she customarily would do when entering a flat. "Ma," Auntie Angie exclaimed. "Do you think he might be accepting Carla and Pietro being together as a couple?" "I don't know Angie, but it's encouraging." Auntie Stella had enough; she was not as forgiving as the rest of the family. "Never!" she said emphatically. "That old *cafone* will never accept Pietro. He wants Carla under his thumb." "Stella, you don't trust anyone," Auntie Angie shot back. "Why can't we hope for the best?" "Yes, Stella," Mom joining in. "Maybe he has changed his mind." "Oh, now we are hearing from the Little One," Auntie Stella replied tartly. As always, Auntie Stella would call Mom the Little One when Mom got under her skin. "He's a *cafone!*" Auntie Stella said more emphatically. "You 're all dreaming."

"Stella, enough!" Grandma responded with a nervous tone in her voice. "Put the eggplant parmesan in the oven. We have a lot to do before our friends come this evening." "Every year is the same," Auntie Stella exclaimed, an exasperated tone in her voice. "Platters of eggplant parmesan, stuffed mushrooms, macaroni with meatballs and sausages. We cook up a storm for the relatives and neighbors. They come, stuff themselves, burp and fart, and on to the next house. We are left to clean up the mess." Grandma responded, "Stella, enough! We do it for the Saint; we do it for the family. This is our tradition." «Tradition, tradition, I'm sick of tradition. We're not in Italy." Auntie Angie then stepped in. "Stella, you are making Mama mad. You always do this. Now put the eggplant in the oven." Mom, opening the oven door, hoping to calm things down, calmly instructed, "Stella, I have the oven heated. Put the eggplant on the bottom rack."

Picking up the tray of eggplant with one hand, Auntie Stella walked over to the oven, tray in hand, and shoved it in so hard, it bounced off the back wall. This she did while adding, "I 'd like to hit them with this." Auntie Stella's attitude further angered Grandma. "Stella, tonight you will ask for God's forgiveness for what you said." Mom then spoke up: "Yes, Stella, you must ask for God's forgiveness." "Oh, the saint spoke," Auntie Stella responded sarcastically. Auntie Angie continued to work through the entire episode. "While you were arguing, I made up three platters. Let's put them in the oven. Mama brought good news. Let's enjoy the evening and our friends." Auntie Stella, having said her piece, calmed down.

Auntie Angie then laid out four cups of coffee. The women all took their seats at the kitchen table, the phone clearly in sight. Looking at Auntie Stella, Grandma decided to have some fun while they waited. "Too bad Angie, if I knew you were having coffee, I would have brought some taralli." Auntie Stella, knowing what Grandma was up to, decided to turn the table on her. "Angie, give me the last half of the éclair I saw in your refrigerator." She said this, knowing how much Grandma loved éclairs. With her eyes fixed on Grandma, she added, "I think I saw a taralli in the refrigerator. Give it to Mama." Mom began to laugh, knowing what Auntie Stella was trying to pull off. Not giving an inch, Grandma took the taralli and dunked it in the coffee. After biting a piece off, she looked directly at Auntie Stella, smacked her lips and exclaimed, *"Delizioso."* Auntie Stella polished the éclair off with two bites. After swallowing the last piece, looked at Grandma, smacked her lips, and repeated, *"Delizioso."* Auntie Angie, acknowledging the latest skirmish, looked at Mom and said, "They're at it again."

Before another word was spoken, the phone rang, and everyone went silent. As usual, Grandma turned to Auntie Angie and said, "Angie, pick up the phone." Instinctively, Mom and Auntie Stella drew their chairs closer to Grandma, huddling together for support. "Uncle Gerardo, how are you?" Auntie Angie said in a voice louder than usual, as if to compensate for the distance between Rome and Boston. "How is Aunt Velia and the family?" Gerardo responded in Italian, *"Tutto Bene"* (All is well). *"E' questa* Angelina?" Calling Auntie Angie by her Italian name. *"Si, si. Questa e' Angelina. Carmela e Stella sono anche qui e tua sorella,* Lucia."

After announcing who was in the room, she handed the phone to Grandma, who was gesturing for it. "Gerardo, this is Lucia. Let's speak in English for my daughters." *"Perche'?"* (Why), Gerardo exclaimed. *"Non parlano italiano* (Don't they speak Italian)?" "Yes, Gerardo. They speak Italian, but not fluently." "Lucia, I am speaking for Velia who is right beside me. Velia preferring not to speak, simply nodded in agreement. What is happening to our son?" Gerardo began. "I am so disappointed in you, and Velia is worried sick." Grandma looked at her daughters while shaking her head from side to side, in typical Italian fashion, indicating this is serious. All three remained silent. Grandma was now in charge. "Gerardo, what happened with Pietro is something that no one can explain. How do you explain love? It just happens." "Lucia, what does he know of love? He is only 19 years old." "Gerardo, I was a year younger than him when I married. Like Pietro, I had my heart set on religious life. You know the story. Bernardo and I met, we fell in love, and I chose another path, but I have been very happy. It also happened to Papa, if it didn't, we would not be around. Can you say, it worked out badly, when you know how wonderful our lives have been?"

Auntie Stella whispered to her sisters, "The old lady is really making sense." "Lucia, you are right. We have had wonderful lives, but this situation with Pietro is different. He is in a foreign country. He is inexperienced, and he is infatuated with a beautiful woman. He is not thinking straight." "Gerardo, whether or not you are right, Pietro is in love with Carla, and Carla is in love with him. You cannot force him into the seminary if he doesn't want to go. If you do, he will always wonder how his life would have been; his vocation will become a burden rather than a blessing."

"Lucia, what do you want us to do, just let our only son give up everything for a woman? What about his mother? You remember what she went through when we lost our son, Umberto, at Anzio. It's happening again with Pietro. Will we lose him to America and to some unknown woman?" "But Gerardo, won't you be losing him to the priesthood?" Grandma asked. "Although we will be losing him to the priesthood, we will have him in Italy, and we have come to accept this." Gerardo replied."Gerardo, listen to me. You must be able to offer an alternative plan. If he does not go into the seminary, what do you wish for him?" "Lucia, he is our only son and our one remaining child. What I wish for him is what any father would wish, that he would follow in his father's footsteps and join my law firm." "Bravo Gerardo," Grandma exclaimed excitedly. "You would take him into your law firm." "Lucia, let me repeat myself.

This is the dream of every father, that his son follows in his father's footsteps." "And what of Velia?" Grandma asked hesitantly. "How would she feel?" Velia, taking the receiver from Gerardo answered, "Lucia, even though my heart is set on Pietro entering the seminary, like every mother, I only wants the best for her son, therefore, I know I would accept it in time if this is God's plan." "And will the two of you accept Carla? Remember, Pietro is very much in love with her," Grandma pressed on. "Lucia, you are asking too much too soon. Let us leave it at this for now. Lucia, should we come to America?" "No, Velia, I will call you next Tuesday at the same time after speaking with Pietro, pray to God to inspire all of us." Gerardo, taking the receiver said wistfully," Lucia, I can still hear the nun in you,". "Si, Si Gerardo, I'm a nun with four children. I will call you on Tuesday. Give my love and the love of my children to Velia. *Ciao Ciao*, Gerardo."

Grandma was off the phone, turned toward her daughters who were stunned by the wisdom of their mother's words and reasoning in this very difficult situation. Opening her arms, Grandma, in somber, measured tones urged, "Now my daughters, we must pray for a miracle." Auntie Stella, in similar measured tones replied, "The Pope has spoken." Auntie Angie and Mom snickered, while Grandma once again shook her head from side to side, this time the gesture meant, "She will never change."

CHAPTER 73

Preparing the Saint

"Carla, the crown of flowers on Saint Theresa's head is crooked. Straighten it out." Claudia Risoto observed. The women of Saint Theresa Society were busy preparing the statue of their patroness for her annual procession through the streets of the North End. As usual, Rosa was searching for gossip, and Carla had become the hot topic of the Society ever since Pietro arrived from Italy. "Carla, the night of Saint Andrew's Feast, you disappeared, and Pietro Petruzelli disappeared also. Everyone knows you and Pietro are stuck on each other, but something must be wrong. Sandra Lo Russo saw you and your father coming out of the church rectory. You were crying and calling out Pietro's name while your father was pulling you away. People know how strict your father is. Have you broken up with Pietro?" Rosa questioned. Angry from Rosa's questioning, Carla snapped back, "Why are you asking, Rosa? Are you interested in him?" "Don't be smart Carla. I'm not interested in any of the imports. When I get married, I want to marry a 100 percent American man. "Carla was about to respond tartly but thought better of it. "Rosa, Saint Theresa's banner needs to be straightened out. Why don't you pay attention to what you are supposed to be doing?" scolded Claudia. "I know what I'm doing Claudia, but don't you want to know what's going on with Saint Carla?"

"That's it," gasped Carla, stepping down from the stool. "I've had it with you Rosa. You accuse everyone in this Society of running around with guys, and now you are accusing me. There is nothing wrong in having a boyfriend. The problem with you, is that you can't get one. "What do you mean, I can't get one? If I wanted a boyfriend, I could have one anytime I wish, including Pietro," chided Rosa. "Enough of this!" scolded Claudia. "Rosa shut your mouth. We have to get the statue ready for the procession." "You're always taking Carla's side, Claudia." Who countered, "Rosa shut up and fix the banner. We want Saint Theresa to look pretty when we process her through the streets."

More members of the Society began filtering into the Shrine. They were beginning to set tables around the perimeter of the Shrine for the neighborhood guests, who would be visiting the Shrine during the Saint Theresa Feast. As Carla worked on the head piece of Saint Theresa, she couldn't help thinking of Pietro and the words Rosa had spoken. She became increasingly sad; her eyes began filling with tears. Not wanting Rosa or any of the members to see, she stepped down from the stool, turned her face to the wall and wiped her eyes. Claudia, noticing Carla's distress, shouted out, "Girls, why don't we take a break and have a cup of coffee! Some of us have been here for a while and before the new arrivals get going, it's a good time to have a break. Carla, come sit with me over in the corner. I have some ideas for a new crown for the Saint and I want to speak with you about them."

Rosa knew something was up, but the table Claudia had chosen could only accommodate two people, there was no room for her, furthermore, she wasn't invited. She sat across the floor with Gina and Paula Bucco, her eyes never leaving the two friends. She knew they were discussing Pietro and was dying to find out what they were talking about, so she did the next best thing, she tried to read their lips and interpret their body language. Claudia, speaking cautiously, observed, "Rosa is trying to listen to what we're saying. She is watching every move we make. Carla, what is happening between you and Pietro? Do you love him? Does he love you? Answer quietly and don't look around." "Yes, Claudia, I do love Pietro, and he does love me. The time we spent at his Aunt Elena's house in East Boston was very beautiful. It was there I came to realize, I truly love him. People talk about young love, impressionable love, but our love is not that way at all. Our love is deep, and it is true." "And what about Pietro, Carla? Is his love true?" Claudia asked, trying to remain as expressionless as possible, knowing Rosa was watching intently. "Claudia, I have never known the love of a man in the way Pietro loves me. It is not the love of a father toward his daughter or a brother toward his sister; it is the love God puts there between a man and a woman meant to be together. He loves me deeply."

Claudia's eyes began to fill with tears. Slowly, Claudia put a handkerchief to her eyes as if to rub away some makeup, a pretense for Rosa's sake, she was really wiping away her tears. "Carla, what you're saying to me is so beautiful. You are so lucky to have this love." "No, Claudia, it has been a curse to me. I'm saying this to you as my best friend. You know how protective my father and brothers are, they will never let me marry Pietro. Furthermore, he comes from a noble family who wants him to become a priest. They see him becoming a Cardinal one day. They will never accept me or allow our love to continue." "Carla," Claudia responded sympathetically, reaching over to caress her hand. "I had no idea you were going through so much." Say no more, Rosa is watching every move we make. You know she can be vicious."

Carla stood up, went back to her stool, and resumed arranging the little crown of flowers on Saint Theresa's head, while Claudia remained at the table considering all she had heard. She had great sorrow for Carla, but was also enthralled by the beautiful and tragic love story Carla just revealed to her. It was like a romance novel she had read, and for a few moments, she sat wistfully recollecting all Carla had spoken.

CHAPTER 74

Opening Night of the Saint Francis Feast

Saint Francis of Assisi is venerated by most Italians regardless the region of Italy they come from, along with many non- Italians, so universal is the Saint's appeal. "Carmela, move the table closer to the building so people can get by on the sidewalk. Angie cover the card tables with the oil cloths. We want to make *una bella figura* (a good showing)." Grandma was busy giving commands, as she and her daughters began setting up for their annual Saint Francis Feast street celebration. The platters of eggplant parmesan, stuffed mushrooms, macaroni with meatballs and sausages that had been prepared earlier in the day, were now being brought down to the street for friends and family to eat. It was a tradition Grandma followed since arriving from Italy. She was determined to feed every stranger that approached her table.

"Ma, you made too much eggplant," Auntie Angie complained, "and there aren't enough mushrooms." "Angie, there will be enough. Just put the platters on the tables," Grandma replied. "That's all, she wants to feed everyone in the neighborhood," Auntie Stella, adding her two cents to the conversation. Mom continued to run up and down the stairs, bringing additional napkins and paper plates for the feast about to begin. "Lucia, what a wonderful spread you put out this year," commented Louisa Pizzano as she sized up Grandma's tables, to see if her spread of a week ago for The Saint Andrew Feast was outdone by Grandma's. Grandma feeling confident about her display and abundance of food, made up a sandwich and handed it to Louisa. "Try the eggplant Louisa, it's delicious." Louisa bit into the sandwich and exclaimed, "Lucia, you're a wonderful cook, but the eggplant is a little greasy." This hit a nerve. "What do you mean my eggplant is greasy? Grandma responded. "I used the best olive oil to fry it, and I blotted off the excess oil."

As Grandma was talking, Aunt Elena arrived. "Lucia, *hai fatto una bella figura quest'anno*" (Lucia, you made a good showing this year). "Si, Elena, my daughters helped me make a very good showing of food," Grandma giving her sister a big hug. "Mangia, mangia Elena." Elena had brought over her entire family; they attacked Grandma's tables like locusts. This infuriated Auntie Stella, who was watching a day's work of food preparation being polished off by one family. What Elena's children weren't eating, they were wrapping in paper napkins and shoving into their pockets. "Put that back!" Auntie Stella shouted. "You're acting as if you are all starved." Grandma, who normally would have scolded Auntie Stella for such a remark, remained quiet, silently agreeing with her. Elena's family was cleaning off the tables. When Grandma couldn't take it any longer, she yelled out, "Elena, *basta!* (enough)! Your kids are eating everything." Auntie Stella took Grandma's remark as a signal to blast away. "You people are a bunch of *cafoni!*" It was her opening salvo. Elena's daughter Antonietta, who had a short fuse, shot back, "Skinny Stella never has anything good to say about us."

Auntie Angie, knowing that comment was going to start a fight, tried to mediate. "Zia Elena, tell your kids to take it easy, they are going to clean out everything. The food has to last the night." Grandma began waving her hands furiously at the ravenous bunch. "Vattene, vattene (Go away, go away)! You ate enough, go and find another table." Mom was emerging from the building with another large platter of eggplant. When she saw what was happening, she turned on her heels, and returned to the flat. "Zia Lucia, your daughter just ran away with the food," Antonietta fired again. Auntie Stella at this point was furious. She picked up two platters of food as if to say, "The party is over." They got the message and pulled back from the table. Elena, knowing they overstayed their welcome, kissed Grandma on the cheek, and wished her a *"Buona Festa* (Good Feast). Before I leave, how is Pietro and Carla? Did Padre Francesco make things right? They make a beautiful couple." "Elena, things are not better. Padre Francesco didn't help. I don't know what we are going to do." "Lucia, this is nobody's business but Pietro's and Carla's," Elena cautioned. "Elena, it is not that simple, and you know it. The family in Italy wants him to be a priest, and you know how protective Carla's family is of her. They want no man to get near her." "Lucia, when they were at my house, I could see they love each other. People should leave them alone," Elena commented. Before Grandma could respond, Paola Fontana came to the table to wish the family a *Buona Festa.*

Elena was about to take her leave, when shouting at the far end of Garden Court Street caught everyone's attention. Elena's kids descended on another table and were picking it clean. It was Regina Romano hollering at the top of her lungs for Elena's kids to stop eating. Then came the inevitable remark, "You are a bunch of *cafoni,* go back to East Boston!" This was too much for Elena. She shouted, "Lucia, *buona festa!"* and quickly made her way down the street to Regina Romano's table. Regina was in for it.

It has been a while since I have had something to say to the readers. Saint Francis is a very popular saint among Italians. My daughter Lucia has always had a special devotion to Saint Francis. Every year, her feelings of joy and gratitude to the Saint inspire her to set tables on the sidewalk, like other devotees, overflowing with traditional Neapolitan food in honor of the Saint; inviting all the neighbors to eat and enjoy her fine cooking. This year is an exception for Lucia and the family, they are greatly troubled. Sitting up here in the company of so many of our family with whom I have consulted, I think I know how it will all work out, but that is for me to know and for you to discover, but I will say one thing, this is a situation that arose in our family many years ago. Let it be enough to say that a solution is at hand, as it was then, and will come to pass in the very near future. For the moment, Lucia seems to be very busy with her neighbors, and I will remain quiet and allow the story to proceed.

It was six o'clock in the evening when Anthony, Bobby, Charlie and

Pietro appeared at Grandma's table. Mom, Auntie Stella and Auntie Angie were serving the neighbors, when the four of us appeared at the table to have supper on the street. Grandma, immediately cut slices of bread out of a Scala loaf and filled them with eggplant parmesan. Handing one to each of us, she simply said, "Mangia, mangia, mangia." As usual, Grandma's eggplant was delicious. Anthony, Bobby and Charlie gulped down the sandwiches, but Pietro didn't have much of an appetite. Grandma kept urging him to eat, when she couldn't get anywhere with him, she turned to Mom, knowing she had a special relationship with him. "Carmela, tell Pietro to eat. The food is good." "Pietro, listen to Mama, you have to eat." Pietro reluctantly took a couple of bites but didn't seem to have much of an appetite. It was obvious to everyone, he was thinking of Carla. Grandma was about to urge Pietro once more, when he interrupted and said, "Aunt, I 'm not hungry. I feel like spending some time in church." "But Pietro, you hardly had a thing to eat," Grandma responded. "Aunt, I'll be back, but for now, I would like to spend some time in church."

As Pietro turned and walked in the direction of the church, Grandma cast a worried look at Mom, who then turned to her sisters as if to say, "What should we do?" Not a word was spoken, and the four women continued to serve the guests, who came to their tables the rest of the evening.

CHAPTER 75
The Big Night

I f the Saint Francis Feast was one of the most popular events happening in the North End during the year, then Saturday night, the busiest night of the feast, was the most popular night of the year, when the entire North End turned out to revel in the streets. A colorful bandstand served as the focal point of the feast. A temporary Shrine, honoring Saint Francis, opposite the bandstand, housed a figure of the Saint. Colorful strands of lights stretched across streets near the Shrine, announced a feast is taking place. "O Sole Mio," "Santa Lucia," "Mamma" and other old Italian favorites, were played repeatedly over a loud speaker throughout the night.

It was a hot August evening, the feast was in full swing, the air filled with the smells of grease and thick smoke from food vendors serving meatball subs, stuffed peppers, calzone, sausages and anything that could be quick fried. The smell of smoke and fried food became trapped between the buildings of the narrow streets, coating the revelers' sweaty skin, impregnating their clothing with an acrid smell that immediately identified them as having been to a feast. A steady stream of devotees of the Saint, made its way to the Shrine, where offerings of a dollar or more were handed to members of the Society, who in turn, pinned them to white ribbons that radiated from the shoulders of the Saint. A visit to the feast is a plunge into an Italian-American world of noise and smoke, grease and sweat. It's laughter and shouts, heartburn and indigestion, all mixed in an atmosphere of devotion and respect for the beloved Saint at its center. In 1949, the feasts were essentially a local affair for North Enders and their families.

Our family gathered at Grandma's entry, from there, we slowly made our way down Prince Street in the direction of the Shrine and into the Neapolitan swirl of activity. It was six in the evening, as usual, we would be spending the next 4 to 5 hours with close friends, who were more like family. There were no strangers at the feast. Such was the way things were in 1949. If the North End was considered one big family, it was made crystal clear during festival time.

"Anthony, take your brothers and Pietro through the feast and get something to eat. I'm going to sit for a while by the bandstand with Grandma and your aunts," Mom instructed. The food vendors brought in for the feast suited Mom just fine, she knew we could easily find things to eat as we roamed our way through the makeshift stands. She would never allow us to eat fried dough, but we could try the meatball sandwiches. Charlie and Bobby were interested in the amusement rides, particularly the Whip. The Whip was made up of cups you sat in, that spun wildly while rotating, as you held on for dear life to a bar pulled across your lap. As we spun and screamed, Anthony and Pietro continued to walk through the feast.

Anthony ran into his friend Gaetano and Gaetano's latest girlfriend. Gaetano had to be the dirtiest kid in the North End. His overalls were a patchwork of rips and caked-on dirt, echoed on his face and hands. "Gaetano, who's your friend?" Anthony asked, amazed that Gaetano could attract any member of the opposite sex. "She's Frances Perillo, we met yesterday." Gaetano, who's your cute friend?" Frances asked, her voice squeaky and somewhat shrill." "He's Anthony. We go to school together." "Hi Anthony," she squeaked. "You're a cute guy. I love guys with red hair." "I bet your friends call you Fran," Anthony replied. "I've never seen you around here. Where do you come from?" Anthony continued. "I live in East Boston," Frances squeaked in response. "And who's your friend, Anthony? Isn't he the fancy one, all dressed up in his fine clothes." "He's my cousin Pietro and he comes from Italy." Anthony could see Fran eyeing Pietro like a cat with a mouse. It was then he decided to throw a monkey wrench into her plans. "Pietro is becoming a priest." "You got to be kidding," she squeaked. "No, I'm not kidding, he's going into the seminary this fall." That last statement put a damper on her plans. Knowing she had hit a dead end, she turned back to Anthony. "Are you also going into the seminary?" She asked, in the tone of a smart ass. "No, only Pietro," Anthony replied. Pietro, listening to the conversation was impassive; his mind on other things.

Gaetano, who was fuming over Frances making out with Anthony, decided to piss her off. "I just saw the best-looking girl at the feast by the Saint Theresa Shrine, Carla Ricci. She's quite a dish." "Don't be a wise guy," Frances hissed. "That stuck up broad wouldn't give you a second look." "She would give this a second look," Gaetano responded, gesturing to his crotch. That was the final straw; Pietro couldn't take it any longer. He turned and walked away without saying a word. "Pietro, where are you going?" Anthony cried out. "Nowhere, Anthony, I just want to be alone. I'll return to the bandstand in a half hour."

Pietro began walking away, when he was out of sight, he circled back, heading to the Saint Theresa Shrine, where Gaetano just reported having seen Carla. Pietro was working his way toward the Shrine, hoping to get a glimpse of Carla. Saint Theresa's Shrine was located on Prince Street, just around the corner from the Saint Francis Shrine. Pietro noticed the front door to the Shrine was open, and as custom dictates, the statue of Saint Theresa was brought close to the entrance for the traditional visit of Saint Francis and Society members. The Saint Theresa members were gathered in front of the Shrine. They were both observing what was happening at the feast and getting the Saint ready for their feast which would be happening in several days. Pietro found a vantage point, just across the street by the fried dough stand, where he believed he would not be seen. He decided to remain there, hoping to catch a glimpse of Carla, but Pietro's stealth could not outwit Rosa's craftiness. She spotted Pietro while talking to a friend in front of the Shrine. Never a friend of Carla's, she decided to cause trouble.

Breaking away from her friend, she turned on her heels and entered the Shrine, where Carla could be seen in its deep recesses, adding flowers to the crown Saint Theresa would be wearing in her procession through the North End. Carla was aware of Rosa approaching, but would not acknowledge her; she just continued to work on the crown. Nudging Carla, Rosa questioned, "Carla, guess who's across the street trying to stay out of sight behind the fried dough stand? It's that cute Pietro Petruzelli. You know Pietro, he's the guy you're not interested in, or maybe you're not interested in him because your brothers would break your legs if you fooled around with him." Carla, not acknowledging her, continued to attach little rose buds to Saint Theresa's crown. Rosa decided to turn up the heat. "He's really a great-looking guy, Carla. I wouldn't mind putting my shoes under his bed." Carla's fury kept gathering, as Rosa continued to push her buttons. "I think I'm going across the street and get further acquainted. See you Carla."

Rosa turned, had not even taken her first step toward the door, when Carla exploded. She grabbed Rosa by her shoulders and spun her around. Looking her straight in the eye, Carla shouted out," You little bitch! You leave Pietro alone!" "Why Carla? Just because you can't have him. Go back to making your crown and ask the Saint to forgive your language." Rosa turned, and once again began making her way to the entrance. Carla was ready to chase after her, when some of the Saint Theresa girls, standing outside, entered the Shrine attracted by Carla's shouts. "What's happening in here?" Claudia asked. "I can hear you guys arguing from outside." Rosa used this opportunity to slip out of the Shrine and began heading across the street to the fried dough stand and Pietro. Seeing what was happening, Carla pushed Claudia aside, making her way out the door. "Come back you little bitch!" She screamed out.

Pietro spotted what was happening and advanced toward the two. Carla looking up, caught sight of him. Rosa, caught between the two, continued to advance toward Pietro. Carla caught up with her and shoved her to the ground. "Stay away from him!" She shouted. Pietro, anxious to break up the argument, took Carla by the arm and hurried her in the direction of the Saint Theresa Shrine, a decision he might not ordinarily have made, but one that became necessary, given the attention the women were attracting.

CHAPTER 76

The Altercation

The moment Pietro and Carla stepped into the Shrine, Pietro paused, gently turned Carla by the shoulders and drew her toward himself. "Carla, what are you doing? What is happening to you?" Pietro asked, as he desperately searched Carla's face for an answer. "Pietro, what's happening to us is terrible," Carla sobbed. "Everyone is interfering in our lives. Why can't they leave us alone?" Carla rested her head on his shoulder and together they stood silently rocking back and forth, while the girls from the Saint Theresa Society silently looked on.

While this was happening, Rosa, seething with jealousy, made her way through the feast toward the bandstand and the Ricci brothers. She found the four brothers seated at a table, nursing a half empty bottle of Chianti. Without wasting a moment, Rosa approached the brothers' table and announced, "Your sister is in the Saint Theresa Shrine making out with that Pietro guy from Italy." She said this while punching Frank Ricci's back, to awake his anger. It worked. The brothers shot up, immediately left the table, and headed directly toward the Saint Theresa Shrine. This time, nothing would hold them back. "I'm going to beat the shit out of him!" Frank shouted to his brothers. "Don't any of you touch him, he's mine. No one is going to accuse the Ricci brothers of ganging up on one guy."

Claudia, seeing the four brothers advancing toward the Shrine, let out a shriek." Carla, your brothers are coming, and they look very, very angry." Carla instinctively pushed Pietro behind her, wanting to shield him from her brothers. Pietro would have no part of it. He was not going to be made a coward in front of Carla. The brothers entered the Shrine in a rush, and in a second Frank was on Pietro. Frank punched Pietro in the stomach causing him to crumple to the floor like a paper bag. He then reached down and pulled him to his feet. Warning his brothers to stay back, he shouted out, "Now, I'm going to work on your pretty face!" Carla lunged toward Frank and was able to dislodge Pietro from his grip. Pietro immediately dropped back to the floor, still reeling from Frank's powerful blow. Carla then dropped to one knee beside the stricken Pietro, looked up toward her brothers, and clawed her face in a sign of despair. Her anguish was unbearable. Through her tears, she shouted, "Leave us alone! Why can't you leave us alone?" Carla then threw herself over Pietro's crumpled body, once again shielding him from her brothers.

The pitiful scene of his sister and Pietro in a heap on the floor of the Shrine, tore into Frank, as words could not. He immediately pulled back, standing over the couple, cried out, "What have I done?" He motioned to his brothers to leave. Frank would have no more of this. The four brothers pushed their way passed the women of Saint Theresa's to the entrance, where Rosa was standing. Frank paused for a second, glared into Rosa's eyes, as if to say, "You caused this," knowing full well the responsibility fell upon him, his brothers and their father for the anguish of their sister. The Riccis left the Shrine and returned to the Saint Francis bandstand, leaving Carla and Pietro sobbing in each other's arms on the grey cement floor of the Shrine. The women, who were motionless, then advanced toward the grief-stricken couple. Claudia bent down, stretched her arms around the couple, and there they remained in silent despair, while the women looked on.

Once the brothers were gone, Claudia motioned to the women gathered around them, to back away, leaving her alone to console her friends. "Carla, your face is scratched and bleeding. Let me get a wet towel and clean you up. Claudia was back in a moment with a wet towel and soap, handed it to Carla who attempted to clean her face, but she was too distraught. Claudia, taking the towel from Carla, wiped her face, cleaning away the tears of anguish and tended to the scratches Carla had inflicted on herself. Pietro, having recovered from Frank's blow, got to his feet. Making certain Carla was okay, he kissed her on the cheek and said, "I must go. I caused enough trouble. I'm tearing your family apart." Reaching out to him, Carla implored, "Pietro, it's not you. The problems in my family existed long before you arrived." "Carla, I must leave. I'm going to spend the evening at the church rectory. I know Father Francesco will have me." "Pietro, when will I see you again?' Carla implored. "You won't go back to Italy without telling me." "No, Carla, I must be alone, at least for tonight. I can't go to Cousin Carmela's or Aunt Lucia's; I need time to be alone."

As Pietro exited the Shrine, Rosa made a halfhearted attempt to grab his hand, still not giving up on meeting him. Pietro seeing what she was up to, stepped sideward away from her, and exited the Shrine, leaving Rosa standing in the doorway. Claudia got Carla to her feet and sat her on one of the chairs lining the walls of the Shrine, while the women of the Shrine kept their distance, still observing the dramatic events unfolding. Walking over to Rosa, Claudia grabbed her by the shoulders and shouted, "You did this! You've always been jealous of Carla, and this is what your jealousy led to." "I have never been jealous of Carla!" Rosa shouted defiantly. "Rosa, I'm not going to argue with you. You caused all this trouble, instead of being sorry for your actions, you remain defiant. I don't know what's wrong with you." Claudia returned to console Carla, still seated near the statue of Saint Theresa, while at the same time, Rosa slipped away. The disapproving looks of the women of the Society proved too much for her, she drifted off into the crowd, to spend the rest of the evening away from the Shrine.

CHAPTER 77

Distressing News

G randma and her daughters were seated just outside of Tomaso's Pizzeria, not far from the bandstand, when Grandma became aware of a commotion taking place near the Saint Francis Shrine. Frank Ricci, racked with guilt from his actions toward his sister and Pietro, with slight provocation, got into a fight with one of the Saint Francis members. The news of the fight spread like a wave over the revelers, drifting over to Grandma, whose look of concern aroused Auntie Angie, Mom and Auntie Stella. "Ma, what's wrong?" "Nothing is wrong with me Angie, but something is happening over at the bandstand. Send Carmela over to find out what's going on."

Mom, hearing what Grandma asked, needed no instructions. "Angie, I'm going to the bandstand to see what's going on." Auntie Stella, concerned for her sister, offered, "Carmela, I will go with you. You're a shrimp, you will get hurt in that crowd." Together, the sisters took off in the direction of the bandstand, before reaching it, Vivian Penta rushed up to them. "Carmela, Stella, have you heard what happened? Frank Ricci beat up your cousin in the Saint Theresa Shrine. Someone told him that Pietro was in there with Carla, and Frank went crazy." Before Vivian could say another word, the two sisters changed direction, turned on their heels and ran toward the Saint Theresa Shrine, where they found Carla still seated by the Saint with Claudia consoling her.

"Carla, what's happening here? Where is Pietro?" Auntie Stella let Mom do the talking, while she remained on guard, watching the entrance of the Shrine for the approach of further trouble. Tearfully looking at Mom, Carla replied, "Carmela, I'm so sorry, I never meant to cause trouble for Pietro. We love each other, and it seems only trouble can come from it." Mom responded, "Carla, what you're saying is foolish. You shouldn't talk that way. Mom then asked, "Where's Pietro now?" "Carmela, he's at the church rectory with Father Francesco. He said he wants to spend the night there," Carla responded. "Carla, I have to get back to Mama and Angie, to let them know what's happening. They are very concerned, but I will reach Pietro and get in touch with you."

As Mom readied to depart, Claudia quickly turned to Carla and asked, "Would you like to go home?" "No, Claudia, not tonight. Can I stay with you?" "Yes, gladly, but your family will worry about you." Before Mom left, Carla asked, "Carmela, could you please do me a favor? Let my family know I will be with Claudia tonight. They won't like it, but they will understand." Mom brushed her cheek against Carla's, looked approvingly at Carla and Claudia, then left with Auntie Stella to inform Grandma and Auntie Angie of all that had happened. Mom and Auntie Stella headed back in the direction of Auntie Angie, knowing the news they carried would greatly disturb Grandma.

They worked their way through the crowd, coming upon Grandma who was talking to a *paesano*. Mom caught Auntie Angie's eye and pulled her aside. After hearing the full story, Auntie paused for a minute, then turning toward her sisters, sternly said, "We have to stop this. Someone is going to get killed, and if that happens, it will kill Mama. Let me tell her the story, and Carmela, you back me up. I know how to break news to her without getting her all nerved up." When Grandma finished with her conversation, she looked up to see Auntie Angie standing beside her. "Angie, what is it?" Auntie gave Grandma an accurate recount of the story, but in her own artful way, blunted the serious aspects of it. Instead of saying Pietro was punched hard, she simply said he was pushed, and she didn't tell her the incident created quite a public display.

Grandma's first reaction was to say, "Angie, this is terrible. Where is Pietro now? If something happens to him, I will never forgive myself. The relatives in Italy will disown us. This is the worst thing that has ever happened to our family." "Mama, don't get upset," Auntie Angie responded reassuringly. "We will work this out. I already told Carmela and Stella, we must solve this situation and we will. First, Ma, Pietro is safe. He's going to spend the night at the rectory with Father Francesco." "Why doesn't he stay with me or Carmela?" Grandma questioned. "Ma, he wants to be alone and he will be safe with Father Francesco," Auntie Angie replied. "And what about Carla?" Grandma asked. "She will be spending the night with her friend, Claudia. She is too upset to go home," Auntie Angie replied. "Angie, they may think the two of them will be spending the night together." "Ma, Carmela will speak to the Riccis and explain what's happening. I know they will believe her."

"No, Angie, this is something I must do myself. I will speak to Egidio. These troubles don't start with the children, they start with the parents. It's time we sit down and make peace, if not for ourselves, for Pietro and Carla. Our family has become the talk of the North End, now it must come to an end, it must be for the good of Carla and Pietro." Grandma's suggestion drew the three sisters closer around her. Auntie Angie, as usual, spoke for them. "Ma, what are you planning to do? These people are unreasonable, and who knows what he will do to you." "Angie, he will do nothing to me. We will speak as heads of each of our families. As heads of our families, we will have respect for one another." "Ma, one of us must accompany you." "No, Angie, this is something I must do alone, and he must do alone. It is the way we have always done these things, and it is the way we will do it now. Angie, you must have faith in God and faith in the old ways, for those are the ways that have proven best. Egidio and I know the old ways better than you and your sisters and better than his sons. We will sit and talk, have something to eat, and work things out in the way it's always been done. This is about family and nothing is more sacred than family."

Grandma's suggestion was too much for Auntie Stella to take. "Ma, what are you talking about? That old bastard will kill you. This is America, not Italy. Why should Carla and Pietro listen to what you and Egidio have to say?" Once again, Auntie Stella was setting Grandma off. "Stella, your tongue is too sharp. You think because I have gray hair, I don't know what I'm doing. That's the trouble today, no one believes in the wisdom of the old ways. We have been solving our family problems this way forever, and we will solve this problem the same way." "Ma, you're in America!" Auntie Stella shouted." *"Basta* (Enough) Stella. *Faremo a modo mio* (We will do it my way)!"

Grandma then rose to her full four feet eleven inches, asserting her authority. Auntie Angie, speaking for her sisters, nervously asked her mother, who had suddenly once again become the matriarch, "Ma, where do you plan to have this meeting, in your flat or Egidio's?" "Angie, we will have this meeting not in a flat but in the upper room of the Saint Francis Shrine. We will ask for the blessing of the Saint, and we will do it now."

Auntie Stella, now saw her chance to get back at Grandma. Sarcastically she asked, "Crazy old lady, why do you think Egidio will talk with you, when he blames our family for all the trouble he has had with Carla?" "Stella," Grandma replied, "Go with your sister Carmela to the Shrine and if Egidio is there, as I think he will be, one of you tell Giuseppe the president, that *la vecchia pazza* (the crazy old lady) Lucia, wife of your old friend Bernardo, wants to speak to Egidio Ricci in the room on the second floor, and we want to be alone. Also, we would like two glasses of Chianti," Grandma knowing wine would be on hand for the visiting guests. Seeing an opening, Auntie Stella asked, "Ma, are you planning to speak with him or make love to him up there?" "Stella, watch your mouth," Auntie Angie scolded. As for Grandma, she didn't say a word. She just cast one of her scolding glances in her direction, knowing Auntie would say no more. The matriarch was now in control, and no one could stop her.

CHAPTER 78

The Pow Wow

Mom and Auntie Stella quickly made their way to the Saint Francis Shrine. Entering the Shrine, they soon spotted Giuseppe, the Society's president. He was greeting visitors who entered the Shrine. Within seconds, Mom picked out Egidio Ricci from a small group gathered together at the rear of the Shrine. Mom, following Grandma's instructions, pulled Giuseppe aside and asked if Grandma could use the room upstairs to discuss family business with Egidio Ricci. Before even mentioning Grandpa's name as Grandma instructed, Giuseppe agreed to the use of the room. Mom, then went over to Egidio and explained Grandma's request. He, with no sign of reluctance, agreed to meeting Grandma. As Egidio made his way to the room upstairs, Mom quickly returned to Grandma, who was waiting near Tomaso's Pizzeria, to inform her everything was ready. Mom, Grandma and Auntie Angie hurried to the Shrine, but before Grandma ascended the stairs to meet with Egidio, she asked Giuseppe if he would kindly send up to their temporary conference room, two glasses of Chianti. She then asked Mom to go to Tomaso's Pizzeria to pick up two plates of spaghetti with meatballs. Grandma ascended the stairs to the upper room where she was greeted by Egidio.

"Egidio, how good of you to meet me on such short notice," Grandma opened. "Lucia, I respect your family and have always thought kindly of you and your daughters. The fact that we are having this problem with your nephew does not reflect on how I feel toward you and your family."

"Egidio, I feel the same," Grandma responded. "Let's sit and talk and maybe we can solve the problem of Carla and Pietro. I hope you don't mind Egidio, I asked Giuseppe to send up two glasses of Chianti, and I sent Carmela to Tomaso's for two plates of spaghetti and meatballs. Food and wine always make things go better."

They took their seats, sitting at right angles to each other. Further pleasantries were exchanged, but before they could get into their discussion, Giuseppe entered the room holding a tray with the two glasses of wine and plates of spaghetti, placed it on the table, and left discreetly without saying a word. Each plate was filled to the brim with spaghetti in marinara sauce and adorned with two meatballs, the size of small baseballs. "Egidio, I can't eat two meatballs, have one of mine. You're a man with a big appetite." "Thank you, Lucia," Egidio responded, taking a meatball from her plate. He then pushed one of the glasses of wine toward Grandma, and as if on cue, they both lifted their glasses and toasted each other. "Salute Egidio." "Salute Lucia."

The couple took a sip, then had two or three forkfuls of spaghetti. Egidio quietly asked, "Lucia, you asked for this meeting. What is it that you want?" "You know what I want Egidio. I want a solution between your Carla and my Pietro." "So do I, Lucia. Carla has never been so unhappy. Before your nephew came, we were a happy family and now he filled her head with nonsense and confused her."

"Egidio," Grandma countered. "The couple is in love and love is never nonsense." "You women always think of love. Love this, love that. I will decide who and when my Carla marries." "Egidio is this the way you met your wife, Antonia? Are you saying it was an arranged marriage, because I know it wasn't. Your mother and father would not accept her, because she was not Neapolitan, but you loved Antonia, and you married her against their wishes. She gave you four sons and a beautiful daughter. Everyone knew how much you loved her. When she died after giving birth to Carla, you went into mourning for a year." "Lucia, I wish you would not bring up Antonia. We must let the dead rest in peace," he implored. "Egidio, I must bring her up, for the situations are very similar. You don't want your Carla to marry Pietro, yet the couple is in love. Don't you think I'm having a problem? My brother and his wife are expecting him to enter the seminary in September. They will blame me if he doesn't go along with their wishes. Do you think they expected him to find a woman in America? Egidio, these things are out of our hands. If God wills this to happen, who are we to stand in the way?" The couple stopped talking, and once more began eating.

While they were meeting upstairs, Mom, Auntie Angie and Auntie Stella were sitting uncomfortably in the downstairs chapel, next to a second statue of Saint Francis, kept in the Shrine. "Girls, why don't you have a glass of wine," Giuseppe offered. "Those two might be up there for a while." Handing them the wine, he then asked, "How long do you think the two of them will be up there?" "I don't know," responded Auntie Angie. "But thank you for the wine." The three sisters toasted each other, then lifted their glasses toward Giuseppe, as if to say, thank you. "Angie, do you think Mama will be alright with Egidio?" "Of course, Carmela," Auntie Angie responded reassuringly. "Egidio respects our family, and Mama knows what she's doing." It was then that Gino Gallo came up behind Auntie Stella, who was sitting with her back toward the doorway, placed his hands on her shoulders and gave her a peck on the cheek.

Gino was medium height, slim, and had a thick black mustache that was like a slash across his face, thick eyebrows and dark wavy hair. He was a reasonably good-looking man with a quiet disposition, a printer by trade and considered a man of means, but for some reason was always passed over by the women of the North End. "So, what's the occasion that Saint Francis Shrine should be graced with the presence of you three lovely sisters?" Before anyone could answer, Giuseppe responded, "Lucia, their mother, is upstairs with Egidio. They have important business to discuss."

Using the opportunity, Gino offered, "Then let me sit with the sisters and keep them company." He sat closest to Auntie Stella, whom he seemed to take a particular interest in. "Stella, you know I have always had an eye for you." It was obvious that Gino had a drink too many and the wine had loosened his tongue. Auntie Stella didn't say a word. She just let Gino continue to talk. "Stella, you're the best-looking girl in the North End. I wanted to ask you for a date for years." "Why didn't you?" Auntie Stella snapped back. "I never thought I had a chance with you," he responded. Before Auntie Stella could respond with one of her sharp remarks, Auntie Angie offered, "Gino, it's never too late. Why don't you ask Stella now?" Gino was caught off guard, but before he could respond, Auntie Stella waved her hand, signaling her irritation. "Never mind, never mind. No one is going to fix me up. Angie, you act as if you were in Italy. Don't try to make a match for me, I can find my own man. You're just like Mama." Johnny Spadaro then entered the Shrine, spotted Mom sitting with her sisters and made a beeline in her direction. He stood in front of Mom, opened his arms and began singing, "I'll be down to get you in a taxi honey." When Johnny finished the opening line, he paused. Mom then responded, "You better be ready around half past eight."

Johnny was about to pick it up again when Auntie Stella asked, "What's going on? Every time you two meet, you sing that song because you were both in La Strada, the church musical." "That's right Stella, Carmela was my Rosita." For a moment, Auntie Angie was enjoying the performance, but then remembered their reason for being at the Shrine. She stood up and said, "Johnny, leave us alone. We're here for important matters." "What important matters?" Johnny asked. "What's more important than singing a song and having a good time?" The whole situation was getting under Auntie Stella's skin. Totally irritated, she snapped, "Johnny leave us alone. Go back to the feast and take Gino with you." Mom then waved him off, he knew something was up, and although he normally would not listen to Auntie Stella, he did this time. He grabbed Gino by the arm and left. They both disappeared into the crowd just outside the door.

"Egidio, the spaghetti is good. Its al dente, just the way I like it." "Yes, Lucia, and the meatballs are not spicy, just the way I like them." Grandma taking a sip of wine, continued, "Egidio, do you agree that we should not interfere with Carla and Pietro? They know what is expected of them, they are not children." "Lucia, what are you suggesting?" "Egidio, I'm suggesting we don't encourage or discourage the couple. Pietro must return to Italy within a week. He knows his parents want him to enter the seminary." "Lucia, do you believe Pietro will enter the seminary?" "I'm not certain Egidio. How can I answer that question? He must be questioning his vocation." "And what about your Carla?" "My Carla is a good girl who has always listened to her father. She will do what I ask." "Egidio, what do you ask of her?" Grandma responded. "I want her to be our old Carla, close to her brothers and father and keeping our house." "Egidio, do you think that's fair. What about Carla? What does she want? Don't you think she desires a family of her own?" "Lucia, when the time comes, I will do it the old way, and find a good man for her." "But Egidio, this is America. Things are different here, and Carla believes she found her man. They are in love with each other." "Pietro is returning to Italy and he will take my Carla with him." "Is that what you fear Egidio? Do you fear losing your daughter?" "Lucia, all fathers fear losing their daughters." "Egidio, if they decide to be together, remember, Pietro is a good man. He's my brother's son. You can't make a prisoner of your daughter. Didn't we have to say goodbye to our parents when we left Italy?" "Lucia, you said enough. I know your mind, and you know mine. I won't promise you anything. Let's go downstairs and return to the feast." "Egidio, will you put your faith in God?" Grandma asked. "And trust in His judgment for your Carla." "Enough Lucia. It's time to go downstairs. We've spoken enough."

Grandma and Egidio left the upstairs room and returned to the chapel. Mom, Auntie Stella and Auntie Angie turned in their direction, all searching Grandma's face for a hint of what had just transpired. Grandma remained impassive. She had plenty to say but was not going to say it in the Shrine and in front of Egidio. She preferred to talk in the privacy of her home. The three sisters stood, each left a small donation to the Saint. Grandma thanked Giuseppe for the use of the upstairs room, and Egidio took his seat back with his friends who hadn't strayed from where he left them. Nodding to the sisters, he turned his attention back to his friends, but the thought of the meeting with Grandma remained vivid in his mind.

CHAPTER 79

Back at Grandma's

G randma and her daughters made their way back to her flat, Grandma remaining silent as to what had happened between her and Egidio. When Auntie Angie asked why she refused to say a word, Grandma simply responded, "When we get to the flat, we will talk." As they were approaching Grandma's building, Auntie Stella walked ahead of the group, made her way up the winding iron staircase to the flat, and quickly turned on the stove to make a pot of espresso. Entering the flat with Mom and Auntie Angie at her side, Grandma's first words were, "Stella, you must have read my mind." The women took their usual places around the kitchen table, Auntie Stella joined them, the moment she placed the prepared pot on the flame. "Mama, you said we would talk when we arrived, so what happened between you and Egidio?" Auntie Angie asked anxiously.

"Listen to me," Grandma began. "You know Egidio is a hard man, but he loves Carla. He wants only the best for her." "Ma, he doesn't want to let her go," Auntie Stella responded. "You're right, Stella. He doesn't want to let her go, when he does, he plans to arrange the marriage." "What?" Auntie Stella shrieked. "No one does that anymore. This is America." "Stella be quiet," Auntie Angie barked. "Let Mama continue." "I tried to convince him that we should leave the couple alone and let them make their own decision. What I was saying is to leave it to God."

Mom then spoke up. "Ma, you know they love each other. Why

don't the two of you just give them your blessings?" "Carmela, it's not that easy. Why say those words? In this matter, it's not for me to give them my blessings, it's between the relatives in Italy, Egidio and his sons. What I tried to do, is to convince him to leave them alone, as we will leave them alone, and see what happens." "Did he agree to that Ma?" "I'm not certain Carmela, but he didn't say no." "*Che vergogna*" (What a shame), Mom exclaimed, continuing, "The couple should have the blessings of their family." "Carmela say no more. Let's put everything in the Hands of God," Grandma countered. Noticing the espresso was ready, Grandma asked Auntie Stella to go to the stove and pour out four cups. "Stella don't forget the taralli." Even before pouring the coffee, Auntie Stella cut four taralli from the string hanging near the kitchen window, tossed them on the table one by one, each hitting the table with a thud. Grandma simply responded by saying, "Stella get the coffee."

Looking for clarification, Auntie Angie asked, "Ma, we're just going to do nothing and Egidio will do nothing?" "Yes, Angie, we will do nothing, and I believe he will get his sons to do nothing. Angie, vediamo cosa succede (Angie, let's see what happens)."

The four women began breaking up their taralli, dunking them in the coffee. Auntie Angie then said, "Ma, isn't Pietro leaving in a week?" "Yes, Angie, he's buying his train ticket at South Station for New York City this week, where he will take the boat back to Italy." "Thank God," Auntie Angie sighed." Then it will be over." "Yes," Grandma repeated." Then it will be over." She then turned to Auntie Stella, with a grin on her face, said, "Stella, enjoy the taralli, I made them just for you."

CHAPTER 80
Sunday at Grandma's

Sunday is the day of the feast when the statue of Saint Francis is paraded through the streets of the North End, when thousands of people will show up to pay homage to the Saint, reuniting with friends they haven't seen for the past year. On Sundays, our family went to church at different times. We went with Mom and Dad to the Children's Mass at 9 o'clock, while Auntie Angie, Uncle Jimmy, Grace and Theresa would go to the 10 o'clock Mass, and Auntie Stella and Grandma would go to the 12 o'clock Mass. It was agreed the night before, whoever ran into Pietro at Mass would invite him to dinner at Grandma's. Everyone was anxious to speak with Pietro, especially after the awful incident the night before. It was Grandma who ran into Pietro at the 12 o'clock Mass. He was assisting Father Francesco, who made it a habit of celebrating the noon Mass.

With the completion of Mass, Grandma waited for Pietro at the family shrine, knowing he had to pass that way on leaving the church. When the sacristy door opened, and Pietro exited, he quickly walked over to Grandma and kissed her on each cheek. "Aunt, you waited for me," he whispered. "Yes, Pietro. I know it's short notice, still I would like you to come to dinner. The whole family will be there, and I promise no one will discuss what happened yesterday." Pietro immediately agreed, joining Auntie Stella and Grandma on the short walk across North Square to Grandma's flat. Within an hour after arriving, the adults were seated around Grandma's dining table, and as usual, the children around the card table. There was a certain sadness that filled the air. It was understood Pietro would be leaving for Italy within the week, and this would be our last family meal with him. We had all grown quite close to him and as so often happens in Italian families, he easily became one of us, as if we had known him for a lifetime. Not a word was spoken of the incident of the night before. The conversation was kept to food and drink and what was happening in the North End.

As dinner was coming to an end, the sound of an approaching band could be heard. It was the Saint Francis procession making its way to North Square and the church, where the procession would stop and be greeted by a peal of bells and a blessing by Father Francesco. Grandma had a bird's eye view of all the proceedings from her vantage point at her bow window. Once the ceremony was completed at the church, the Saint was turned and began heading in the direction of Grandma's flat, following its traditional route. By now, the entire family was gathered at the window. Grandma had hung a Saint Francis banner from her windowsill, a signal to the statue bearers that they should stop under her window.

Acknowledging her banner, they stopped. Grandma threw open her window, appearing as if a queen on her balcony, with the rest of the family standing just behind her. She motioned to the statue bearers to wait a moment, a signal money was to be sent down, all pinned on a ribbon, meant to be hung around the Saint's neck. "Pietro, you lower the donation to the Saint. I want you to do this, while doing it, make a wish. Saint Francis is a powerful saint, and if you make your wish with love and with all your heart, he will take it to Our Lord." Grandma handed the ribbon with dollars pinned to it to Pietro. He took his place at the window, closed his eyes for a moment, his lips barely moving, formed his wish, and lowered the ribbon ceremoniously to the cheering crowd beneath. Once the ribbon was hung around the Saint's neck, the crowd cheered while the band played *"La Marcia Reale"* (The Royal March), the traditional song acknowledging a donation. All this, while Grandma and the entire family clapped in unison to the rhythm of the march. It was a wonderful moment, one that none present would ever forget.

CHAPTER 81

The North End Warriors

Abaseball game was planned for Sunday afternoon at the North End Park between the North End Warriors and the East Boston Rockets. The rivalry had been going on for years between the two baseball teams. The game seemed to become an unofficial part of the Saint Francis Feast, even though it was not connected to it in any way. Anthony would be playing on the team for the first time and our cousin Vinny, who was one of the coaches of the Warriors, wanted all the men in the family to go to the park and cheer on the team.

We finished dinner at 2:30 in the afternoon. Grandma was upset because we rushed through the meal, anxious to make the baseball game. Her preference would have been to spend the rest of the day at the dinner table talking and going over the affairs of the week, but that was not to be. Vinny was pushing hard for the men to get down to the park as the game was to begin at 3 o'clock. "Pietro, you have to come with us this time," Vinny requested. "I know you don't understand the rules of baseball, but we need your voice cheering on the Warriors. Anthony, this is your first game, so I placed you in right field where you won't see much action. I wish the aunts were coming with us," Vinny said hopefully. "And you too Grandma." But Grandma would have none of it. "What about you, Auntie Carmela?"

Mom was just about ready to say yes when Grandma finally spoke up. "Who is going to entertain our guests when they visit? We always have guests for the Saint Francis Feast, you know they will be visiting this afternoon." "Ma, you don't need me," Mom insisted. "Carmela, I want all my daughters present, our guests expect to see all of us. Let the men go to the park and enjoy the game, I want my daughters here to entertain the guests." Grandma made her intentions clear, and that was that. Once she finished speaking, the guys quickly made their way out the door. They were on their way to the park. Grandma, Mom, Auntie Angie and Auntie Stella cleared the table, making ready for the afternoon guests that were sure to come. Grandma was a wonderful cook; their guests would be coming to enjoy her traditional Neapolitan dishes.

It was 6 o'clock when the men returned from the park. They could be heard coming down the street toward Grandma's flat, and they were in a great mood. The North End Warriors beat the East Boston Rockets 8 to 1; it was no contest. As they entered the building, Vinny could be heard shouting out, "Anthony, you made a great catch." That announcement caught Mom's ear. She ran into the hallway, grabbed Anthony, and gave him a big congratulatory kiss. Anthony tended to pull away, but he was happy Mom was so delighted. Even Pietro was excited, though he barely understood the game. He was proudly wearing a Warriors baseball shirt, Vinny had given him at the park.

As the men entered the flat, they were greeted by an apartment full of people, friends of the family and distant relatives. People were coming and going, sampling Grandma's food, and heading out for other buffets of regional Italian cooking. Auntie Angie was anxious we all eat something. She began taking food from the oven she had put aside for us. Before she would allow anyone of us to eat, she demanded we all wash. Her nostrils were fully flared as always, when she detected unpleasant odors; they were filled with the odor of sweat that the guys worked up at the steamy ball park. One by one, we made our way to the bathroom sink where we could wash off some of the day's grime. Auntie Angie kept bringing out platters of food from the oven, placing them on the card table she always brought out for these occasions. She placed the table at the far end of the kitchen, away from the guests. As each of us exited the bathroom, we went straight to the table, while Auntie Angie stood guard over the table warding off ravenous guests. The food was meant for her family.

The rest of the evening was spent with the women entertaining the constant stream of guests, some invited, some uninvited, that continued to enter Grandma's flat. The guys were off to enjoy the feast, and on this special night, boast of their triumph over the East Boston Rockets. Pietro joined the men as they made their way through the crowd at the feast, stopping often to wish friends a *"Buona festa."* He continued wearing his Warriors shirt, and for the evening, became caught up in the joy of the victory, temporarily liberated from his sadness.

CHAPTER 82

The Saint Theresa Feast

"Carla fix the wreath of flowers on Saint Theresa's head, it's tilted to one side." Claudia was a perfectionist and before she would allow the Saint to be paraded through the streets, she made certain everything was in order. Saint Theresa was one of the last feasts of the festival season. For many, it was their favorite feast because of its simplicity. The procession began about 6 o'clock in the evening, within three hours of making their way through the streets of the North End, the procession was over. It was set apart from other feasts by the fact, the statue of Saint Theresa was carried by both men and women. As mentioned earlier, unique to the Saint Theresa Feast, many of the faithful processed behind the Saint in either their stocking feet or bare feet. They were either looking for a favor from Saint Theresa or thanking the Saint for a favor received. The presence of these devotees created an atmosphere of silence and deep devotion.

There was much to do at the chapel before the Saint was ready to be processed. Flowers needed to be pinned to the stand that held the Saint, and the statue needed to be firmly attached to the litter that would be carried through the streets by the litter bearers. In addition to making the statue ready for its annual procession through the North End, prayer cards and buttons imprinted with the image of the Saint were gathered into baskets, members of the Society distributed. The women carefully tied pale blue-ribbon streamers around the neck of the Saint, held by members of the Society, as they walked alongside the Saint. Offerings from spectators were pinned to the streamers as the Saint processed through the streets. It would be several hours before the Saint began her annual tour through the North End, time to clean the chapel, and lay out some food and drink for the guests that surely would be filtering into the chapel during the feast.

While Carla was busy preparing the chapel, Pietro was helping Mom carry bundles of groceries back to our apartment. It was Mom's tradition to march with Grandma, seeking Saint Theresa's blessings and grace for the family, and to thank her for the help she gave Bobby years earlier, with a serious eye infection. Grandma wore shoes in the procession because of her diabetes, for fear of an infection from a cut that she might receive by walking barefoot or in stocking feet. Mom, on the other hand, would walk in stocking feet, both women once again, taking part in this annual event.

"Pietro, please go to the refrigerator and take out a loaf of bread," Mom requested. Today, we are going to have something that I can make quickly. We will have ham and cheese sandwiches and for the first dish, pastina with eggs." Making fast dinners was Mom's specialty, and it often came in handy. Even though it was 2:30 in the afternoon, Mom planned to get dinner out of the way and take us over to Grandma's flat where we would leave for the procession. Mom called out to Dad, "Joe, we will be eating with you today, so by the time you go to work at 3:30, we will be on our way to Mama's." Pietro called Anthony over to help make the sandwiches, while Bobby and Charlie helped set the table.

During the midst of preparing the dinner, Dad motioned to Mom to come into the parlor. "Carmela, how are things going with Pietro and Carla?" He asked. "Is there going to be more trouble with the Ricci family, and has anyone heard further from your relatives in Italy?" "Joe speak softly, Pietro will hear you," Mom whispered. "There has been no word from Italy. The last thing we heard is, they are very unhappy with us because of all that's happened and are anxious for Pietro to return." "What about the Riccis? Are they making trouble for our family because of Pietro and Carla?" Dad asked, while anxiously watching out for Pietro. "No, Joe. They are not making trouble for us. Ever since Frank beat up Pietro in the Saint Theresa Shrine, they have been quiet. Mama has met with Egidio, and there appears to be a truce." "Carmela, what about Carla and Pietro? How do they feel about this?" Dad asked. "What do you think?" Mom impatiently responded. "They love each other, and everyone has interfered with them. The kids should have been left alone. Now it's a mess, and our family is the talk of the North End." Dad cautioned, eyeing Pietro glancing in their direction. "Carmela, Pietro is getting wise. Is dinner ready?" "Yes, Joe, everything will be ready in five minutes." "Why don't you call the boys and we will all have dinner together." We sat around the table, eating and discussing Mom's yearly act of devotion offered up to Saint Theresa, for her continued intercession for our family.

With the conclusion of dinner, Dad got ready for work, while Mom and the rest of us prepared to go to Grandma's house, where we would meet up with Auntie Angie, Auntie Stella, Grace and Theresa, and eventually make our way to the church, joining the procession. At 3:30, we said goodbye to Dad, who was off to the newspaper, and left for Grandma's flat. As we walked toward North Square, Mom turned to Pietro and said, "Pietro, today I will be marching in the Saint Theresa procession for two intentions, one is for the family, and the other intention will be for you." "For me, Cousin!" Pietro responded somewhat surprised. "Pietro," Mom responded, "Saint Theresa has always been good to our family. I'm asking her to bring peace to our families and to bring happiness to you and Carla." "Cousin, that is wonderful of you, but I think you are asking too much from Saint Theresa," Pietro said haltingly. "No, Pietro. Nothing is too much for Saint Theresa. She will help us, and she will help you and Carla."

We arrived at Grandma's flat to find the entire family waiting for us. Everyone was sitting around Grandma's kitchen table, enjoying an icebox cake Auntie Angie brought with her. She could whip up one of these confections at the drop of a hat. "Carmela, have your boys and Pietro sit at the card table with Theresa and Grace. I saved a seat for you beside me." You could always count on Auntie Angie to have food in abundance. When everyone was seated, Auntie Angie cut her icebox cake, making certain everyone had a piece.

After doling out the servings, she waited a moment or two and turned to Mom, a grave look had come over her face. "Carmela, Carla will be marching in the procession and the Ricci Family always greets the Saint on Garden Court Street, in front of their building. Do you think there will be trouble?" "Angie don't worry. I'm certain everything will be okay," Mom responded. "What are you two talking about?" Auntie Stella questioned nervously. "Are you talking about Carla and Pietro, and maybe there will be trouble tonight?" "Stella shut up," Auntie Angie demanded. "Pietro will hear you." "Where's Mama?" Mom asked. "She is in her room, dressing for the procession," Auntie Angie responded. "Angie," Auntie Stella said anxiously. "Mama wants to walk barefoot in the procession. With her diabetes, if she gets a cut and it becomes infected, she could be in a lot of trouble." Auntie Stella no sooner finished her warning, when Grandma exited her room and walked over to the kitchen table to join her daughters. Each kissed her on the cheek as always, then they all took their seats to enjoy a cup of espresso and icebox cake before heading out to the Saint Theresa procession.

Before taking her seat, Grandma closed a pair of pocket doors that separated the dining area from the kitchen to achieve some privacy, knowing the conversation would certainly turn to Pietro and Carla. Ignoring the icebox cake, Grandma walked over to the kitchen window, cut off four taralli from the garland that never seemed to be depleted, placed them on a plate, and put them in the middle of the kitchen table. "Mangia," she said firmly. Auntie Stella decided not to say a word, figuring an exasperated look would be enough to make her point, and she already had a piece of icebox cake in front of her. *"Angie, ho paura di stasera* (Angie, I'm frightened about tonight)," Grandma said anxiously, directing her comment to Auntie Angie, knowing Auntie Stella and Mom would realize she was also speaking to them.

"Carla will be in the procession, and we will be going down Garden Court Street where Egidio and his sons are sure to greet the Saint. Pietro will be with either us or Padre Francesco, but certainly he will be in the procession." "Ma, as usual, you are worrying too much. Things will be okay," Mom responded. "Forget that," Auntie Stella said nervously." "The old lady is planning to walk in her bare feet for a special favor. You know what the special favor is, it's for the two of them, that they get together." While she was saying this, her leg was rocking back and forth, betraying her annoyance. "Ma," Auntie Angie gasped. *"Sei pazza!"*

(Are you crazy)! Like Grandma, Auntie always went to Italian when she wanted to drive her point home. "You have diabetes. You know what the doctor said. You have to avoid an infection, and if you get one in your feet, you could lose your toes and even your leg."

"Stella," Grandma responded, with exasperation in her voice. "You have a big mouth. I know what I'm doing." "For those two, she's going to kill herself," Auntie Stella shot back. "Stella, *basta* (enough)!" Grandma scolded, wanting to shut her up. "Ma, for once, Stella is right," Mom joined in. "It's too dangerous for you to march in your bare feet or stocking feet." "Even you, Carmela," Grandma responded with even greater exasperation. "Yes, Ma, even me. I will march in my bare feet. I will do it for both of us." "Stella, you march for Mama. You go in your bare feet." Auntie Angie offered. "Never!"

Auntie Stella responded emphatically. "You do it Angie," she slyly countered, knowing Auntie Angie would never do it because of her obsession with cleanliness. Auntie Angie crooked her mouth and in measured words responded, "Stella, you're always a wise guy. You know I skeeve (find disgusting) the dirty streets." "That's right, that's right," Auntie Stella, once again countered, keeping her voice down so Pietro would not hear her. "I'm a wise guy, but I'm looking out for the old lady." Once again, Mom implored, "Ma, I will march in my bare feet, you do it in your shoes." Grandma did not respond. She simply dunked her taralli in the coffee and began munching on it. The three sisters stared at each other, not knowing what to make of her silence, but there was a consensus, Grandma would not march in her bare feet. Everyone began sipping their espresso before getting ready to meet up with the Saint Theresa procession, arriving in about forty-five minutes in front of the church.

CHAPTER 83

The Procession

The faint sound of band music could be heard in the distance, a sure sign the Saint Theresa procession was heading in the direction of the church. "Stella, get me my pocketbook and hat. It's time to go." Auntie Stella quickly disappeared into Grandma's room and returned with a little black, straw hat with veil, plus a black, leather handbag. "Stella, that's the wrong hat," Grandma said curtly. "Oh, here we go again," frustration evident in her voice. "Ma, what difference does it make? They all look alike." "Stella don't talk back. You brought out the wrong hat. I want the one with the half veil; you brought me the one with the full veil." "Why do you wear a veil? You look like you're always going to a funeral." "Stella don't talk back. I wear the veil out of respect for my husband, your father." "Ma, he passed away eight years ago." "Stella, enough. Go to the room and get me the right hat." "Stella, stop arguing with her!" Mom shouted anxiously. "Be thankful she decided to wear her shoes. Get her the right hat. The procession is coming. We're going to miss it." "You get her the hat," Auntie Stella said defiantly. "There are twenty hats in there and they all look alike."

Mom grabbed the hat from Auntie Stella's hand and quickly ran into Grandma's room. After a minute or two, Mom yelled out from the bedroom," Ma, the hats all look alike. Which hat do you want?" "There!" Auntie Stella shouted triumphantly. "They all look alike." Grandma was fit to be tied. She marched into her room, on the top of her dresser was a little black hat with a half veil, surrounded by four or five other little black hats. She took the hat, placed it on her head angrily, and pinned it to the back of her head with the long hat pin with a pearl at the end. She then exited the room and was greeted with another caustic remark by Auntie Stella, "That hat looks just like the hat you wore this morning. They all look alike." Grandma simply said, "Saint Theresa is coming, let's go to the church and greet her." Auntie Angie opened the pocket doors, Grace and Theresa and all the boys were there, but Pietro was missing. "Where's Pietro? We're getting ready to leave." Auntie Angie asked. Grace responded, "Ma, he left as soon as he heard the sound of the band." "Did he say where he was going?" Auntie Angie asked. "No," Grace responded. "He just got up, left, and simply said, he would meet us at the procession." "He went to meet her," Auntie Stella speculated. "He knows Carla will be in the procession. Where else would he go?" Grandma, heading to the door, simply said, "Let's hurry, Saint Theresa will soon be here, and I want to get to Pietro before any trouble happens."

We left Grandma's flat and headed toward the church. Saint Theresa's procession was just minutes away. "Angie, here comes Saint Theresa," Grandma announced. Her voice tinged with a sense of anxiety and expectation. "Ma, let's stand near the entrance of the church. I want to see Father Francesco greet Saint Theresa," Auntie Angie responded. "Angie, keep an eye out for Pietro. I want to get to him before he does something foolish. Remind Stella and Carmela to keep an eye out for him," Grandma warned.

The procession was now entering North Square; the familiar strands of "Mama", played by the band, heralded the coming of the Saint to the faithful gathered in the square. Saint Theresa was hoisted high on the shoulders of the litter bearers. Blue silk streamers pinned with money, donations from the faithful, each streamer held by a Society member, radiated out from the front, sides and back of the Saint. It was a sight from Southern Italy recreated in America. Carla walked to the right of the Saint, gracefully holding one of the streamers in her left hand. She was wearing a white dress with a tiny yellow floral pattern, contrasting beautifully with her tanned skin. The dress had a scooped neckline and flared at the hips, and as usual, draped gracefully just beneath her knees. Her auburn hair was being gently tossed in the early evening breeze, blowing across her face then brushed back by a sweep of her hand, as she gracefully swayed to the movement of the procession.

Suddenly, the bells of the church began to peal, welcoming the Saint into the square. A roar came up from the crowd waiting at the church, followed by applause of the faithful. Father Francesco majestically emerged from the interior of the church, resplendent in his robes, with Pietro at his side. He stopped at the entrance of the church, waiting for the Saint to be set down in front of him. Pietro was still dressed in civilian clothes, not in the cassock and surplus that an assistant to Father Francesco would normally be wearing. He was carrying a small gold metal urn filled with holy water, to be used by Father Francesco to bless the members of the Saint Theresa Society, as well as the faithful gathered. Finally, the procession stopped, and the Saint's litter was set down upon legs attached to the underside.

Suddenly, a silence fell over the crowd, shouts and applause turning to silent reverence. There were people standing with their heads bowed, and others kneeling on the pavement in front of the church. It was time for Father Francesco to pay homage to Saint Theresa by blessing the statue, then the litter bearers, and finally the crowd beyond. He motioned to Pietro to come closer, dipped the aspergil in the urn of holy water and began sprinkling profusely. He then lifted his hand and blessed the crowd. With the final motion of his blessing, the crowd erupted into applause, spontaneously, the band struck up "Mama", as the crowd sang the words of the beloved song. It was as if they were serenading the Saint.

As all this was occurring, Pietro and Carla stood only a whisper away from one another. Their eyes never separated. They seemed to exist in a silent world, a world apart, a world known only to lovers. Grandma observing the lovers, nudged Auntie Angie to take notice. She in turn nudged Mom, who in turn nudged Auntie Stella, who didn't need to be nudged, she was already observing on her own. The four women stood breathless not knowing what to expect, yet anticipating something momentous was about to happen. Suddenly, a Society member shouted out, *"Avanti,"* a signal for the litter bearers to hoist the litter back onto their shoulders and continue the procession through the North End.

With the litter now firmly in place on their shoulders, the procession was about to get underway. Carla, once again, took hold of the streamer bearing donations to Saint Theresa, her eyes never leaving Pietro. As they pulled away from the church, the bells began to peal. It was then, Pietro seeing Carla departing, caught up in the emotion of the moment, could no longer contain himself. He handed the little gold urn of holy water to Father Francesco, stepped out of the church and reached for Carla's free hand, which she gave him lovingly. Not a word was spoken between them, but words weren't necessary. The lovers were finally together, their commitment to each other made in front of the church, Saint Theresa, and the crowd surrounding them. Nothing would separate them again. As the procession turned and left the square, Pietro walked silently by Carla's side, a simple gesture of commitment, the couple yearned for, had now become a reality. The procession was now heading toward Garden Court Street where Carla's father and brothers traditionally greeted the Saint.

"Carmela," Grandma gasped, "They're walking together, heading toward Garden Court Street and Carla's family. *Avremo bisogno di un miracolo* (We're going to need a miracle). Saint Theresa must make a miracle to prevent bloodshed." Grandma, in desperation, kicked off her shoes, removed her knee-high stockings and stood in her bare feet in front of the church. "Ma, what are you doing?" Mom shouted. "You promised you wouldn't walk in your bare feet. You know the danger. Remember your diabetes." It was as if Grandma heard nothing. Bending down, she took hold of her shoes and stockings and tucked them into her handbag. She then stood up, linked her arm around Mom's, who was standing in her bare feet. Auntie Angie, seeing what was happening, called out to Mom to do something. Mom, knowing how determined Grandma was, assured her, she would be guiding Grandma to make certain no harm came to her. Auntie Stella called out in a panic for Mom to stop her. Once again, Mom gave assurance she would be guiding Grandma's every step. The two women began to walk arm in arm behind the Saint, each performing an act of penance and devotion, each seeking a petition for a loved one, Mom for her family, and Grandma for a peaceful solution to a forbidden love affair.

Auntie Angie and Auntie Stella were following just behind, followed by Grace and Theresa, Anthony, Charlie and Bobby. As the procession pulled away from the church, Aunt Elena emerged from the crowd, grasping Grandma by the hand, she nervously asked, "Lucia, where are Pietro and Carla?" Grandma nodded in the direction of the Saint. Elena turned and spotted Pietro and Carla. She then squeezed Grandma's hand all the harder, signaling to Grandma her own anxiety, joining the family and the procession heading to Garden Court Street and the unpredictable reception of the Ricci family.

CHAPTER 84

The Miracle

"Angie, I'm going to throw up," Auntie Stella warned nervously as she and Auntie Angie walked toward Garden Court Street. "Stella calm down," Auntie Angie said reassuringly. "The Riccis won't make a scene in front of this crowd." "Angie, that old man is crazy. You don't know what he will do next. He has that fish hook and takes it out whenever there's trouble, and his sons are as crazy as he is." Grandma and Mom walking ahead, were only several yards behind Pietro and Carla.

The procession turned onto Garden Court Street, making its way to the Ricci building, where traditionally, money pinned to a long blue ribbon would be sent down from their second floor flat. "Carmela," Grandma asked nervously. "The Ricci window is open. How can they not miss seeing Carla and Pietro together?" "Ma, please be careful. Look where you're going," Mom cautioned. "If you step on glass or a nail and get cut, you can get an infection in your feet. Please put on your shoes. Saint Theresa would not want this." Knowing how anxious Mom was for her feet, Grandma struck a bargain. "Carmela, I know what I'm doing is making you nervous. I must do this, at least on Garden Court Street. Once we turn onto Hanover Street, I will put my shoes on." Mom, somewhat relieved, gave Grandma a quick kiss on the cheek and said, "*Grazie* Ma. In the meantime, watch where you step."

Just when Mom was feeling somewhat relieved, Aunt Elena spoke up, "Lucia," she said nervously, "Egidio and his sons are standing in their doorway. By now, they must have seen Carla and Pietro walking together. What should we do?" "Oh Madonna!" Shouted Grandma, "They are there. Carmela, Carmela," she repeated anxiously while tugging on Mom's arm. "All the Riccis are on their steps. They must have seen Carla and Pietro." In desperation, Grandma turned to Auntie Angie who was only several paces behind. "Angie, all the Riccis are in their doorway. They're going to do harm to Pietro."

"Ma, calm down. It will be okay!" Auntie Angie shouting above the noise of the crowd. "Angie, I think I'm going to pee myself." "Stella, you're going to disgrace us." "That's all Angie, you're always afraid of what people will think. The old bastard is standing in his doorway with his cafoni sons. They're going to kill all of us." "Stella shut up!" Auntie Angie implored. "And don't disgrace us." "What are you talking about?" Auntie Stella screamed. "You're worrying about a little piss and those bastards are going to kill us." Turning abruptly, just ahead of them, Grandma scolded, "Stella, I can hear what you're saying. Be quiet. Saint Theresa will protect us. The Riccis won't do anything." "Oh, that's right, Saint Lucia is praying to Saint Theresa and everything is going to be okay," Auntie Stella snapped. "Stella, don't talk about her that way!" Mom shouted.

Before Auntie Stella could respond, the procession stopped directly in front of the Ricci building. The crowd went silent as the procession stopped, anticipating the Riccis ceremonial donation to Saint Theresa, but something was different, Egidio's eyes and those of his sons were fixed on Carla and Pietro. The unexpected sight of the couple walking together reignited their anger.

Ignoring the crowd around them, their eyes remained fixed on the couple. Seconds passed, which seemed like an eternity, and the crowd began to murmur. Grandma, increasingly alarmed, began moving in the direction of Pietro and Carla, who were standing just an arm's length from Egidio and his sons. As she pulled up abreast of Pietro, she looked directly into Egidio's face and could see the anger mounting in his eyes. She then maneuvered herself between Carla and Pietro and grasped both their hands. Once again, she looked at Egidio, the anger in his eyes did not abate. His sons, standing behind him, remained silent, waiting for their father to make his move. The crowd continued to stir, aware of

Egidio's hostility toward Pietro, and well-aware of the drama happening before their eyes. He appeared to be contemplating something. The fearsome look in his eyes filled Grandma and Mom with dread, alarmed by the fact, one of his hands remained in his pocket as if clutching at something. Grandma, once again, squeezed Carla and Pietro's hands, and Egidio took note of it. When at last, he seemed ready to advance, someone in the crowd bumped the litter upon which Saint Theresa stood, causing the statue to rock in place, shaking the wreath of flowers from the Saint's head.

Falling from the Saint, the wreath hit Carla on the shoulder and landed at Grandma's bare feet, catching everyone by surprise, and stopping Egidio in his tracks. Instinctively, he bent down to pick up the wreath. It was then he noticed it had fallen onto Grandma's feet. The sight of the delicate floral wreath lying on Grandma's bare feet tore through his anger, reaching deep into his soul. He immediately understood the significance of the moment, and the sacrifice Grandma was making for the couple. He seemed to stay an extra moment or two on his knees, as if in prayer.

Taking the crown from Grandma's bare feet, he gradually stood up, to the amazement of Grandma and Mom, his eyes were filled with tears. The anger harbored within him, dissolved away at the holy sight he just observed. He stood motionless in front of Grandma, as if in a spell, holding the wreath but not handing it to her. Grandma reached out and took the wreath from his hands. Egidio offered it up and gently bent over, kissed Grandma on one cheek and then the other. Grandma, slowly pulling away, nodded in the direction of Carla, as if to say, "Now, your daughter." But instead, he turned to Pietro and repeated the gesture of peace. Mom whispered to Grandma, "Ma, Saint Theresa made a miracle." Grandma simply nodded and whispered, "*Si, Carmela. Santa Theresa ha fatto un miracolo.*" Egidio turned to Carla, put his arms around her, and whispered in her ear, "*Figlia mia, figlia mia* (my daughter, my daughter), forgive me." They stood for a moment, rocking back and forth.

When finally he pulled away, he motioned to his astonished sons, standing behind him, to attach the ribbon filled with their donation to Saint Theresa. It took only a second for Frank to loop the ribbon around the Saint's head. When he stepped back, the crowd began to cheer as the band struck up *"La Marcia Reale"* in tribute to the Riccis' generosity. Grandma and Egidio, along with Carla and Pietro, began clapping in rhythm with the music, joined by the rest of the family and the crowd. All were aware a miracle had taken place and finally, Pietro and Carla could be together. Egidio motioned to his sons to join the procession. They took up their position behind Carla and Pietro, aware of the change that had come over their father, responding in kind. Someone shouted, *"Avanti,"* and the Saint, her floral crown once again in place on her head, was lifted onto the shoulders of the litter bearers. The procession continued down Garden Court Street where it would turn onto Hanover Street. Before turning onto Hanover Street, Grandma pulled Mom aside, reached into her handbag, pulled out her shoes and slipped them on, leaving her stockings in her handbag. "Carmela," she said with a grin on her face. "Are you happy now?" Mom gave Grandma a big hug, with tears in her eyes, responded, "I'm very happy Ma." Together, they re-joined the procession.

Turning onto Hanover Street, Auntie Stella whispered to Auntie Angie, "Angie, I wet myself." Characteristically, Auntie Angie responded, "Stella, shut up!"

CHAPTER 85

Searching for an Answer

"Anna, the Saint is crooked in her niche, please straighten her out." As always, with the conclusion of a procession, Claudia was in charge of straightening out the Saint Theresa Chapel, while at the same time, seeing to the needs of the dozens of well-wishers who had followed the Saint through the streets, and now returned to the chapel for refreshments.

Before entering the chapel, Pietro drew Carla aside and revealed, "Carla, I have made a decision. I want you to come with me to Rome when I return. I want you to meet my parents. I know Papa secretly has always wanted me to follow in his footsteps as a lawyer. I would like to enter university this fall; I'm certain Papa can arrange it, but I must have your approval. I'm thinking for the both of us, no longer just for myself." "Pietro, I only want what you want, but your parents will never accept me." Carla forewarned. "Carla, listen to me. They only want the best for me; I know they will accept you." Carla responded, "Pietro, I just want to be with you." They then entered the Shrine.

Like so many in the procession, Grandma and our family entered the Shrine ostensibly for refreshments, but this time it was different. Both families had finally accepted Pietro and Carla should be together. Carla was now standing with her arms around Pietro, radiant with delight. She appeared to be admiring the Saint, now bedecked with streamers and offerings, but in truth, her mind was on Pietro and the miracle that just occurred. Every so often, Pietro would kiss Carla on the cheek, pull away, and simply remain staring at her, his eyes full of love for the woman, a few hours ago, was forbidden to him.

Egidio, having entered the Shrine, caught sight of Grandma and her daughters and walked over to them. He motioned to his sons to join them. They pulled up little metal chairs and formed a circle in a corner of the Shrine. Pietro and Carla, seeing their families together, walked over to join them. "Signor Ricci, now that I 'm not entering the seminary, on my return to Rome, I will attempt to enter Law School this autumn. Although the university is not expecting me, I believe there is a strong possibility they will accept me. I plan to follow in my father's footsteps and become a lawyer and enter my father's law firm. I always surmised this is what he really wanted of me. He was trying to please Mama by agreeing to let me enter the seminary and study for the priesthood, a vocation I considered from a very early age. I would like to take Carla back to Italy to meet my parents, with your permission, Signor Ricci.

Egidio responded, "Carla, if I agree to this, I must insist you travel with a chaperon, and return to Boston after spending three or four weeks getting acquainted with the Petruzelli family." "I will ask one of my cousins or my Aunt Lucia to accompany us," Pietro responded. "Will this satisfy you, Signor Ricci?" Carla then spoke up. "Papa, I would like to go to Italy to meet Pietro's parents, why can't you come with us?" Slightly irritated, Egidio responded, "Carla, I'm not a millionaire. I'm a humble fisherman, and I have responsibilities to your brothers and my family." "Papa, you're not a poor man, you have never taken a vacation." "Carla, you must let me think about this. You are both going too fast for me."

CHAPTER 86

The Answer

"Before we go any further," Egidio said sternly, "I want to hear what Lucia and her daughters have to say. Lucia, you and your daughters have been listening to all we've been saying but have remained silent. Do you agree with the request, that you or one of your daughters accompany my daughter and Pietro to Italy?" "Bravo," Grandma responded. "It's a wonderful idea, and Egidio, you should come with us, Grandma having already decided to go. It's years since I've seen my brother. I would love to go to Italy with Pietro and Carla." "Ma, what are you saying?" Auntie Angie shouted out, distressed at the fact that Grandma planned such a trip. "The ocean voyage will be too much for you. You're too old to travel so far." "Angie, I will be fine. If you're worrying about my diabetes, Carla can help me with my insulin, and there will be a doctor on the ship."

"Lucia, I never thought you would accept this idea," Egidio responded incredulously. "Egidio, they're young; what was denied us when we were young, we can now do for them." "Lucia, it's out of the question that I go. I have responsibilities." "Egidio, you have worked like a dog all your life. This is a wonderful opportunity for you. If not for yourself, then do it for Carla. She would love you to come." "Lucia, you know my weakness. You know I would do anything for my daughter." "*E' fatto, andremo insieme* (It's done, we will go together)!" Grandma exclaimed joyfully. Pietro, if I'm not mistaken, there is a guesthouse on your family's property. I'm certain your family will allow us to use it while we're in Rome. I will call my brother Gerardo and ask him if we can use it." "Aunt Lucia, I'm certain my family will allow this," Pietro said reassuringly. "Then it's done. I will call Gerardo in the morning. I promised to do so anyway, when I spoke with him last Friday," Grandma responded. Auntie Stella listening to all that was being said, could hardly believe her ears. "Ma, are you crazy? You can't do this," she blurted out nervously. "The trip will be too much for you." "Stella, I know my mind, and this is something I want to do." Now Mom spoke up. "Ma, you know I don't always agree with Stella, but this time she's right. You can't do this. The trip will be too much for you." "Even you, Carmela," Grandma replied. "I might never have another chance to see my brother again. I'm the head of this family, by accompanying Carla and Pietro, I will show our family's approval of Carla. I want them to be happy."

Listening to Grandma's remarks, Egidio became convinced it was the right course of action. "Lucia," he said sternly. "I will accompany my daughter to Italy, and I will be there to help you. If you want the best for the couple, and Pietro is simply your nephew, and you are willing to do so much for them, how much more is expected of me, Carla's father?" He then turned to his son Frank. "Frank, I'm going to accompany Carla to Italy. You will be in charge while I'm gone. But Lucia, I must caution you before we begin the journey. It's true, the Riccis are good people, but we are humble fishermen, Carla is the daughter of a fisherman. Pietro is from a noble family, another world, an aristocratic world, a world of boundaries that are never crossed. I believe they will never accept Carla.

"Egidio, listen to me," Grandma responded. "It's true, my brother's wife's family, the Contes, is an old aristocratic Roman family, but they are different. Things are different from when our families were in Italy before the Great Wars. Barriers that once existed have been lowered. Did they not accept my brother, a commoner? How could they not accept Carla, knowing how much their son Pietro loves her?" "But Lucia, won't they blame Carla and say she was the cause of his change of heart, that she turned his head." "Egidio, I know my brother. His family will accept this as God's will. This is what we will do. We will go to Italy with Pietro and Carla. Pietro, you will call your parents and inform them of your plans to return to Italy with Carla, letting them know Egidio and I will accompany the both of you. I promised your father I would call on Tuesday. We can make the call together, you will speak first, then I will talk. It will reassure your family and express our approval." Pietro nodded in agreement. They would call on Tuesday at noon from Auntie Angie's flat.

CHAPTER 87

Tuesday Morning

Tuesday was a bright sunny day. It was 11 A.M., everyone had gathered at Auntie Angie's house including Egidio. A feeling of relief as well as excitement filled the air, now it was time to give Pietro's parents details of the plan both families had worked out the previous day. Auntie Angie had placed two pots of coffee on the stove and pulled out of the refrigerator an icebox cake, she made the night before. She took her place at the head of the table, cut the cake, and methodically plopped a piece onto a plate drawn from a stack just to her left. As she plated each piece, she called out the name the piece was to go to, maintaining an etiquette that seemed to come natural to her. As always, the first went to Grandma followed by her guests, Egidio, Carla and Pietro, finally Auntie Stella and Mom. Everyone agreed, Auntie Angie made the best icebox cake. Because of the seriousness of the situation and not wanting any distractions, Auntie Angie arranged that Grace and Theresa would take Anthony, Bobby and Charlie to The H where they would spend the afternoon. Auntie Angie got the conversation going, "Ma, you have to speak to Gerardo when we call in fifteen minutes. Do you know what you want to say?" "Angie don't worry. Gerardo is my brother. The words will come to me when we talk."

Auntie Angie then caught sight of Mom and Auntie Stella laughing over some private joke, while digging into the icebox cake. Auntie Stella was already motioning for a second piece. Exasperated, Auntie Angie called the two of them by name, "Stella, Carmela pay attention. This is important. Mama is going to speak to Gerardo in ten minutes." Mom responded by asking for a second piece of icebox cake. "Stop with the icebox cake," Auntie Angie said impatiently. "We need to prepare Mama." Egidio then spoke up. "Angie, your mother is a wise woman. She knows her brother, and she will know what to say." "Angie, give me another piece of icebox cake," Auntie Stella demanded. It was more than Auntie Angie could stand. She pushed the platter of cake to the middle of the table, with exasperation clearly in her voice, ordered, "Help yourself." Auntie Stella and Mom dug in. Before Auntie Angie could say another word, Pietro spoke up. "Cousin, I know you are concerned. Aunt Lucia will speak from her heart and she will say the right words." Grandma then asked Auntie Angie to call the operator and place the call.

While Auntie was busy placing the call, Grandma reached across the table and motioned for Carla's and Pietro's hands, took them in her hands and squeezed them tightly. The simplicity of her gesture said it all, reassuring the three sisters, Grandma would say the right words. Grandma then turned toward Egidio, gave him a smile, took his hand and continued to hold it while Auntie Angie handed her the phone. A minute or two later, a voice could be heard. It was the overseas operator announcing that Gerardo was on the line.

Squeezing Egidio's hand a little tighter, Grandma began, *"Gerardo, Questa e' tua sorella Lucia. Parliamo in inglese* (This is your sister Lucia. Let's speak in English). We are all here sitting in Angelina's kitchen." Grandma automatically turned to her daughters' Italian names when speaking with relatives from the old country. "Stella and Carmela are here, and your son Pietro and Carla, as well as Carla's father, Egidio. Do you want to speak to your son Pietro?" *"Si si, Lucia, per un minuto* (Yes, yes, Lucia, for a minute)."

Pietro took the phone and first spoke in Italian. *"Papa', questo e' Pietro. Come stai? E' mamma e' li* (Papa, this is Pietro. How are you? Is Mama there)?" *"Si, si Pietro, tua madre e' qui accanto a me* (Yes, yes, your mother is here beside me)," Gerardo handing the phone to Velia. Pietro then said, "Mama, let's speak in English so our cousins can understand. Are you okay?" "Si, si Pietro. I am okay. It has been so long since we have spoken. I have been so worried about you. When are you returning home?" "Mama, I am leaving for Italy by boat next Monday. Aunt Lucia will be with me as well as Carla and her father, Egidio." There was a silence on the other end of the line.

The next voice was that of Gerardo, who Velia handed the phone off to, not wanting Pietro to hear her sobbing. "Pietro, why are you bringing Carla and her father with you? I can understand Lucia. I haven't seen my sister in years, but it's too soon to bring Carla and her father." Before he could answer, Grandma hearing every word, gestured for the phone, which Pietro handed her with a look of distress on his face.

"Gerardo, this is Lucia once again. Your son wants you and Velia to meet Carla. Egidio and I are coming as, *come si dice la parola in inglese, accompagnatori* (how do you say the word in English, *accompagnatori*)?" Gerardo responded, "chaperons." "Si, Si, chaperons. I would also like to see you and Velia. Pietro wants to follow in your footsteps and become a lawyer. He admires you and he wants you and Velia to meet the woman he loves. They are seeking your approval. Consider the alternative. If you turn your back on them, you will drive them away. What could be worse? Gerardo, don't you think I know how you and Velia feel, particularly Velia? She's disappointed. Listen to me. You will not be disappointed. The Riccis are a fine family. I have known them for many years. I'm sorry to have to speak this way in front of them but time is short, and a great distance separates us. Trust me, trust your sister. I would never disappoint you. I promise you, Carla could be the daughter you never had."

The phone went silent. Grandma then cast her eyes at her daughters, searching for their approval which they gave by simultaneously nodding their heads in her direction. Finally, the silence was broken, but this time it was Velia on the phone. "Lucia, this is Velia. You are all welcome at our home. Come for as long as you like." Pietro then reached for the phone. "Mama, *molte grazie* (many thanks). Carla and I have already made plans. She will only be in Italy for three weeks. She wants to meet you and Papa. I will go on to Law School." "But Pietro, you have not applied to University." Gerardo could be heard in the background. "Velia, don't worry. Your son is very wise. He is like his father. He knows our family is a big contributor to the University, his grades are very strong, he knows there is a good possibility we can get him in, even at this late hour."

Velia then spoke the words Pietro and Carla were longing to hear, "Pietro, you know I am disappointed. I wanted you to enter seminary, but if this is what you desire, then I must accept it as God's Will. Carla and her father will be welcomed to our home." "Mama, we will be leaving for Italy next Monday. I'm looking forward to seeing you and Papa. Please have the guest house ready. Aunt Lucia just blew a kiss in your direction." The three sisters then called out, "Uncle Gerardo, Aunt Velia, we love you." Pietro simply said, *"Dio ti benedica"* (God bless you) and hung up the phone. Everyone breathed a sigh of relief. Finally, there was approval by all families, and the way had been prepared for a happy visit.

CHAPTER 88

Una Famiglia (One Family)

I t was 9 o'clock in the morning, the day of the departure for Rome. The plan was everyone would meet at Grandma's flat. Uncle Jimmy and Uncle Tino would drive as many as could fit in their cars to South Station, where we would see the travelers off. Pasquale would provide the third car carrying Egidio, his sons and luggage. The train for New York would be leaving at 11 A.M. for the four-hour trip.

Anthony, Bobby and Charlie ran to the North End Park to pick up a surprise for Pietro, and would then head to Grandma's flat. Dad planned to help Pietro carry his bags to Grandma's. "Pietro are your bags all packed?" "Yes, cousin Carmela. I completed my packing, and I'm ready to leave. It seems as if I just arrived." "Pietro, we're going to miss you terribly. You've become one of our family," Mom said tearfully. "Shortly, you will be so far away." "Cousin Carmela, I will be returning next summer, time will pass quickly, and more than ever, I will stay in touch with the family during this period."

Mom went to the refrigerator and pulled out a package of sandwiches she made for the four travelers. "Pietro, this is something to eat on your train ride to New York. I made meatball sandwiches for the four of you. I know how much you and Mama love my meatballs, I'm certain Carla and Egidio will also enjoy them. Everyone loves meatball sandwiches." Mom had wrapped two sandwiches for each of the travelers. She put them in a small shopping bag and placed them on top of Pietro's suitcases. She then called to Dad who was in the bedroom, "Joe, we're ready to go."

Dad came out, pulled from the stack two of Pietro's leather suitcases and brought them to the doorway, leaving the other two for Pietro. Tearfully, Mom repeated, "Pietro, I hate to see you go. We will miss you." Before Pietro could respond, she hugged him and then kissed him on both cheeks. Pietro pulled back, his eyes began to well with tears. "Cousin Carmela, *Ti amo* (I love you). I love your family. You have changed my life. It is here I found my true love." He returned Mom's embrace, took one last look at the apartment, which had been home for three months, then they left for Grandma's flat with Dad leading the way.

As they entered Grandma's building, Mom could hear Auntie Stella arguing with Grandma. "Ma, you want your travel hat. Which hat is it? They all look alike." "Stella, don't make me nervous. You know the hat I want. It's the one with the feather and no veil." "Here we go again," Auntie cried out. "Ma, why do you call that your travel hat?" "Stella don't talk back. Find the hat with the feather and no veil and bring it to me," Grandma scolded. "Things never change," Mom said laughingly, turning to Pietro. "They're still fighting over the hats. Let's go upstairs before they kill each other."

As they entered the apartment, Auntie Stella was standing in the kitchen holding a little black straw hat with a black feather sticking up from the brim. "Carmela!" She shouted, clearly exasperated. "She insists on this hat. What makes this a travel hat? They all look alike." Grandma yanked the hat from Auntie Stella, placed it on her head and fastened it with one of her hat pins, the one with the pearl at the end. Having placed the hat on her head, Grandma turned to Mom. "Carmela, where is your sister Angie? We're going to be late for the train." "Ma, its only 9:15. The train leaves at 11 o'clock." "South Station is ten minutes away." "Carmela, if your sister is not here in five minutes, I want you to go to her flat and bring her here."

Before she could say another word, Auntie Angie could be heard mounting the stairs with Theresa and Grace. Auntie entered the room, eyed the situation, and asked, "What's going on? Are they arguing again? Everyone looks mad." "*Niente* (nothing) Angie," Grandma responded. "Everything is fine. Your sister Stella is making me nervous as usual. Angie, I want to drink a toast for good luck. Bring out the bottle of Five Star brandy and get the little glasses from the cabinet. Carmela, go, bring Carla and Egidio here. We will drink a toast to each other as *una famiglia* (one family)."

Mom, not wanting to waste time, immediately shot out of the flat following Grandma's request. As she quickly descended the stairs, she passed Anthony, Bobby and Charlie excitedly running up the stairs. Charlie was carrying a bag which immediately caught Mom's attention. Mom stopped, turned on her heels and shot out, "Charlie, what's in the bag? What tricks are the three of you up to now?" "Nothing Ma," Charlie responded. "It's just a going-away gift for Pietro." "If there's something alive in that bag, I'm going to kill the three of you," her eyes never leaving the bag. Anthony then grabbed the bag, opened it, and pulled out a North End Warriors baseball cap. "Ma, we got this gift for Pietro to go along with his baseball jersey. This way, when he returns next summer, he will be all set to play on the team." Mom let out a big grin and a sigh of relief. "Wonderful," she exclaimed. Excitedly, she quickly kissed all three of her sons, dashed down the stairs and left the building for Carla's flat.

Crashing through Grandma's door in excitement, Anthony quickly ran over to Pietro with Bobby and Charlie following, and handed him the bag. "Pietro open the bag, open the bag," Anthony insisted. "It's a gift for you." Pietro quickly opened the bag, pulled out the cap and held it up for all to see. *"Molto bello"* (Very beautiful), he exclaimed. "Put it on Pietro," Anthony urged. "We want to see how it looks on you." Pietro quickly placed it on his head and walked over to Grandma for her approval. "Bravo, bravo, Pietro. You now look like Joe DiMaggio." "Now, its official, you are a member of the North End Warriors," Anthony said excitedly. When you come back next year, you will be on the team." Pietro beamed with delight. The three boys could not have given him a better gift.

Mom, Egidio, Carla and her five brothers then entered the flat. Carla, immediately spotting Pietro in his baseball cap, ran over to him, tugged at the cap and said, "Pietro, how handsome you look in your baseball cap. I can't wait to see you play next summer." Grandma began filling the small glasses, half full, with Five Star brandy. For Anthony, Bobby, Charlie, Theresa and Grace, she filled their glasses with Coke. Looking around, seeing Uncle Jimmy and Uncle Tino were missing, motioned to Auntie Angie and asked her to look out the window to see if they had brought the cars around. "Ma, I can see them sitting in the cars in front of the church." "Angie, call to them. Ask them to come up for a minute." Auntie went to the window and after two or three calls, caught their attention. She motioned for them to come to the flat.

Uncle Tino and Uncle Jimmy quickly left their cars and began walking briskly to the flat. In a minute, the men were up the stairs, taking their places in the family circle, each given a glass of brandy. Looking directly at Egidio, Grandma lifted her glass and gave the toast. *"Una famiglia,* Egidio," she said proudly. *"Una famiglia,"* Egidio responded, his gaze never leaving Grandma. With a sweeping motion, glass in her hand, Grandma repeated the toast once again, both families responded, *"Una famiglia."* Glasses clinked, everyone took a small sip and as if on cue, began hugging each other. The miracle was complete. The blast of a horn interrupted the happy moment. It was Pasquale pulling up behind Uncle Jimmy and Uncle Tino's cars, signaling his arrival, departure time had come.

CHAPTER 89

The Departure

The two families left Grandma's building and walked to the cars parked in front of the church. As we walked from the building, Grandma turned for a moment, and looked back at her apartment. Teary eyed, she raised her hand and made the sign of the cross as if to bless the apartment.

"One more thing before I leave, I must visit the shrine of the Madonna." "Carmela, Angie, Stella come with me." As she opened the door to the church, she called to Carla, Pietro and Egidio. "We must visit the shrine before we leave." The little group walked down the side aisle, passed the shrine of Saint Theresa to the shrine of Our Lady of Pompeii, Grandma's shrine. All stood for a moment in front of the shrine, making their silent prayer. Grandma then lit three lamps, one for her family, one for Egidio's family and one for Carla and Pietro. Not a word was spoken, it wasn't necessary. They stood watching the flickering candles for a moment or two, then one by one, they slowly began to drift away. Grandma was the last to leave the shrine. Kissing the tips of her fingers, she reached over to the picture and touched the foot of the Madonna, then offered a prayer for Grandpa Bernardo, her family and safe passage. She crossed herself and joined the group that paused momentarily at the shrine of Saint Theresa, the shrine Carla had cleaned so often.

Carla lit a candle, offered a silent prayer, and the two families left the church to find Father Francesco waiting for them just outside the door.

Placing a hand on one of Pietro's shoulders, Father whispered, "Pietro, my son, you are leaving us." "Si, Padre Francesco," Pietro responded. "I am returning to Italy to enter Law School." "Yes, Pietro," Father Francesco responded. "And Carla, Lucia and Signore Ricci will be accompanying you to Italy." "Si, Padre. Carla and Signore Ricci will meet my parents, and my aunt will be visiting her brother." Father Francesco, embracing Pietro, whispered, "The Holy Spirit moves like the wind. He will inspire you my son. Go with God." Pulling away, he stood erect and said, "Now, I will bless the group." We all gathered in front of Father Francesco; Pasquale simply stuck his head out the car window. Father lifted his hand, and with sweeping motions, formed a cross in the air, first to the left, then to the right, and finally to the center. The families responded by crossing themselves. *"Grazie,* Padre Francesco!" Grandma shouted. Father Francesco repeated, "Go with God."

Grandma turned from Father Francesco, faced the group, and with a sweep of her hand, shouted, *"Andiamo!"* With that, we all piled into the three waiting cars and were on our way to South Station. As we made our departure, the church bells began to chime, a final blessing from Father Francesco.

Within ten minutes, the three cars pulled up in front of South Station, doors opened, and the men ran to the rear of the cars to pull the luggage from the trunks for the four travelers. After taking the luggage into South Station, Pasquale, Uncle Jimmy and Uncle Tino returned to their cars. Uncle Jimmy and Uncle Tino parked on Summer Street, while Pasquale returned to North Square, figuring those of us who remained could easily return in two cars. We arrived at South Station to find Uncle Carmine, Aunt Loretta and their two children, Edward and Caterina waiting for us. Mom had given Uncle Carmine the time of departure, and he and his family came to see Grandma and the travelers off. A nervous energy passed through the group, revealing feelings of anxiety and sadness over the fact, only twenty minutes remained until the train would be departing for New York, and the first leg of a long journey. "Ma, I want you to call home at least once a week." Auntie Angie was emphatic with her instructions to Grandma. "Carmela and Stella will be with me when you call. If you call at 5:00 P.M. Rome time, it will be 11:00 A.M. in Boston. Call on Saturday." "Angie, I will call. You worry too much." Grandma responded reassuringly. Pietro then spoke up. "Cousin Angie, I will make certain Aunt Lucia calls. You know we will be watching over her through the entire voyage and visit. She will be surrounded with love." "I know Pietro," Auntie responded. "It's the only thing giving me peace of mind."

Auntie Stella walked over to Grandma, straightened the little black hat on her head, somewhat choked up, whispered, "You're right Ma, this is a good travel hat. You look beautiful in it. I should never have questioned you." "Stella, you are a faithful daughter and you have revealed some of the secrets in your heart. On my return, we will invite Gino Gallo to our home for coffee and…" Grandma was about to say taralli but caught herself. Wanting to please Auntie Stella, she continued, "for coffee and cannoli." Grandma's eyes then filled with tears. Auntie Stella hugged her and whispered, "Ma, I would like that very much, and taralli will be fine." Then they separated, and Grandma kissed her on both cheeks, and etched out a small cross on her forehead as a blessing.

Grandma then turned to Mom, motioning for her to come close. "Carmela, you were the first to recognize the love between Carla and Pietro. I've always called you the Foxy One, I knew what I was talking about. Take care of the boys and Joe, and watch out for your sisters as they will watch out for you." "Ma, you're making me cry," Mom said in a hushed voice. "I want you to be very careful on your journey. Be certain to take your medications and stay close to Egidio, Carla and Pietro." "Carmela, you worry too much, but I'll do as you say." They then embraced. Grandma kissed Mom on both cheeks and once again, etched out a small cross on her forehead as a blessing.

Turning to Auntie Angie, Grandma became quite solemn. "Angie, in my absence, I want you to watch over your sisters and the family. I know you and Carmela have your husbands, they are the strength, but the women are the heart of the family. Listen to me Angie, I know what I'm talking about. You are my eldest child, I have always turned to you when I needed help or advice. I'm asking you to watch over the family while I'm gone. I know I can count on you." "Ma," Auntie Angie responded. "I'll do all you ask and will pray for you while you're away." The two then embraced, tears flowed from their eyes. *"Dio sia con voi"*

(God be with you), Grandma whispered. Auntie Angie returned, *"Dio sia con voi."* She kissed her on both cheeks and etched out a small cross on her forehead as a blessing.

Grandma then called Uncle Carmine over. "Carmine, you are the man of the family, I know you are busy with your career and family, but I ask you to please stay in touch with your sisters while I'm away. She kissed him on both cheeks and etched out a small cross on his forehead as a blessing. She called Aunt Loretta over and repeated her blessing.

The grandchildren then came forward and surrounded Grandma. She motioned to them to come over one by one, kissed each from cheek to cheek and once again, etched out a little cross on each of their foreheads as a blessing. Grandma completed her departing ritual with Dad, Uncle Jimmy and Uncle Tino.

While all this was happening, Egidio was saying goodbye to each of his sons, mirroring Grandma's parting gestures and blessings. The sons then came over to Grandma, each kissing her and wishing her well. Everyone now turned to Carla and Pietro who were quietly observing our parting rituals.

Mom shouted out, "Before you leave, we want to see Carla and Pietro kiss each other!" Auntie Angie and Auntie Stella seized on the idea and joined in, "Yes, yes, one kiss before you leave." Grandma then spoke up, "Carmela, you're embarrassing the couple." Egidio, prompted by Mom's suggestion, gleefully added, "Carla, Pietro, it would be a wonderful way to say goodbye." Grandma, taking Egidio by the arm, shouted out, "Carla, Pietro, *fa'cosi"* (do it this way)! With that, she gave Egidio a peck on the cheek, catching him totally by surprise. Delighted, Egidio returned the gesture, causing Grandma to blush. Egidio's sons then yelled out, "Bravo, bravo!" Finally, Pietro turned toward Carla, shrugged his shoulders as if to say, "What do you think?" Carla burst into a huge smile, all her pent-up emotions released. Throwing her arms around Pietro, she kissed him on both cheeks and lightly on the lips, then whispered, "Pietro, I love you." "I love you, Carla," Pietro responded. We all began to clap. It was a wonderful moment for all of us, but particularly for Carla and Pietro. They were beaming with love for each other. "How close we all have become," Grandma exclaimed,

"*Santa Teresa ha veramente fatto un miracolo*" (Saint Theresa truly made a miracle).

In the distance, we could hear the conductor shouting, "All aboard!" Suddenly, we knew it was time for us to say goodbye, and once again, emotions bubbled up and tears flowed.

"Lucia *aspetta*, Lucia *aspettami*," could be heard rising above the noise from the crowd in South Station. It was Aunt Elena and her eight children coming to say goodbye. It would only be minutes before Grandma would be gone, Aunt Elena intended to fill them with as much emotion as possible. Tearfully, she embraced Grandma, then turned to Pietro and Carla embracing each of them. She then shouted out, "*Ti voglio bene!*" (I love you). And as if in a chorus, we all shouted out, "*Ti voglio bene, Zia Elena!*"

Gradually, we made our way to the train, the family surrounding the departing travelers. Dad and Uncle Jimmy helped carry their bags onto the train, placed them on the luggage rack above their seats, then stepped back onto the platform. Pietro and Carla stood on the upper steps of the train, their arms wrapped around each other. Grandma remained on the platform close to her family. Egidio also stood close to his sons, kissing each of them goodbye.

Before mounting the steps, Grandma called her daughters to her. "Angie, Stella, Carmela, before I leave, you must promise me something. I want the three of you to clean and take care of our shrine and promise to keep a candle lit in front of the Madonna, as I know you will. *Non lasciare mai la Madonna nell'oscutita'* (Never leave the Madonna in darkness)."

One by one, each of her daughters gave her a parting kiss, then Grandma motioned to Egidio to help her onto the train. The train lurched and slowly began to move. Egidio grabbed hold of Grandma, steadying her on the steps. It was a gesture instinctively done, reassuring her daughters that Grandma was in good hands. Carla and Pietro were on the top steps waving their goodbyes. The conductor, who had been watching our parting scene, motioned to Grandma and Egidio to step up into the train, prompting Carla and Pietro to move into the compartment. Not wanting to lose sight of Grandma, Mom, Auntie Angie and Auntie Stella began walking beside the moving train.

Suddenly, Grandma appeared at the window along with Egidio, Carla and Pietro surrounding her. Grandma began waving her little handkerchief, catching the attention of her three daughters. In a final parting gesture, Mom stopped, placed her hand on her heart, kissed it, and waved in their direction. Auntie Angie and Auntie Stella followed. The sisters stood side by side, waving to their parting loved ones. They stood, not moving, until the train was out of sight. Finally, they turned and slowly walked to rejoin the rest of the family. With their arms around each other's waist, they walked the distance separating them from the family. Mom stopped, turned to her sisters, with a burst of joy erupting through her tears, shouted, "Angie, Stella, let's go to the church to light a parting candle at the shrine as Mama asked!" Auntie Stella joined in, "Then we can clean the shrine." Followed by Auntie Angie "Yes, we will clean the shrine, as Mama wished." With that, the sisters joined hands and continued to walk toward their waiting family.

EPILOGUE

S o, we have come to the end of the story. I would like to thank those
of you who have taken the time to read this book. It has given me
great pleasure to look over the shoulders of my great grandsons, as they
filled these pages with some of the experiences of their early lives. At the
beginning of this book, I said you will be reading about the lives of my
family, and a love story very close to my heart. In these pages, you have
come to know my family, and the joy we bring to each other, sharing our
lives in the most intimate ways. It might interest you to know Pietro and
Carla did get married. Theirs is a story for another time. My children
and many of my grandchildren are now with me, and the light still
burns at the shrine of the Madonna, kept burning bright by my great
grandsons. "Till we meet again, *va con Dio.*"